A PLACE
IN THE
COUNTRY

By Sarah Gainham

SARAH GAINHAM

A PLACE

IN THE

COUNTRY

HOLT, RINEHART AND WINSTON
NEW YORK   CHICAGO   SAN FRANCISCO

F
G12

Library of Congress Catalog Card Number: 69-11800

Published in German under the title of *Frau an der Grenze,*
Copyright © 1968 by Verlag Fritz Molden AG. Zurich.

First Edition

Designer: Ernst Reichl
SBN: 03-076430-0
Printed in the United States of America

70-9   12-4-69   GELTMAN 695/590

BOOK ONE
1946-1947

I

It was Georg Kerenyi who brought into my life both Lali, my wife, and Julia Homburg. So that it seems only fair to begin at the beginning, with his appearance. That was December 1946 and he was dumped, literally dumped, on the unit I then served in, as one of a grotesque transport of repatriated prisoners collected haphazard into a closed rail wagon which wandered for weeks from a camp probably on the far side of the Ural Mountains until it was near enough to be pushed over a border where it could no longer be refused. That was the border of Austria. Because the wagon found itself on a side-line of the Hungarian railways it crossed the border on a single branch track and ended in the only siding of a small provincial station in the extreme south-east of Styria instead of at a railhead in Vienna where there were facilities for dealing with such 'freight'.

He was only one of a nameless gaggle of scarecrows at that moment; jetsam of the vast and meaningless storm the rage of which ended in official documents on May 8, 1945; one small eddy of the squalls still blowing millions of human beings to and fro all over Europe and Asia. There was nothing to distinguish the common soldier from a Colonel of the Staff of the Sixth German Army; or the lowest ranker of the Allgemeine SS from Georg Kerenyi, Doctor of Philosophy and former editor of a large Vienna newspaper. That he was suspected—rightly—of having been involved in the plot against Hitler's life was the cause of his being transferred in August 1944 from the comparative ease of Zagreb, or Agram as he called the town in Croatia, to a combatant infantry regiment on a front about to break where he could be expected to disappear for ever. This starving derelict was a force in Austrian politics before 1938 and the friend, or enemy, of almost every figure known in Vienna and many known to the whole world. The mind now switching in and out of half-consciousness like the lighting that flickered weakly in every city of Europe and for the same reason—lack of fuel—once gave

3

sound, and unwelcome, advice to the President and Chancellor of his country. If he had been listened to, the warring Austrian parties might have shown a combined front to the encroaching Nazis, before it was too late. Not that the course of that history could have been changed, and certainly Kerenyi, as I later so well knew him, was the last man in the world ever to claim that possibility as a chance of his own achievement; but it could have recovered the pride of a people whose place in history is not less than our own. That this *was* a mind became clear as soon as he could talk to us; but I think nobody then could have believed that the cadaverous long form from which we cut the filthy rags of uniform to dress its injuries was once the object of desire and rivalry to beautiful and talented women and was to become so again. But that, with Julia Homburg, belongs to the future of this story; for the friendship I formed with Kerenyi brought me into his own world.

This was a winter that, even in the capital of our country which still thought itself as a victor, if not the victor, in the war recently ended, was attended by more privation than at any time during the war itself. If in London the lights went out and rations were shorter than at the deepest moments of the war, the condition of people in enemy countries and the countries laid waste in turn by the German armies and the Russian armies can hardly now be reconstructed in the imagination by any description of mine. Austria was comparatively better off than either Germany itself or anywhere in eastern Europe except for small islands where the peasants could count on their own crops, and Czechoslovakia, which had been spared both bombing and the fearful, rambling land battles. People were near starvation even in France; in Hamburg, as I heard from a friend stationed there, older people dropped dead in the streets from exhaustion and undernourishment. Italy was in a state of destruction that makes the survival of its glorious cities seem in retrospect a miracle—I myself had been posted two months before to my present unit after a year in Trieste. And to reach Trieste meant driving up from Bari in the late summer of 1945; through the Abruzzi and then the string of famous towns crowned by Venice.

I saw much destruction, but always destruction both caused and suffered by others. Being as I was, an interpreter-interrogator, I neither destroyed by my own actions nor suffered the ruin in my own person. A war spent in Alexandria had provided me with a curious perspective, I am prepared to believe; one small ratchet of the overweighted Staff machinery could easily see war as a gigantic complex of paper. The journey to Trieste cured me of the guilt and envy of one who did no fighting; I was glad not to be responsible for the results, as I saw them through the protective mask of never having fired a shot myself. Trieste itself was, though vastly complicated, also vastly amusing as a job. The ferocity and pride of those Balkan bandits who wished to take the city and equally the ancient slipperiness of Italian nationalism were balanced precariously by our presence. My posting to Austria was a drop into boredom; a boredom I greeted with pleasure for I was using the plentiful spare time and the Army's educational facilities to pass examinations which would replace the lost university years.

We were an interrogation unit concerned with dredging through former soldiers of the enemy armies; concerned too with some members of that even more melancholy army of nomads then moving about central and eastern Europe. Homeless and often nameless, they were called displaced persons; if they seemed either to the Austrian police or to the British authorities to have some other background than the helpless misfortune of war, they were sent to us to discover what that background might be.

It was, then, in accordance with his normal function that the police chief of our small town telephoned, for though the Austrian police were in civil control they still hesitated to take any measures that must concern the occupation power—in that district the British—without checking back carefully. Not even in urgent matters and this, it seemed, was urgent. I happened to be on duty and took the call in the interrogators' room, as it was called. At first I could not understand what he meant when he said it would be better to wait for darkness to unload the truck.

'Herr Captain,' he said in a breathy undertone, 'I don't want to speak too loudly or my clerk will hear—no need for anyone to know what does not have to be known. We shall have to cordon off the siding and clear the truck very quickly or I shall have trouble here in the town if the public sees or hears anything of it. I think many of them may be dead. None of them can walk properly. Or hardly move, so far as we can tell. There are no freight papers that we can find and the engine driver speaks no German and pretends to know nothing. You see, it is already suspicious that the truck came over the border as it did, with a Hungarian engine. He insists on being allowed to return at once with his engine and since the line is, naturally, always clear to the east, there is no ground for holding him.'

I heard him out and then said helplessly that we possessed no stretchers and no medical facilities.

'I have stretchers still from the old air-raid shelters,' he said. 'I can recall enough men for special duty to keep off strangers if you can arrive immediately after the local train leaves for Graz at five-twenty. It is the last train of the day and after that there will be nobody about that we can't control. Of course, it will be all over the town by tomorrow, but at least nobody will see anything. I have already informed the morgue and the priest.'

'How many men are there in the truck?'

'We don't know yet, but at least fifty. The station-master was fetched at once and ordered the truck to be closed again until he could talk to me. Fortunately the two men who unsealed it are on duty until the passenger train goes and you can imagine, I made it pretty clear to them that they'd better keep their mouths shut if they don't want a riot on their station.'

'But how do we know they are returned prisoners of war, if you haven't found any papers?'

'The men lying nearest to the doors are all wearing the remnants of Wehrmacht uniforms. And the wagon itself is Russian— you know, the kind that can be lifted on to flatcars for the gauge-change . . . ?'

I didn't know, but took his word for it that such wagons existed. We checked the time and I rang off. I must at once find the transport officer, Tom Wallingham. The 'pen' included a car-pool with four two-tonners, and only these were going to be any use for stretchers.

I found Tom in his little office in a fug of cigarette smoke, reading an issue of *Horse and Hound* three weeks old in the company of the unit security officer, Major Baxter. This was a bit of luck, to find them together.

'One truck is due for overhaul,' he objected when I told him we should need all four that evening. 'And the Colonel borrowed one for the afternoon. Wilder's gone off in it somewhere.'

'I thought you never allowed any of your pool to be "borrowed"?' grunted Baxter, taking the chance of poking fun at Tom's known dislike of any irregularity and at the same time hinting disapproval at the use the borrowed truck was undoubtedly being put to; attitudes he himself shared.

6

Tom registered this double-edged remark with a rueful grin and, swinging back in his chair, shouted through the door to Sergeant Benson to see if the truck due for servicing was in fact in a state to be used. Of course it was, the overhauling was a routine matter of army regulations. Sergeant-Major Benson then went off to dig the drivers out of their lair where, like all soldiers, they spent most of their spare time sleeping; and to round up such of the guards who could be spared from night duty or had not yet repaired to the dirty little beerhouse nearby where they normally took a couple of glasses of the thin local brew of an evening.

'I expect this police chap is exaggerating, anyway, Robert,' said Tom. 'It's a nuisance about the other lorry, but Manley asked me himself and I could hardly refuse. But it'll be all right, I dare say.'

'I don't think he was,' I answered dubiously, already worrying about the contemptuous telling-off I should get from the Colonel if all this fuss was for nothing. 'He wouldn't have agreed to the wagon being closed up again if it weren't in a pretty terrifying state.'

Tom looked up sharply, the possible situation striking him now in all its force in the only way he was capable of being touched by human suffering.

'We must get organised, quickly,' he said, losing his customary drawl and moving swiftly to the door with his lurching limp. 'Beds have to be set up. I'll get the men together. They'll be dirty—we'll get the spare boiler going—it'll probably blow up on us. Belongs to the year dot. Fifty—we shan't have enough bed linen. Listen, Robert, come on, we must call Keeler at once.'

Keeler was the Major of the Medical Corps who cared for our health as part of the town garrison, and for anything needed by our charges. As we crossed the courtyard between the cars and trucks from the Transport and Administration Office to the pen, it was slowly getting dark; it was, too, bitingly cold. Lights were going on in the house next door which was our Mess. The whole compound of the two large suburban houses with their gardens was surrounded by high wire fences covered inside with rush-matting to shield the pen from the curious eyes of the civilian world and outside with barbed wire; security in the military sense was taken care of by a double installation, of electric bells wired to the top of the inner fence and by a light-flashing apparatus somewhat like the oldfashioned call-boards for servants in hotels. Both of these were connected to the signals office where one of Baxter's men always sat on duty over the telephones. The only exit—the others were wired over—was the main gate from this house to the road, which, of course, was guarded as well as permanently locked.

After talking to Keeler, who was always impatient and irritable and now inclined to minimise our fears, I called the anteroom in the Mess. But the Mess steward told me that none of the officers was there; by bad luck there were so few men actually held in the pen that week that everybody not on duty was taking the chance of some unofficial free time. Especially that evening when Colonel Manley was known to be in Graz, miles away, with an old fellow-officer from the Indian Army. I could guess where they all were. Wilder was still ranging somewhere with the borrowed truck going about his extensive black-market business. David Stephenson, who was in fact on the duty roster, was dining in the town at the Officers' Club with his pretty red-head, the latest of an apparently endless supply of girls which was the cause of a good deal of envious teasing. The two serious interrogators, both German immigrants of the thirties called Morgenstern and Johnson, were at the theatre in Graz and would return with Manley in his Humber late at night. In what we considered to be the hardships of military existence, every one of us took what advantage he could of the chance to do what he wanted and not what the Army ordained; I myself had intended to study that evening and felt the arrival of the transport to be an interference in my restricted personal life.

We were met at the side road that led to the railway station—as often in small towns, the station was outside the town itself with its own roadway leading to it—by a railway official in uniform who was clearly the station-master. He directed the trucks over a clattering wooden track laid to level off the rails, to the siding where normally only goods wagons were loaded and unloaded. At this time such installations were always guarded by railway police, for the hunger made thieving endemic and this was where the official rations for the townspeople were delivered and where valuable timber from the district was loaded for removal. This evening it was also guarded by the civil police, all of whom carried hand lamps although the area was lit by tall lamps which swung in the bitter north-easter. These oil lamps not only gave an even more secretive appearance to a place that must in any case always appear strange and suspect at night but were a great nuisance in themselves. Either the police must carry them, putting one hand out of action, or they must be stood down and constituted an obstacle to movement and the danger of fire.

'Over-organisation,' muttered Baxter under his breath to me with the usual scorn of the highly trained Special Branch officer for local, and foreign at that, police forces.

'It is pretty dark, though,' said Tom Wallingham. Nobody else said anything as we piled out of our trucks and the men began to take stretchers off a high stack indicated by a gesture of the station-master. This official knew that the men at any rate could not understand anything he said to them, but his lack of any greeting to us apart from a formal salute gave me a strong and unpleasant sensation; apprehension suddenly mounted almost to fear and I became aware that the man before us was full of a sullen anger only just held in check by his nervousness towards the occupiers. There were three long timber carriers on the rail; behind them at a distance I could already see the bulk of a closed goods wagon rearing against the dark sky and the tall swaying electric lamps and dwarfing the numerous uniformed police moving about to keep circulation going while they waited. Being a goods track there was no platform, and the wagon looked immensely high, silent, black.

'We're going to have trouble getting the stretchers up and down, Sir,' said Sergeant Benson behind me to Tom; he too spoke in an undertone just audible above the scrunch and slither of our boots on the hard, stony and cindery ground which was uneven enough to make us uncertain of our footing in the cross-lights that illuminated everything in conflicting shadows and outlines. It was already clear even to my inexpert eye that no temporary ramp we could lay against the double side-entrance of the wagon would be shallow enough in its slope to afford anything more than an additional hazard.

As we reached the wagon, the police chief stepped out and saluted us. He was an elderly man, probably called out of retirement, and his long meagre face showed lividly pale with the dark shadows in its eyes and under the cheekbones. I greeted him in German and he replied; he was obviously nervous and disturbed to the point of sub-hysteria. I said something about the height of the wagon doors. One of the police was now climbing the narrow steel ladder at the side of the door, and with a great clatter and rattle, released the bars. Two other policemen, standing on the ground pushed the sliding doors apart from the bottom, having to use all their force to do so. The instant the doors began to open a filthy odour billowed out as a visible cloudy miasma into the fresh cold air of the night.

We three looked at each other and Tom's and Baxter's faces showed the rigidity of a fearful realisation which I knew was reflected in my own features; behind us the men made a concerted shuffle and a murmur of shock. I heard a coarse voice use a familiar soldier's curse and another voice answered.

'The poor buggers must be rotting alive.'

'My men will get up and hand down the ones on this side nearest the door first. Then we can clear the wagon bit by bit,' suggested the police chief. His voice shook audibly with the effort of controlling it.

'Get the stretchers as near up under the doors as you can carry them,' shouted Baxter, recognising with a long experience of handling men that he must rally them with clear orders in this instant, before shock could degenerate into disorder. 'Each stretcher will be handled by two men and laid out behind us on the ground until we have the wagon cleared. Form up in line holding the stretchers and as soon as you lay one down the same two men fetch another stretcher. Clear?'

'Okay, Sarnt-major,' said a voice. Nobody else spoke.

'Inglis, you stand right by the door—here to the side or you'll be in the way. You may have to interpret for the police.'

I obeyed him, pulling out a handkerchief clumsily with my gloved hand, to hold before my mouth against the nausea already rising.

The first dangling bundle was already being held out at the base of the opening, but though the two men held the stretcher as high as they could there was still a gap and the inert figure sprawled, half on and half off the stretcher, almost felling its bearers. Tom Wallingham moved quickly to the side-ladder to try to get up into the wagon to help the police. Ashamed that Tom, almost disabled as he was by wounds, should have thought of it before I did, I held him back.

'I'll get up,' I said, 'you try and help the ones already laid out.' Baxter got up after me, and by pushing them out as gently as we could, feet first as we took the forms from the policemen, and by tilting the stretchers lengthwise up to the base of the opening, we managed not to drop them. By now everyone present was carrying stretchers, railwaymen, police, Baxter and the police chief; for it became clear at once that not more than three men could help inside the black dark of the wagon in the hopeless confusion of heads, bodies and limbs. As soon as we got a space cleared to one side of the doors we could use the lamps passed up to us and this made the dreadful task much faster, but with the disadvantage that we could now see the extent of the disaster. After a few minutes one of the policemen had to jump down and reeled off to one side where we could hear him retching loudly. Another man took his place without a word.

I did not see the priest arrive, nor the hearse. Nor do I know how long it took us to empty the wagon. I recall seeing the black-robed figure with the cross bending over one prone form after another, but the memory is confused. Eight were dead. About half of them could still move and rather more were able to speak; presently a confused murmur of sounds rose inside the wagon as the half-conscious men understood that they were being unloaded. There were sixty-two altogether.

As soon as the wagon was empty except for the mass of filth on the floor, an altercation arose over the police hearse which, naturally, was not intended to carry eight corpses. Baxter intervened but his German was inadequate and I called in the priest to decide what should be done. It was decided that the overriding urgency was the removal of the bodies to the morgue, even if they had to be piled up inside the hearse; the dignity of death must wait a little longer. By this time trucks were already coming back empty from their first loads and with the second one came Major Keeler to inspect the situation. He went off with the station-master at once to telephone his medical station of half a dozen orderlies. They were already at the pen and at work when we finally got back there ourselves. In the meantime we had discussed with the priest and the police chief the problem of burial and arranged that all eight dead should be buried the following evening after dark, the same priest officiating. Since it would be in a way a military funeral, Tom volunteered to attend, with Sergeant Benson and four men. This duty was easy to leave to Tom for he was the only Catholic among the officers of our unit. It was clear even without the police chief's openly expressed fears and the pervading atmosphere of sullen horror, that the funeral must not only be as speedy and secret as possible, but that we, as the British occupiers, must behave with all due formality and respect for our dead enemies.

II

That these precautions were necessary was proved the next night, when the cemetery was surrounded by a silent crowd. The following day the row of graves was covered by home-made wreaths and crosses of evergreens, the only tribute the townspeople could manage. There was, however, no demonstration of any other kind, unless a letter of formal thanks for our military presence from the mayor can be counted. But for the time being none of us had any attention to spare for such considerations except for Colonel Manley, who expressed his opinion that the letter was an impertinence; and indeed its perfectly correct formality did somehow convey an air of irony.

By the time all the returned prisoners were bedded down and provided with some kind of food the greater part of the night was past and we three and the men snatched a few hours of exhausted sleep. It was not until the following day that the real shock hit us, for somehow in the nightmarish haste and unreality of emergency the condition of these prisoners did not sink in. They were starving, of course, for everyone in Russia was starving at that time except the Party bosses and these men were the last of a long waiting list in a society needier and more incompetent than anything in Europe; a society moreover thrown back into chaos by war.

Wounds two years old were still open. Neither flesh nor skin had been able to form anew in that climate and with that diet. Tuberculosis, dysentery, vermin internal and external, mental aberrations, edemas and that strange—to Europe strange for centuries—disease of hunger in which holes appear in the cheeks and whole pieces of jaw drop out leaving the inner mouth exposed; all these and much else were present among the sixty-two men. Worst of all was the frostbite. I had never seen it before but those among the men who had agreed that nothing like this for virulence, extent and, above all, smell was anywhere in their experience.

You would hardly have said they were human, or even alive.

Gaping jaws, even where other holes were not visible, gasping groans of foul-smelling breath, the filthy torn rags of leftover scraps of any kind of cloth that bound their feet, hands and heads; yes, these latter were all mixed up in a mess of wrappings with old scraps of what seemed once to have been newspaper, ground in with skin and flesh of rotting feet and hands—for they certainly spent two weeks if not longer in the wagon getting to us. It seemed clear that the rail truck must have been wrongly shunted at some unknown point on its journey so that the routine stops usual with prisoner transports at which food was handed in had been missed and the wagon remained sealed, perhaps even from its starting point, which remained unknown.

For two days and nights we attempted to care for these men ourselves with the aid of Major Keeler and his orderlies, who were never all present for they had their own responsibility to the garrison to take care of. The pen included nothing more than the usual Red Cross first-aid kit of its own. This was the first time such an emergency had arisen, as Tom Wallingham told me, so that the need for some proper medical arrangement was only now obvious. Most of our charges arrived in small batches from regular prison camps, or singly as suspected criminals. From the east we received single displaced persons, or Russian deserters disguised as them, usually sent on to us by the civilian bodies, official and voluntary, that ran the refugee camps. For security reasons we had no contact with Austrian doctors and the hospital in the town was obviously out of the question for the reasons that inspired the police chief's original secrecy; besides, it was full and overfull with the Austrian sick.

The seven inmates of the pen already under interrogation were crowded into one room to make space for the newcomers and, needless to say, there were no interrogations for the next few days. We had enough cot beds but not enough blankets or linen; rations could be indented for, but there was almost no fresh milk or greenstuff even for ourselves except what came up at irregular intervals from Udine—Wilder did succeed quite often in buying blackmarket stuff but that, naturally, was for the Mess and not for prisoners entitled by military law only to the basic rations. There was nothing of that sort to be bought legally in Austria then, even supposing we had funds to buy it.

The first day was an appalling experience and, as I knew only later, it was a turning point in my own life. It is hard to put into words what it was like.

The repatriates were put into their beds in the night as they were. In the morning light it became clear that the first need was to wash them; since their condition had already fouled their bed linen this entailed washing everything touched by them. Tom Wallingham's diagnosis of the old house-boiler which was not normally used—we had installed our own system—proved correct. It did not quite blow up, but neither did it produce hot water. Sergeant Benson sent the men searching for tubs and buckets and I—without it occurring to me to ask permission—authorised him to organise a chain of men to fetch hot water from our own supply in the Mess, and to stoke like fury in both houses. The use of the Mess hot water proved to be a great mistake.

Somehow we organised a laundry in the cellar washroom. We worked steadily all day without stopping, making some sort of a fist of cleaning up the helpless scarecrows who lay for the most part silent and apathetic, when they were even conscious, under our hands. In spite of all our efforts half of them were inevitably laid back into bed with damp sheets until Keeler's long list of requirements was brought back in two of the trucks by Wilder and Sergeant Benson. In any case, after their privations a state that would give a pampered officer pneumonia was nothing to them; in their condition any ill-effects were unnoticeable. On the recommendation of Major Keeler the kitchens of both houses produced a thick soup, the basis of which seemed to be oatmeal; it was not unappetising. I tried it myself before it was issued. The starving men were extravagantly grateful. Some of them tried to say so and that was the worst of the day's trials, I think. It took a long time to feed them for many of them were not able to help themselves.

It was at once clear that the problem of sanitation was beyond our powers; more than half the men could not crawl to the lavatories. It is things of that sort that cause the biggest headaches in emergencies, as I now learned. Even when Keeler's stock of bedpans arrived we were pretty unhandy with them; what we needed was a flock of nurses, but those we lacked.

Rather to my surprise, Wilder rallied to help and the men who, as the saying goes, would do anything for Major Wallingham worked like heroes more for Tom's sake than for the prisoners'. It surprised me less that both Morgenstern and Stephenson turned to with a will, Jack dropping his sarcasms and David his schoolboy jokes, at least for a day or so; and Martin Johnson displayed an unsuspected talent as organiser of the makeshift laundry. Because they arrived back late the first night, neither Manley nor his two theatre-going passengers could have known until the next day what had happened. Just the same, David and the two former Germans worked hard and long, while Colonel Manley was not seen all day. For all I knew, he did not even know of the emergency until late the next day for he was, as usual, shut in his own office most of the time. That nobody noticed much on the evening of the transport was not so strange as it may seem, since lights always burned all night in the pen. They would see nothing out of the ordinary unless their return coincided with the arrival of a truck with stretchers, and these had all come and gone by the time Manley's car got back.

We had no notion of the passage of time. But finally the last man was laid in a clean bed in some sort of decency, two corpses were laid out in the cellar and Keeler was making a round of the beds while I took notes of his rapid comments on what treatments were needed. Tom stretched, his face twitching with pain, for he was almost lame on one side of his body.

'Benson,' he said yawning, 'be a good chap and go and fetch a bottle of whisky you'll find in my room. We all need a drink.'

Benson was a tubby, hearty chap with an almost square red face. He came back with the whisky looking shaken, as the sights of that day had not been able to shake him.

'Sir, I am to inform you that dinner was announced over an hour ago,' he reported stiffly.

'Dinner?' asked Tom blankly.

'I hope they've kept something hot for us,' said Keeler round a cigarette he was just lighting.

Then Wallingham and I looked at each other. He said nothing, but shrugged slightly, catching his underlip in his teeth for a moment as he had a habit of doing in embarrassment.

'Drink up, Benson,' he said, 'we've earned this drink.'

'Your health Sir,' said Benson, without smiling.

We were, now we stopped to notice it, so tired that it was impossible to make the effort to sit down for a few minutes so that we drank standing up.

I stopped to make sure that those men who could move would

report to the men on guard duty if they needed anything while we were gone and then followed Keeler and Wallingham across the well-beaten path to the Mess. The cold, starlit air was a startling relief. I lingered for a moment to light a cigarette, by the overgrown hedge that ran down the dividing fence between the two gardens and drew in the frosty keen smell of clean air. Great stars sparkled and flashed overhead. The hard snow glittered and crunched underfoot. In the distance through a gap in the ordered trees of the garden I could see a gleam of white on the mountains where the moon was coming up, for the sky tonight, unlike yesterday, was perfectly clear.

There was nobody in the large hall. I went straight to my room and hastily cleaned up.

Entering the anteroom prepared to have to apologise, I found Keeler and Wallingham just walking in before me. I did not, after all, have to speak because Manley was at that moment refusing their excuses with a face set with such anger and resentment that for a moment I was bewildered by it.

'I am not accustomed,' he was saying, 'to being kept waiting for dinner by my officers—or guests. Particularly not by uninvited guests.' He removed his spectacles to glare past the others at me. 'You are improperly dressed,' he added.

Then he actually walked up to me and looked me over from top to toe as if I were a horse for sale and a poor horse at that. 'You appear not to have bathed,' he said venomously. 'Which is hardly surprising since there has been no hot water today. Perhaps you would care to explain?'

Someone must have told him that it was I who thought of getting Benson to fetch water from the Mess.

'I'm sorry, Sir,' I stammered like a fool. 'The new batch of repatriates are . . .' I was going to say starving, but got stuck and Keeler spoke first. He sounded almost hilariously incredulous; the whisky on an empty stomach, I suppose. And then, he did not know Manley.

'We had to clean up those sixty men, you know, Colonel,' he said as if making a joke. 'Unless we wanted typhus to break out, you know?'

'In this weather?' snapped Manley, positively through his teeth. His forehead went suddenly red although he had whitish patches under his cheekbones. This was too much for Wilder, who gave a slight snort, whether of shock or laughter I could hardly tell. Probably laughter; he had a strong sense of the ridiculous.

'Exactly, Sir,' said Wallingham clearly. 'The temperature is fifteen below freezing centigrade tonight. The prisoners could not be left in the state they were in unless half of them were to die. Which', he added, without raising his voice but cutting into whatever it was Manley was about to say with obvious and contemptuous intention, 'I was not prepared to do.'

The syntax was odd but the meaning clear.

'I am not aware, Major Wallingham, that the prisoners are your responsibility. I believe you are Administration and Transport officer at this station.'

'You might say that those men were a transport, after all,' chipped in Keeler, still not able to take Manley's rage seriously.

Wallingham said nothing, and nobody spoke for a moment, leaving a silence weighted with our general realisation that Manley had trapped himself. For the condition of the repatriated prisoners was his responsibility.

It was Stephenson, with his instinctive tact in managing the Colonel, for which we had frequent reason to be grateful, who saved the situation.

'Honestly, Sir,' he volunteered eagerly as he joined us. 'They are in a pretty bad state. It really gave me an idea of what conditions in Russia are like. If they, with their ideals, have to let prisoners get into this condition, they must be really starving there. I think we have no idea of how bad things are in Russia. The destruction has completely wrecked the economy, things must be far worse than we have any idea . . .'

Manley must have been grateful to him for going on talking, which after a stuttering pause, he did. 'I saw a bit once at Archangel when I was liaising on the convoys, but not much. They have to be so careful of strangers, we hardly ever saw a Russian from where we were. Well, what we did see was bad enough, but I never really had any idea of how bad . . . I mean, we just don't know what they suffered.' He turned towards Wallingham almost appealingly. 'Leningrad . . . I've read . . .'

David's fair, regular features were vivid with idealistic enthusiasm and he looked even younger than usual. He was several years older than myself, nearly twenty-eight, and had finished the University before his call-up, but I often felt him to be younger than I was

17

and his unsophisticated view of the world made me both protective and envious of him. Indeed, we envied each other I think. He would have liked to have my boyhood experiences, and said so sometimes when I would have been glad to keep quiet about them or even have shed them altogether. And I envied him his sheltered family background, the influence which he denied existed and the air of unquestionably 'belonging'; so we each would have liked to possess what the other would have been glad to be rid of—or imagined so. We both, as we all do, drew what advantage we saw from the given circumstances of our lives, but this universal practice does not imply that everyone equally accepts what is given him, even if it seems good to others. And I often had the impression that David accepted his circumstances as much and as little as I did mine; this made me feel that we had something in common.

His extraordinary charm, the way he put just enough affectation into his manner to give the Colonel the flattering impression that it was of the greatest importance to beguile him, and not because he was our Commanding Officer but because he was himself, succeeded for the moment in calming Manley's touchy self-importance. We went into dinner superficially courteous and Manley looked almost embarrassed because his rage had made him inflate our breach of etiquette into a scene and put off the meal until we appeared.

The food was dried up and half cold but I was without appetite in any case. As soon as the question of responsibility ebbed from Manley's mind and he therefore might suppose it had also left ours, he began to nag again about the hot water. We three were too tired to care and the monologue may not have seemed much different from the usual one, to an onlooker not familiar with the usual subject of some aspect or other of the Labour government's stupidity or wickedness. Keeler, it was clear, was bewildered by the whole thing; but as a guest made an attempt to answer Manley and to converse. As soon as he decently could he took his leave and sent the Mess servant out to call his driver and the orderlies, who could not stay away from their billets overnight because of regulations.

I managed to get Wallingham to go and sleep then for a few hours while I went back to the pen. He relieved me there at three and I slept like the dead until nearly eight when somebody, racketing about on the landing outside my room, woke me.

Breakfast was over but the Mess Corporal got me some filthy coffee. Morgenstern was there, having nothing to do that morning.

'I've been waiting for you,' he said in his odd accent and turned his prominent, intelligent tired eyes on my face. 'Has it occurred to you good samaritans yet that this sort of emergency will be repeated? As I understand it, we have no means of stopping the repatriation transports and I doubt if we ought to even if we could. Unless we want a serious disaster in the pen here we have to get the idea across that some proper arrangements must be made to receive transports in this condition. You see what I mean?'

I must have looked stupid for he went on patiently.

'It is only December and these transports may go on all winter. For all we know there may be others on the way now. The Russians are simply getting rid of the prisoners to die somewhere else. One can find Stephenson's starry-eyed nonsense absurd, but the Russians can hardly be blamed for their attitude to these men even though one knows quite well that it is simply their attitude and has little to do with the fact that these are enemy prisoners. But we ought to start making some proper arrangements for nursing and medical care here.'

'It isn't certain by any means that anything of this sort will happen again,' I pointed out. 'This transport seems to have been lost or something. We had no papers of any sort with them. The military rail people at Sopron over the border signalled for permission to send a short train on, and since it was a military transport the Austrian railways simply let it through and it was diverted to us as the nearest repatriation unit.'

'It's still incredible that nothing was done when the gauge transfer was made at the Russian border. Something must have been noticeable by then . . . ?'

'The station-master said it's the kind of truck that can be reloaded on the different gauge.' I finished my cold coffee with a shudder. 'But you're right. If nothing gets done today, somebody will have to do some heavy hinting.' Neither of us mentioned Manley's name.

I glanced at the notice board automatically as I went out. A new notice was up, forbidding the use of any Mess facilities for repatriates or prisoners.

But we underestimated Manley's sense of self-preservation. He knew very well that a repetition of this transport would mean a scandal for which he could be blamed. Keeler was bound to make a report, if nothing else.

I realised from the delicate way Manley handled Wallingham during the next few days that it was the way Wallingham had spoken to him that made him think. Wallingham was not a man who normally found it necessary to be rude or even blunt.

Baxter was talking on the telephone to the local rail transport officer when I reached the pen. Manley sat by his desk, listening, and from the conversation it was clear that the transport papers had been found.

'Morgenstern was asking what he could do to help,' I said when the call was ended. 'Shall I ask him to take a car and collect them?'

'Yes, do that, Captain Inglis,' said Manley as if I had made the suggestion to him. 'I'll come over with you. I have an office full of work to get through. Perhaps, Major, you would be good enough to ask Major Keeler to come over when he has finished his rounds?'

Wallingham changed his mind over something he was about to say and let Manley go. I realised what that was when we found Keeler bending over one of the starving men a moment later.

'I thought Manley was going to make an inspection?' he said with the sarcastic sharpness that often goes with medical rank in the Army.

Wallingham did not answer.

'This man is not too badly off. I think he'll be all right when the old wound has a chance to heal properly.'

The man in question opened his eyes languidly and whispered in good English.

'I was lucky. In the middle of the truck. It was the men on the outside who got the worst of the cold.' Exhausted by this effort he closed his eyes again and seemed to drift off into a kind of sleep without any interval at all.

'He may be able to tell us who some of the others are when he's in a bit better shape,' said Wallingham. 'We must bear him in mind.' He always forgot that we did not need to rely on someone speaking English; it was as if the other languages did not actually exist for him and it was one of the most lovable things about him that he was in fact rather lacking in brains.

He limped off to the far side of the room, taking Keeler with him to a case he had decided was particularly bad. It was, indeed. Both feet black and formless; the foul stink of gangrene; and the jaw joggled loosely as the man dragged in painful breath. When

Keeler and the orderly had done what they could, Keeler stood up and turned to us.

'It's not much use wasting time and effort on him. Quite unconscious, won't live past today. But I'd like to get some photographs of his face. It's very interesting, I've never seen a case before. I think its gangrenous stomatitis. If he does live a few more days I should expect the jaw to break right out.'

They moved to the next bed. From the door Johnson was signalling to me. He would not come in, he had a fear of sickness and Keeler's remark about typhus last night evidently worried him, for he held a handkerchief to his face—against the smells, I suppose. But you got used to those almost at once.

'Look here, I've had an idea,' he said out in the corridor. 'There is a big convent only a mile or so from here. Why don't we get the Mother Superior to bring some of her nuns over? The Colonel wouldn't have any objection to them, would he? I mean, they are not likely to be a security risk?'

'But where would they sleep?' I objected. 'They are useless if they don't stay here, after all.'

'They can take care of that. There is room in the house, if we make room. It's supposed to hold a hundred and twenty at full capacity, so the Admin-corporal says. Manley was asking him; he thought he might get rid of this lot by saying we were overcrowded.'

'You want me to suggest it?' I was pretty dubious about that. Manley would hardly take any more notice of me than he would of Johnson.

'I'll suggest it to Wallingham,' I said. 'He'll do it all right.'

When Johnson had gone I went back to the man who spoke English. He was a big man, wide shoulders and long legs. His only slightly frost-bitten feet stuck out past the end of his cot. He opened his eyes again when I bent over him. They had fallen back into his head under deep brows and a prominent, bony nose jutting upwards made them seem even deeper set, I suppose, than they were. He was not quite conscious and spoke in German with a slight accent I could not place.

'Where am I? Is this a hospital? Why does nobody speak Russian here?'

'We are British,' I said and for some reason the statement tightened my throat. 'You have been repatriated to Austria.'

21

'Austria . . . Vienna?'

'No, we are way down in Styria here. But don't worry about that. Can I get you anything—something to drink?'

He did not answer for a little, then faintly. 'Will the arm have to come off?'

'The surgeon says not. He's cleaned it up; it was a flesh wound and he said it would heal.' What Keeler in fact said was: 'It won't look very pretty but after what he's been through I don't imagine he'll mind that.'

'I thought it was gangrenous,' whispered the big man, 'but it may have been the man next to me.'

'No, it was, but we have those new healing drugs here that stop it going further. Of course, the tissue that was already gone can't grow again, but it won't be too bad.'

'I dreamed there was something with a leg, too?'

'Yes, a bone broken in the left leg, tibia or phibia, I don't know the names. But that was a fresh break—I can't think how that happened. It's been set. You'll limp a little I dare say, but nothing more.'

There was a long cut on his head and neck, too, but he seemed not to feel it. That, too, according to Keeler was fresh; there was caked blood on it and it could not have happened more than a few days before. There were a number of these fresh injuries among the transport and it was one of the things I had already made up my mind to question this man about as soon as he was fit.

In the next bed a man started to moan aloud and at this sign of life I moved over to him, the jug of some concoction brewed by Keeler's orderly in my hand, which was supposed to stop the dysentery. I lifted the man by putting an arm behind him as I saw the orderlies did, but he spilled, or I spilled the drink. We needed those spouted cups but there were none—they arrived the next day.

'Wait a moment,' I said, 'I'll get a spoon.'

He caught at my arms as I made to move away with a hand so emaciated you could have used it to demonstrate anatomy; it felt like dry leather and not like human skin at all.

'Don't go,' he said in a clear, small voice. 'Stay with me.' The strange clearness, unblurred and steady, of his remote voice chilled me with fear. 'I'm going,' he said. 'Is there a priest here?'

There was a strange sound in his throat or his chest, and thinking he was choking I called to an orderly who was passing to help me lift him. But before I grasped what was happening, the man was dead. He had not seemed so badly off as some of the others. The orderly pushed his hand in under the clean shirt, the collarless washed-out khaki shirt borrowed from one of the men.

'Cor, it don't half make you think, don't it?' he said. 'I've seen a few things in battle, but I never did see anything like this lot.'

Outside the door, I could hear Johnson's pedantic voice explaining his idea about the nuns to Tom Wallingham.

'I'll go and ask the Colonel at once,' said Tom. 'You're a genius, my dear chap.'

'You think he will agree?'

'I shall baffle him with speed and science,' replied Tom. 'He won't have time to think up an excuse.'

At dusk, the nuns arrived. They were not of a nursing order, they were teachers but that was all one to them. They asked no questions not immediately concerned with the task proposed to them and those they asked in the charming lilt of cultured Austrians with all the exact courtesies of speech they were no doubt used to drilling into their pupils. They sent back at once for some lay sisters and by the next evening we were so well organised that there was little difference between the pen and a proper hospital. I suppose they must have been glad of something to do, their pupils scattered, I gathered, except for one or two girls with no settled homes. It was a very odd situation for them as for us, but during the two weeks they stayed with us until the worst was over, it somehow seemed quite natural. It even seemed natural that we should all be terrified of them, though they never raised their voices above a murmur—perhaps because of that. And at any rate, while they were with us the dreary, eternal swear-words stopped.

III

That the pen was turned into a hospital under an almost absolute although unobtrusive control by women so strange to the military life brought with it the contrary effect that our own life in the Mess next door reverted with an effect of suddenness to its normal routine. We returned to our duty times, luncheon and dinner re-established themselves according to the custom of the Indian Army brought with him on his secondment long before I knew the unit by Colonel Manley. That is, junior officers—and we were all Captains with the exceptions of Major Baxter and Major Wallingham—spoke only when spoken to while the Colonel was present. This rule, no doubt reasonable in its former home, was peculiarly inappropriate to an interrogation unit whose officers must always be to some extent outsiders to the martial hierarchy.

Siegfried Morgenstern, who had no connection with the Edward Lear of German literature and who naturally preferred to be addressed as Jack, was older than Manley and all of us by years and possessed several academic degrees. He was named Siegfried during the time of most passionate patriotism among German Jewry and became British just before the war broke out. Martin Johnson was more fortunate, having a name equally easy to pronounce in either language, and fitted more smoothly than his much older compatriot into our company. But he was just as German as Jack Morgenstern, his father having been a Socialist deputy in the Prussian parliament for years before 1933, and this in spite of emigrating young enough to have been educated in England. These two and myself were the only three men there who spoke the German language with any intimacy and nearly all the interesting cases were allotted to one of the three of us. David Stephenson was simply waiting out his time until demobilisation, which he could not normally expect for some time. Wilder, who for some reason was always called by his surname even in intimate conversation, hardly counted as far as work was concerned. He was the son of a builder who made a large fortune on ribbon-building outside London in the thirties and retained the crude but effective business concepts of his upbringing. He possessed a shrewdness which his lack of intellect made it impossible for him to express easily in words and it was easy to think him a fool, a part he often played to the extent of clowning, as half-unconscious camouflage for his merchandising activities. These activities were made use of by Colonel Manley to increase his own income, but this did not prevent him looking down on Wilder as being socially impossible.

The two Majors, who could not be banned from talking at meals, both had their own reasons for not co-operating any more than they were obliged to by good manners in this rule, as in much else. Baxter was a professional policeman, only in the Army for special duties and belonging to a different branch of the service in the disciplinary sense; that is, he was outside Colonel Manley's jurisdiction, a fact which was never mentioned but equally never forgiven him. The Transport and Administration officer, Tom Wallingham, was not outside Manley's jurisdiction, but he was outside his moral and social reach. His full name was Major the Hon. Thomas de Grey Wallingham, and his uncle was an aged Marquis who lived beleaguered in a decaying mansion in Ireland, in a state of undeclared and permanent war with both the British and the Irish; Tom was also a regular soldier of the Grenadier Guards and his posting to us was the consequence of disabling wounds that would have procured his discharge from service if faithful friends had not been able to arrange his retention. His reasons for not wishing to go home were of a nature he never mentioned. It was some years later that I discovered from Lali, to whom everyone told their secrets, that his own small house was occupied by a wife of whose existence I was unaware and her current lover; they later went to Canada or somewhere and had the goodness to leave the house vacant for him. It is clear, then, that Tom was enormously grand, but this was not noticeable and indeed I did not know it until I happened to see his name and rank in Part I Orders, weeks after I joined the unit. What was, on the other hand, at once clear about Tom was his goodness.

Under the appearance of a return to normality, the arrival of the transport really made great changes. It exposed the dichotomy of our official purpose as an interrogating team; it split us into two groups as human beings; to myself it was a shock that made a permanent change in my attitude to the world. Or rather, to people. I suppose that most men and women, sometimes long after they are supposed to be adult, discover the reality of other human beings through sexual love or through having children of their own. For me it was those repatriated men and Wallingham's attitude to them. For Tom they were human beings, nothing less or more, suffering as he had suffered when seriously wounded and left for dead, he lay for days in the shadow of a great rock among the weapons as broken as himself. When the troops who had retreated returned to that spot in the desert it was by accident they found him; they recognised the rock and sought shelter from the sun there as both they and the Italians had done before.

The first interrogations were carried out in the wards, as we now called them, the three main rooms of the house turned into a hospital. The packet of papers—really, not much more than way-bills—found in the railway truck were so fouled and torn and crumpled by the journey that its contents were unreadable and useful only for beginning a check on the identities of the men. Of the sixty-two men delivered to us, seventeen died in the first few days, the rest lived except for the men who did not survive the journey. It took us two days working hard to deduce the identities of the thirty-seven men lying there at the end of the first frantic period, by which time we could be more or less sure that those left could be saved. One man turned out to be a Pole who spoke no German—that was how we identified him—and he was removed as soon as his condition allowed it, to the sickbay of the nearest Displaced Persons Camp. There were two Hungarians who had been in the Wehrmacht, three members of the Waffen SS and one of the Allgemeine SS and the rest were Wehrmacht men. Of this remainder, oddly enough exactly half were Germans and the other fifteen Austrians. How such a motley group came to be entrained together and what happened on the journey do not belong to this story, but we could roughly deduce the course of events from piecing together what individuals had heard or seen.

Naturally, none of the men knew at the time what was happening to them; prisoners everywhere are transferred and transported without explanations being given to them. It seemed that a remnant of a large train of repatriates had been uncoupled by one of the endless mistakes that such postwar conditions entail and was recoupled to the wrong train, a goods transport of empty trucks returning to be refilled with 'reparations from current production', which was the phrase for postwar looting when it was official. That was why it took so long. At some stage a mixed bag of odd men had been shoved into the truck, up to then containing Wehrmacht men. At this point there was some kind of riot. Either the Army men in the truck tried to break out, or tried to resist the addition of others to their number, or were simply struggling to get whatever food was being passed in to them. It was from this struggle that the new injuries I have mentioned resulted. The truck was then resealed and resumed its wandering course, each section of rail getting rid of it to the next until it was near enough to the border to be finally pushed into other hands. Ours, as it turned out.

As soon as the nuns had taken over the nursing, Manley began to hint that many of the men could be transferred to other authorities. I watched how Wallingham managed these hints and copied his method as best I could. This was to murmur agreement and then do nothing, finding ever new grounds for delay; the papers were not decipherable and we must wait until the men could identify themselves. Then, checks must be made from man to man as to the identity of his fellows and this excuse was true because in fact the Wehrmacht men all knew each other and had clearly been in the same POW camp together. Then, we must make sure that the Hungarians, the Pole and the SS men had not been put into this truck for some reason the documentation of which was lost. The Pole was the first to go for he talked his own language in his sleep so that even Manley could tell he was no German soldier.

'Now what are we going to do with the two Hungarians?' Martin asked one evening when the transport had been over a fortnight with us. 'We can't put it off much longer. And if they can be identified in Hungary they'll be interned or transported again.'

'They actually were in the German Wehrmacht, were they?' Morgenstern wanted to know. Manley was dining out with the Colonel of a neighbouring infantry unit that evening, so we talked all through dinner. 'I mean, not in the Hungarian Army?'

'They both claim to have been picked up by a vagrant unit of the Sixth Army in the autumn of 1944 somewhere east of Balaton and there captured,' said Martin Johnson, who had questioned these two.

'That hangs together,' I agreed. 'All the Germans and Austrians are Sixth Army remnants from the Hungarian battles.'

'I don't quite understand your question, Jack,' Tom said. 'What difference does it make?'

'If they were in the German Army their papers may have survived. In that case we had better treat them as repatriated prisoners of war who have the right to stay here or go to Germany. If they were members of some irregular unit who just joined up with a broken lot of infantry for rations and so on, then they are in danger of being put back over the border or turned over to the Russian liaison team in Graz.'

'You mean Arrow Cross men?' interrupted Stephenson, who, so far, had taken no part in the discussion. 'If they are, we don't want to have anything to do with protecting them. That bunch of Fascists! As a matter of fact,' he pushed his hair off his forehead with a characteristic, nervous gesture, 'I don't know why you all take so much interest in these men at all. Once they are on their feet they can take care of their own lives. Provided they are not to be kept here as prisoners, I mean.'

'We can't put them where they can be transported again to Russia,' said Tom.

'Why must you talk like that about the Russians, as if they were a fate worse than death?' David was suddenly excited with a characteristic effect of suppressed violence that he sometimes showed. 'You would think these men hadn't laid waste the whole of Europe to hear you talk; as if they were a bunch of helpless women and children.'

'I was just judging by the state they were in when they came,' said Tom apologetically.

'We don't know that they laid anything waste,' I said. 'It's not up to us to judge them. We know nothing about them.'

'That's just what it is up to us to do.' Stephenson was right there, I knew; that was exactly what we were there to do. But I was startled by a tone of anger that had already prejudged all of the prisoners in a blanket judgment.

'They may not have been soldiers at all,' put in Morgenstern. 'Several times we've had men in scraps of uniform just picked up and transported, and then repatriated with Army men because they were of military age.'

'In that case they are Displaced Persons,' said Johnson. Here was something definite that could be pigeonholed. 'As soon as they're fit we can turn them over to the camp.'

'It seems to me,' said Morgenstern, 'that would be the simplest thing to do with them. Their names are not on our lists of wanted men. They can be transferred like that Pole and if they want to go home the liaison team in the camp will send them back.'

'So long as they understand what they have to do,' Johnson insisted. 'One of them seems to be rather dumb; it would have to be explained to him with some care. Pity none of us speaks his language. I don't have much confidence that he really understands German.'

'Explain to him!' protested David, laughing. 'What a bunch of nursemaids. Why should you care whether this booby understands or not?'

'Indeed. Why should we?' Morgenstern sighed and took off his thick glasses to polish them, showing his prominent eyes in all their shy helplessness. 'I suppose because we are civilised people.'

'I suppose you mean by that remark that I'm not civilised.'

'No, no. Just rather young, my dear chap.'

'Now wait a moment,' said Johnson. 'Let's stick to the point and not start arguing among ourselves. The Hungarians must understand what is happening if we turn them over to the DP camp because we shall otherwise land ourselves in trouble. And the point of turning them over to the DP camp is to free ourselves of men we have no use for and no charge against.'

'Exactly,' I said gratefully. 'No question of right and wrong, or sympathy.'

'We have nothing against either of these men,' interjected Baxter. 'We shall keep records of them. But apart from that, let's get them off the strength as quickly and tidily as we can.'

'I agree, we must explain to them—for our own sakes, of course.' Tom took up Johnson's version. 'And I'll tell you what—that big man you are dealing with, Robert. He speaks Hungarian, didn't you say? Could he put them in the picture—is he well enough?'

'Kerenyi?' I answered. 'He's well enough now; as a matter of fact he's almost fit. He gets about on his crutches though I gather from sawbones that he should stay in bed for weeks. Would that be all right with security, Baxter?' Nobody was supposed to talk to the prisoners in a language we could not check on.

'Oh-h, I think so,' said Baxter judicially, pulling his tunic straight over his rounded front and finishing the wine in his glass. 'You can be there too, Inglis, and check in German with Kerenyi.'

'You got the most interesting man of the whole bunch, there, Robert,' Johnson said, referring to Kerenyi having been allotted to me for interrogation.

'Oh no,' Stephenson argued excitedly, 'I don't agree. That horrible SS man is much more fascinating. Probably Kerenyi wasn't with this famous resistance group at all—they all say they were against Hitler, after all. But this Benda, he really is the genuine criminal article, a most sinister specimen. The worst I've ever seen, I think.'

'You've been talking to him, David?' asked Morgenstern mildly. 'He seems to me to be of a very low level of intelligence. I have the impression he wasn't with the others all the time, didn't you think that?'

'I don't know,' Stephenson was suddenly shy. 'I wasn't poaching on your job, Jack. I hope you don't mind me talking to him? I wasn't really interrogating him; just talking. The way their minds work, this SS type—I can't help being interested in it.'

David suddenly dropped his aggressive manner and grinned so appealingly that nobody could hold his momentary nervous irritability against him. He filled up our glasses now and called to the Mess Corporal for another bottle.

'Let's celebrate,' he suggested. 'Since we have the chance, eh?'

'Yes, good idea. We have cause to celebrate, getting supplies today; the cheese is excellent.'

Gorgonzola and Bel Paese had arrived from Udine with other supplies and Jack Morgenstern had a particular liking for cheese. We were lucky to get these occasional supplies brought by a liaison Major when he came to visit us and other units. He was dining out in Manley's company.

Stephenson stubbed out his cigarette and lit another. He chain-smoked sometimes and liked to drink for drinking's sake. He and Manley would often sit up and finish a bottle of whisky and when they drank together they got on famously, the only one of us who did get on with Manley spontaneously. We were grateful to him for his diplomatic talent with the Colonel and admired the way he took on the ungrateful task of amusing him.

'What makes you think this Benda was not with the other men in Russia, Jack?' I asked Morgenstern.

'I'm not certain. I just have the impression that he tries to hide a lack of intimacy with the others, the Wehrmacht men.'

'That might be because they don't care for him,' Stephenson

pointed out. 'I notice that nobody seems to want to sit and chat with him. Not even the other SS bastards!'

'There's a Benda on my black list, I believe,' said Baxter. 'What's this fellow's Christian name?'

'Ulrich. I'm sure he's on some list.'

'I'll go and have a look now,' Baxter got up and went out to his little office, rattling his keys as he turned over the bunch. Stephenson filled our glasses again, and I took the opportunity to top mine up from the water jug on the table. The heavy, red Chianti we were drinking was very strong.

When Baxter came back he was carrying his black list, which was literally as well as symbolically so, being kept in a black plastic folder. It was not a list but a thick handful of short biographies of men wanted for specific crimes. Benda was in the automatic arrest category, being of the General or Allgemeine SS; but by no means all such men appeared individually in wanted lists and certainly not in such black lists as Baxter began to read from. This was of men already known to be the worst kind of sadistic criminal and was made up of names to become infamous all over the world. It is one of the consequences for Germany of losing the war that this series of crimes and criminals has been accepted by the entire world as surrogate for the cruelties of all totalitarian regimes. This was altogether so then and even now, ten years later, is hardly different although much is now known of crimes just as widespread and terrible in other countries. Yet nobody is interested in why men like other men do such things. It is a matter for great regret that there were no trained psychiatrists in units such as the one I was attached to who could have made valuable researches into the real grounds for such crimes, for the superficial questioning we were capable of resulted in consciously or unconsciously lying answers, coloured by all the contingency of the prisoned state.

As Baxter now read out to us, Benda joined the then illegal SA in his district of Vienna in 1934 and was involved in several brushes with the police. He seemed to have been a casual labourer and spent six weeks in gaol for bashing his foreman's teeth in during 1935. He was again arrested for beating up a prostitute in 1937 but not sentenced. During the Anschluss he was in trouble over a rather vaguely described outrage but there was no police charge, probably for the same reason he was not charged with violence to the streetwoman—membership of the feared SA. He joined the Allgemeine SS as soon as recruiting started in Austria after March 1938 and was attached to the Emigration Board under Obersturmbannführer Eichmann for some time. Recommended by his chief for special duties in Lodz late in 1939, he was stationed there with only short absences until the end of May 1944. He was in trouble with his own SS people in 1942, suspected of embezzlement of valuables confiscated from transportees, and only got away with it on the intervention of his very much senior officer Odilo Globocnik. The threatened SS court of honour was reduced to a disciplinary enquiry in camera, held in Krakov. There was not much doubt that Globocnik's help to his junior was motivated by his own involvement; since Globocnik himself was tried by an SS court of honour later for corrupt financial practices. Benda's protection was good; unlike Globocnik he was not even transferred but stayed in Lodz and was several times promoted after that, reaching the rank of Obersturmführer—Lieutenant—although he was almost illiterate. The final note read by Baxter was that Benda's commander at Lodz, a man called Biebow, was then on trial for his life in a Polish court in Lodz, but there was no mention of Benda being wanted either as witness or accused.

'Yet he was in the forced-labour hiring office in Lodz, didn't you say, Baxter?'

'According to this record, yes. Evidently the Polish authorities haven't got a file on him though, or they would have demanded his extradition.'

'Did he make any attempt to hide his identity, Jack?' I asked Morgenstern.

'None at all. Which is suspicious. We had better assume that he took his papers with him when he left Lodz by some means and they—the Poles—haven't caught up with him.'

'Some of the witnesses will certainly bring up his name in court, and then he will be asked for,' offered Johnson, it seemed to me in order to reassure himself that justice would be done. For a man who had been in that position in Lodz must, we all knew that, be as guilty as hell.

'Is he married, Baxter?' asked David Stephenson. It was such an odd question that I looked at him, startled, and saw Jack Morgenstern observing him with a curious look of understanding; curious because I thought he understood not the question itself but the reason it was asked. David went on, with his own naïveté, which was as if he had never been to school and been taught by the crude methods of boys to recognise his own motives. 'I mean, one can't imagine how any woman could have anything to do with such a man.'

'She wouldn't know,' pointed out Jack. 'Besides, any woman who would marry a man of his type would probably not be able to see what he was.'

'In fact, he is not married, as far as our records go,' said Baxter in a tone of blunt disapproval. He did not like David.

'You didn't ask about Benda before,' said Morgenstern to Baxter. 'Is he new on your list?'

'Yes, a batch of information sheets came today from Vienna.' A courier had arrived from the capital that day, but we hardly noticed him since there was nothing from Vienna—unlike Udine—that we personally wanted. 'The source of the entry on Benda is the files of the Ministry of the Interior; they seem to have taken some interest in him during his career.'

'Probably the file was turned up in connection with Biebow's trial,' I suggested.

'No, Biebow is not an Austrian. But there is a general search unit now in Vienna—part of the "Haystack" lot from London.'

'Haystack! Looking for needles? I wonder who thought of that?' David was delighted at this small joke of official nomenclature. He was now well down the big straw-covered bottle only started upon half an hour before and I wondered, not for the first time, what it was gave David that air of being driven. As far as I knew he had no problems not common to all of us; rather the contrary, for his father had been a very senior civil servant up to his sudden death a year before and though David had no private fortune he was pretty well off for influence.

His voice was beginning to slur and he turned pale, as always when drinking, looking even younger than usual. He began now to throw the wine corks at a large, furiously dark and confused picture that hung opposite his place at table and I knew that soon he would suggest playing leapfrog over the massive furniture. I looked at Tom and, without making any gesture, agreed that we should retire in time to avoid being drawn into any such games. I knew Tom not only hated the games in themselves, but disliked exposing his lameness; this made us allies in a small deception on such evenings and now we got up, stretched, and put out our cigarettes. But we did not get away easily, probably because Wilder, who was usually not

33

averse to horseplay, shouted at David not to play the fool. 'You damaged a picture last week, you ass,' he said. 'We shall have to repair it out of Mess funds.'

'We bloody well won't do anything of the sort,' replied David furiously. 'It's enemy property, isn't it?'

'Not quite,' answered Wilder, pulling a face and laughing. 'We do a bit of business with the owner now and then; that makes a difference.'

'Oh stop a bit and have another drink, you two,' David almost begged. 'I shall be all alone here.' Neither Jack nor Martin counted as drinking companions and he was hurt at our desertion.

'I still have some work to do,' I hedged, embarrassed at refusing him, for I liked him enough to wish he would not get drunk, a habit widespread at that time, mainly because drink was so absurdly cheap for us.

'You haven't a thing to do,' he countered, 'you just want to chat with your Nazi boy-friend. You're supposed to be a Russian interpreter as well as German, but I don't notice you ever chatting to any Russians . . .' This idea amused him for he liked to tease me and would have liked to make fun of Tom too but some, perhaps inherited, prudence stopped him doing that. Tom's family had great influence, even if Tom himself never made use of it.

'There aren't any Russians here at the moment,' I pointed out to show that I kept my temper, because my Russian-speaking was a sore point in more ways than one, as David well knew.

'The real reason you don't like the Russians is because they won the war,' called David after us. 'They're too tough for you, Robert, you're a mother's boy!' He shouted with laughter. 'And they're going to win the peace too—you wait and see . . .'

'You and your politics,' called back Tom indulgently. 'You don't mean a word of it.'

'It's true in a way,' I said. 'I do want to talk to Kerenyi, though he certainly was never a Nazi.'

We went through the Mess pantry and took a bottle of the Chianti which I signed for as if it were going up to my room. It was, of course, against every military law to take alcohol of any kind into the pen.

'It's true that I don't like the Russians, too,' said Tom easily, 'but David doesn't rag me about it. You should answer him back, Robert; he's only a kid really; he gets at you because you're shy.'

IV

'I think it's boredom, really,' I said as we emerged into the still, hard cold of the night. 'You real soldiers, it's different for you. But conscription is pretty hard on a clever, ambitious chap like David. He's marking time for months, just waiting about for real life to begin again. So he can't take much interest in what he does here— it's only a stop-gap.'

It was clear and the moon, now full, sparkled on the powdery snow of the garden wherever it was not trodden. The trees made lovely bulks and patterns of blues and silvers subtly threaded with the black of branches and twigs. I thought suddenly of the night after the transport, when I first noticed the stars so brilliantly flashing and caught the glimpse of the distant mountains, never seen before. We both stood still.

'It's beautiful, isn't it?' said Tom quietly. We absorbed the quiet, made more profound by a railway engine that faintly clanked from the far side of the town, and then hooted. An owl called, as if answering.

'Just the same, we're pretty lucky, though,' I muttered. 'Just a trick of birth and we might have been inside the pen and not outside it, ourselves.'

The thought was obscurely related to David Stephenson, whose rebellious and changeable moods reflected all the worries about my own future to which I could not openly admit. David's impatience implied an expectation that I certainly could not feel and the remark that we were all fortunate was really an inversion of what I meant. This was not something I could expect Tom to understand without explanation, for his position in the world was so settled that he could not know the feeling of chanciness my unorthodox upbringing had produced. But, by now I relied on Tom to understand me without any intellectual process. No need to explain everything where he was concerned, and that may be one of the reasons I had so quickly and completely become fond of him.

We moved now, scattering showers of snow that glittered in the arid moonlight, from the bushes as we went through the gap in the hedge. Sometimes the knowledge of the high and double wire fence that surrounded the two houses and their grounds gave me a feeling of protection, of being privileged.

I unlocked the outer door of the pen and nodded at the man on guard duty, a Corporal from Durham. Like most of our guards, he was seconded to us from his regiment after a wound that made him unfit for regimental duty.

'All quiet, Sir,' he called cheerfully. Tom looked at his watch and I took the hint.

'D'you want to get a beer at the pub before they shut, Collins?' I turned to lock the door behind us and then unlocked the inner door to the hall. 'We shall be here for half an hour. Tell Sergeant Benson I said so.'

The man thanked us in his Tyneside accent and left with alacrity, having switched the telephone over to the administration office inside the house where we could easily hear it from the 'wards'.

Kerenyi was up, sitting talking to an emaciated wreck of an artillery officer whom we had expected to die but who evidently was tougher than he looked and would survive. I hardly knew this man and therefore could not trust him, so I jerked my chin at Kerenyi and after a moment he limped up to the office door which stood open and looked inside. I waved him in and indicated the fat bottle.

'Come in. Sit down. You know Major Wallingham?' I spoke English because of Tom, and Kerenyi came and sat down in the visitor's chair.

'Good evening, Major Wallingham,' he said rather formally, 'this is very kind of you. I haven't seen a bottle like that for a long time.'

Meanwhile Tom had removed the cork and poured out three liberal drinks in tumblers. He pushed over his packet of Players. 'Don't you rat on us now,' he said.

'Rat? Ah, yes, I know. My English is a little rusty.'

Kerenyi lifted his stiff arm, the left one, onto the armrest of his chair and held the cigarette awkwardly in the left hand.

'Major Keeler keeps telling me I must use the arm,' he explained.

'You ought to be having massage and what d'you call it—therapy,' said Tom, shaking his head. 'I shall get Keeler to have a word with the nursing sisters and see if we can't arrange something.'

'This place is not a reconvalescent hospital,' said Kerenyi, shrugging his wide shoulders. 'You are incredibly good to us all, as it is.'

'We want you to do something for us now, if you will,' I seized the opportunity. 'It's the two Hungarians. They ought to be transferred to the DP camp next week and we want you to talk to them. Make sure they understand their rights, that they can choose to stay here if they don't want to go back home. We don't want to have any queries about them after they are discharged.'

'I wondered what they were doing here,' said Kerenyi, and drank wine with lifted eyebrows of appreciation. 'And so do they. They weren't even in the Army according to their own accounts. One, the dark one, was a skilled workman in a steel works in Budapest and the other a waiter. They were both picked up in a roundup when the Russians took Buda, to work on rebuilding.'

'They weren't with you in the prisoner of war camp, then?' asked Tom.

'I never saw either of them until I came to my senses here.'

'We suppose they were among the men who were pushed into your truck somewhere on the journey,' I explained. 'You haven't remembered anything more about that?'

'I'm afraid the whole journey is very misty in my mind. Somewhere the doors were opened; it was black dark. The truck was full to begin with and there was a lot of pushing and struggling. I wasn't near the doors or I suppose I wouldn't be here to talk to you now; the men on the outside of the truck were all frozen. I recall the doors opening because of the wind and the outside air more than any real memory, and that is about all I can tell you.'

He sat leaning a little sideways in his chair, to relieve the pressure on his leg which was in plaster with a metal support under the foot to keep it off the ground. When he moved his hand to put ash off the cigarette in the big ashtray on the desk the muscles of his jaw tensed with the effort of not wincing and I pushed the ashtray nearer to him. He put down his glass and touched with his fingers the scar on his neck, healed but still very visible, where the fresh cut was when he arrived.

'I think the new men who were put into the wagon must have had bread with them,' he said. 'There was much struggling and shouting and I was flung against one of the uprights of the truck.

37

Perhaps I became unconscious then, and that is why I don't remember much of what happened? And it was dark, too, you see, all the time in the sealed truck . . .'

'Do the two Hungarians know where they were when they were put into the wagon?' asked Tom.

'None of us does. They were taken from one train over the lines and pushed into the wagon already filled with the rest of us. It was night; they saw nothing but the railway lines and the trucks. But the others can tell you all that, in German.'

'Yes, I just wondered if they'd said anything more—to you, in their own language?'

'No, nothing. But they certainly are neither of them soldiers.'

'Yes, I'm sure we had just better send them over to the UNRRA people. They are well enough now. They were not in too bad shape when they got here. Hadn't been so long in the truck as the rest of you.'

'You might ask some of the others in the later group if you need to know more. Did no travel documents come with them?'

'That lot had no papers at all. Not even the sort of way-bill that was originally in the holder; the Austrian railwaymen did eventually find the list belonging to the original group in the mess on the wagon floor. The container had been wrenched off and smashed, like everything else in the truck. But we suppose the second group were loaded without any papers at all. Major Keeler worked that out, because the group that was not in such bad condition is the same number as the men missing from the original list. And that is all we know. All the others have been interrogated and know as little as you. And there is no official reason why we should try to find out what happened. It's really—officially—only a matter of checking the identities of these two Hungarians before we release them. The rest is really only our own curiosity.'

'I can't identify these two men, since I don't know them,' said Kerenyi, 'but if you will take my word for it, they are just what they seem. A pair of workmen, nothing more. Their accents and manners are quite typical. If you asked me to speak up for others of that group, I should have some hesitation. But I think those two are just the victims of circumstances.'

'You mean Benda, don't you?' I asked him. 'He was put in the truck with those two, wasn't he?'

'Benda was certainly not in the prison camp with me,' said

Kerenyi, 'and I rather think he was not in Russia at all. But where he came from and how he came to be in the truck, that I don't know.' His manner had become reserved and I knew he suspected me of trying to trap Benda through him.

'What makes you think he was not in Russia?' I asked.

'Benda? He doesn't use the prisoner of war slang.'

'You need not be afraid of giving him away, you know,' said Tom suddenly. 'We know about him.'

'He's a bad lot!' Kerenyi moved awkwardly and put down his glass on the desk. 'But I don't want to have anything to do with it—either with him or with your side of it.' He knew, I was sure, that it would be against the rules about prisoners of war for us to interrogate him about a fellow-prisoner, but that was the most often broken of all the rules of the Geneva Convention. Tom gave Kerenyi more wine and poured himself out some; I shook my head, knowing my very limited capacity for alcohol.

'One of the things I put off—I hope for good—in Russia, was the habit of involving myself in the unhuman generalisations of politics. This man, Benda; I can no longer concern myself with him although I know you expect it of me in some sense. I mean, in the sense of agreeing with your condemnation of him and I do agree with you but the judgment is your affair. The victors arrogate justice to themselves. It may still be justice. But I, you see, can have nothing to do with it.'

'But surely,' stated Tom gently and without protest, 'everyone must have to do with a common criminal of Benda's kind?'

'Not that anyone expects you to give evidence in any sense at all,' I intervened hastily, thinking of the legalities. 'But your whole personality must be against him, just as much as ours is. This is not a matter of the different sides . . .'

'I can't let myself be drawn into judgment,' said Kerenyi hastily, and frowned uneasily. 'I'm not fit for it. As Captain Inglis can tell you, Major, there is a sense in which I can be judged myself. I maintained contacts with the Gestapo when it suited me. Both at the beginning, before the war started, and later.'

'The Gestapo!' muttered Tom unhappily, turning to me as the source of understanding in such complicated matters.

'The conspirators did,' I admitted. 'They had to know what the police were thinking, you see.'

'Not all the conspirators, by any means, Captain Inglis,' Kerenyi corrected me, and a derisive look I had been puzzled by several times before this occasion crossed his haggard face. 'Such contacts were left to outsiders like myself. The aristocratic officers never dirtied their hands with policemen. But I should hardly have been able to survive if I had not known where to turn for help when it came to the point. So I owe my life in a way to a man not very far removed in evil from Benda himself. Who am I, then, to judge him?'

'Blaschke?' I asked him. 'I thought you considered him quite a decent chap—for a policeman?'

'Not Blaschke, no. He was dead by then. I made a bargain with SS-General Tenius, who was police commander of the Breslau district. He put in a quite false report to the Albrechtstrasse to the effect that I had been reporting to him on my activities with the conspirators against Hitler. In return I took a white-washing report of his own views on the Final Solution to *my* friends. As the war turned out, it may not have been needed, this manoeuvre. But I could not know that in July 1944.'

'But you knew by then that the war was lost, surely?' asked Tom.

'Of course. Long before that. But the nearer disaster came, the more savage the police were and I was afraid someone of my fellow-conspirators might have written down my name or mentioned me under torture; such things happened.'

'If you knew the war was lost and if—as you have told me—you made up your mind that the conspiracy against Hitler was useless even before the assassination was attempted, then why did you continue with it to the bitter end?'

'I could not play the coward and get out while better men were prepared to give up their lives,' he replied to my question. 'There is a logic of conspiracy which includes the logic of involvement—in both directions, the friends and the enemies—that is, the police. It is that logic I am determined no longer to belong to. And, in any case . . . I know that it is all of no use. Opposition, political activity . . . of no use.'

There was a silence; Tom said nothing out of modesty, I because I could guess that Kerenyi had more to say. We waited while he collected his thoughts into the foreign language for us.

'Once power is out of hand, or the situation produced by power is out of hand, there is nothing anyone can do. The problem everywhere is to control power. I acted instead of thinking. But we were impotent.' He stopped again and we again waited. Then he burst out with great energy, looking from Tom to me with that derisive look.

'You too were impotent. You could not control your Churchill— or even know what was happening. Only while situations are not of vital urgency and importance do controls work. As soon as a crisis is upon a community, the circumstances take on a being of their own, and the need to act reduces the freedom to decide between several courses of action to an iron law—reaction to the actions of others. This is true of natural catastrophes, like floods or earthquakes. But it is equally true of political catastrophes, above all, of war. The paradox is that this loss of freedom is what gives men the sensation of liberation in war—they no longer need to choose but must do what they must do. Men flee from choice into obedience to the laws of action. The only exceptions are those who remain attached to the most primitive loyalties; loyalty to a person or a family. Occasionally a priest, a pacifist, women . . . There was a priest in the camp with us, but he is not here now. He must be one of those who died. I remember him faintly on the journey, trying to talk to Benda. He persuaded us to go to Mass in the camp, and we went for companionship; it took one's mind off the hunger. He was not one of those very pious priests; a simple man who believed if we went to confession and ate no meat on Friday all would be well. In the truck I could hear him praying for the men who were gnawing those already dead—Benda shouted him down and someone struggled. Perhaps he was killed then? I can't recall clearly, it was very confused.'

'How did you know it was Benda in the pitch dark truck?' I asked.

'From the voice, of course . . . His was a new voice and the only one speaking Viennese dialect, oddly enough. I recognized him here just because I'd never seen him, until I heard his voice again when I was still half conscious.' Kerenyi turned to Tom. 'You remember, Major? You moved him from the bed next to mine a few days after we got here.'

'So we did,' recalled Tom, 'he was moved to be with the others who were not too badly off and needed less attention.'

'I was confused about him and about where I was at first. I knew, of course that we were not in the train any more. There was light and it was clean, and no rattling or movement. But at first

Benda seemed to have something to do with our being here . . . he was a connection between the two states, the wagon and the bed here.'

'I'm afraid I don't quite get . . .' Tom was bewildered, as indeed I was myself. Never having been shut up in the dark, I did not know of the disorientation it produces.

'You see, when we were put into the train, he was not there. Then the new group was pushed in on top of us in the wagon, I did not know how long afterwards or where, how many days and nights later. But that was the only clear event of the journey, and after that I heard his voice. Oddly enough, I don't recall hearing the two men speaking Hungarian, but Benda must have been nearer to me, I think perhaps on the other side of the priest from me . . . when I came to myself here, his voice was here too. So, being half conscious, it seemed to me that he had something to do with us being here. I can't explain it any better than that.'

'I am afraid the priest must have been one of the dead,' said Tom. 'There is no priest among you now, I am sure.'

'He was not very strong,' said Kerenyi, his control making him sound indifferent, for he forced always a calm exterior to us, the last pride of the conquered. 'But it occurs to me—am I allowed to write a letter from here?'

'Yes, certainly. But it has to be censored, you know that?' I was uncomfortable saying that; it already seemed unfitting that his privacy should be invaded except in that area of his life about which I was engaged in interrogating him, his military career. That part of his life did not, somehow, belong to him; Kerenyi was a very unmilitary man.

'Well, naturally,' he replied, surprised; he was long used to censorship. It was well past lights-out and when I had fetched the letter-card for Kerenyi, we left. On the way back to the Mess, as we strolled with our hands in our pockets—the cold was not noticeable because the air was so dry—Tom asked me about Kerenyi's contacts with the German police.

I tried to explain, as he had explained it to me, what Kerenyi called the involvement of conspiracy. How men determined not to conform must look all the more as if they do conform. But I think Tom did not grasp it for no such conflict existed in his world. His suffering was physical—and emotional though I did not know that then. The kind of uprooted suffering so well understood by Jack

42

Morgenstern and Martin Johnson, the suffering of the exile whose loyalties are destroyed, was unreal to Tom. Yet he did understand and showed it when he stopped and answered me, nodding slowly, his eyes on the snowy ground.

'Yes, I feel sorry for these chaps. They never had the fun of war. I mean—of course, it's hell to be wounded or killed; and for the side that loses, especially for their families. But at first it was tremendous fun too—like playing with great toys, and betting your life on them. Much better than hunting. They never had that; they were forced to disapprove of it all the time. I mean, look at Martin. It must have been sheer murder for him, knowing he was fighting his own chaps, and the hell of it when he read about Berlin being bombed and thought of his family . . .'

'Has he talked to you about it? He told me one day all his family were killed by one bomb except for an uncle—the only member of the family who was a Nazi. Weird, isn't it?'

'Yes, I made a boob there—said I'd pray for them and he was most upset. He thinks he's an atheist, poor fellow, of course.'

I couldn't help laughing in the bleak light of the hall; dear Tom, such a fool and so much wiser than the rest of us.

V

The letter was short. 'My dear Hansi,' it ran. 'I am in a British repatriation camp in Styria. I have no idea when I shall be finally released, since as you know I had some dubious acquaintances during the war and though these people here are—as I remember from visits to London in better days—rather inconsiderable on the surface they are not by any means all as inexperienced as their manner might make them appear. But compared with some other kinds of people who will not need to be more closely described to you, they are unbelievably easy-going with me and have been much more generous in their treatment than I expected. It is, in fact, a great relief to find oneself among people one can get to terms with. What I want you to do for me is to let me know how and where Julie is, and if you are in touch with her, to let her know, as quickly as possible, where I am. I will put off asking all other questions until I hear from you, or from Direktor Schoenherr, to whom with you I shall address this letter. With my thanks and the best of wishes for your own well-being, your old friend George Kerenyi.'

I had to cross out the name of the Province, since we were still technically on active service, and added the military address at the head of the card. I did not need to ask Kerenyi why he put two names on the card; I knew it was because he did not know whether any or all of the three people mentioned in his enquiry were still alive and in Vienna. I did ask him, however, why our correct treatment of prisoners of war should surprise him.

He looked at me cautiously out of those deep-set eyes which gave him a secretive look. The surgeon, Keeler, had prescribed exercise in the open air for him and some of the other repatriates, and we were standing together—I was on my way back to the Mess for lunch—in the snowy tree-filled garden of the pen under a purplish steely sky. He leaned on a stout cane, his plastered foot enveloped in a thick ski-ing sock and a bundle of waterproof material torn, I suspected, from a camouflaged groundsheet that one of the men must have found for him.

'Because I know what you think of us all,' he said at last, having clearly decided not to try to be tactful.

'We are still bound by the rules of the war,' I said rather stiffly. I did not care for the implication of a general overall judgment by us being extended to my own attitude. He glanced at me again with that cautious look that showed how little he wanted to continue the conversation.

'What's on your mind?' I said sharply. 'Tell me.'

'No,' he said, 'it is not my business. You are running this place. Not me, thank God!' And he limped away, leaning on his stick, without further ado.

I thought this was the hostility of the prisoner, although he had shown nothing of such an attitude before this. Rather, what so much impressed me about him was his quite unselfconscious air of being our equal; he showed none of the servility of fear that so often made one dislike a prisoner or repatriate. Kerenyi did not know that we were only waiting for a reply to our check in London on his past, to free him. As far as he was concerned he might, without being told of it, be transferred from the 'repatriate list' to the 'wanted' or 'witness' list and be in for a long and gruelling course of further interrogation. I had said nothing to him of his approaching freedom; partly it seemed unfair to raise his hopes before they were certain of fulfilment and partly because the inmates of the pen, like all prisoners, operated such a close grapevine system that I feared someone else would hear of my giving him the news and get me into trouble with Colonel Manley. Manley did not in the least mind my being friendly with Kerenyi; from his infrequent comments on such matters I knew he assumed that we used the repatriates and prisoners against each other and accounted for any friendliness in that way. But he would have been annoyed at what he would, rightly, consider a breach of security.

Although I ought to have known that Kerenyi would not suddenly change his whole attitude without reason, I thought no more of this until I went down to the punishment cells the next afternoon. I wanted to ask Jack Morgenstern about a man whose adjutant he had interrogated some time before and whose name now appeared on one of Baxter's new information lists.

It was dark down there, and stuffily cold; it smelt of old stores, the dried, earthy smell of potato sacks, a sourish whiff of wine, with an overlay of men in confined quarters. The inside door was double locked, which was unusual in the daytime. I switched on the powerful lights with a feeling of surprise at their being off, so that only the pilot lamps, the original lighting of the cellar, provided a weak glimmer of light. Almost immediately the far cell.door opened and David Stephenson appeared in the doorway. In the harsh lighting he was pale and his fair hair disordered, falling forward over his forehead. He breathed hard and his eyes looked strange. In his hand he gripped an officer's cane; a piece of equipment I had never seen any of us carrying, not even on trips to town in service dress. I experienced that feeling of shock that feels like a thump inside one, and went, as the saying quite truly has it, hot and cold. There was never the least doubt in my mind as to what his appearance meant: that cell was where Benda was confined.

'What do you want?' he said abruptly, as if I had no business there. 'I thought you were off duty!'

'I'm looking for Jack Morgenstern,' I said, trying to sound as if I had noticed nothing.

'He isn't down here. Wait a moment, I'll come up with you.'

The attempt to sound casual made matters worse. David pulled his collar straight with a self-conscious gesture and turned to look over his shoulder into the cell behind him. Then he pulled the door shut and locked it twice, taking the ring of cell-keys—there were only two rings and one was permanently locked up in Baxter's office for emergencies—from the inside of the cell door. I never did become a military man, but this breach of regulations and of ordinary common sense shocked me more profoundly than anything else about the matter. The man in that cell was a multiple murderer and a desperate character who must know by now that his chances of escaping the gallows were of the slightest. To leave his cell-key within his reach was incredible foolhardiness. And as David reached me where I stood by the main door, I saw that he was not even armed. Unless his short cane counted as a weapon.

I was so much troubled by this little incident that I went up to my room instead of looking further for Jack. There Tom found me a little later, staring out of the window at the far hills.

'Can I come in?' he called, doing so. 'There are some letters for censoring, look at Sergeant Benson's there's a good chap, for me. I don't feel up to reading about his daughter's illness today.' He gave me the bundle and I scanned them perfunctorily. Sergeant Benson and the guards, all professional soldiers, were much less likely than I was myself to commit breaches of security. There were no 'bad soldiers' in the pen.

As I gave them back, sealed, he caught my eye, in spite of my care. 'Is something the matter?' he said, and turned the bundle of letters over with a puzzled air, as if I might have seen something improper in one of them.

'Of course not.' I laughed. 'I think I must be homesick or something.' This was a constant joke of Manley's.

'Why don't we drive into the town and eat at the Officers' Club tonight? It's Wednesday and you haven't taken a day off for weeks.'

'Good idea. Ask the others if they want to come. I'm going to have a bath—if there's any hot water.' This too had become a standing joke, but not of Manley's. I felt as if I must wash myself clean.

The use of force, or even the threat of force, on prisoners is strictly forbidden precisely because it is so often a temptation, especially in interrogation centres. Once or twice in Alexandria there were cases of great urgency in which quick results in questioning a prisoner might save the lives of our own troops or even affect the course of military operations. And once or twice the threat of force was used to obtain those results; but that was in the heat of battle and I was lucky in never having been in the position of choosing between leaving a captive in the heat for an hour or so without shade or water and forgoing details he could give us of what his comrades were intending. Physical violence, though it must have occasionally been used, was a military and personal tabu not only because it was unprofessional and inefficient but because it could easily become a habit, a short-cut, the effects of which are almost as bad for the interrogator as for his victims. And underlying the rational basis of the tabu lies the fear of any physical relationship between soldiers that is bound to be strong in large bodies of men living close together for months on end without feminine company. In the case of Benda there was no need for haste. We knew who he was; the rest was a matter of patient collection of details to which Jack Morgenstern was pre-eminently suited.

While I dressed I was struck by the contrast between Jack, who might have been forgiven for feeling hatred of Benda personally, and who could not be imagined as expressing that hatred in physical action, and David, who had no cause for anything but that dislike of depraved criminality which is a kind of superiority and shuts out any possibility of personal relations. We were all so much Benda's accusers that it seemed to me impossible even to speak to him with anything but a cold and distant formality. The thought of touching the man filled me with a superstitious dread as if he could transmit his own evil by contagion.

So I was glad and relieved when I found on going downstairs that only Wilder wanted to go into the town that evening. Both Tom and I liked him, although we then preferred to ignore his business activities, about which he instinctively maintained silence in front of Tom.

'David's going on special leave to London next week—did he tell you?' asked Wilder.

'No. Why? He went on leave only a few weeks ago,' I said.

'He's going to sit for the Foreign Office entrance exam. Rum he didn't say anything. He's known for days, I know, because old Manley told me. Manley is delighted that one of his chaps is going into the FO. Seems to think it's all his doing, of course.'

'He's got to pass first,' I said, with envy.

'Don't you worry about his passing, old boy,' Wilder said, exaggerating his South-London accent deliberately. 'It's in the bag. All his dad's old chums are putting in a little word for our boy David.'

'Will he transfer direct from the Army?' I wanted to know because David would be going quite quickly if that were the case and then I should be relieved of doing something about what I had seen in the afternoon.

'He probably will,' said Tom. 'There is this new selection system now.'

'Isn't that just for the Control Commission?' Wilder objected. 'I didn't know it was laid on for the real Foreign Office.'

'I think so. A man I know transferred from my old regiment direct into the FO. I heard from him only a week ago. But he's by way of being an Arabist, so you may be right, Wilder. It may only be for people with special jobs waiting.'

'No, it's part of this general reorganisation,' I corrected them. 'Neither of you reads the *Times* with care, that's clear.'

'Old governess Robert, teaching again,' jeered Wilder with friendly scorn that had no sting in it. 'I just wish they'd reorganise the rules about fraternising, so that we could bring Austrian girls to the Club. That would really make some sense. I like to dance.'

He stared with a somewhat disparaging look at a quartette of female officers on the far side of the dining room.

'One of them is rather pretty.' I narrowed my eyes to see across the distance. 'Oh, it's the girl David goes with. I hadn't seen them before. Don't you think it's just the uniform that is so off-putting?'

'I'd rather bring a local girl dancing,' argued Wilder, 'that lot are always toffee-nosed. Last time I took one out, she talked about "my people" and what a good lot they were in the Mess. As bad as a man. Though you're right about the red-head, Robert, she's a poppet. But booked for David, lucky so and so. He knows how to handle them. He treats them as if he couldn't care less and they just eat out of his hand. Especially Betty—that's the red-head.'

'I don't know her, but the girl on the left I know. I'll go and ask them to dance if you like,' I offered, hoping he would refuse for I was shy of making myself conspicuous walking across the empty dance floor and accosting, as it would seem to onlookers, a tableful of girls. The one on the left was a very quiet Scot called Agnes Macdonald, whose mild company I found undemanding and pleasant.

'Not a chance,' said Wilder. 'Once was enough for me. They'd start chatting about Daddy and Mums and what a splendid time we had in Rome before we came up here . . .'

He put on a mincing, delicate falsetto, lifting his shoulders and bunching his wide lips together as if for kissing while flicking his eyes open and shut. He had dark, smiling eyes with long, curling lashes and the effect was so exactly like a very affected young girl we both burst out laughing, which was just what Wilder wanted for he knew the girls across the room were covertly watching us.

Just then, David came in. He stood at the door, lounging against the moulded frame and glancing about him looking for someone. His eyes—I was facing towards him and the incident of the afternoon made me aware of every slightest thing about him—slid round the large dining room, wavering over a mixed group of senior officers entertaining some visiting Americans, over the local band, over the table where the women officers sat, over to us. It was quite unnecessary for he knew we were there, having been invited to come with us, and the always half-empty room usually allowed us to sit at the same table together. Units tended to do this even if they were not of a special kind like ourselves.

The *frisson* that went round the table where the girls sat was so much in keeping with what Wilder had just been guying that I began to laugh again. David, meanwhile, raised a hand to greet us and strolled across the room, taking no notice at all of the other table. I could not tell whether this indifference was put on deliberately or whether he really did not care whether they noticed him; I rather doubt if he knew himself.

'David!' called the red-headed girl. She really was very pretty, I saw, as she turned her head and waved at Stephenson.

'You see what I mean?' asked Wilder. 'Now you watch . . .'

'Don't pretend you don't see us,' called the girl in her attractive lively voice, spoiled by just the affected accent Wilder complained of. Forced to notice her, David pretended surprise and went across to speak to the group. But as he leaned negligently on the back of one of their chairs—not that of the red-haired girl—he gestured towards us as if excusing himself, and then came at once across to our table. It was a complete demonstration of the lack of interest that attracted women to him. I wished I could assume it. All the four girls had now turned and looked across at our table and I was forced to smile and wave to Agnes and could feel myself blushing. She sat with her back to us and had not seen me before but she waved now, and again I liked her quiet and pleasant smile. But I was furious with myself for blushing and was sure David never did so.

'I got bored after all, and followed you over,' said David, drawing up a chair from the next table, without asking its two occupants if he might do so. One of them, an elderly Colonel with the black buttons and badges of the Rifle Brigade, frowned at this discourtesy and I did not know whether to admire David's casualness or condemn it. 'I got stuck with old Baxter and he's a terrible bore; a genuine Blimp.'

'For a copper I find him rather decent,' said Wilder. 'What are you drinking?'

'Whisky, please.' David took it quite for granted that someone should order drinks for him. 'No, I can't agree about Baxter. But I dare say you look at him differently from Tom or myself.'

'I haven't any attitude to Baxter at all,' disclaimed Tom with the effect of gentleness he always gave when David said something outrageous. 'I just like him!'

But Wilder was, for once, not prepared to accept David's snobbery, which was not infrequent; he quite often made remarks intended to show a gulf between the classes and sometimes made hints to me that I was inferior to himself because of not having attended a school that would be called 'public'.

'If I'm not good enough for you, old boy, perhaps you'd rather somebody else ordered your booze for you,' said Wilder and ignored the waiter now answering his waved hand.

'Oh, I say!' protested David, immediately hurt. 'I didn't mean it like that . . .'

'Yes, you did and I don't give a damn. I'm just not buying you drinks if you can't be civil,' replied Wilder.

'A double Scotch and soda with ice, if you've got any,' ordered Tom.

'It will go on our joint bill anyway,' Wilder pushed his advantage. He was the only one of us who complained that David tried to avoid paying for things. The rest of us were ashamed of this streak of carefulness with money and, as men usually do, tried to ignore it.

'I hear you're going off to London.' I changed the subject.

'Next week,' David was grateful. 'I'm scared to death. Not of the interviews—I can manage those old buffers. But the written exam!' He gave an exaggerated shudder.

'That'll be all right, you'll find,' said Wilder and offered Tom and myself the wine bottle. We had just finished our meal when David appeared, and we now emptied the bottle and ordered coffee.

I wished strongly that he had not followed us; I found it hard to speak normally to him. And yet, nothing had happened. But something *had* happened, and this was proved by the way David kept glancing at me sideways, seeming to expect something or perhaps trying to guess whether I had said anything to the others. He was doing most of the talking now for the casual and pleasant atmosphere of our dinner party was gone. He talked about politics of which he knew little and that little so distorted by irrational emotionalism that the subject served only to supply him with a reason for anger.

This evening it was a renewed promise by the British government to supply food to the British Zone of Germany, an act of self-preservation that appeared reasonable to me. I said as much.

'If they starve by the thousand we shall have all the trouble of food riots, and disease in the summer. Besides, it would take the entire Army and Navy to police the area. I don't see what we can do except feed them as far as we can.'

'I don't agree. You lived in Germany, too long, Robert. The Morgenthau plan was right, the population should be drastically reduced to the level where their own agriculture can feed them.'

'You don't mean that, David,' protested Tom. 'Think what you're saying for goodness' sake.'

'That's just what *they* did, in Russia. And Poland of course.'

'Come off it, man,' Wilder laughed. 'You want us to behave like the Nazis?'

David, as usual, was beginning to get excited with his second large whisky. He had been drinking before he came out, I saw. I was bored and annoyed, as well as embarrassed, with the way the evening was going so I got up and went over to the girls' table to ask Agnes Macdonald to dance. She was a nice girl, in the sense that Wilder would have meant sarcastically and I wished we could go off together for an hour or so, just to talk. I wanted somebody to ask for advice, somebody who would not know what specific people and happenings my description referred to.

Even to go into the bar to talk was out of the question in the circumstances, but just chatting through the vaguely South American rhythm of the dance music was a relief. My partner talked of the hostel the girls were living in—Wilder would have laughed— and how their small possessions kept disappearing and what could be done about it. She said, what I had noticed myself, that in chance communities such as officers' quarters, there was often one light-fingered member. I suggested the way to tackle her problem was to talk about it openly at dinner or some other occasion when all of them were together, and in such a way as to suggest she knew who did the pilfering. She was pleased at this simple idea and promised to let me know if it achieved any result. I took the opportunity to ask her to come out on Sunday for a long walk and proposed the Army cinema afterwards. Going back to our own table the advice I had so easily given to this girl now gave me an idea about my own problem. I would hint to Morgenstern that he should keep the key to Benda's cell himself and not leave it with the guards, who held the cell-keys because of the feeding, exercising and 'ablutions' of the men in punishment arrest. There were two other men down in the basement cells besides Benda, who was there as a dangerous criminal during his interrogation. This and punishment up to ten days were the only categories of our charges who could be put down there and it struck me now that the rules deciding whether prisoners were bad enough and the suspicion of their guilt strong enough to justify their being in solitary confinement were a bit too loosely framed.

To my surprise, the other three had moved round to that subject, as I found on returning to our table.

'He's not a Russian, he's a Ukrainian,' argued Wilder as I sat down. He turned to me. 'Isn't he, that chap in the cells who went barmy?'

'Poor brute, yes. I'm putting in a chit to get him removed to the DP hospital at Judenberg. We can't keep him down in the cells long and he can't be put back with other men.' This man had been sent to us as a Russian deserter picked up by the Austrian police near the border of Slovenia. Two days after he arrived he ran amok with—fortunately—an ordinary dinner knife and tried to stab the repatriates at his table. They managed to sit on his head and he was removed to the cells, screaming and foaming at the mouth. I was trying, in my capacity of Russian interpreter, to discover his identity. 'He certainly speaks Ukrainian or something like it and I can sometimes hardly understand him.'

'Is it so very different from Russian?' asked Tom.

'Different enough to be damned confusing when the chap is raving half the time,' I said. 'And sometimes he isn't speaking the same dialect as other times. I rather think he isn't Ukrainian at all, or even a Russian deserter. I think he's probably a Pole, in fact.'

'At any rate, it's a disgrace he should be down in the cells next to a brute like Benda,' cried David with generous heat. 'He ought to be in hospital.'

'Well, I'm doing my best,' I said. 'It's not my fault that he has to be restrained from murdering his fellow-men.' I was pretty sure, in fact, that the madman was simulating and had a good deal to hide. This was why I wanted to get him over to the hospital where he would be among men who spoke all the various Ukrainian, Ruthenian and similar dialects that I could not differentiate one from another.

'Why bring Benda into it again?' protested Wilder. 'He's an obsession with you, Stephenson. Like King Charles's head—who was that fellow in Dickens who always dragged King Charles into everything he said?'

'As a matter of fact David is quite right that this chap should not be down in the cells,' I said deliberately. 'There is nothing we can do with him really, until we can get him certified and in hospital, but the rules about the cells ought to be much tighter than they are. I'm thinking of speaking to Baxter about the whole cell system.'

It went home. It was David now who flushed and flung himself back in his chair. He muttered something about the strengthening of the top-floor security cells not being finished. Indeed, the work had only just started. He swung himself on the back legs of his chair for a moment or so and then let himself fall forward again with a bang and began to talk about his trip to London, for which we were all grateful.

David sulked for days after that, blaming me for his having been caught out. He watched me, too, listening and coming up behind doors to find out if I said anything specifically about having seen him in the cells that afternoon. What I did do was hint to Jack Morgenstern that it was not safe to have the cell-keys hanging in the guard room. Anybody, as I said, could help themselves when the duty man was called away, or even turned his back to switch the telephones. Either there should be custodians who carried the cell-keys all the time or they should be permanently locked up and anyone who took them should have to sign for them. The rack where they hung was often not even closed; we assumed that the pen was secured from the outside. When I said that, Jack gazed at me through his thick glasses with that blank look of extreme intelligence which made people who did not know him sometimes think he was stupid. Manley, for instance, who never lost an opportunity of ridiculing Jack.

'So!' he said quietly, his Berlin accent very strong. 'You too have noticed that someone has been visiting Benda, have you?'

I was startled and shook my head warningly, frowning at him; the door was open behind me. We were in the little office called the interrogators' room where we kept our records and notes. There were three roughly sound-proofed interrogation cubicles of which this formed the entrance and anteroom, a kind of inner hall. Martin came through at that moment, glancing at his watch and shouting over his shoulder to the guard to bring out the artillery officer for questioning.

'Isn't he David's body?' I asked when I heard the name.

'David's gone into town to get his travel papers,' he replied. 'And Keeler wants this chap finished with because he's got TB.'

I must have betrayed something at the news that David was not in the pen; relief perhaps. It was extraordinary how guilty I had become to feel about him. At my look, whatever it was, Jack raised his eyebrows.

'I thought as much,' he said, as Martin Johnson disappeared.

'How?' I asked, knowing he referred to Benda.

'I saw weals on his neck and made him strip. He obviously thought I was going to start beating him up too, and started whining and offering me compensatory pleasures . . .' I could not help shuddering and Jack gave me that considering look again. 'I just could not think who it could have been.' He stopped and then the solemn honesty of the German, for despite his Jewishness he was, of course, totally German, made him correct himself. 'No. I knew it was—you know.'

'How did you guess?'

'I might ask you that, Robert, eh? But it was just a guess. You must have noticed it—he—is a little queer?'

I didn't ask in what sense Morgenstern used the word; I had only too clear a vision of what he meant and felt again that sense of shock like an inward blow, but this time of an unwilling recognition of something I had known before.

'How did you know?' Jack asked directly. 'You saw something?'

'I went down unexpectedly, to find you,' I said. 'Hence the remarks about the cell-keys.'

'Ah, yes—I will speak to Baxter about the keys. No need, perhaps, to take it any further . . . if we are careful from now on.'

We sat, I suppose apparently relaxed, looking at each other. Things like this happen so quietly that it is only afterwards, sometimes long afterwards, that the fact of something crucial happening, becomes clear. Presently Jack pulled out his top drawer and took out a bar of chocolate, for he did not smoke and had a sweet tooth. Munching on it with the silver paper pulled back over his fingers, he went to the window, curtainless and dirty.

'We must ask Sergeant Benson to lend us a man for window-cleaning,' he said slowly. 'You know, of course, that we ought to report this matter, Robert?'

'Yes, I know. But we aren't going to. Are we?' He turned and looked at me, peering; his lenses can't have been correct for he always peered at any distance.

'I suppose not,' he agreed dubiously. 'Time will shortly relieve us of the responsibility to do so. Or at least, we shall hope so. Unless someone else has noticed something? One of the prisoners, perhaps?'

'How could any of them know? Benda is isolated from them.'

Then I remembered Kerenyi's remark, in the garden. One of the

prisoners who helped the guards with carrying food . . . ? We were
not supposed to use them for work, but they quite genuinely volunteered for the sake of having something to do. They knew every
breath that was drawn in the pen.

'If it comes out, I shall be in trouble,' said Jack.

'It won't. They take that sort of thing for granted, remember.'

I knew some of them did not, Kerenyi himself for instance, who
knew very well not only what the law was but was familiar with the
British and their ways.

'And if that is so, and it is, all the more reason that we should
not allow such—methods.'

It was part of Jack's Germanness that he would say such a thing
where an Englishman would have left it unsaid and contributed to
misunderstanding. For as David had painfully demonstrated, it
cannot be taken for granted that 'we' are sure not to do such things.

'Don't be so worried about this, Robert,' Jack advised me. 'My
dear boy, such things happen in all interrogation units. I've been in
one or another prisoner-cage since the war began, and I assure you
one must always keep an eye out for such lapses.'

He liked to use very English idioms and when he did so, he
would raise his eyebrows and smile in a particular way as if inviting
the compliant amusement of his hearer.

'You're worried about it yourself,' I argued. At that moment the
artillery officer was brought through by the guard and taken to
Johnson's room, so that I stopped speaking until the door was shut
again.

'It was the other aspect of the matter that worried me,' he admitted. 'But as you will find with experience, there is always something sexual about sadistic impulses. David was just reverting to
some schoolboy incident in all probability. It is a good thing that he
is to leave this atmosphere—he's not fitted for interrogation. Too
emotional altogether. And since this last transport arrived we have
all been on edge here. You must have noticed?'

'Yes. My God yes. I still feel as if I'd been hit by an avalanche or
something.'

'This, you see, is what we have made of our world,' he said
softly, still staring out of the dirty window. 'Suffering so terrible
becomes meaningless, like a catastrophe of nature—as you say
yourself, like an avalanche or an earthquake. We can't any longer
look upon it as punishment for wrongdoing. It just exists as a fact

56

so intractable that it is like a rock in the mind—you can't get round it or over it, and neither can you forget it. But David cannot admit the existence of this rock for that would upset all his carefully constructed beliefs. That is why he gave way to a bad impulse over Benda—d'you see what I'm trying to say? He must reassert the wrongness of Nazi war crimes and demonstrate that that wrongness is so great—as indeed it was—that *anything* goes.'

'Well, why doesn't it affect Tom in the same way, then?'

'Because Tom's beliefs are real,' he said simply. 'David's nonsense is just war hysteria. And, don't forget it's shared by a large proportion of the British population. You see . . .' he turned from the window and smiled shyly at me, propped against the desk with my hands in my trouser pockets. 'You have the disadvantage of having actually seen Russia for a short time, even if before the war. You simply don't understand how anybody could be so starry-eyed but lots of people can be—it's plain ignorance. I will demonstrate what I mean in a way you will think very cynical. You know, of course, that David volunteered to travel as liaison officer on one of the northern convoys? At once on his return, as I know because he went to a unit I know well, he asked to be reposted to another branch of Intelligence. You may suspect that this was because of the extreme discomfort and danger of those sea convoys. But I am willing to take a large bet with you that it was nothing of the sort. It was because he had caught a glimpse of reality, and wanted, instinctively, to see no more.'

I was still trying to digest this when the duty clerk came in and gave me an ordinary civilian letter addressed to Dr. Georg Kerenyi.

'He's your bod, isn't he, Sir?'

The censor's stamp was in the interrogators' room so I went back there. Jack went down to bring up Benda from the cells for questioning. It was a thin, greyish envelope of the poorest quality and the sheet of paper was no better; it was written in a large, firm, feminine hand.

'Dearest Georgy, Hansi gave me your card and I can't tell you how wonderful it was to know that you too have survived. I had almost written you off, like almost everyone else I ever knew. We use the Ronacher now, since the Burg was destroyed, as perhaps you heard. I will not tell you personal things, because I know you don't want to read a long list of the missing; life is bad enough without dwelling on the past. The important thing is that you are alive and

I hope well. I found out where your repatriation camp is and I think I may be near there in the next week or so. I suppose there is no hope of seeing you? You will remember my mother's house? I have managed to establish my claim to inherit the property and shall come to look at it. It has been empty for over a year and may be quite ruined, but it is an excuse to get out of Vienna for a little while and if it is inhabitable I want to arrange for Nando's mother and sister and her baby to live there. In case you have forgotten, the name of the house is Gut Schwering, near Leibnitz, Steiermark. I have to go first to Graz about the papers and passes for going into the border area where the British are rather strict because the Yugoslav Communists are a trouble on the border, as they tell me here. The British are very stuffy, but correct. They cannot make up their minds whether I am a Nazi or a Communist or both, but are sure I am one or the other at least. However, since the lawyer in Graz is still alive and even rescued his papers with my mother's will, they have agreed that the house must provisionally be mine. It belonged, in fact, to my mother's second husband but there are no other heirs, it seems. You will wonder at my taking so much trouble over a house I can't need to use but you do not know, of course, how things have been for Lali von Kasda and the Countess but you remember where they lived, don't you? I am not sure what I am allowed to say in this letter so have to be cautious, since the British officers here tell me that you are technically, as they say, a prisoner of war still. I shall telephone from Graz. If you are freed before I can get away, go to the house . . .'

The unknown writer's notion of caution was very much awry; almost everything in the letter was censorable and I knew I ought not to give it to Kerenyi because half of it I could not understand and what I did understand could easily have been coded messages. But I took it to him at once; he was sitting by one of the beds, reading to a man whose eyes were damaged.

'Read it through twice carefully,' I told him, 'because it's censorable and I shall have to take it back and file it.' I drew him over to a window to show it to him, so that the other men in the room should not know exactly what I said. Of course, they heard or guessed most of it—letters did not often come for them.

Kerenyi gave me a quick, startled look almost of fear when he saw the writing which, I assumed, was of his wife. I was worried at showing him the letter, which was written on ordinary paper and not on a prisoner's letter-form and therefore should really have been returned to the sender, and his painful emotion added to my embarrassment. He would think me unfeeling not to leave him in privacy with his letter, but I dared not do that. I turned my head as he finally dropped his eyes to the paper and looked out at the garden.

It was one of the influences of that time that I had suddenly become sensitive to physical beauty and the tangled, overgrown shrubs and trees of the garden made in the snow a series of designs in black and white and many tones of grey, purple, blue which touched me deeply; so deeply that sometimes I could feel my eyes fill with tears and I became unable to speak for a moment. Especially at night these patterns and shadows were unbearably lovely and mysterious, with a significance of their own that has no words. This is an area of living for which we have no adequate, meaningful words. Those abstruse poetical or 'literary' ways of describing physical beauty that are used by real writers seem to me to attach only the ego of the writer to his apprehension of beauty and not to describe the beauty itself at all.

In the meantime, Kerenyi had read his letter and now touched my arm. I put out my hand and he put the paper into it, without our looking at each other or speaking. I can't explain the current of awareness that made me sure of this letter's significance for him; but I felt it strongly. I went away and for some reason which I am also unable to name, I looked up his papers when I got back to the interrogators' room. I had not noticed it before, but saw now that he had been divorced from his wife for many years; so the writer of the letter was not his wife, who married again years before and emigrated to America.

I determined that even if his release did not come through by the time he—or rather, we—heard that the letter-writer was at her mother's house, I would arrange to take Kerenyi there to meet her. This is not quite so incredible an idea as it may seem because we did, from time to time, take a man out of the pen on a visit to the town, usually to give him the shock of seeing a more normal life and incline him to talk.

Baxter came in while I was doing this, with a fresh batch of messages; one of them direct from the department of the War Office in London to which we belonged. There was a list of further questions to ask Kerenyi and an order to release him provisionally when

59

he had answered them. Provisional release meant that he must remain at a certain address approved by us until our masters should decide that he could tell us no more. I already knew, yes I was quite sure, although the letter had made it clear that the house might be a ruin, what that address was going to be.

VI

When Tom and I went over to the pen after dinner that evening, Kerenyi was expecting us as I saw from the sharp lift of his head when we came in. Tom brought books and—illicit—sweetstuffs to distribute to his various friends, and I the questions to ask Kerenyi.

He followed me into the interrogators' room, where the office chairs were hard and had no seat cushions. As always, he shifted his weight sideways to relieve his plastered leg. It was not so bad for me, who had too much fat in any case, but the chair must have been pretty uncomfortable for him. When I made some joking remark about this, he stared for a moment and then laughed.

'You can never understand the sensation of luxury we live in here,' he explained. 'To be in a heated house, just of itself, is incredible. We discuss the chances of the heating continuing, all the time. And sheets . . . well, you can't imagine. Some of us have extravagant theories about the way we are treated. They think we are to be induced to join some invasion army to attack Russia, or recruited as spies—all sorts of things.'

'But you don't believe anything of that kind—do you?'

'No,' he said, consideringly, 'not really. Though I should not be surprised if something of that sort happened. But why do you ask? Have you a surprise for me in store this evening?'

'Yes, I have. But a pleasant one. You are to be released. Only provisionally and you have to live wherever we direct, but still . . .'

I could not understand the obvious disappointment in his face.

The idea of being able to move about freely, it seemed to me, must be the height of happiness to one who had been a prisoner. But I was not able to transpose myself into Kerenyi's state of mind, having only seen prisoners—up to that time—as objects. I understood nothing then of how hard life was outside the occupation fences. Still less did I understand what life appeared like as a prospect to those grown used to Russian labour camps, who must suppose conditions in their homeland to be similar to those of Russian peasants. For Kerenyi, then, and many thousands like him, imagined central Europe to have been reduced to Siberian conditions of poverty. Their imaginations naturally failed to take into account the great differences of long-established wealth in the form of habitable houses, real furniture, window frames with glass in them, leave alone industrial building and communications, and the old-established working of distribution. Everything they knew before, they believed to be now lost.

Just as primitive people cannot envisage taking the apparatus of 'normal' life for granted, so the ideas of these prisoners were reduced to the extremes of privation in which they had existed in the Russian camps. There all the news, apart from rumour which outdid even the reality of the early occupation days, was naturally coloured by the perfectly understandable Russian determination to reduce the conquered areas to the level of their own ruined society; that is, to Asiatic conditions. They were unable to do so because many generations of a civil polity had built up huge reserves of what, from the Russian point of view, were unrealisable assets in central Europe. That is, they could not be physically removed. But this could not be taken into account by men just returned from Russia and still confined in what was, in fact, a prison.

Such thoughts were then coming into being in my own mind from the assumptions made about their future by men such as Kerenyi. I had the great advantage over my fellow-officers that I had seen parts of Russia as a boy in 1938, and was therefore better able to understand both the fears of the returned prisoners and the determination of their former gaolers that their future should at least be no better than the general state of their conquerors.

'Where shall I live?' Kerenyi asked me, and I felt for the first time the reality of his remarks about heating and beds with sheets; to him the pen was a haven of warmth and the guarantee of enough to eat.

I told him he would have to remain for the time being in the district, and could not return to Vienna, where he had a home, and, presumably work. Until he was finally freed he could not return to his world of newspapers.

'The letter that came today,' I suggested. 'From its name I gather that the house stands in its own estate? Can't you stay there and do some farming, perhaps, until you can go back home for good?'

'Farming?' he said blankly. 'But I hardly know a pig from a bale of wheat.'

I was forced to laugh, he looked so dismayed. 'I mean, grow vegetables, keep chickens so that you could live, or something of the sort. From what I've seen of the towns, it is a good thing to be in the country here.'

'Cultivate one's garden, eh?' he said, looking down at his hands with little confidence. 'Perhaps you are right.'

'Rations are very poor,' I argued. 'And in the town you are dependent on them. However bad a gardener you are, and I suppose you're about as used to country life as I am myself, you'll be better off out of towns.'

'You mean, this chance of the house came just at the right moment?'

'It seems providential that the two pieces of news should have arrived together.' I did not want to pry into his affairs further than my job made me; he gave one this feeling of a strong reserve and of having the right to personal privacy which, in his physical circumstances, expressed his strength of character. Though I was extremely curious about him, I had by now a feeling of impertinence when I questioned him.

The new list of queries was evidently part of a complex crosscheck, about a man who appeared to have died in Breslau or been shot there by the SD, at the end of the war. I say it must have been part of a cross-check, because it was clear that the conversation was almost unintelligible to Kerenyi as to me and nothing to do with the plot against Hitler's life, which was the subject of all his other interrogations. Presently, he asked me what could be the purpose of the questions, saying he could be more helpful if he knew.

'I don't know. I haven't been told the reason for the enquiry. Maybe a query from the Poles or the Russians. We get a lot sent on from London.'

'Even about dead men?' Kerenyi seemed dubious.

'That letter, this afternoon,' he went on at last in a constrained even voice. 'Can you tell me what it meant—the sentence about knowing where the von Kasdas lived?'

'I'm afraid I can't. I never heard the name before.'

'No, you wouldn't have. They were friends of the woman who wrote to me. Their house was just on the Vienna side of the Enns river in Lower Austria.'

'It's in the Russian Zone then. That must be what she meant.'

'Zone? What does that mean?'

'But you surely know that Austria is divided into zones of occupation! Originally, I believe three—British, American and Russian. Then the French got a piece, so there are now four zones. It's the same in Vienna, too, the city is divided into four sectors with the old city controlled by turns. The Austrian administration is operating under the instruction of the Allies all over the country.'

'Ah, Yalta,' he said. 'But the Russians really dominate the country, don't they?'

'By no means,' I said sharply. I was used to this supposition from the stupid and fanatical among the repatriates—the two characteristics often coincided—but did not expect to hear it from Kerenyi. 'Rather the contrary; they were obliged to withdraw from some districts to the lines agreed at Yalta. Here, for instance. Red Army units occupied the whole of this area for several months, right up to the ridge of the Lower Tauern and then had to pull back. In fact, they have even left Yugoslavia, by agreement with Tito.'

'That must be why Julie implied surprise in her letter about the survival of the lawyer and his papers in Graz.' He sat, looking down at his hands. 'I wonder what Vienna is like . . .'

'I don't know. I've never been there.'

'Perhaps you're right about me staying in the country. Perhaps better not to go back to Vienna. I don't know that I want to see its ruins.'

'Accounts vary a lot about the amount of damage. Some say it is badly knocked about. But Wilder, who was in Hamburg before he came here, says it's hardly touched in comparison.'

Kerenyi looked up at me under his brows.

'Hamburg was bombed,' he said, 'but have you ever seen a place just taken by the Russians? No? I thought not . . .'

I went over to the cupboard where stationery supplies were kept and where we had stowed away the straw-covered bottle of Chianti on the unused top shelf.

'Let's have a glass of wine,' I suggested. 'You ought to want to celebrate your release. Come along, now, don't be so gloomy!' I looked dubiously at the two tumblers in my hand. We put them away dirty and they now looked pretty sordid so I went out to the washroom to rinse them under the tap. Baxter would have had a fit at the idea of leaving even a released prisoner alone in the room, but I knew Kerenyi would not stir from where he sat.

'So much news in one day,' he said, making an effort to be jovial when I returned. 'It makes me quite dizzy. I'd been living without a future here, and now it all has to be faced.'

'I wouldn't worry too much about Vienna,' I said as we drank. 'Graz was taken by the Russians, after all, and by the time I first saw it there wasn't much sign of disorder. And Vienna being the capital, all the Allies must be concerned to get things going again. Honestly, I'm not trying to comfort you with phrases. Graz really didn't look half as bad as some of the Italian towns I drove through, in the summer last year. And the war was over in that part of Italy in 1943, remember . . .'

'Yes. I wasn't thinking of how it must be now, though. But of during the siege and just after.' He stopped and drank as if he needed the wine. 'But they must have got away,' he said. 'They must have gone. There was plenty of warning. Budapest fell in December 1944 and after that everyone knew . . . I remember hearing of the fall of Budapest in camp . . .'

'I'm sure everyone who could, would have left.'

'That's just it,' he said uneasily. 'Everyone who could. But could they? You could get shot for quitting a job then, you know.'

We fell silent until he said suddenly, 'I see why Julie needs her mother's house, if Nando's family are living in the Russian Zone. Poor Nando. He wasn't made for war.' He looked up at me as he emptied his glass, which he held in front of him, elbows resting on his long knees. 'You'd have liked Nando. Everybody did. But, of course, you don't know who he was, do you?'

I shook my head and refilled his glass.

'He was Julie's lover,' he said, with a curious air of determination. 'They are a very old family. I believe they owned that land there in lower Austria since the Babenbergs . . . well, perhaps that is a slight exaggeration.'

I understood less than ever the depth of Kerenyi's reaction to his letter. This Julia was not his wife and evidently not his mistress either. And he was not the man to feel strongly about the partner of a casual affair, I was sure of that; not even after so long an absence, although I was used to the sometimes immoderate affects of prisoners to any sign of feeling from the outside world. Dealing with repatriates I was already accustomed to the prison neurosis with its febrile and exaggerated emotions. But Kerenyi gave the impression of so detached an intelligence that I could not think of him as unstable; that he was not even in the first few days. Whoever this woman was whose handwriting could make him tremble, she was evidently a woman of stature and I began to feel a very strong curiosity about the writer of Kerenyi's letter.

VII

I did not have long to wait. About a week after our conversation that evening, the various papers which assured Kerenyi's release were all signed and stamped. In the intervening evenings, leaving this job until after the day's work, I completed my interrogation concerning his part—which he belittled—in the plot against Hitler's life, the details of which are today well known. Tacitly Kerenyi evidently agreed with me that he should go, for the time being, to his friend's house for there was no accommodation available in the district, and he was very lucky to have a place to go where he would not be charged the inflated rent then asked for any weatherproof room—if the house proved to be habitable.

I came into the pen on the evening before his release and found him sitting with the almost blind man I have already mentioned, and since they both seemed to be engrossed in what Kerenyi was reading aloud I went quietly round the 'wards' and talked to some of the officers and men I hardly knew. Tom was there, as he was every evening, with his illicit sweets and coffee brewed, also illicitly, by the signals clerk who complained that when Major Wallingham made the stuff himself, it proved undrinkable and he liked a good, strong cup of coffee himself if the prisoners were going to be pampered. It was very curious to see Tom talking, usually with the aid of some officer who could speak English, to all manner and condition of men, none of whom could understand why this tall, shy, limping Major should bother with them. If Tom had known that most of the lower ranks of the repatriates and not a few of the seniors believed him to be what they called a *Spitzel*—that is, a police spy—he would no doubt have laughed; his blamelessness was so complete that I am sure he would have felt no anger but only amusement at the confusions due to language difficulties. A majority of the men could now get about and there was usually much going to and fro between the beds after the nuns retired for the night until lights-out. Colonel Manley never visited the pen after dark and therefore this unmilitary and 'insecure' behaviour remained unknown; Baxter winked at it because he knew that either Morgenstern, Johnson or myself was bound to hear every hint of what went on, for the repatriates had nothing else to do but sleep, eat and talk endlessly. They produced in the process some wonderful rumors and war against the Russians broke out every other day.

'Forgive me that I did not come at once,' said Kerenyi round the door of the interrogators' room a little later. 'But I am leaving in the morning and I didn't want to disappoint that poor devil by not finishing this.' And he laid down on the corner of the desk a copy of *Anna Karenina* in German; needless to say, it was Tom who drove to the town to drum up any kind of reading-matter he could find from lists written out by one of us who could write German which he could then present to the bookshop owner.

'What a strange thing for him to want,' I said.

'Not really. Many of the men who have been in Russia want to know what the *other* Russia is like. Naturally, they think of Tolstoy or Dostoevsky—they've heard of them. I am sure it's the same with your people? Men who have heard only of Nazis must want to know what else there is to the German-speaking world?'

The thought of Sergeant-Major Benson driven by a longing to understand Goethe's theory of plant-life reduced me to helpless laughter, but the intellectualism of central Europe failed to understand our contempt for culture and Kerenyi shook his head at me.

'You pretend to be frivolous—the English always do,' he said. 'But I found on this reading that the end is disgusting. Though it is a great, great novel.'

'The end? Anna's death, you mean?'

'No, no. That was contained in the story from the first. No, I mean Tolstoy's childish nationalism. One can understand it well in *War and Peace* but it drenches much else of his writing, quite taken for granted. It is, after all, a quasi-invasion of the Balkans to which Vronsky is going with such enthusiasm—so absolutely right for Vronsky, who is altogether a brilliant portrait of a type Tolstoy must have known well in his military youth. But Tolstoy himself obviously shares Vronsky's attitude . . . that reduces his stature—don't you agree?'

'D'you know, I'd never thought of it like that at all . . . ?' I stopped short as an idea occurred to me. 'Look here, why don't you write something about this war—you're a writer, after all.'

'Emulate Tolstoy, you mean?' He asked. 'You are making fun of me for being serious.'

'On the contrary—I am being serious for once. You could earn money and re-establish your reputation.'

'I shan't starve,' he said, 'and I have nothing to say about the war, from my point of view or anyone else's. What could anyone write about this war that would not be an impertinence, a piece of crass presumption?'

'Not, perhaps, on a small scale?' I suggested. 'Simply about what you experienced?'

He shook his head. 'That would be even more an impertinence. How could I write about Stalingrad, when I was an *onlooker* there? I was flown out in the last aeroplane almost; and not because of a ridiculous wound I recovered from in three weeks, but because reporters were included in the list of those who on no account were to fall into the hands of the enemy. A splinter through my thigh— God it would be laughable if it weren't so horrible. I saw the columns of prisoners, black, curving lines on the snow, as the 'plane rose and circled. The gunfire was frightful, we were all sick from the twisting and rolling of the aircraft. My sufferings! Yes, that would really be a fitting comment on my own survival, to write about it and complete the picture of a survivor without even the proper shame of having survived.'

'I don't see any shame in surviving,' I protested. 'It seems to me wonderful that anything has survived at all, and I've seen only the edge of the catastrophe from the outside. I was never even in a combatant unit. And don't you feel any—well—not pride, but satisfaction, at having opposed these really terrible people? I'm not trying to talk propaganda about the Nazis, but they really were well worth opposing, to put it mildly. And you did, almost from the start, oppose them.'

'You are sentimentalising the situation,' he said harshly. 'I did nothing. I began to oppose them by co-operating with the Gestapo man watching me. I continued by carrying messages for a marginal, a tangential plot which I knew could never succeed, and which none of our enemies would have treated with, had it succeeded. The real plotters suspected me, rightly, as an intellectual—a word that was an insult to them, as it may well be—and I felt scorn for them as political innocents who didn't even know how important it was to include the signals staff in their plans. In the meantime, while I was playing at opposition, and before while I was simply marking time, enjoying life under the shelter of my Gestapo agent —who had the decency to get himself shot by the Tito "bandits", by the way, and didn't survive to be hanged by his enemies, or reprieved by them, like myself—in the meantime . . .' He stopped abruptly in the middle of his tirade.

'You underestimate yourself,' I said feebly, startled by his passion, so different from his usual manner.

'Meanwhile, other things were happening,' he finished his sentence. 'Yes, other things, things that—as Himmler himself is supposed to have said—will never be written. You know nothing of me. Nothing. Everything you asked me and I answered—just as I used to answer the Gestapo—truthfully; all that has nothing to do with what was really happening. I've told you nothing about me, in spite of the reams of paper you have covered with my answers. Not one of them deliberately untrue or misleading. But you still know nothing. One can talk for ever and tell the truth and yet never reach what was real, what really mattered. That one can't talk of.'

He looked up at me; he was leaning forward with his elbows on his knees, half sideways towards the table and his deep eyes, shadowed by the uncovered overhead light were black holes, above a beak-like nose, making his face ugly and mask-like. He could not be called a good-looking man in any case but now he was almost frightening.

'Lublin, that summer,' he said. 'That was real; that was the presence behind my little chats with the police. And that I did nothing about.'

'You could hardly have done, since you never saw Lublin until after you joined the Wehrmacht news service; and after that you never met the Gestapo man again, according to your own account. Which, by the way, has been cross-checked by other evidence.'

He grinned at my attempt at astringent common sense, which I suppose must have sounded pretty weak. I was unutterably dismayed at his outburst, not because of the abyss of self-accusation it exposed but because I suddenly feared that he had deceived me, or I had deceived myself about him, and there were things I ought to have discovered in his past, things that could matter in the context of my job. He seemed to guess this; of course, his experience of men and the world was far wider than mine and, I was aware, made him immensely superior to me if he wanted to fool me.

'Yes, you are right; Lublin was after I left Vienna.' He said the word 'Lublin' with a grinding emphasis of hatred like a man gritting his teeth together with a bad toothache—or did his reference to the last chapter of *Anna Karenina* bring that simile into my mind? I hardly knew; I was very much at sea. He looked up at the clock on the wall.

'It is well past lights-out. I'd better go.' He limped to the door, saying goodnight over his shoulder.

'The arrangements about tomorrow are quite clear, are they?' I asked. I was to drive him, privately, to the house near the border; we were able to use duty cars on days-off for a nominal charge if they were not being used on duty. I was arranging to buy an ex-German Army vehicle for my own use but the purchase was not yet completed.

'Look,' Kerenyi said, at the door, 'I was being histrionic. There's nothing in what I said but very personal matters. Really. I promise you. It is very good of you to take me tomorrow, and I would not want to reward you with suspicion and stupid mysteries. I felt I wanted to talk about my private affairs, and found I couldn't. That's all.'

It was a most beautiful day, a spanking frost of glittering intensity with the sun blazing in a clear heaven of purplish, winter clarity. It was cold enough to make even the nuns show signs of human feeling, in that one of them shivered as she closed the ward windows, and the priest had a red nose. It was Saturday and he was already making his round, taking the confessions of those in the wards who wished to communicate at Mass next day. They had a strong influence, those nuns; nearly all the repatriates now listened with attention to Mass celebrated at the table covered by a sheet which had been consecrated for them. They grasped, with an intense gratitude that I ought to have understood, at the symbols of certainty.

Tom had agreed that I could drive his precious motor myself, a breach of regulations which ordained that a certified driver must always drive Army vehicles. He, too, was early about and I knew he would have liked to take this adventurous outing with me, though he said nothing but good wishes for a weekend off.

'How can they?' I said to Tom, looking at the priest murmuring by one of the cots. 'You'd think they would all be atheists, after the things they've seen.'

'Men need order,' he said. It was the only theoretical remark I ever heard him make.

71

I went into Colonel Manley's office, where Kerenyi was waiting, attended by a guard for the last time, outside the door. He had a small, roundish bundle with him. He signed his parole declaration and it was countersigned by Major Baxter. Manley was not yet up. Then we left, and it was all very simple.

'Have a good time!' called Baxter after me. 'Don't get too near the border!'

It was the first time since I was at the pen, and I think probably the first time at all, that anyone had gone off on a completely 'civilian' trip, or as we would then have said, ventured into the 'economy'—the real country. I felt like a pioneer.

Kerenyi looked taller, standing outside by the car. He had no overcoat, but from somewhere—the other ranks were much more percipient than we were about such practical matters—had acquired proper boots of which the one belonging to his still plastered foot lay in the back of the car; someone had written off a pair of ammo boots. I had borrowed Tom's big sheepskin driving coat so I could lend him that and wear my British warm for the car was not heated. It fitted him well; Tom was taller than me, and wider in the shoulders, but not so well fleshed and I was too plump for his coat.

The back seat was piled with stores. I had been into the town, to the main Army shop, the day before to buy everything I could think of, out of fear of going short and also of seeming mean. Kerenyi hardly said a word; he was visibly nervous of his entry into civilian life. From the very fact that I was driving him to a house put at his disposal, it was clear that this was a man with friends so that the question of his survival could hardly be worrying him. Millions of men must have feared the approach of an unwanted freedom and responsibility when being freed from military servitude, whether of their own people or of their enemies. There is nothing strange in that and I felt it myself later and understand it very well. But there was a strong feeling that it was his private life Kerenyi would have been happy to avoid and not fear of responsibility for his own earnings, which he appeared, then and later, to view with the indifference of a man who always has managed very well and has no thought of doing otherwise.

We took a map but as it turned out we did not need it, for Kerenyi had been to the house before, years ago, and remembered the way. We only lost ourselves once after leaving what was for centuries a main, a military, road; and that I can fairly claim was because the landscape was blurred by masses of snow while the few signposts surviving from the holocaust of war were covered with most seasonable and annoying decorations of drifted whiteness, like old-fashioned Christmas cards. Twice we were stopped by patrols who examined our papers; mine induced them to believe we were respectable. There had been shootings on the border and that made adventurous travellers officially unpopular.

'Listen, Sir,' said the Corporal of the second border patrol plaintively, 'don't lose your way and go up any lanes to the east from here, will you? Or you'll have to start talking Russian or Serbian. We're sick of digging chaps out of the drifts—they get deep as you go up. And the last car we dug out had two dead men in it. Shot. Them partisans.'

I did not credit his story but assured him that I felt less than no desire to prove my patriotism by chancing my arm with the Yugoslav soldiers who were then still commonly referred to by our troops as partisans and who, apparently, treated our side of the border as fair game and their own as sacred. He and his men were typically enjoying their arduous and dangerous chance to grumble about something for once worth grumbling about.

The snow did indeed get deeper as the road—it is a euphemism —rose fairly steeply, but some kind of track was beaten by local people from outlying farms concerned to earn the high prices of food and fuel. The heavy car waltzed up the curves slowly but surely, the engine thrumming heavily and with a constant rattling from the wheel-chains. What I did begin to fear was to find a total ruin at a time, now afternoon, when retreat would be hazardous.

'There's the house,' said Kerenyi, leaning forward. 'See—down to the left.'

Later I recognised that it was every solitary's dream of seclusion; then I only registered with still suspicious relief that the roof seemed to be intact.

'There's somebody there,' said Kerenyi sharply.

'How can you possibly see anything at this distance?' I snapped, pulling the heavy car out of one more skid. My wrists and forearms felt as if I had been bound on a medieval wheel for hours. From nervous strain on the pedals and from the cold, both thighs were bound tight in muscular cramp. We slid and slewed the last couple of hundred metres. Kerenyi was right, as I saw when I could look away from what I was doing so incompetently. There was smoke rising. By that time the car had skidded, by purest luck, under an archway and I cut the engine—brakes were useless, of course—so that we came to rest a few inches from a formidable barn door on one side of a large farm courtyard. It was what we would call a manor farmhouse.

A moaning wind had arisen, I realised, as I pushed my door open and swung my stiffened legs out. I staggered, we were both half frozen and only the tension in Kerenyi's face stopped me laughing; our comical appearance was suddenly forgotten in his attention to the back door of the house. It was very closed; it seemed secretive.

'You go first,' I said nervously, 'your friends won't welcome a British soldier in uniform.' Then I caught his arm. 'No, I'm armed. I'd better make sure, in case there are strangers here. Or did you expect anyone?'

There was no sound or sign from the house except thick, yellowish smoke from a wide chimney, where damp wood was being burned.

'No. I don't know who it could be—anyone; tramps, I suppose.' He glanced about him and then again at the door. 'We're very exposed here.' He moved as quickly as his stiffened limbs would take him, to the side of the rather wide doorway. There was a carved wooden frame in a niche in the grey stone above the door with the broken figure of some saint, the remains of a withered old votary wreath still trailing from behind the headless carving. The house was built of stone blocks which looked very solid. I followed Kerenyi as quickly as I could, consumed by that desire to laugh which cramp always brings on. He tried the curved iron door handle, and quite simply threw it open. Feeling histrionic, I pulled at my holster, or rather at my revolver which I had never fired. I slid round the edge of the doorway, Kerenyi close behind, and stepped onto ringing stone flags. It seemed almost dark inside. There was no sound, except the whining moan of the wind which would prevent anyone in the house hearing the approach of the car.

After a moment I could see that a figure stood by the long, coal cooking range on the far side of what was obviously a farm kitchen. It was a woman and she turned after a moment filled by the piping of the wind; the draught or the increase of light, had warned her of the opened door.

'Who is that?' said a voice quickly. There must have been fear in it but what I also heard was a demanding arrogance. The tone was clear, ringing, not deep; an extraordinary voice.

'Julie!' cried Kerenyi, and stumbled past me. 'You're here!'

'Georgy!' There was a clatter as something metallic dropped on to the iron stove, and the hiss of liquid on hot metal. A powerful vegetable odour arose. I could see that Kerenyi gripped her shoulders and pushed his head against hers as if he meant to force her onto the stove. She clutched him with equal force and maintained her balance. It was no embrace but a demonstration of ferocity. Then the woman pushed Kerenyi off to stare at him.

'What have you done to yourself?' she accused him. 'And who in the world is that there, by the door?'

Our positions were so irretrievably reversed that it did not even seem astonishing.

'That's Robert Inglis,' said Kerenyi. 'He's my gaoler, one might say. Come in, Captain, and close the door. We shall blow the fire out.'

I pushed the door shut, fumbling with the handle. 'There's no key,' I said stupidly, 'and please don't call me Captain.'

'But how did you get here?' asked that extraordinary voice.

'We drove,' I said, 'if one can call it driving. And if it comes to that,' recovering myself a little, 'how did you get here without the help of an Army vehicle?' I translated this military expression into German exactly, with that desire to relieve tension by schoolboy jokes that belongs to such overcharged occasions.

With the outer door closed, it was almost dark; the afternoon of December was drawing in. I could see no more than outlines.

'I found a lamp,' said the voice. 'No glass, of course. And some oil in the bottom of a drum in the cellar. Just a moment . . .' There was the scraping, several times as they broke off, of matches. 'God, these frightful . . .' Then light bloomed, yellow, soft, intimate.

'It's bound to smell,' the voice prophesied. It did and I have never since smelled paraffin without seeing the farmhouse kitchen just as it was then, and the first glimpse of her face. Especially of recent years, since the jet age began, I feel again that moment folding into other moments that came later whenever one of those splendid machines takes off and away leaving me on the tarmac, with the somehow demonic whiff of paraffin floating in its wake. It must have been the sudden gift of light that created the effect of a revelation; as I have said, beauty had recently acquired a new reality for me. The long, strong, nervous hands holding the lamp base disappeared as she set it down and the lines of her face became visible. Spare, it was, honed down by some privation that was not hunger which produces laxness, a blurring of contour; this was a face drawn to a pitch of power by stringent discipline, and a naked but infinitely civilised expression of acceptance and humanness defined it. It was a moment not of discovery but of recognition, and in that moment everything I had felt and learned in the previous few weeks took on both form and reality, acquired a personal expression for me which I never again lost.

I stepped forward, shoving back into its holster the revolver I could not succeed in freeing, and bowed formally.

'Robert Inglis,' I said, as the custom is in that country. 'My homage, Madam.' There was no exaggeration about the formal phrase on that occasion.

'I am Julia Homburg,' she replied. 'You have a north-German accent.'

'Treat him as a friend,' said Kerenyi. 'He's a good chap.'

'You are very welcome, Captain Inglis. Don't take any notice of Georgy. I really have nothing at all against north-German accents, I assure you.'

She said my rank in English, and not in German, which was at that time universal practice. But there was the sound of some hostility or perhaps derision in her voice which she was not in the least afraid to show. Perhaps, I thought vaguely, she took me for a former German, an emigrant, who in the occupation armies were often unpopular.

'You still haven't told me what you've been doing to yourself,' she turned back to Kerenyi. 'Oh! My heavens, the soup!' She took up a rag from the dirty table and moved a large pot to one side of the hob. Kerenyi bent awkwardly and picked up the fallen ladle and she took it, looking at it dubiously.

'I'd better wash that. The floor hasn't been cleaned for ages, as you can see.'

'Oh, you know, I got a bit knocked about,' said Kerenyi.

She turned away to the flat, old sink of stone and rinsed the soup spoon under the tap. When this was done to her satisfaction and her hands dried from the freezing water, she stirred her soup and tasted it, blowing on the ladle so that the thick liquid crumpled in it as I remembered from my childhood when my mother's

Russian friend made cherry jam. 'Good,' she said and put the ladle on a wooden chopping board. 'Now, come along in. I've made the stove work in the living room and it's quite warm in there.' When she spoke to both of us, she used the plural of '*du*' naturally, since she and Kerenyi were on intimate terms and this gave the occasion an incongruously cosy atmosphere, in spite of her indifferent coolness to me. I remembered the things on the back seat of the car.

'You go on. I'll get our bags. Everything will freeze in an hour, out there.' He looked at Frau Homburg, who had turned towards the inner door, and I said quickly. 'Yes, go on; no need for both of us to get cold again. I won't be a moment.' He knew, of course, that I was embarrassed at being there, interrupting their meeting.

We had only Kerenyi's bundle and my holdall as luggage, but there were the two boxes of supplies and two sleeping bags—I congratulated myself on thinking of everything. Everything except that Frau Homburg could already be at the house. I found that the barn door was only loosely fastened and the vast, echoing space inside quite empty but for an unrecognisable pile at one end of what could be sacks. When the headlamps were on, I could see very well to drive the car in, lock it and remove the rotor-arm which we were instructed always to remove from the motor.

There was no smell of a farm courtyard outside when I pushed the heavy door shut again. It was clear the place had been abandoned for at least a year. It was now almost dark. A heavy, starless night was coming. The piping wind shrilled from every direction, in different notes, as it forced its way through crevices, keyholes, broken windows. It was beginning to snow again. I fumbled my way across the kitchen by the reflection of lamplight from the almost closed inner door. The cover was now on the fire and it made only a slight glow from the firebox. I felt deep familiarity, like going back to a place known many years before.

It was indeed warm in the living room, which was much smaller than the kitchen. A square room with three smallish windows, now shuttered outside against the weather, but uncurtained which looked quite natural. She was speaking of the furniture there.

'. . . It was clever of me, wasn't it? I wrote to the priest here—it was easy to find out his name—and warned him I should be returning to the house and of course he told everybody, and quite a lot of the stuff they had taken was back here when I got here. All the farm implements and machinery are gone, but they knew I shouldn't make a fuss about that if the house was habitable. How cunning the peasants are—one has to admire them. Ah, come to the stove, Robert. Georgy says I must call you Robert. You have been kind to him, he says, and I am grateful to you for bringing him in your motor car; he would never have managed it alone without money. The local people have reverted to their natural savagery, you know, and won't move a finger except for money or goods, and he couldn't have trudged all this way from the last bus stop with his leg.'

'Julie hates the peasants, like all Viennese,' explained Kerenyi, who was seated on a bench that ran round the curved body of the big stove, green ceramic tiles gleaming up to shoulder height and dusty whitewash above that almost to the low ceiling, with here and there a blob of the deep green jutting from it. It had a conical top, very satisfying in shape, rather different from the usual half-sphere. I rubbed my chilled hands together.

'This is wonderful,' I said in English. 'Listen Georg, I'm sure Frau Homburg's food is much better than any of those horrible tins we brought, but perhaps she would allow us to donate some drinks, do you think?'

I avoided using his name when possible, for in our former relationship I could not address him formally and to use his name without a handle, either surname or first name, would have been impossible. Now it came quite naturally to use his Christian name while retaining the impersonal 'you' which is one of the things that makes other languages so much more graded than English. To us everybody is 'you', and we have even forgotten the intimate forms. Kerenyi insisted on unpacking the box of bottles, and took a yellowish candle on a cracked blue saucer to see by, leaving the lamp where it was on the heavy table in the centre of the room. Frau Homburg watched him as he limped out and carefully pulled the door shut to conserve the warmth.

'He won't say anything,' she said abruptly. 'Is he all right? What happened to his leg—that can't be an old wound?'

She had a sovereign, a completely real unselfconsciousness that left all the conventions of strangers simply to one side, like a queen who knows she can do as she pleases, can commit no solecism since it is she who makes the customs. She was not even imperious, there was just some unassailable position in her that took itself for granted.

'There was some kind of a mix-up on the journey from his

78

prison camp,' I explained, grateful that she now accepted me if not my nationality, as a party to the occasion. 'He is all right now . . . you should have seen him three weeks ago. His physique must be terrific, he recovered so quickly.'

'It was very bad, then?'

Faced with formulating an experience still not inwardly consumed, I could not answer. She quite rightly took this silence for an answer in itself.

'I see,' she said, and looking across as the door opened again. 'He can't tell me anything either, so it must have been quite dreadful.'

'Let's not talk about it,' said Kerenyi. 'There are limits to the power of words. Let's drink instead and release everything without the need of them.'

I had stolen some tumblers from the Mess. 'Cognac or whisky?' he asked, 'I know you prefer cognac, Julie.'

'I've never tasted whisky. Give me some, I'll try it.' I was proud of that bottle, which was a month's ration. Whisky and real cigarettes were the currency of prestige. In the Mess we could drink as much as we wanted, but to buy for outside it was strictly rationed because of its immense value on the black market. For the moment the presence of that full, unopened bottle asserted a superiority.

'Mm. A curious flavour. I think, rather pleasant.'

It was curious, but not the taste of whisky. I knew from Kerenyi's manner when he saw this woman's handwriting that there was some deep bond between them and that they must have many questions to ask each other. But, and it was not my presence I was sure, neither said anything except casual chat. They avoided anything that could be in the least serious. An area of years was bypassed, as Kerenyi said, without words. The content of that time, whatever it had been, was simply adopted into the present. A little later, when I knew what that content was, this seemed unbelievable; but it was so. The nearest they came to reality was when Frau Homburg talked of the people for whom she needed to recover her mother's house.

'I'm afraid it may not come off. It seems to be impossible to get permission for them to move, because both the women are supposed to be housekeeping for Russian officers, officially. If Frau von Kasda leaves illegally, the house and the land will be sequestrated and she can't agree to that. Besides, she would have to leave Pohaisky. He's been very much adopted by the occupiers, having been in Dachau, and he's now so crippled with arthritis he can't be moved without transport. They can't even think of getting him over the Enns secretly.' She turned to include me. 'You know, that would mean a small rowing boat—hopeless, he can hardly walk. And it's such a small river! But he'd have to be carried about three kilometres to the bank. We've gone round and round the problem and there seems to be no answer. Margarete—you never met Frau Pohaisky, did you, Georgy?—she's tried every trick either of us can think up. And it's not only the old man, there's the baby. He is just the age, about two, when he would make a tremendous noise all the time— no hope of secrecy there, you see. And anyway, they won't agree to try an illegal crossing of the border.' She turned again to me, this time very personally. 'I tried to get the British to help in Vienna, but they suspect me and it seems hopeless. And I really see their point; there is no legal way of including these people in any transfer of domicile. They have no land outside Lower Austria, no jobs, no relationships . . .'

'Could you sign over this place to them,' I suggested, 'if possession of property would give them the right to move?'

'I tried that. But to establish my own claim to this land, the question of its ownership was gone into so thoroughly, there is no room there for manoeuvre. If only I hadn't thought of the house here *first* . . .'

'I don't at all understand how you came to think of it,' said Kerenyi. 'Could the von Kasdas not have come to you in Vienna? I mean, why here?'

She stared, astonished. 'But of course, they have to go to one of the western zones. Vienna is almost as bad as where they are now. That is the point where the whole question of this house came up, don't you see? It's in the British Zone!'

'I only discovered about the zones a day or so ago,' he said. 'I'm still not clear about it.'

'The child's mother?' I suggested nervously, feeling my way. 'Would she leave without her own mother and the old man?'

'Yes, she would come over with the child, for the child's sake. But how? If she goes secretly, the Russians take it out on Frau von Kasda. How can she do that? She dare not even admit openly that she wants the child to be brought up out of their influence—she's supposed to be supporting their ideas! That is the only way they've kept the property together up to now. Other abandoned estates have been totally plundered. They have a Russian General living in the house—that's their only protection.'

'That's a lot of protection,' said Kerenyi.

'The only kind there is, there,' she said astringently. 'Frau von Kasda tells me he's a very decent man, correct and easy to get along with. I've noticed it before, although I don't care for soldiers much, they are often scrupulous as human beings and apparently the Russians are no exception. It must be the discipline.'

Kerenyi moved lips and brows to speak, but changed his mind and only stared at her with the rather grim and impassive look that made him seem secretive.

'I'm not sure I wouldn't rather be without protection,' I said, thinking of the condition of some of the repatriates and their accounts of Russian camps.

'You have the luck not to have to make the choice,' she said. Then abruptly and coldly, 'It was even worse at first than you can possibly imagine, but that was obviously . . . the looting was uncontrollable. And one has to be just. It was the Red Army that fed me while millions starved. And though they did it for their own good reasons, they opened up the theatres again and that gave me back my place in the world. My short experience of life in a jungle at the mercy of the mob makes me appreciate that, no matter what your Control Commission thinks of me.' She was suddenly really angry and her eyes flicked over my battledress with the hostility I had felt on my arrival.

'Denazification! Boys of your age judging situations you haven't even words for in your language. The crazy questions, impossible to answer, even if one could remember half of it. Naturally, the real Nazis have their answers all off by heart . . . and it makes a festival for the informers. But democratic, of course!'

'I didn't invent the system you know,' I said, putting up my hands as if to protect myself from a physical attack. 'I just do as I'm told.'

'That's just what everybody said on our side,' she countered. 'But don't take what I say personally, Robert. I'm bound to feel very differently from you about such things, but I don't want you to feel that you have to agree with me against your own people, just out of politeness.' She laughed suddenly. 'And I checkmated them, really. They can't touch me and that is what annoys them all, for they are sure there's something wrong with my politics. As if I had any politics!'

'But why?' Kerenyi wanted urgently to know, 'I just don't understand how your political attitude could ever be in question. Doesn't . . .' He stopped; here was some intimate part of their lives not to be spoken of in front of a stranger.

'*Au fond,* the British and Americans suspect me because the Red Army took care of me in hospital, immediately after the fighting was over.'

'Hospital?' he cried. 'Were you ill?'

'I was injured. See, I still have a scar, here . . .' She pushed up the dark hair from her left temple and we could see a puckered white triangle. 'You don't suppose only men were injured, do you?'

There was a silence filled with the fear of going further.

'But your record,' Kerenyi said at last. 'That must be enough for anyone. It speaks for itself.'

'What record?' she said. 'The authorities deal with documents, and all the evidence on paper speaks against me. There is nobody but you who can say anything in direct evidence in my defence. Frau Pichler was killed and he's a bit dotty since then . . .' She turned with what I already knew to be typical swift energy towards me. 'The Pichlers were the house janitors. And you, of course, were not there, Georgy.'

The bitterness of her voice made him shrink.

'What documents do you mean?' he asked at last.

'The transfer of property to me in 1938. Lawyers' papers over the divorce. Part of the record of my interrogation in December '44 survived.' She was brusque, businesslike.

Kerenyi was staring at her, on the point of some vital question; but he did not frame it. Whatever the question and its answer, he was forced to read them from her face.

'I see,' he said at last.

'Your whisky makes me dizzy,' she said to me. 'We'd better eat. I managed to get some vegetables and potatoes and some bread. There's plenty of soup.'

We opened a couple of tins of meat to mix into the thick soup; I did not realise until I ate how hungry I was.

'How long have you been here?' asked Kerenyi. 'Clearly, long enough to come to terms with the peasants . . .'

'I haven't come to terms with them,' she said, ladling more soup with unpractised movements into the stoneware bowls. Kerenyi was cutting the bread, which was heavy, moist and dark; delicious. 'Money is the only thing that does that. And I have some money. That's all anyone does have since there is nothing in Vienna to buy. I've been here three days, that's all. But I mean to stay for at least a month.'

He seemed startled. 'A whole month?' he said, his mouth full.

'Yes. I've gone on strike. I'll tell you about it, but let's eat first.'

But we did not go back to the subject, talking instead of inconsiderable things in the drowsy heat of the big stove, until we all three began to yawn behind our hands.

'One thing the peasants did not return was the bedding,' she said. 'I have only one bed properly furnished. There are lots of rooms but no bedding or mattresses. What are we going to do about you two?'

She was delighted with the sleeping bags.

'Proper mountaineering ones. Where can one get such wonderful quality nowadays?' They were army-surplus sleeping bags, offered for sale at our Army shop as 'ski-ing equipment'. 'You can't sleep upstairs; most of the windows are broken up there. Look, there's a cook's room on the other side of the kitchen. If you can manage to pull another bedstead into it, that will do for tonight. It's warmed from the kitchen fire which backs on to it.'

It was as warm in the little room, its shutters firmly closed, as in the living room. I was now pleasantly stiff and my face burned from the weather invading the unheated car. I went to bolt the heavy bars inside the door and put my head out; it was snowing hard. The last thing I heard was the piping of the wind and I wondered at this obviously pampered woman coming here alone, with no one to do anything for her. The thought expanded and slid into sleep.

VIII

In the morning, the pump was frozen and the tap in the kitchen as dry as the Sahara.

'It ought to be lagged, I suppose,' hazarded Kerenyi. We stood, still crumpled from deep sleep and half dressed as Frau Homburg had roused us, staring with ludicrous respect at the intransigence of inanimate objects, and shivering.

'Hot water?' she suggested. 'But there isn't any. That's obviously what the tank in the cooking stove is for, but I didn't think to fill it last night. Hmm. I shan't forget that again.'

'I've heard somewhere hot water makes it worse,' I offered. Kerenyi, I could tell from the helpless way he stood there, would be of no practical use at all. I went in and pulled out my sleeping bag, as warm as a central heating plant, and wrapped it about the base of the pump. 'It can't be frozen right through. It isn't that cold.' It was a dark morning, late dawn just breaking, no promise of sun. 'You can see, it used to have a wooden housing that protected it from changes of temperature, but that seems to be all broken off. We must work the handle very gently until it gives.'

At this simple instruction Kerenyi co-operated with a force that would break the handle if it really were frozen fast, and I stopped him, laughing at his lack of practical sense which I had not suspected. Rattled gently to and fro for half an hour, the thing at last began to produce water, as Frau Homburg called with satisfaction from inside where she watched. The fire was burning brightly and the kettle soon sang. She came outside with me again.

'It used to have a sort of casing of heavy wood and stood in a little hut. I never remember it freezing before.'

'Wood is an insulator of heat,' I said. 'We must get it covered before the weather gets worse. I must find some planks and straw. There must be some about.' I knew enough about farms—just—to know that and I found some, away from the house in a lean-to in the corner of what was once the orchard; planks formerly used to protect saplings. In the barn, the heap of what seemed like sacks proved to be filthy, rotten straw. It was, though unpleasant to carry, better than nothing.

The smell of coffee was piercingly good long before I pushed open the door and went in, feeling pleased with myself. 'It'll take all morning,' I said heartily, rubbing cold hands together, 'but then I think it may be all right . . .'

My pleasure at being part of even so temporary a community was as abruptly cut off as my words; neither of them listened in any case. Kerenyi sat sideways at the kitchen table, his head down; in the half light of the shuttered room there was an acceptance of despair so drawn in his attitude—I could not see his face, which was turned to the fire—that in dismay, almost in fear, further prattle died in me.

'What d'you mean, I *must* know?' said Frau Homburg's voice in a vibrating, furious tone. 'I was five weeks in hospital—two of them unconscious. When they carried me home, everything was cleared up, as tidy as if nobody had lived there. I've never been down in the cellar from that day to this—I mean from that day when I was carried up. Nothing would get me down there—nothing. If it were possible to get the work done, I'd have the doors bricked up, so nobody could ever go down there again . . .'

He must have muttered something; I did not hear it, but she insisted so that she was almost shouting, battering at him with her voice.

'Of course I asked! I nagged and bullied—them and Hansi too. Finally, that fool . . . I've forgotten his name, I forget everything from that time. Not that he matters. Finally he produced two numbers. I suppose you don't know—but graves have numbers. Gate so-an-so, Path C, row 44, and then the actual grave number. Only *these were big graves.* People laid down in rows. That's not admitted, of course. But as the cemetery man said, the city had to be cleared up before it became any warmer. And nobody talks of it; you can't get anybody to tell you anything. Because it isn't supposed to have happened, you see. We were *liberated,* you see. Only SS men were *killed.* Not people who were supposed to survive.'

I could see that Kerenyi turned his head, lifting his chin to look up at her, his eyes squeezed half shut.

'So. We are the survivors? You and I?'

'That's all,' she said.

'Nando?'

'Dead. I didn't hear until long afterwards, from his mother. It must have been about the time you were taken prisoner.'

He nodded slowly and turned his head away again.

'You knew I was a prisoner?'

'Not until I got your letter.'

There was a silence and I longed for a noise so that I could back away without either of them noticing me. Still staring towards the glowing fire-cage, he said at last, almost as if to himself . . .

'So you thought there was nobody left. You were quite alone. No wonder you've changed. Completely changed.'

'Yes,' she said, quiet now, 'even the survivors are not really survivors, but quite different people . . .'

In a stir of wind sound, a door closed with a thump upstairs somewhere, and I moved quickly, rattling the door and coughing. Kerenyi did not move but Frau Homburg turned, moving a hand to indicate my chair. She reached for the enamel coffee pot on the stove and poured the dark, sparkling rush of coffee into one of the large cups, gave it a brisk, little shove towards me with her left hand and then pushed the grey packet of sugar after it. Tate and Lyle, I read. I spite or because of the gloom, everything that moved was extraordinarily sharp and real, as if the movements came out of depth in a fourth dimension. The oblong packet of sugar brought by myself, its upper side torn unevenly away, increased the reality of the foreignness, rather than making itself or other things seem absurd in its domestic familiarity. Stirring, I watched her hand slide into the flat pocket of the old, blue overall she wore. It was pulled in at the thin waist by a masculine looking strap almost like a luggage strap; the folds of coarse stuff softened by much washing, bunched upwards under the strap, and sprang outwards again above it, almost formalised. As I sipped cautiously at the stinging hot coffee, her hand jumped up again out of the pocket and flicked in the air, a gesture so accomplished, so refined, it was almost hilarious in its inappropriateness.

'But nobody speaks of all this,' she said. 'You'll see, when you get back, it is never mentioned.'

'But that's impossible!' Kerenyi was abruptly upright, outraged. 'Half Vienna must know—just as they knew before!'

'What do they know? They know, everyone knows. But—what? Franz was just gone, as if I never had a husband. When I went to the first meeting, nobody knew what to say. Greetings all round, then silence. Chatter, a lot of questions that nobody quite finished and I didn't answer. I could feel everyone withdraw. At the first rehearsal, they made a more determined effort . . . Willy, Walter Harich, Hella, Thorn. I knew Hansi had warned them not to push me, but they had to try . . . What's the matter?' She broke off with pretended surprise, 'Don't you want to know? But you wanted to know . . . You forced me to talk of it. Now you can listen! You wanted to drag it out in the open, just as they did. Yes, I felt it.' She leaned over the table and over his bent head, speaking now very quietly, with a savage, intense quietness. 'They wanted to adopt it all; that whole time, when they knew nothing and wanted to know nothing—now it could come out. Now it was safe and I was a heroine. Now they could claim it as theirs, too. I could hear them, before a word was said, saying, "Of course, I knew all the time . . ." '

'You are being desperately unfair,' he said.

'Yes. I knew that even then. But I had to stop it growing into a kind of cosy legend. I didn't talk, so nobody else could. Now nobody says anything and it suits them, really. It could all have been rather awkward, though nobody thought of it like that at first—the deaths, and me in hospital—you see? If it is talked of now, somebody might ask why no one tried to help! Above all, they might have to ask themselves that question . . .'

'How you've changed! Before, you could hardly have been bothered with such bitterness. You would not even have noticed other people's little calculations!'

'You're being sentimental. I always noticed, and used, the meannesses of others. But things didn't touch me. Or I believed they didn't.'

'Sentimental' seemed a strange word to use of Kerenyi, but no doubt it was a case of using any stick to beat a dog with.

'I can see I've been taking a good deal for granted,' he said and he turned his hands over before him, as if he did not recognise them.

'Oh, you can do that,' she agreed with cheerful scorn. 'You can have your job back. You'll be a hero. You can do anything you like, when you get back, I expect. Naturally, the Allies don't care too much for anyone who thought it a good idea to kill a tyrant. But, equally naturally, none of them actually mentions it, in case they should seem to think of themselves as tyrants . . . who could be threatened. But if you don't make too much of it—just talk about freedom and democracy—you'll be asked to write your memoirs, I shouldn't wonder.'

She stopped, catching a breath, and unable to prevent herself, went on with histrionic coldness.

'You'll have to get a new secretary, though. Fräulein Bracher's dead.'

'*What?*'

'She was shot. You didn't hear? Yes, over the manuscript.'

'Franz's manuscript . . . ?' He stared up for a moment and then sank his head into his gripping hands and clutched his thick, grey hair. 'God. I'd forgotten.'

He said something else, but he was muttering at the floor and what he said could not be heard. After a bit he rose slowly and went to the door, rather unsteadily, and went out. The door swung to and fro. Frau Homburg shouted after him.

'You wanted to know! Now you know! I'll never speak of it again. Never. Never in my life. You hear me? Never . . .' She was beating on the table with the side of her fist, and without thinking what I did, I pushed out my hand, palm upwards, so that her next blow struck me instead of the wood. It hurt. But she was too intensely human to feel flesh without noticing it, and it stopped her. She looked down at my hand and caught her breath in the middle of a cry with a groan, almost a cough. Instantly, as if without her own volition, a hand flew up to her throat. Then she pushed her hair away from her brow with both hands, which shook. She put out a hand behind her, found the back rail of a chair and scraped it towards herself on the stone floor. Slowly she seated herself so that her eyes, slightly reddened in the inner corners, were now on a level with my own.

Her eyes looked stripped, horrified. She pushed her hand over mine and gripped it where it still lay on the dirty table top.

'Thank you,' she said hoarsely. 'Thank you.'

I curled my fingers over hers and held her hand, which shivered coldly, with a feeling of astonishment.

'Why do you thank me?' I asked stupidly.

'You stopped me saying more . . . How could I say such things, to him . . . ? How could I . . . ?'

I was astonished that I should be thought to have done something helpful, for inside myself I felt like a schoolboy faced with adult passions for the first time in his life. Against my own will, I sniffed and, forgetting dignity, added, 'It's cold. Is there anything to eat?'

'Cheese,' she said briskly, 'you brought it yourself.' She shot up from the chair and brought a packet of cheese for the dark bread, from a side cupboard. After a few minutes, Kerenyi came in again and drew up his chair to the long table, and she poured him out a fresh cup of coffee. Curiously enough, there was no feeling that I was unwanted, or the cause of embarrassment to either of them. Rather the contrary, they needed a third person there to take some of the weight of their desperate communion; and it was an added advantage that I understood little of what they were talking about. I was for both a neutral, a referee to whom neither would appeal but whose presence was a relief. But it was painful to be a witness of Kerenyi's humiliation, half understood as such; he had not shown signs as he now did, in the most terrible state of privation, when reduced to a condition hardly human, that he felt himself weak, lacking in some essential dignity.

'I'm going to explore the outhouses,' I said. To change the subject seemed the only possible thing to do. 'If I'm to lag the pump, I need some sort of hammer and nails or screws. There must be something about that we can use.' While I spoke I gathered up my cup and plate and put them in the sink. After a search of some time through the stables, byres, an empty toolshed, even the deserted chicken house, I did find a rusty hammer with a split haft, but nails had to be knocked with it out of used planks and laboriously straightened for re-use. Everything was rusty; it would not hold for long, but it would be better than nothing. Since I could find no means of cutting up the planks I commandeered, the structure was ludicrous—shapeless, botched. I found one or two rags of old saddle cloths, a torn waterproof, a piece of tarpaulin; all sorts of useless junk not worth the attentions of the local peasants who had plundered the place of everything they could use. These I stuffed between my structure and the iron pump, putting the foul straw on the inside so that it was covered and would not blow away in the first real gale of wind. There was a scuttering under the heap of straw when I first pushed in a mulch fork with one of its three tines missing and I was glad nobody was there to see how I shuddered at the thought of the rats I was disturbing. By the time it was done as well as I could manage, the short day was darkening and pathways were tramped through the lying snow so that the courtyard no longer looked like a calendar picture of romantic winter. From the deep hollow boom under the pump I could tell that the well was very deep and was unlikely to freeze and I hoped that now the pump would not freeze up again. Kerenyi came out early on to try to help, but he had no talent for using his hands and I suggested he would be better employed in collecting any wood he could find and stacking it in the woodhouse—more rats—where it would at least be out of the weather, if not dry. It was obvious from stumps and chips that someone had been felling about the place which must once have been enfolded, and in summer hidden, by trees. I heard later that a good deal of timber was stolen.

I wondered why the local people were so confident that they would not be called to account. That was something Frau Homburg had not mentioned, although I supposed she must know something of what happened to her mother and step-father. She was busy all day, wrapped in the old, blue overall much too wide for her. I could see the kitchen floor was now clean, and I took off my boots and padded across to the cook's room for slippers. Tomorrow, Sunday, I would see if I could do anything to cover the broken panes in the upstairs windows. It is strange how the windows of abandoned houses get broken as if they break themselves.

It must have been a sedate gentleman's farm until a few years before, I thought, as I went from room to room upstairs and through the attics looking for material to cover the various shattered panes of glass. I decided I could use the linoleum covering the floor of the large attic, once the dormitory of the farm hands I supposed, and now empty but for its heavy beams showing a faint gleam of whitewash in the dusk—here there were no shutters.

Among her other business of the day Frau Homburg had cleaned up the bathhouse and although the whitewash showed patches of damp it looked almost normal and I could wash myself properly. She had found the small hanging lamp that belonged there and it burned fitfully through a broken glass. I wondered, looking at it, what had become of the servants—had they just run away or were they involved in whatever had happened to their employers? There had been no violence inside the house that I could see evidence of; it seemed as if the peasants had come and carried off what they could and left the structure. The carved handrail of the stairs, for instance, which must appeal to the acquisitive sense of such people, was still in place. I wondered at that and other signs that the house itself had been spared. I reached the upper story and the attics by the back stairs and saw the entrance hall of the house by coming down the main stair, for the first time. There was a large, well-proportioned room off there with smaller rooms beyond and a considerable dining room with a huge open hearth surrounded by an untrimmed stone fireplace. This was once a handsome place. Peering out of the dark windows in the shadow of my own head, I could see the outlines under the snow of a formal garden and groupings of small trees and shrubs; large trees were absent. Coming in by the back door, as it were, I had underestimated the place; it was bigger than it seemed.

'Did you find anything for the broken window panes?' Frau Homburg greeted me; I was already familiar with the practical turn of her mind.

'Yes, I did. There is a big attic with linoleum on the floor, and I can use that if you agree.'

'Of course,' she said, 'I shall be thankful not to have the weather in the house.'

We were now in the back living room in the even heat of the big stove and my skin burned, the various scratches and cuts of my untutored efforts as a carpenter stung.

'This room has all its window panes as well as its proper complement of furniture,' I said while we were eating. 'It's odd nobody seems to have stolen much from here.'

Frau Homburg laughed. 'This room is supposed to be haunted,' she said, waving her spoon at the space about us. 'That is why the house itself hasn't been much damaged. They would be afraid to have parts of the house in their own homes, or to tamper with it.'

'Haunted! So that's the explanation. I simply couldn't understand the lack of damage.'

'And is it haunted?' asked Kerenyi, who took no part in our housekeeping talk.

'Of course not. But everybody about here believes it is. Very useful.'

'What is the story, do you know?'

'Something to do with a girl, generations back, who rejected one lover and accepted his rival and a short time afterwards she is supposed to have died from no cause that could be discovered. They say it was witchcraft—there are witches in all these outlying districts, as you know. It was almost certainly poison, I suppose. In any case, the girl and the jealous lover haunt the place, turn and turn about.'

'Did the lover die mysteriously too, then?'

'No, he lived to be a very old man, all by himself, and it's an old man with a beard who so terrifies the locals. The girl is rarely mentioned and almost forgotten. I don't think they believe her ghost exists, but they certainly do believe in the old man who used witchcraft to kill her—that's what they are afraid of, his knowledge of magic.'

'I hope he doesn't penetrate to the cook's room,' I said, looking about me at the homely room.

'He can't do or no servants would have ever stayed in the place. In the old days they used to have the priest up here regularly, to keep the old man in his place although he couldn't be exorcised.'

'His witchcraft must have been very strong,' said Kerenyi.

'Strong enough to have saved the house anyway,' she pointed out. 'I certainly shan't try to exorcise him!'

'I'm glad I know why it's undamaged.' I nodded round at the room again. 'That was puzzling me a good deal. Do you think that story is the reason the Russians never came here, too?'

'Oh no, they wouldn't hear a local legend like that. The peasants are very close about such things; the Church would put heavy penances on them if anything were said openly. No, we are too far off the road, that is all, and the hills are higher to the east here than just a little further down towards the village. But the Turks were here once, on a raid, and burned the place to the ground as it then stood. The front part was rebuilt about the turn of the eighteenth century. It's all in the local records, if it interests you.'

'The haunting explains too why they cut down the trees while leaving the buildings intact.' I said it half to myself and was then horrified at going so near to the fate of the property and therefore, of her mother.

'Yes,' she said, giving me a look of comprehension. 'That is shrewd of you, to see that they weren't afraid of human justice.' She drew a breath and forced herself with an effect of brutality, not least to herself. 'The priest swore to me that she died quickly, my mother. She had only this short stretch from here to the village, to suffer and then the first shot went straight through her head, thank God!' She crossed herself at the words.

'Here!' cried Kerenyi, his face rigid again with that look of despairing humiliation. 'In the village?'

'In the square between the post and the inn. They were land-owners, you see.'

'And you heard this—this horror—only the other day, when you arrived here?'

'Yes, I went straight to the priest's house—I had written to him, as I told you yesterday. He said, quite rightly, that I'd better know at once what happened, rather than hear it in hints and whispers. He knows his local people! I knew, naturally, that something had happened, otherwise I must have heard from them long since. What I was afraid of was that they might have been taken for slave labour, like so many people in Vienna. So the news was really a relief.'

'And I made you answer my childish questions . . .' Kerenyi gripped his thick grey hair in long, bony hands, sinking his head forward. 'God, how right you are about male egotism.'

'Don't, Georgy,' she begged. 'It's bad enough to live in a world where one must thank God that people one cares about are dead. Don't let us make it worse with reproaches that can't do any good.'

'I just wonder what other horrors are in wait for me, to hear, that I contributed to with my self-important business, making little plots to trap just the people I should most want to help.'

'No more. Or not from me. And there's the egotism again; it all had nothing to do with you. It is simply the price of defeat.'

'But you were never a Nazi,' I cried with an absolute conviction. 'You can never have wished their victory.'

'Ah, but don't you know,' she said, with the effect of something theatrical in her resignation, 'it always is those who haven't de-served it, who suffer in defeat.' I knew, only too well from the pen, that those who deserved to suffer did so too, but there was in the cliché something of essential truth so that I recognised it as real, the great injustice of suffering.

There was a long silence and then we began, all three, to draw normality and the surface of living over the unbearable truths of impotent involvement. The meeting again of these two human beings must in any circumstances be infinitely painful; I already knew enough to understand that. But there were many things we could talk of without being either unreal or kicking each other in the guts; I was beginning to feel my own frightening responsibilities enough for me to include myself with them, at least as a novice, in the guilt of responsibility. We talked, as they say, of other things. We were all three social by nature, talkative, in the habit of being in company. Our converse was built on the agreement of whole worlds of meaning under what we said; meaning we were not to fumble at, or not with words and not now.

We opened a bottle of Italian wine with our soup and bread.

'Your German is really awfully good,' said Frau Homburg, laughing at my use of some slang phrase. 'How did you learn it? So few real English people speak German.'

'He speaks Russian just as well,' said Georg. 'How many languages do you speak, Robert?'

'Four,' I admitted. 'It makes me pretty unpopular with my fellow-officers. I try to keep it quiet.'

'You mean four apart from English?'

'Oh yes, I wasn't counting English. I think my French is better than my German, but it's a bit rusty.'

'Come along, don't be so British,' Frau Homburg urged me. 'How on earth did you come to learn Russian?'

'My father was an engineer, a heating expert. He was in Russia during the First War. You may think it rather odd now that we know what happened there but in 1916 he was actually installing a new heating plant in the house and stables on an estate about the size of Belgium that belonged to a Russian prince. He met my mother there; she was the senior governess. The contract was finished about May 1917, I think—just in time to be destroyed in the revolution, I've no doubt. When he left, it was already clear that awful things, much worse than the Tsar's abdication, were going to happen. So when he was going, he took my mother with him. She is a woman of great character, my mother, and I can just imagine her pointing out to him that he could hardly leave her there. The idea was, he should escort her to Petrograd, where she would be safe. But they got stuck there because the prince had not paid my father's fees and they had to wait. There was some problem over her salary, too. So when things began to get really hot, it seemed best for them to be married—she's very funny about it, if you can get her to talk. The various authorities who had to give them passes and so on kept changing, and they always had trouble with having different names. So they got married. My mother is a great feminist and didn't care

94

for the idea of needing the protection of a man's name—but the Bolshevik revolution was too much for her principles.'

'What marvellous irony!' she cried, delighted. 'Go on . . .'

'Well, I'm the only result of the marriage. And mother has this obsession about languages. She believes that half the trouble in the world is caused by people not being able to talk to each other. Moreover, though she couldn't cope with the Bolsheviks, she was able to deal with the refusal of the British government to let in Russian émigrés, and she rescued a woman friend of hers, who spoke not a word of English, only Russian and French. Until I was twelve, they educated me themselves, and that's how I come to speak languages.'

'But what about compulsory schooling?' asked Frau Homburg, astonished.

'My mother is a teacher with university degrees,' I said, 'and that got round the school regulations. So was Elisaveta Michaelovna, but only an elementary school teacher and in any case her diplomas didn't count in England. But later, when I was at school and my parents were abroad again, it was she who lived at home and took care of me—including the famous languages.'

'What a perfectly astounding story,' said Georg. 'No wonder you are a bit different from the other officers over there.' He nodded sideways more or less in the direction of the distant pen.

'I know,' I answered unhappily. 'It's followed me all my life.'

'Come now,' said Frau Homburg, seeing at once that I hated the idea of being different from my fellows. 'All your life is a bit of an exaggeration. How old are you?'

'Twenty-three,' I admitted and we all laughed.

'Yes, but you don't know,' I protested, but laughing still. 'You don't have to live in the Mess with Colonel Manley and his rimless glasses. He's always saying he doesn't like bilingual men and looking at me. Of course, I'm not bilingual in any of the languages, but it seems like it to him. All the interrogation officers speak German, but he can recognise that mine sounds more like the former German citizens than the other Englishmen. So he classes me with them, and them he doesn't like at all. They're much too clever for his liking. He suspects us of making fun of him. As a matter of fact, we do, too. But not the way he thinks.'

'What is your fourth language, then?' she asked.

'Italian. It's all quite ordinary, really, you see . . .'

'Well, I must admit I don't quite see what the fuss is about. I speak four languages including my own and I don't at all think it extraordinary. Lots of people I know speak six or seven—Georgy, for instance.'

'You don't know about Indian Army Colonels,' I assured her. 'Manley thinks a few words of Hindi or Urdu are all a gentleman should permit himself to understand.'

'Urdu?' she asked, awed. 'What on earth is Urdu?'

'It's an Indian language. As a matter of fact, I don't think I mean Urdu at all—I mean what they speak on the North-West Frontier, but I can't think what it's called.'

'The North-West Frontier,' said Frau Homburg. 'I read a book about it, years ago. Something about The Great Game—was it?'

'Ah, that's something Vronsky would have understood,' I looked at Georg, reminding him of our conversation before we left. 'That is where Vronsky must have made his later career—don't you agree, Georg? You should write that—yes, the later adventures of Colonel Vronsky.'

Georg's face changed and I knew I had made a mistake.

'No more pastiches,' he said, and he shifted uneasily in his chair, 'I've written my last pastiche.'

'Yes, but that one you did in 1939 was very good . . .' she began and then the lovely voice faded and the look of stringent control, the first thing I had seen in her face, returned. 'No going back to the past,' she said sharply, as if to herself. 'But *Anna Karenina*— what a part—hopeless on the stage, of course. They are going to do it in Vienna in a modern Russian version . . . with thirty-two curtains!'

We were over the bad moment before I really knew it was there. The two of them began a lively argument as to how many curtains really were contained in the stage version of the famous story.

We worked all day on Sunday, patching up the windows with squares of linoleum that Kerenyi cut for me, using the edge of a loose tile we found which still had one perfect right-angle, an iron rod for the long sides and a broken kitchen knife to cut with. This knife I sharpened on the edge of the stone sink, using some child-hood memory I could no longer place—the action and the way the knife-blade was held almost flat against the stone were still quite clear in my mind's eye, but I could not recall whom I had seen doing it—and I was absurdly proud that Frau Homburg and Georg showed astonished admiration at this small skill. Kerenyi looked so unhandy that I made him wear my driving gloves, fearing he must cut himself. We needed to be muffled up in any case; it was now very cold and once away from the kitchen or the living room, the house was arctic. At breakfast we discussed my staying until Monday evening—my leave was only for the weekend and I should have to drive to the hamlet below the road to telephone. There was no difficulty about extending my absence from the pen, for I was owed much unspent leave, but I knew Tom would worry if I did not return on Sunday night.

Kerenyi hardly spoke all day, cutting anxiously away at the tough, rather brittle linoleum with the concentration of one unused to manual work. He was probably glad to have an excuse for silence. The hammering of the nails, almost every one of which had to be straightened on a flat stone before it could be used, made small talk impossible. Every now and then Frau Homburg came in with a fresh harvest of nails of all sizes and in every condition of rust and angle which she doggedly searched for all over the house and buildings. We must work as fast as we could for the day-light was short.

The unaccustomed physical exertion made it easy to think, behind the hammering, the echoing tread of our steps to and fro on the bare floors and the naked, hollow stairs. Every sound we made was counterpointed by the hundred voices of the wind through window panes and past broken shutters, each different inlet forming a different sound, like a large and undisciplined orchestra endlessly tuning up.

She seemed to me a strange woman, for I had no means of knowing what had formed her mind. Strange in the atmosphere of indifference—or was it resignation?—that underlay her vigour. Strange in her changeableness, for it was impossible even for one as inexperienced as myself to think of her as 'feminine' in the masculine sense. She attacked Kerenyi with fury and her fierceness that morning before was more than an outraged protest at probing questions unheard by me; she wanted then to damage him, to lessen his own worth to himself—and perhaps for herself? Yet when she spoke of her mother's death, it was not at all as if the appalling event forced itself into words instinctively to be shared with others and so lessened, as events are lessened by being talked about. She did herself, as well as us, violence in speaking of the murders. But in a world in which people could feel it was a lesser evil for their own parents to be murdered I could faintly envisage a state of mind where relief could set in at knowing the worst and relief, too, that the anguished fear of their suffering was over.

'I can't imagine Frau Homburg going on strike,' I said suddenly. The idea came into my wandering thoughts as something so ludicrous that I said it aloud and Kerenyi jumped as if he had cut himself.

'Strike?' he asked, and remembered. 'Of course, she did say something about it.'

'What can she have meant?'

'I don't know, but she can only have meant from the theatre. But that's absurd. Theatre people don't go on strike.'

'Perhaps just a phrase?'

'Julie,' he said bitterly, 'doesn't use phrases. She must have meant something by it. You did know she is an actress?'

'No, of course I didn't *know*. A famous actress?'

'In the German-speaking world, I suppose you'd call her famous. At any rate, a very good actress. Had you never heard her name? . . . But you would be too young before the war, and cut off during it. Strange thought . . .'

After a pause for hammering a square of lino over a window frame, at which he watched me, he spoke again and I saw that it was easier for him to talk of the remoter past than of the war.

'As I remember London, the theatre is quite different there, and what you mean by a famous actress would hardly be understood by us. At the Burg, where Julie has always worked, they don't have "stars" because they never had to finance their own productions, each separately for itself. Productions are not built round favourite players to draw audiences, and often the public's favourites are to be seen in quite small parts that they happen to be well cast in. As for fame; there are two kinds of fame. There are several actors and actresses in Vienna better known than Julia Homburg, especially abroad, because they have made more films. Hella Schneider, for instance. But real theatre-lovers would hardly hesitate between Hella and Julie for talent, or for versatility.'

'So it all depends on what one means by "fame"?'

'It goes even further than that—of course, it's a kind of snobbery too—and the word itself would be considered almost an insult used about a member of the Burgtheater. If anyone reaches what in England or America would be called fame, they would have to live it down in Vienna; it would be anything but a help. Its considered almost a kind of prostitution—for men and women.'

'That I can understand. That would be my mother's attitude.'

I thought of those two formidable women of my childhood, my puritan mother and her feminist Russian friend. Any comparison was impossible with the powerful and harmonious person and personality of Frau Homburg, but there was some relationship in my mind between their integrity and seriousness and what I felt already to be the fortitude and the uncompromising independence of Julia Homburg's inner relationship to her world. Just as my mother and Elisaveta Michaelovna were hardly in a conventional sense women at all in their actions and views, so I felt in Frau Homburg none of the defencelessness or dependence my small experience of the other sex had impressed on me, doubtless in contrast with the two pillars of my childhood. My adult experience was, I suppose, typical of war and military service; that is, financial and fleeting with girls who made themselves into sexual objects for men and whose real nature was hidden from their temporary lovers. The only young woman I knew who could be considered as inhabiting the same world as my mother, was, until this weekend, Agnes Macdonald.

The thought of Agnes struck me with a sudden idea. Frau Homburg said that a job would enable the young woman she was trying to help, to leave the Russian Zone. Agnes was about to become the administrator of the new library in the town; she could give this girl, to whom I could give no name in my mind, an official position. I decided, however, to say nothing of this idea until I could test it out on Agnes Macdonald. It would not endear me to a woman as practical and forthright as Frau Homburg if I bragged largely of achieving what she had failed to do and then could not bring it off. But I would telephone Agnes as soon as I got back to the Mess.

Frau Homburg came in as I made this silent decision, with another handful of bent and rusted nails. 'I think those are really all I can find,' she said. 'The house will fall down if I pull out any more.'

I was standing at one of the windows of the long room, which we had left until last to mend, because our linoleum covers shut out the light.

'There's someone coming,' I said, startled and resentful as if it were my own property being invaded. 'Look, crossing from the lane.'

Frau Homburg rested a hand still holding the crude wirecutter she had been using to pull out nails, on my arm. She must be cramped and aching, I thought.

'It's one of the local people,' she said. 'I'd better go down.'

It was certainly a peasant, one could see from his tilted hat well forward over his forehead and from the way he walked, or rather, trudged, up the lane. Then he disappeared from view.

A few moments later I heard my name in her wonderful voice.

'Robert! Robert, come down! You're wanted!'

The man stood just inside the kitchen door, not leaving the old sack that did duty, since the floor had been cleaned, for a foot mat. He did not remove his filthy old hat, the surly fellow. It was only the atmosphere of adventure, strangeness, that attended this week-end that made me feel he must be after something sinister. It was really very simple. He wanted to speak to the British officer with the thick-tyred vehicle. In short, the tyres were the right size for a small delivery truck that he could use again if only he could get a fourth tyre. I explained that the car was not mine, and in any case in such driving conditions to be short of a spare wheel was little short of insanity. At my refusal, the man became excited. He spoke so fast and in such thick dialect that I could not follow him and Frau Homburg, between gusts of laughter, had to help me. He had a pair of fowls. The wife would wring their necks, pluck and clean them in a few minutes—all I need do was say the word. When I grasped that his offer was serious I began to laugh with my hostess; but then a gulf of complementary greed and hunger opened in my mind, in which two chickens were worth a heavy-duty-tyre costing the British Army something like eight pounds sterling. But I thought of roast chicken. I was very sick of tinned food.

'You can't have this tyre,' I said, 'But I have a friend, a fellow-officer, who can arrange such things. If you'll sell me the . . .'

Frau Homburg gripped my arm and her fingers were like steel.

'No, that is not the way,' she said in English, entering into the spirit of the thing. 'Let me do it.'

'We don't want your rubbishy old fowls, probably layers, too old for eggs any more, they'd take four hours to boil—roast, you say? Ha, there isn't a roasting chicken between here and Graz!'

'That's where you're wrong,' he said sniffing scornfully. 'They're roasters, come out of the egg last April, God's holy word on it. Two of 'em, beauties!'

'Be off with you,' she cried derisively. 'No tyres for you. The poor birds are probably as tough as the tyre would be. Come along, now, you're wasting our time. This Englishman is a very senior officer, not one of your common soldiers, he is used to real chickens. He could get you a whole set of tyres, but not for stringy old fowls, my poor friend.'

She glanced over her shoulder as she spoke and I saw the scrawny neck muscles of the man stretch as his rheumy eyes followed her look to the boxes of supplies on the kitchen table.

'Ah, but he's going away, I'll be bound. Then where's my tyre? I'm not selling my birds for money; and food, we've enough of that.'

'But I'm coming back,' I said, getting the idea but wishing Wilder were there. 'I shall be back next week, with a friend who imports all kinds of things. Tyres, petrol, seeds. But of course, if you are not interested . . .'

She gripped my arm again enjoining silence. I could taste roast chicken. After two days of soup, however good, roast chicken.

He half turned away. I could feel her holding her breath. Then he stopped, but did not turn back.

'Seeds, you said?' He pushed at the brim of his hat with a thumb blackened to the bone. 'I'm not interested in grain seeds, if that's what you mean.'

'All kinds of seed,' I said airily. I had heard Wilder talking, but only vaguely, about seeds; but at that time I was self-righteous and not interested in roast chicken. He looked at me like a rasp, if a rasp had eyes, under the brim of his hat.

'Tell us what you want. He can get it for you,' said Frau Homburg, 'but you get nothing now for your chickens but money, you understand? Do you suppose a gentleman like this travels with his pockets full of lettuce, or peas, or cabbage seed?'

'Well, how can I know he'll come back? Money's worth nothing. You could stuff pillows with it. I need tyres for the little van, not money. Seed, well now, that might be . . .' he dropped into muttering as he again made to leave.

'And what good is your little van, if you have nothing to deliver with it?' she said swiftly. 'If you have the wits to think two minutes ahead you can have the tyre *and* the seed. But not this minute.'

He snuffled again, twisting the end of his nose in the most cruel way by pushing it with his dark thumb. After another ten minutes Kerenyi and I got into the car with him and while his wife plucked the chickens under Kerenyi's eye. I went to the tavern where the border patrol lived to telephone. As I came out of the stuffy little office, the patrol Corporal hailed me across the hall, or rather, the coach passage—it had once been a posting house—from the tap-room.

'Did the old boy come up with the chickens, Sir?' He came across, smelling of the local spirits. 'You didn't run into any par-tisans then! Cor, them partisans! The old devil came round asking who you were. I told him you would be sure to want some chickens, if they weren't too dear.' Struck by a sudden thought, he frowned. 'I hope you didn't pay too high? Spoil the market if you did, you know.'

'I'm sure I did,' I said. 'You should have warned me.' I named the price we had agreed and he nodded, pulling down the outside corners of his mouth in surprised respect.

'Not too bad,' he said, 'not too bad.' He looked at me with a slight puzzlement as if he had not expected me to be so sensible.

I glanced round the shabby and comfortable room with its wooden benches and tables and big metal counter. It was steamily warm in there.

'You've got a snug little place here.'

'Not too bad,' he said, 'not too bad,' and he smiled his thin, cockney smile. 'Let me know on the old blower when you're coming up again, Sir, and we'll get you some fresh veg.' He closed one eye. 'Just give us a ring and let us know when you're coming—on account of going so near the border, of course.'

I thought suddenly of what Colonel Manley would say to this and smiled in spite of myself as I promised to do so. What he and Wilder did was one thing, but what others did was very much another; using military communications for black-marketing—and with other ranks!

'Will two chickens be enough, d'you think, Sir? The old boy claims that's all he's got, but I dare say, if I asked about . . .'

It dawned on me that the Corporal was curious about the house and its occupant, of whom he must have heard. But I said nothing, thinking that if I satisfied his curiosity he would lose interest, whereas if he did not know quite what went on, he would continue to take an interest in the outlying manor house and would keep an eye on it on patrol.

The headlights blazed over the snowy hillocks, and as we lurched upwards on a curve I looked over to the east. It was impenetrably dark over there. It could have been uninhabited country marked on an old map 'here be dragons'.

Julie was waiting, fiddling with the dampers of the cooking stove and pushing fresh wood blocks into the firebox.

'There you are,' she said. 'I've used the wood that was still in the house because that's all there is that's really dry. But I'm not sure about the oven . . . Are they all right for roasting?' She sounded anxious. 'I wouldn't want to let you both down. I've never roasted a chicken before.'

We looked at the two soft, bony corpses judicially. When she looked at the separated heads and claws, Julie shuddered.

'What did you bring those horrible things for?'

'They're good for soup,' said Georg. 'At least so the woman said.'

'Let's put a little water in the roasting pan with them and they will half steam. Then they'll be tender,' I suggested, finding this gem of wisdom from heaven knows where.

'The things you know!' she said almost crossly. 'That's the sort of thing I ought to tell you.'

'They'd better be good,' said Kerenyi, rubbing helplessly at his thick grey hair. 'I picked the brutes out very carefully . . . I asked the woman and she said forty-five minutes.'

Unlike me, he could put his advice so delicately that she did not notice it. The chickens were, in fact, wonderful. They were a feast of delight and we ate the lot, carefully saving the picked bones for soup. We sat, faces glowing with Italian rosé, for hours at the table, completely, as it seemed, at peace as if nothing had ever happened to any of us.

IX

I did not, after all, need to telephone Agnes Macdonald on Tuesday, for the only subject of conversation at breakfast that morning was a Club dinner party arranged for the following Friday, to which I too was invited. It would be, I thought, much easier to discuss my idea with Agnes in person, and a few days would not make any difference. I looked forward with an eagerness that surprised me slightly, to seeing her again; we had enjoyed our walk two Sundays ago, but she did not inhabit my mind in the interim. But now, I found, I wanted to describe my weekend to her.

David Stephenson arrived back from London on Thursday evening but remained invisible, closeted a long time with Colonel Manley; it was clear his departure was already as good as arranged, and I recalled Wilder's prophesy that the outcome of the civil service examinations was certain.

'You do look smart, Robert,' David called patronisingly as I came into the Mess anteroom, bathed, shaved and in service dress. 'Come and have a drink.' There was already a certain languidness in his manner and voice in preparation for his new profession, I noticed. He acted moods and feelings almost like a young girl who is never just driving a car but being a pretty girl driving a car, or being a trim, young housewife importantly marketing instead of simply buying food. I said I would have a glass of sherry, which made him laugh at me, but I already knew Agnes Macdonald did not like the smell of whisky. And in any case, I did not want to start drinking, for I knew that would spoil my enjoyment of the party which was a special occasion in two ways; Agnes was transferring to the services' library and the girls were all going to wear real dresses for the first time. The Order allowing them to do so had just been 'posted'.

'How was London?' I asked, meaning London in general.

'Everything went off all right, I rather fancy,' he replied, assuming the question to refer to his own affairs. 'The old boys were very lenient with me. My mother really prepared the ground very well, the poppet.' He finished his drink and called through the door for another, without using the Mess-servant's name, a bad habit that made him unpopular with the staff.

'Sir,' said the soldier, putting the whisky smartly down on the table. 'Can I bring you another sherry, Captain Inglis?'

'No thanks, Wilson, I'm all right for the moment.'

'That man is very abrupt,' complained David as the soldier disappeared. 'I don't think he's a good Mess-servant.' One could already see the butler hovering in the background of diplomatic grandeur. 'I shall be glad to be demobbed and get back to civilisation again.' He laughed. 'All I need now is a rich wife. Perhaps I shall be posted to Washington. I could marry an oil heiress.'

'Are you going so soon?' I was surprised, for the examination results would take some time to come through.

'They're taking me on some temporary transfer thing,' he said negligently. 'It will be changed over later to the regular service.' I saw that the ground really was well prepared, and was suitably impressed and envious. Wilder put down a two-day-old *Financial Times* and came across the room to us. He, too, had taken trouble to dress properly.

'Did I hear you saying you were looking for a rich wife, David? Doesn't go very well with your Commie notions, does it? But then, they don't go very well with being a diplomat, either, so I suppose one more contradiction makes no odds.'

'My notions, as you call them, are not Commie.' David was annoyed and defensive as always at any sign of disapproval or of his not being a universal favourite. 'I suppose you can't imagine it, but not all diplomats have to be semi-Fascist members of the Tory Party.'

'Is that meant to apply to Robert?' jeered Wilder. 'It certainly doesn't to me. I don't know one party from another and don't want to. Except the sort of party we're going to tonight.'

'I'm a socialist, but until things change, I have to live in the world as it is, and that takes money.' David was now sullenly rude. 'It's all right for you. You've got a stinking rich father.'

'Thanks,' replied Wilder, now furious himself. 'And you might remember sometimes that the brotherhood of man includes the way you talk to Wilson and the other men. You speak to them as if they were slaves. As for a rich wife, I have news for you. You don't have to wait until you get posted abroad. We have an heiress of our own at the party tonight and you can make up to her. I'm sure you'll be successful—you always are with girls, I believe.' There was a slight emphasis on 'girls' which went a bit too far and I interrupted quickly, saying to David he should rush up and change because the car would be round in ten minutes to collect us.

'Oh, Lord, do I have to? God knows what my service uniform looks like. I'm not sure it's even been unpacked.'

'Well, Tom is dressing and we've all put on tunics,' I said, uncomfortably joking. 'You'd look a bit conspicuous . . . besides, if you want to impress Wilder's heiress . . . ?'

'With a senior in service dress, it wouldn't be the cat's pants for you to appear all scruffy,' mocked Wilder. 'You must begin to think about keeping in with your superiors.'

'Superiors! Cat's pants! You do use some horrible expressions, my dear chap.' David decided to adopt a condescending tone, and made his way, reluctantly towards the hall to go upstairs and dress.

'Yes, I'm a common bastard, I know.' Wilder said it without a smile.

'Are you two on bad terms again?' I asked as David's footsteps faded up the stairs. 'Have you had a row?'

He looked at me with those dark, laughing eyes, which never told you what he was thinking. 'No, he just bores me with his silly airs. Now he's going I don't trouble to—what's the word—dissemble, like I did when I knew we'd got to live together.'

'Where did you get this news that one of the girls is rich?' I asked then, idly. 'I've heard nothing of it.' Wilder always had the news long before anyone else.

'You hadn't?' He seemed surprised and I wondered if he thought everybody talked about money all the time. He was assuming that Agnes must have told me, but in fact she did not know herself the last time we were out together. Tom now came in and the subject changed. David was bound to keep us waiting, so I went out to tell the driver to come into the hall; it was ten degrees of frost, centigrade, outside. After a few minutes, Tom looked for the second time at his watch.

'Wilson, go up and tap at Captain Stephenson's door and tell him the time, will you?' he said, and to Wilder and myself. 'We're going to be late if he doesn't hurry.'

It was over twenty minutes before David appeared. His tunic was so crumpled that he must have known beforehand it was not unpacked. We three were all wearing cloth belts, but Tom looked distinguished in a properly cut tunic and chestnut-polished leather.

'I wish I had a Sam Browne,' said David with a sulky look. He was humiliated, I suppose, at knowing he was keeping us all waiting.

'I couldn't find a tie without food stains on it,' he excused himself. 'That bloody batman is no good at all!'

'You should clean your own stuff, as I do,' said Wilder, deliberately making matters worse. Wilder always looked smart. He was wearing highly polished and very well made low shoes of non-regulation style and his trousers were narrowed almost like trews. I noticed too late that David's belt was twisted and one shoe-lace coming undone. Tom, following him out, frowned at this. Tom did not care a bit about rank but was a professional with a strong sense of correctness, apart from the habit of neatness of the soldier.

'You'll have to drive fast,' said David to the driver.

The man did not reply but glanced at Tom who said nothing. Tom had given renewed orders about breaking the speed limits in bad weather—he was very strict about that with his drivers. The man stolidly drove out into the road and proceeded at the allowed speed, which it would certainly have been dangerous to exceed with the surface iced as it was. Although there was practically no traffic it was never safe to assume that horses and carts without lights would not loom up ahead, even in December. We were ten minutes late and our guests were assembled. They were, besides Agnes, the very pretty red-head, whose name was Betty, an older woman of tall, aristocratic ugliness with greying hair whom I did not know but who was an acquaintance of Tom's, and a little, dark, round girl also unknown to me.

'Hello, Veronica,' cried Tom, limping forward to kiss the cheek of the tall woman. 'How nice to see you again, my dear. How's Bertie?'

'Bertie's fine; at least his last letter seemed all right,' she said in a big, hearty voice. 'How are you, Tom? How's the leg now?'

'Perfectly fit, thank you,' he replied and began to introduce her as Veronica Masters. The dark, round girl's name turned out to be April, which seemed unsuited to her jolly appearance of good sense. Betty was the only one who looked pointedly at her watch.

'David kept us all waiting,' said Wilder at this—we were all moving towards the little bar now. 'He's hopeless at taking care of himself.'

Betty blushed vividly with annoyance at herself for having hinted at a fault which turned out to be David's but he did not notice and seated himself beside her with a careless air, looking about the little room. The Club, being the town's only good hotel, was well appointed and the service was good for the staff had been requisitioned with their hotel. Agnes asked for sherry, as I knew she would. Veronica Masters drank whisky and the two other girls ordered those dreadful concoctions then popular called Alexanders, which if they really were christened after the Field Marshal, were an insult to a great man.

'We drank them all the time in Rome,' said April, laughing as she spoke. 'They taste so delicious.' I caught Wilder's eye and grinned, knowing what he was thinking. I was looking forward to this party, but suddenly the thought of the bare, warm living room at Julia Homburg's house came into my mind and I knew clearly that I would rather be there drinking the Italian wine I took with me.

'I'll keep you company, then,' said David and looked into Betty's hazel eyes. His little smile made her face rosy with joy and she began to sparkle, positively to sparkle, with happiness.

'Did you get my letters?' she asked him in an undertone. 'You asked me to write, so I did.'

'They were splendid letters,' he answered with caressing condescension, 'though I had absolutely no time for writing myself.'

'It's better to have you back than to get letters,' cried April, laughing again. She looked meaningly at Betty, who pretended to take no notice.

From the way April said this I saw that matters were much further on between David and Betty than I had supposed.

'Has your transfer gone through, Agnes?' Tom asked and she replied in her shy way, yes, she should start in her new job on the first of January.

'You'll much prefer the library work,' Veronica Masters assured her. 'Much more your cup of tea.' She turned to Tom with her large air of kindness and explained that Agnes was authorised to engage her own local staff. 'Quite a new departure,' as she said.

This was just the opening I had hoped for and I grasped at it.

'If you really are looking for staff, Agnes, I think I can recommend someone to you.'

'Oh, you Lothario,' cried April, 'two girl friends at once!'

'I've never seen this girl in my life,' I protested. I turned quickly to Agnes. 'It is a friend of a friend—you remember, I told you about the friend of Kerenyi's, with the house?'

'You went, then?' she said softly. Her voice was always soft.

I nodded. 'Frau Homburg wants to find this girl a job so that she can get her little son out of the Russian Zone.'

'Frau Homburg's little son?'

'No, no, the girl's. I don't think Frau Homburg has any children. She's an actress.'

'Doesn't necessarily follow,' threw in Veronica Masters. 'An actress, you said? Would that be Julia Homburg?'

'Yes,' I said surprised, 'do you know her?'

'I saw her last time I was in Vienna, when I had some leave, at the theatre.'

'Lady Veronica is allowed to go to Vienna on leave because her brother is General Masters,' announced April grandly. At that time special permission was needed to spend leaves in the capital.

'Oh, I say,' said David scornfully, 'what favouritism.'

'I wanted to see my brother,' said Veronica Masters equably. 'And I knew Vienna before the war. It's a terrible shock to see it now. I remember Julia Homburg in 1938, as Nora in *The Doll's House.*' She turned to me. 'Do you know her well?' she asked.

'Just this weekend I spent at her house,' I said. Now I knew she had a title I was shy of her and afraid of doing something maladroit. I looked across at Tom, who gave me a small smile of conspiracy. 'You remember the question of where Kerenyi should be billeted? Well, the owner was already there.'

'How interesting,' murmured Agnes. 'What is she like? I've never met an actress.'

'Neither had I. What *is* she like, now? Extraordinary, that's what she is like.'

'I wish I'd been there too,' said Veronica, setting down her glass with a slight ring to indicate she could use another drink. 'There was a lot of talk about her in Vienna in those sort of circles. I gathered, she's said to have been a Nazi.'

'I'm quite sure that's not true,' I countered, too hotly.

'Well,' she said comfortably, 'it's only what "they say" of course.

But there was talk of suspending her from her theatre for a time, until the Allies have got over their objections, or until the question is cleared up.'

'Which Allies?' David wanted to know. He knew, of course, what the answer must be from the sister of a senior officer, for we all knew of the constant difficulties with the Russians, and that was, typically, why he asked.

She raised her eyebrows a little. 'The British and Americans, of course,' she said, and nodded thanks at the waiter who now brought a fresh round of drinks.

'Ah,' cried David with triumph, 'then it sounds to me as if she might be pro-Russian and that's why she gets labelled a Nazi.'

'I can't think why you should assume that,' objected Veronica coolly, and sipped her drink. 'Anyway, let us not talk politics.'

'Why not? It sounds intriguing. And I like politics.'

'I never talk politics,' she said serenely. 'I know nothing about the subject. And Agnes' new job is more interesting.'

I should have liked to hear more of what was said about Frau Homburg, but that was now impossible. Instead, we talked about the services library which was to be transformed into a reading room open to the Austrian public with Agnes, who worked for a year at the London Library before joining the service, to run it. David, not interested in that subject, was whispering with Betty, bending his head close to hers and April, next to me, assured me in an undertone that she was sure the announcement would be made in a few days. This surprised me; she seemed too nice a girl in spite of her coyness, to expose her friend to ridicule with such gossip if it were unfounded, but unless David had been talking only for effect his mind was not running on marriage with Betty. She seemed so certain of what she said that I realised with a little shock that she was in Betty's confidence and that matters had indeed gone far; in fact looking with sharpened perception at Betty's brilliant, joyous eyes, I saw they had gone to the limit.

All three of these girls, in spite of some worldly airs they gave themselves, were really very inexperienced and by that I mean the unfashionable word innocent. Betty, I was very sure, assumed that the stage her relations with David had reached automatically meant marriage. But there was always the point that, even if David had meant his remarks in the anteroom, Betty herself was the heiress.

However, we now went in to dinner, which Tom had ordered

with as much care as the very restricted kitchen of the Club could manage. By comparison with the way even privileged Austrians were living, we did ourselves very well but that did not say much about the refinement of our food. The four women looked charming, moving across the dining room together, in their gay-coloured dresses; they had evidently agreed each to wear a different colour. Only Lady Veronica could be called elegant in her own way and the others were all a bit fluttery in texture and overdone in colour, a reaction from uniforms, in their Italian silks. But they looked delightful to my unsophisticated eyes and the slight emphasis of their femininity added to their general air of being 'nice girls'.

Wilder had, by arrangement, been left last to sign the bar bill, and David remained behind with him, I supposed to make up for the slight unpleasantness between them, which would be like him. Sure enough, they followed us up, laughing and talking in half tones. I was glad David made his peace with Wilder for if they bickered they would spoil our evening, which I was determined to enjoy. I was fated to be disappointed in this small ambition.

Tom was surrounded by the four women, debating who should sit where, a point of organisation he had forgotten. So David, with much laughing and joking, placed himself between Lady Veronica and Agnes and said, with a hand on an arm of each, 'You two sit by me and let's be sociable. The others can sort themselves out.'

Laughing gently, Agnes demurred. I did not hear her words, but he replied gaily, that we mustn't break the party up into couples. This resolved the table order and we all sat down with Tom at the other end from David, the two remaining girls, Betty and April on his either side and Wilder and I between the women. Eight, as someone has said, is the perfect number for a party. As soon as the waiter finished leaning between us to serve the paté, I turned to Agnes beside me.

'Now, Robert, I thought we agreed not to break up into pairs,' cried David, at which Agnes blushed and so did I. In order then, not to embarrass her, I devoted myself to April on my other hand. She prattled with animation and saved me from the trouble of replying with her rapid commentary on everyone and everything in the room. Presently, as we were being served with soup, she appealed to Betty for confirmation of some comment just made and I, of course, looked across at Betty too. I felt a stiffening in April at the distance of our chairs, and saw that Betty, with her head up and a high colour, sat silent while Tom talked quietly on and on about nothing, not looking at her. Seeing us looking at her, she looked at us and to my surprise, her eyes filled visibly with tears. I had the thought that she was too sensitive to make a diplomat's wife. Both April and I began our chatter again at once and the three of us, for the next course, gave poor Betty protection while she recovered herself. I could really see little cause for such depression but supposed she was in an over-emotional state. Wilder, meanwhile, talked to Lady Veronica and very quickly got on good terms with her, they being both quite without class feeling and discovering a shared passion for ski-ing and horses. By the time we were served with roast pork—inevitably pork—the table was full of cheerful noise. Tom ordered claret, which I was then only learning to like, and explained to Betty with his diffident air, 'I hope you won't mind it's not being a Burgundy. I know ladies often don't care for claret, but they really do have quite good ones and I *am* rather fond of a good claret.' At that time the services were importing the finest wines of France which otherwise might have gone without buyers.

'You will have to tell me about wines,' she said, smiling bravely. 'I am very ignorant.'

'No good telling anyone. Experience is the only teacher, and I'm sure you're a natural connoisseur.'

Betty glanced quickly up the table for David's approval but his head was bent, the lock of fair hair falling sideways, his gaze fixed on Agnes.

'You're so restful,' he murmured. 'One gets so bored with people—throwing themselves. I like you.'

'Restful . . . my goodness, I'm afraid you must mean boring,' she replied without any flirtatious undertone. She seemed bewildered.

'You know very well you're not boring. How could I not have noticed you before? I suppose just because you are so restful and gentle. You make me feel you could never hurt anyone or anything.'

I saw her raise her candid eyes to his face from her plate.

'I hope not,' she said. 'But you haven't said a word to Veronica and I must talk to my own neighbour, don't you think?'

'Ah, you feel that Robert has a prior claim, since he recognised you before I did.'

'A claim, certainly,' she said with quiet persistence.

'And I have none? That's my own fault. It always happens, because I am so slow and stupid about people. I miss everything.'

'I didn't mean it like that,' she protested. 'It's only that . . .' She glanced about her quickly, I knew for help, but my tongue was tied by embarrassment. And I was afraid, too, that by intervening I would suggest a claim I did not feel. Across the table—April meanwhile was arguing happily with Tom—I frowned at Wilder but he did not see me, between his food and an arrangement he was just making with Veronica to go ski-ing in January.

The band had been playing for some time now, and when our plates were removed, the chance, or duty, to dance, presented itself. This was the way I could help Agnes, and, putting my napkin to my lips, I turned towards her.

'Let's dance,' cried David in a ringing voice. 'Come on, let's dance. Each take your partner!' With an emphasis on the possessive word he took Agnes' hand, which was in her lap, and pulled her, inertly, to her feet, propelled by the absolute need, so useful to those who know how to use it, to behave conventionally.

In its minor way it was one of the most brutal things I ever saw. I turned, not quite knowing what I did, to April but she shoved my foot with hers brusquely and I don't believe anyone noticed my change of direction.

'Come along, young woman,' I said with idiotic sternness to Betty. 'Heaven help your feet, but duty is duty. You will have to bear my version of—what on earth is this dance called?'

'It's a samba,' she said as she rose, and I think I never heard so much despair in such banal words, before or since.

'Why are you so unhappy?' I whispered urgently. 'He's only trying you out! Come along now, look as if you were enjoying yourself!' We managed the steps somehow and I went on, 'You'll never cope with a temperamental chap like David if you give in like this.'

We moved gradually to the other side of the dance floor between the other pairs before she answered.

'I shall never have to cope with him. Only with . . .'

'With what?' I asked, visited by a frightful thought which I at once rejected. 'You're being fanciful. It comes of being in love.'

'Oh please,' she said. 'You can see as well as I can that he knows. Somebody has told him . . . Was it you?'

'Told him what?' I said stupidly. But I knew. 'I've told him nothing.'

'I thought it was a joke of his when he talked about money,' she almost moaned, her delicious face nearly on my shoulder and her scent in my face. 'But it wasn't. Somebody has told him her grandmother has died and now she's rich.' She spoke with an appalling directness.

It was impossible to break it up. The charade went on until midnight, and as Veronica finally rose with great determination, having been deflected several times, to go, I heard David begging Agnes to allow him to help her with her luggage to her new quarters whence she was due to remove the following week. I saw from her look that she could neither understand him nor believe in his insincerity, which was so foreign to her nature. He appealed like a naughty child that knows it deserves nothing, for everything, and the openness of this appeal, the admission that he deserved nothing, was its guarantee of success. As we all parted, Agnes gave me a look of bewilderment, a look that knew as little as I did myself whether such changes of feeling could be real, or, in such public circumstances, justified by any urgency. For that was what he told her; he must soon leave and the realisation of his going had opened his eyes.

'You wanted me to call you back,' ventured the timid voice. 'I'm sorry I was out the other evening when you telephoned.' I was determined not to abandon the chance of getting the job in the library for Frau Homburg's protégée, so I twice telephoned Agnes and she was out. David, too, was not dining in Mess on these evenings.

'About your staff,' I said stiffly, 'I wish you'd try to take on this girl. I'm sure she deserves help and I can't think of any other way of getting her legally out of the Russian Zone but by offering her an official job.'

She said a little breathlessly, 'It's difficult to leave *any* of the Zones for any other, I hear. But why does she so much want to leave her home?'

I knew David must already have been talking his obsessive 'politics' at her, so I grew careful. 'She has to make her living. It's difficult where she is, right out in the country, and she needs to begin a proper profession. She has the boy to think of, you see?'

I hated the thought that I should manipulate her, too. Especially when, to be vulgar, she rose to it. And even more, because I guessed that he was pressing her to give up her job, a course that seemed insane to me, but now that I had watched David at work, quite possible. She would need reliable staff so that she could leave suddenly without altogether giving up her personal ideas of responsibility; the library was a job she had tried hard to get. I was, even in my own chagrin, sorry for her dilemma and understood it well. Only for a higher duty could she reconcile herself to going back on her contract, and that higher duty David very well presented to her in his helplessness.

She would put the request in at once with every possible urgency. Yes, she knew all the facts and would get the various papers at once. There was one difficulty—the local authorities were cagey about giving residence permits to people, and still more to families, with no home to go to. She needed a signature on a promise to give a home to this unknown young woman and her son. Good, she should have it, and we made an appointment for me to pick up a formal letter from her.

Lady Veronica called that day, too, sounding very unlike Agnes in her unconscious assumption that what she wanted must be done.

'I've been trying to get Major Keeler,' said her big voice. 'They tell me in his office that he may be at your place. Can I talk to him, please?' She sounded abrupt and worried. Keeler, I told her, would be in the pen a little later, should I give him a message? He should telephone her in her office, please, I wouldn't forget? It was rather urgent. As soon as he appeared, I should tell him. I hoped nobody was seriously ill? No, no, she said, her heartiness sounding false, not serious.

I gave Major Keeler this message when he came in and handed him the telephone. I knew he was a very busy man and did not want to expose myself to blame if he should forget. It did not occur to me to go away. I, too, had much to do, for David had practically ceased to work at all and his charges were unofficially divided between the rest of the interrogators. I was behind with my reports and was writing away at one of them.

'Masters,' said Veronica's voice at once; I could hear her quite clearly from my chair with Keeler standing on the other side of the desk. She cut his greetings short. 'Look, I'm sorry to bother you. I know you've enough to do, but could you get over to see me as soon as you finish this evening? It's a purely private matter. I'd rather you didn't come in working hours.'

'Why the secrecy?' he said in his sharp, sarcastic way. 'Can't you tell me what it's about?'

'No. I can't. I'm asking you to do me a personal favour and come over to the Mess.'

Major Keeler hesitated noticeably and then agreed to be there before dinner-time. As he put down the receiver he gave me a sharp look, but I went on writing.

'Hmm,' he pressed his mouth shut and went out with his brisk, businesslike walk. I had to get this job done before I could go into the town to get the letter from Agnes, but try as I would I could not get my report written before Agnes finished work for the day. I would drive straight to the women's Mess on the other side of the town in my new possession, my war-booty car as they were then called, being former Wehrmacht vehicles. Wilder ran up the steps to the house as I slammed the door of the car shut, and hearing me, came over to tell me that he could get me the tyre and the seed of various kinds I wanted, but the latter would take a week or so yet. The tyre I could have straight away. He did not say from where the tyre came, but I knew it was from another unit, for our transport pool under Tom did not engage in the black market in Army supplies.

Agnes was not yet in the women's Mess and April coming in and finding me waiting in the hall, said that she usually went across to the new reading room on leaving the office, to see how the decorators were progressing. April was carrying parcels wrapped in coloured paper. It was a week before Christmas. I must excuse her, she said, she must rush upstairs; Betty was not very well and she had promised to see how she was. I thought her bubbling cheerfulness somewhat subdued. I walked, moodily, to the window. The two most senior women officers came in, letting in a blast of cold. I came to attention and greeted them without enthusiasm. The window looked over the narrow street on the far side of which the new reading room was being fitted out.

As I watched, the lights went out and a moment later Agnes and David came out of its door and she turned to lock up. He pulled up the collar of her greatcoat as she straightened up again and bent his head down to her face. After a moment they crossed towards where I stood watching them. I could see that Agnes looked about her just before the entrance, and seemed to demur at something he said; but he detained her with a hand behind her shoulder, at which she stepped back. They were, of course, both in uniform and bound to behave formally. He was laughing at her objection, as he must often have laughed at more serious scruples, I thought. She glanced then at the lighted windows of her official home and they moved towards the wall, bringing their faces almost to the window where I stood, made invisible by the hangings. David's laughing face teased her with something I could not hear, and she lifted her eyes to him with a look of frightened joy and adoration that touched me to the heart. There was such puzzled, questioning and trusting surrender in that look that I was, curiously, comforted by it for surely no human being could resist her simplicity and goodness. He did not insist then, on kissing her again, and stepped back to salute her. A moment later the street door opened and she came in. As she saw me the dazed happiness in her face faded and she glanced at the window and back to my face.

'Robert, I'm sorry I'm so late,' she said breathlessly. She flicked a look about her, not knowing what to do with me, and then pointed to the door of the common sitting room, smiling with relief. There was no one in there; it was the hour of freshening up for the evening meal and all the inmates of the house but Agnes were already in their rooms.

'I'll just hang up my coat.' She went and put her outer clothes on the rack in a side corridor and came back, smoothing her dark hair with a gesture of her usual neatness. Our business was soon done for the letter was ready, its envelope left open, but addressed to the appropriate authority. In both languages, with four copies and I must get all four signed; we were in the machinery of the bureaucrats.

'They tell me it will take about ten days. So far none of such applications have been refused.'

'I suppose not,' I said. 'By the time they get this far they are already approved. Those that are refused are not heard of.' This was too conspiratorial an idea for her to believe in, but if I went further and explained that the Russians were often glad to supply people who would remain under their own remote control to the western Allies, she would disagree with me and we should part unfriends. Even at that time I had the feeling that I must remain her friend; my protective attitude to David was changed completely after the evening in the Club and I now felt almost a fear of him mixed with the pity he still aroused.

Agnes now hesitated, and I waited, unsure what she wanted me to do or say. Until I spoke I did not know I was going to say it.

'Your names seem already joined. Or haven't you read *David Copperfield?*'

'Oh,' she said, startled, 'I hadn't noticed it.' A dawning secret smile crept into her look, which had nothing to do with me; the chance of the two names belonging immortally together gave her some inner confirmation. Someone, a man, came into the house door, his Army boots clattering on the tiles, as he walked across the hall, and when he spoke loudly to a servant passing towards the empty dining room I recognised Major Keeler's voice asking for Junior Commander Masters. Veronica must have been waiting nearby for only a half minute passed before I heard her voice as she ran down the stairs.

'Good of you to come so promptly,' it said. 'Come up. We can't talk here.'

'That was Major Keeler, wasn't it?' said Agnes. 'Is somebody ill, I wonder . . . ?' She did not know, of course she did not. There was, however, something uneasy in her, and I realised now that a feeling of unadmitted anxiety went right through her new state and was, now and for ever, a part of it. Then, with the effect of suddenness, Agnes spoke again, needing to say it to someone.

'We're engaged,' she said softly. 'He wants me to ask for my discharge at once but I think I must stay a month or so. I wanted to ask your advice. Don't you agree that I ought at least to get the new reading room organised before I leave? But David wants me to go as quickly as I can so that we can be married straight away, in London.' She looked up with her shy smile that was so touchingly and anxiously happy. 'Under his gay ways, he's awfully scared of his new job . . . but you know that—don't you?—because you were a friend of his even before I knew him.' She stopped, nervously aware of a discrepancy and at a loss with a situation—not with me—where an unspoken and unrealised dishonesty complicated everything. 'I mean, before we really met. I did know him a bit before that, of course, but he was always so gay and flirting with everybody . . .' The word 'gay' again; so entirely what David never was. 'I didn't even like him until then, when I saw how different he is, underneath.'

'I hope you will both be very happy,' I said. It sounded both insincere and inadequate but I could think of nothing else. She did not mind it. I was not any longer real to her, but catching sight of the watch on her wrist, said hastily. 'I'm sorry. I must go and change; we're dining at the Club. Do forgive me, Robert . . .' I was already going and she ran up the stairs calling goodbye to me. On the half landing she stood aside for Veronica to come down, frowning with preoccupation. Veronica did not see me but I watched as she came, rather slowly, half way down the stairs. Then she looked back up at where Agnes had stood, with a puzzled look and shook her head. I went quickly, wanting neither to seem to pry nor to be spoken to.

David himself passed me as I turned in at the drive to the Mess, in a unit car, going to his dinner appointment—on time, for once, I noticed.

'Every blessed night,' said Tom, laughing and shaking his head. 'David's really caught, this time. It's splendid to see him so happy. You look chilled through, Robert. Come and have a drink before you go upstairs.'

Wilder was, as usual, drinking beer, in Jack Morgenstern's company.

'We have news, Robert,' said Jack. 'David is engaged to that nice Scots girl. Marriage will settle him, it's just what he needs.' I could not help wondering, and I dare say Jack did too, whether what David needed would be equally good for the girl he was to marry, in the circumstances we both knew of. But I said nothing, needless to say, and if Jack had doubts he showed no sign of them. But we did not crack the jokes men make about getting engaged.

'It is to be as soon as possible,' said Tom, raising his glass to me. 'David wants her to go back to London with him.' Wilder looked sharply at Tom but said nothing, and Tom finished the sentence. 'But she won't be able to do that, of course.'

Wilder and I went up to have a wash together.

'D'you think David really is keen on this girl?' he asked me dubiously. 'I feel a bit—sort of uncomfortable about it, since it was me that first told him about . . . But he seems to be in such a hurry, I'm beginning to believe he really hadn't noticed her before that evening. It beats me—I've fallen in love myself once or twice at first sight . . . but marriage is different. So serious. And what the hell he sees in her—apart from the money, I mean . . .'

'Surely it's obvious,' I said, his own doubts stirring my conscience so that I spoke viciously. 'If he leaves her here for long she will either come to her senses or someone will tell her something. Not that I think she would believe anything against him. But she herself has simply never thought of the money—don't you see?' In the relief of being angry I was going to say more but stopped myself in time from betraying someone else's secret.

'You think he's as calculating as that?' Wilder asked in a tone that denied the question. 'Of course, I haven't had much experience with decent girls, it's true—with the sort we pick up in the town everything is so much simpler . . .' His own calculations were exclusively for business, I realised, and suddenly I liked him better than I ever had. We went on up.

X

Christmas, with implications impossible to ignore, was upon us, bringing with it the first half-hearted attempts on the part of ourselves, the occupiers, to extend a hand to our enemies. I don't describe them, in the cant already then much heard, as our former enemies, because on neither side had the enmity abated. On ours bitterness and the multifarious distortions of propaganda made real sympathy impossible towards individuals we considered culpable by that depressing self-righteousness which has grown with the increase of power to the masses everywhere. They, because their disappointment in the way the western Allies approached them—without the ravaging lust for booty of the Russians but with a cold denial of their claim to have been Hitler's first victims—was tainted deeply with an interested dishonesty that denied complicity in Hitler's later victimisations. The immense advantage the country as a whole gained from the political determination of the Americans and British to admit Austria's plea of having been occupied by the Nazis, which incidentally was the case, was negated in popular opinion even as it was recognised, by the personal and social ostracism which in fact almost universally obtained between the half-starving populace and their encamped and segregated liberators.

But now, to mark the birth of our common Lord, the Commanding General visited the mayor of the provincial capital instead of requiring that dignitary's presence in his office, and presented him with a quite handsome sum of money collected among the troops, and many gifts for children and the sick. The services organisation that cared for our leisure gave a children's party and the Bishop indicated in an addition to his pastoral message written in faulty English that he would welcome the sight of our uniforms at High Mass on Christmas Day. There were also a number of smaller efforts to show charity in something other than words. One of these was suggested by David, but we, of course, could do nothing directly because of the needs of security. Veronica, approached by us, agreed that she would put forward to her own superiors the suggestion that we should help pay for a party to be given by the women officers to the Old People's Home. Our offer was accepted with alacrity and we were asked to lend cars to collect and return the aged guests. It was an occasion of unmitigated misery on the part of the hosts and bewildered overeating on that of the guests. The only people who really enjoyed it, it seemed, were the nuns who cared for the more decrepit among the latter; those stern and practical women were enough to turn the devil himself at once into a pious Catholic and a terrified anti-feminist.

As a reward we were invited to return to the Mess after taking back our passengers to their home, a misnomer in bleak grey stone, if ever I saw one, whose inmates subsisted and died on a diet of oatmeal. A thin porridge or gruel was their usual food, as one of the nuns told me. Even the young and vigorous in full possession of their faculties were permanently hungry at that time; for those in enclosed institutions existence meant slow starvation. The Mother Superior assured me in thanking me (for nothing, indeed, as I was painfully aware) that things were not nearly as bad as after the First World War when, as a young novice, she attended at the funerals of nearly all her patients in 1919. She was handsome and I could imagine how strikingly the idealised notion of a holy woman she must have appeared in her teens. I called Wilder over and assured her, with his agreement, that we would see that the home got enough garden seed to take care at least of their vegetable needs for the coming year. Wilder told her with his happy candour that he was glad to reduce his profit margin for anyone so truly admirable and she replied with the ghost of worldliness in her smile that his sacrifice, no matter what its methods, would not pass unremarked in Heaven. This turned out to be a prophecy, for, to jump ahead several years, Wilder later made a huge fortune as a pioneer of large-scale ski-ing tourism.

'It was a really so awful afternoon,' said Veronica when we were reassembled, 'that I feel I must have a glass of champagne.'

This idea was adopted with enthusiasm. Drinking it, I asked April how Betty was progressing. Betty had not appeared at the party and Agnes had now left to go out with David, who behaved beautifully, being infinitely kind and considerate to the very oldest and most slobbering of the guests under Agnes' adoring approval.

'She is really much better,' answered April, and gave me a look of nervous suspicion that negated her determined discretion. 'It was quite a bad dose of "flu", but she's over it now.' She put on a slightly haughty air of rejecting something. 'She's not as strong as she looks. She ought to go home, really, but she's only just signed on for another year.'

'She'll be all right,' promised Veronica with her large confidence. 'Ronnie and I are going to take her with us in January to teach her to ski.'

Ronnie, as I discovered at that moment, was Wilder. I seemed to be the only one in the group, I thought resentfully, with no amorous entanglement, whether happy or unhappy. For Major Baxter now showed an unmistakable interest in April's company and Jack Morgenstern was flirting with oldfashioned German thoroughness with a terrific woman Colonel, while Martin and Colonel Manley were laughing loudly with two Queen Alexandra's nurses, smart and seemingly untouchable in their pale grey and scarlet. After the second glass of champagne I tried to think of myself as hopelessly languishing after Agnes. But I knew quite well that I was not in love with her; I simply resented having been pre-empted in her regard; and, I must say, deeply shocked at the way David simply forgot or never recognised, any obligation to Betty. That feeling, at any rate, was genuine; and it is a measure of the effect Agnes had in her quiet, brown-mouse way on everyone who knew her, that neither I nor anyone else considered her an accomplice in David's guilt towards Betty.

The next day I rose early to drive to Frau Homburg's house. I was away soon after dawn, in the eery gloom of mist and damp snow. The going was bad, and became worse the further I drove from the district town; a winter that started as early as that year provided on unfrequented roads a series of deep and uneven ruts, rock hard under the later layers of snow, of which only the surface was soft and unreliable. By the time I reached the hamlet where the border patrol was housed, I was already tired and chilled to the bone although the distance was not great.

My leave pass entitled me to share their midday meal, and I sat for over an hour, waiting for the Corporal and his co-driver to come in. There was nobody else in the guest room of the inn which was requisitioned as the patrol Mess and the house was quiet, the room with its empty tables and high-backed benches melancholy, only half lit. Outside it remained dusk all day, the shortest of the year. He came at last, followed by the depressed, surly woman with a crooked eye who had served me my rationed meal. She brought him slivovitz and beer without being asked.

'Have you been sitting here long, all alone?' he asked me, remembering 'Sir' as an obvious afterthought. They did pretty much as they liked, these little outposts. 'I expect the others are still asleep—they were out half the night.'

I did not believe this; more likely they had been drinking half the night, I thought. The atmosphere of bartering, of ummilitary understandings with the villagers of which I was, naturally, already aware, made me feel uncomfortable. It is the penalty of occupation power that men become corrupted by what in itself is good. For my Corporal supplied necessities, it was quite clear, to half the village. Twice in the first few minutes, the woman came in behind the unused zinc counter and jerked her head at him, and twice he slipped out of the door and I heard the pidgin-German conversation in the long, echoing entrance arch which went through to the centre courtyard.

'They think this stuff is just printed paper,' he said the second time he reseated himself. He showed me a fistful of the local money, filthy old Reichsmark notes overprinted, which were still in circulation. 'Your supplies will be here in a minute.' He pushed the money carelessly into the upper pocket of his battledress blouse.

'It isn't much else,' I said.

He glanced at me sideways, pityingly. 'By the time I've changed it into sterling at the legal rate, it is. I put more than twice my pay into my savings account every week.'

'You oughtn't to tell me that,' I said uneasily. 'How do you know I shan't report it?'

'Oh, you're all right, Sir. You won't report.' He did not say what he might have said, that I could hardly report him when I was black-marketing through him myself. I cursed myself for speaking; pompous ass and dishonest too, I said to myself. I really disliked it very much; but there was no other way to get the things I knew Frau Homburg and Kerenyi needed.

'Only thing is,' he said cheerfully, 'I'm always driving to one post after another to change it in. Takes up a lot of time. But you never know, we're inspected sometimes. Better safe than sorry.'

He finished his drink and picked up the half-empty beer glass.

'Besides,' he said, with a puzzled thoughtfulness, 'you feel sorry for the poor sods, don't you, Sir? Where's the harm if I get them a length of rope or something of that?'

I nodded and offered him a cigarette. A few minutes later the ill-visaged old man I remembered put his head round the door, and my companion went out to deal with the delivery. Evidently no one was allowed to enter the requisitioned part of the house; typically English arrangement, I thought, to put up an invisible cantonment. The old man could not be made to understand why the seed was not yet there and I had to join in the conversation. By the time we had done our business and the sacks with potatoes and other root vegetables, and a big leg of pork, which I was warned needed hanging, were packed into the boot of my car, it was dark again.

The corporal and I exchanged Christmas greetings, and he left me for the warmth of the inn. Between the inn and the Post, the thought came without warning into my mind. I crunched the few steps along the square to the next house, pulling up the collar of my new sheepskin coat. This building was not so old as the inn, low and square, with steps up to a battered door, shuttered windows and beside the door the old Post sign on the wall. Covered for seven years by the German insignia, it now showed again, faded and shabby. Between the two buildings was a narrow space. I could see a broken fence leaning outward where the ground fell away beyond it, and one arid winter tree, its branches loaded with snow which drifted deep here. So it was here that it happened.

I turned to the open square, criss-crossed with wagon tracks, a dark space of emptiness around which the low cottages crouched unevenly. The humped lines of the roof tops were broken twice, by the church with its bulbous spire and by the towering naked pole waiting for the spring festival. Somewhere a gable shed its weight of snow with a soft rushing sound and a bump, the scatter of snow dust glittered for an instant in the subdued light from a small square window. On the far side of the square three figures, heavily muffled and close together, left the dark of an alleyway and trudged over to the church. A long shaft of yellow light broke the dark sharply and then the portal shut behind them with a hollow boom in the silence. As I unlocked the car door and kicked my heavy boots against the running board to free them of the clumps of hardened snow, the church clock tolled three-quarters. The car motor exploded energetically into the uncanny night and the wheel chains clanked as I slowly rolled forward. The headlights picked up a moon landscape of snowy lane, scarred by black ruts. I turned the first corner, rocking sideways as if driving over open country; it was slow going. Presently, I came to the turning into the eastern lane where the lack of traffic made the surface at any rate less uneven, if more dangerous.

At first sight I thought the dark shape moving in front of the car a length or so ahead was an animal. But no animal was about in that weather at night; then I thought it must be a drunken man from the village. I was almost on it before I saw that it was a woman, a traveller struggling with the intractable surface masses. Caught in the light stream she tried to hasten her hampered steps and as I stopped the car, she flung herself panic-stricken towards the side of the track, where the drifts were as deep as the ditch and as high as the hedging. My only feeling was a nervous irritation at having to stop the car on the rutted slope. I wound down the window.

'Don't get in there—it must be deep.' I shouted. She may not have heard me, for she fought on, kneedeep, towards the side of the track where even in the pitch dark the larger bushes showed a marking line punctuated here and there by a tree. The figure fell, half sinking in the snow, wrestled to its feet and fell again. There was no earth under her feet, only snow as treacherous as water. As I freed myself from the door handle, caught in between the buttons of my unwieldy coat, I shouted again.

'It's all right. I'm English. Don't be frightened.' I am not sure why my nationality came into my mind—perhaps I thought she was from over the border, less than a kilometre away from the track just at this point. At any rate she stopped, swaying and drooping, and turned a tallow pale oval wrapped in dark shawls towards the lights of the car. She had made a track of deep footprints and I followed her, staggering like a drunk away from me, pulling desperately out of my grip.

'There's nothing up here! Where do you want to go?' I shouted, though there was hardly any wind and the night was rather quiet, as I noticed when my voice faded and the stillness enfolded us.

'The house,' she groaned, 'isn't the house up here? They said . . .' She glared round wildly into the inky dark outside the car lights, which blinded her.

'You mean Frau Homburg's? I'm going there myself. Here—let me help you.'

She might have gone on for a long time without the interruption, but the terror I could see in the frantic glitter of the sunken eyes and the stretched mouth from which no cry came, took the last of her strength. She seemed to fold together and I had to drag her back to the track. There was no means of leverage to lift her in the deep, floundering wilderness of snow. Propped against the car while I opened the passenger door, she seemed to try to fight me off, a nightmare struggle in the empty night, our feet slipping to and fro and her groaning breath rasping loudly. I managed to shove her weight into the car, and lifted the soaked boots, still trying to kick me, in after her, so that the movement swung her back against the seat and she gave up and huddled there, inertly, fighting for breath. She was wet through and there was melting snow everywhere. My foot slid off the pedal, but some roughness of the ground just there enabled the chains to grip and the car started, I fumbling with soaked gloves and peering through the misted windshield which began at once to freeze from our breath gusting in clouds. It was getting colder every moment and I was never so glad to see anything as the lights from the house flowing out over the treeless slope to our left.

The girl roused herself a little when the car stopped, and groaned again, catching breath with a wincing rasp as if it hurt her. This time the motor was heard from inside—my window patching did keep some of the draughts out of the house, it seemed. Kerenyi's tall form showed, lopsided, in the opened door and he called my name.

'Come and help me, will you, Georg?' I shouted. 'I've picked up a starving girl with the rations.'

'She was coming up here, so she said before she collapsed.' I added to Frau Homburg, who was hastily pulling on clogs to come outside.

'We'd better get her inside.' It was easier to carry her than to try to help her walk, but she struggled feebly, still afraid of us.

'That's pleurisy,' said Kerenyi, pulling down his mouth and nodding at the sound of her breath. 'I've heard that, before.'

We laid her on the wide bench in the kitchen, near the cooking stove where once the outside workmen and herdsmen sat to warm or dry themselves.

Frau Homburg brought the lamp to aid the guttering candle, and now drew back the shawl from the girl's face.

She said dully, 'It's Lali.' She seemed stunned. 'I hardly recognise her, but it is Lali.'

'We'd better get her into a hot bath and then bed,' said Kerenyi, taking over with a competence he had not shown before. The effects of cold and exposure were familiar—he knew better what to do with them than with nails and pump handles.

Frau Homburg sat stiff with a helplessness not natural to her. Her hands on her knees, she bent forward to study the girl's pallid, puffy, ugly face, with the mouth half open, the eyes gummed with a rheumy juice of sickness. There was something terrible in her look as she studied the face before her, a look of anger and hatred that frightened me. She seemed like one of those legendary women of the Greek tragedies, about to tear human beings to pieces in some unknowable revenge. Then she shook herself, sat back and spoke quite calmly, her expression normal again. 'You go and stoke the bath fire, Robert,' she said as she stood up stiffly. 'We'll get her into the inside room and I'll undress her.'

I was dubious about the propriety of bathing a pleurisy patient, but reminded myself that it is undoubtedly the quickest way of warming a chilled body. By the time this was all done, and the groaning girl wrapped in blankets in Frau Homburg's bed, it was getting late, but none of us felt appetite; all we wanted was a drink and a strong one. In my absence a large tabby, or tiger, cat had been added to the household and she sat primly on the stove seat, the only one of the circle to show equanimity, as she carefully washed her ears and whiskers. She, at any rate, felt an appetite for my extravagant Christmas gesture of opening a tin of pallid salmon. We stared at each other's gloomy faces. In retrospect my first visit was seen to be of a hopefulness and energy now lapsed into a dogged kind of depression; dogged because there was no cure for anything in the thought of 'giving up'.

'There's no end to it,' said Frau Homburg. 'The only way to bear other people's misery is to drink.'

I remembered the confirmation from Veronica about her being suspect with the western Allies in Vienna, and guessed that this sarcastic tone would not be easily understood, both its content and manner being so near what would only recently have been total impropriety and even vulgarity in a woman of good society.

It was, however, the connecting thought, the contrast with

Veronica Masters, that brought home with shocked force a realisation, a jump of understanding. This girl, Lali, was the daughter of an old family, the sister and daughter of generations of state servants and military commanders, just as Julia Homburg was herself the daughter of a man who in our country would be called a Privy Councillor. The ruin of our civilisation was come if women of their kind could be exposed quite unprotected to the total savagery of war and its aftermath. That had not happened until now in Europe since the Dark Ages. It was impossible to imagine the sister of General Masters struggling exhausted, ill and hungry through snow-drifts alone at night. Yet, until the last year or so, where was the difference between Julia Homburg or Ferdinand von Kasda's sister and Lady Veronica Masters? One only, unless we considered ourselves as making war on women—they were born on the wrong side.

'Well, here's to survival,' said Julia, and we drank.

'No need to keep rubbing it in,' Georg said quietly.

'I'm sorry,' she said, 'I know you've had a bad time too, but the shock of seeing Lali in this state . . . You never saw her before; she was a child almost.'

'Child!' Georg's voice made us jump. 'God, where *is* the child?'

'It stayed with its grandmother for the time being. It's all right. Lali managed to tell me that much.'

'I thought I was going to bring you good news this evening,' I said. 'And about Lali, too. That is why she felt she must get here, I suppose because I've managed to get her a job. Though it certainly worked much quicker than I expected. I thought we'd have time to make some arrangement to pick her up at the zone border.'

Julia looked at me as if she did not understand what I said, for the whole matter was now mentioned for the first time; I was determined not to promise anything until I could be sure of carrying out my plan.

'A job?' she asked blankly. 'You mean with the Army?'

'Not quite that. With the new reading room and library in the town. It's being opened in January and I suggested Lali—I have to call her that because I don't know her name—for the staff. The papers were sent off last week, giving this address as her official home.'

'Her name is von Kasda,' she said and Georg lifted his head.

'The child's father was killed before they could be married. Lali refused a proxy wedding. They told me in the letter I got before the end that there would still be a Ferdinand von Kasda. They were sure it would be a boy and it was.'

'A job,' she went on, after a long pause. 'Work—it's the only thing that saves one, the only thing that can never be taken away. You know, since I've been here I've been puzzling all the time about the way everything that happened has been turned upside down since the war ended.

'I don't think either of you quite understand that. There were the Germans, you see, and things got worse and worse with the police after July '44 and everybody was more and more afraid. And at the same time terrified of the Russians and the end—of course, everybody knew the war was lost though a lot of people did quite genuinely think of the Red Army as liberating us from the Gestapo; I remember thinking myself—it must have been in April, just before the end—that they would take care of us and we should be— well, liberated, from the cellar, from the secrets, from the awful way we lived. People say now, from the Nazis, and it was that, too, but really from the war itself. That mood didn't last long, you can imagine. By the time I was sent home from the hospital the whole city was sunk in black despair.

'It's not quite fair to blame it all on the Russians—it was really the total breakdown of ordinary city living. You know, administration, water, all that stuff we take for granted—though I shall never be able to do that again. I didn't realise this at the time, since I couldn't get about at first and didn't know what they meant when the other people in the house began coming to me to thank me because they had water—the water was reconnected quite quickly— they could do things fast when they wanted to. We even had electricity for the lift when it was on at all. Other lifts were not allowed to be used, but the rations deliveries to my apartment had to come up to the fourth storey. I was privileged, again. What the other people in the house were especially grateful for was the guard on the house; marauders were warned off by the guards who were really there to see I stayed there.

'It wasn't until about June, I suppose, that I grasped all this . . . oh, the smells of summer last year with the dead bodies everywhere under the ruins and half the sewage smashed and no water in parts of the city . . . And it was just about the same time as I began to think of work again, that the rumours about the Americans and

British insisting on their rights in the city became really convincing. Up to then we'd heard only the Russian version and nobody believed that any more than they believed the Germans. But now we heard the radio from Salzburg and Graz. That we believed. Everything the Americans and British said was gospel. But it was still uncertain for some weeks and people prayed for the arrival of the western troops as if they were the Second Coming. The idea that the Russians could be controlled—ah, that was the new deliverance because if things went on as they were it looked as if the whole city, the whole country, would be stripped to the bone.

'And when the Allies arrived things did at once get better, rations were increased, medical attention, hygiene because of the danger of epidemics. And they had their own radio stations. But the really wonderful thing was the new newspapers. The Viennese are great newspaper-readers, Robert, and they just fell on the new papers and again, every word was gospel. But that's where everything began to be turned upside down. You see, the new editors were mostly former German or Austrian refugees and their eyes were on the past, on 1938 and after. And several foreign correspondents came back who were in Vienna until America joined the war, including Colton Barber, who knew one. It was as if all the trouble they were having with the Russians, the disillusionment and conspiracy and constant quarrelling, made them the more bitter against us. The hunt for the Nazis began and naturally it was always the small ones that got into trouble; the big ones were gone or were well covered.

'I was suspect because the Russians had taken care of me—they were mad keen to open up the theatres again. Then, three months ago, the denazification story got into print. It was like being in a looking-glass. I could prove nothing though I kept suggesting witnesses who knew something, however vague. But they weren't interested in all that because they had documentary evidence. They had the papers of my divorce and wouldn't believe it was forced on me. They had the transfer of property. They even had the frightful thing about my giving the book to Fräulein Bracher to type, and her arrest—while I'd been freed after being interrogated, she was shot. The Russians wanted the manuscript and so did the Americans, and I insisted on leaving it in Zurich. I couldn't seem to explain anything, or rather, everything I explained made matters worse.

'Because, you see, it was true. I did get a divorce when the theatre administrator insisted. I was a rich woman from Jewish property. I really was concerned in Fräulein Bracher's death in a way, by asking her to type a proscribed manuscript.

'I remember the worst day; it was some sort of hearing—I never quite understood, really. The man who kept the little pub near our house came, but he hadn't been told to appear and nobody wanted to listen to him. He kept jumping up and shouting that he must say something. "I carried him down to the cellars myself," he kept on yelling, blubbering like a kid. He was so upset he made no sense at all and they thought he was unhinged and he was taken out by some official who kept patting his arm and telling him to control himself. Of course, this great big man crying made me worse. I had a sort of block so that I couldn't talk about—anything, and certainly they thought I was hedging. An actress, after all . . . but every time I had to answer a question I began to weep. It was ghastly, a nightmare of weird misunderstandings and the most humiliating thing . . .'

The slow, quiet voice broke and we sat silent but for the hoarse breathing of the girl in the bed. Presently Julia began to talk again in a trembling tone.

'Then, when I saw the newspaper accounts, I thought I was going mad. After that, people were wary with me; nobody wanted to know me. I was avoided. They were afraid of offending the saviours.'

'It's monstrous, all the same, that somebody belonging to the theatre—Hansi Ostrovsky or Schoenherr—didn't defend you,' Georg said bitterly. 'Almost as monstrous as my not being there— the only one who actually knew the whole story.'

'Hansi cares only about the theatre, first, last and all the time,' she said wearily, and she had clearly said it often before. 'And Schoenherr is retired, a complete invalid. And as for you, Georgy— d'you think you were the only man who didn't want to join the Army? Why do you have to blame yourself, attach everything to your own person? It's the most intolerable arrogance—can't you see that?'

'I suppose it is—as if I'd have been a saviour if only I'd been there. Though I certainly could have helped you.'

She considered. 'I don't think you would have made much difference by then. It was Colton Barber's story about the divorce in the New York press that finished me. He'd known me before and had what they call an inside story. Naturally, the Vienna papers reprinted it. There was no arguing with that—these were the newspapers, like the wireless, that were telling us the truth! After so many years of slanted news, this was fact, hard fact; what people read about me and other people attacked for being Nazis was instantly believed just because the political news was so free from obvious propaganda. And just because for years we had not believed "official" news, only the foreign broadcasts.'

She stopped again and frowned at the blinking cat.

'The night after that inside story appeared, I was hissed in the theatre,' she said at last, flatly. I caught my breath and Georg muttered something unprintable under his breath.

'And the Russians began to keep on about getting the book back from Zurich. I wouldn't have been afraid if the public had been behind me—they wouldn't have dared touch me, then. As it was, I was scared I might just disappear like lots of others. I was lucky, though. By that time the transfer of this place to my name was completed and I could come here.'

'I'm rather surprised they let you leave Vienna,' said Georg.

'I waited until the Americans had their month in the city and left quietly.'

'And the Americans gave you a pass to travel without difficulty?'

'I don't need an American pass to come into the British Zone,' she explained patiently. 'Only a British pass, and that is automatic if one has a house in their zone. It's just that the American month in the city is the safest for moving about. They—the Americans—are quite clear about the Russians. But I don't suppose I'd have had any difficulty about leaving from them or the British, even if they noticed my going. I rather fancy they were relieved when I told Hansi I should not appear again until all this was cleared up. So was Hansi relieved, poor fellow. He was in between, with all sides firing at him. Including myself, of course.'

The girl in the bed had begun now to fidget and turn about, moaning aloud and trying to push away her covers and catching her breath painfully. She had been quieter but now began to toss, moving her hands feebly and muttering to herself.

She was talking to someone, a name recurred, Nikolai Petrovich; she spoke to him formally but in a dignified, personal tone, as one human being to another. Could he not request his successor to continue living in the house; we should be happy to take care of him, as we took care of you, Nikolai Petrovich. But it can't be true that you have no influence, you are a General. You can't abandon us, you know what it will be like. What does it mean, you are ordered back to Moscow? You say that in such a tone, Nikolai Petrovich, I begin to fear for you as well as for ourselves. Yes, I understand you, and nothing is further from me than to wish to wound your patriotic feelings. You have taught us, my mother and me, that Russians are human beings. But this man is a horror, you know it yourself. For God's sake let us not descend to dishonesty between our two selves, that would not be worthy of you. If you could get your successor to take over the house, this man would be under some kind of control. This man, I beg you not to abandon us to him.

All this in very bad Russian, hard to follow, even if she were not rambling, muttering unintelligibly for long intervals. Of the three of us, I alone understood her attempt at Russian, since Georg had only a few words of camp argot. The scene was repeated, over and over, in a droning, disconnected stream of words. Then, with abrupt transfer, in a cold but normal tone as if speaking to an acquaintance on some social occasion, and perfectly clearly in German.

'He was arrested, you know. Yes, the special forces came for him, I recognised their cap-bands. That's the last that will ever be seen of him, poor devil.'

Her mutterings continued so, pleading with the unknown General in ungrammatical Russian and commenting in German on her own narrative. I never in my life heard anything more uncanny. Once she said slowly, in the intimate form, 'You mean, I should leave Nando here, and go alone . . . ?' and wept miserably, without tears, for the fever left no tears to weep with. After a time the mutterings became incoherent and she stopped tossing to and fro. We fetched blankets from our beds in the cook's room to pile on her and pulled her frame bed nearer to the glowing stove so that as much heat as we could produce should stoke the temperature. There was nothing more to be done, but we could none of us think of sleeping so we sat there, waiting endlessly for the dawn or for the outbreak of sweat that would signal a reduction of the fever. The fever might, of course rise and rise until the heart gave out, but that we did not consider. Or rather, I considered it without saying it and I dare say the others did so too. It is a curious experience to sit by the bed of a stranger and know there is nothing you can do to save her; nature, as we often say without knowing what we mean, must take its course.

Presently, about two o'clock in the morning, an absurd gaiety seized us all. We brought a tin of the pressed pork that was such a luxury and that we all disliked and dug it out with a knife to spread on the dark, wet bread. We talked about everything and nothing, helpless except to defend a barrier between us and despair. I told them, as in a story, about David's change of heart—or mind— and Betty's dilemma; it seemed, comparatively, the slight tale of a misadventure and there was not much harm in the telling for neither of them was likely ever to see the actors. Julie told us stories of theatrical intrigues and Kerenyi described the life of splendour lived by the former occupiers of Poland.

The girl in the bed began again to babble; we were all, by now, unsober—I am aware of how disgusting this must appear to my bourgeois readers, but facts are facts. I felt myself sway as I leaned over to feel her brow, moist and cold with the breaking fever. She was now sweating like a laundry, gasping and turning from side to side in her wrappings of blankets which began to smell of damp wool. She begged for something to drink and we fed her with weak tea, continuing ourselves to drink Italian brandy and water. I had no idea, and have none now, whether the tea was a good thing or not. But after a time Lali fell with the suddenness of a spell, into a deep, tranquil slumber. She turned from her back on to her side and fell asleep as if she were perfectly well. We looked at each other and stopped our chatter; we began to yawn.

At a quarter to eleven the distant bells from the village church woke me, pealing for High Mass. It was Christmas. And I had the worst hangover of my life.

At that time Austrians were not allowed to carry any kind of firearms, but the regulations were sometimes unofficially relaxed in favour of sporting guns because of the necessity of making use of whatever food was to be had. It was Wilder, naturally, who found out how to borrow from the official store of confiscated local weapons. We went out every day, Kerenyi and I. One day Wilder and Tom came over and joined us, sleeping the night before at the tavern where the border patrol lived, so as to be out before dawn with us. The butcher in the village smoked and cured parts of our bag; what we could eat fresh we consumed. The larger part went on to the black market through the same butcher. Game was plentiful and neighbouring landowners only too happy to allow us to shoot their fields and woods in return for a proportion of the bags. It was a sportsman's paradise after so long a stop on shooting.

Kerenyi and Tom were good shots, and they got on well together while both Tom and Wilder became fast friends with Julie on a basis of mutual benefits, Julie expanding her meagre housekeeping and we getting the sport. The access to a source of meat was important, too, because it was the one means of getting any of the village craftsmen to work about the place and it was astonishing how quickly a carpenter, a tile setter, a plumber and others found their way up to a house whose owners only twenty-one months before had been shot, if not on the denunciation of one of the villagers at any rate without any of them trying to hide or protect them. I already knew enough of what the district had been like in March and April 1945 to feel no surprise that attempts had not been made to help the hated *bourzhuis*. But I think we all felt more than a suspicion that some member of that small community had deflected the rage of the soldiers from himself by naming the class-enemies up the eastern lane.

I sent a message by Tom that Lali von Kasda would not be fit for work for a week or so, but it was heartening how quickly she recovered from an illness that must have been well advanced even before she undertook her hazardous cross-country journey. She walked into the nearest town from her mother's house, six kilometres, before getting space to stand in one of the overcrowded, unheated and windowless trains of that time. A night spent on the station where she must change, after several hours in the standing train while Russian and American border controls were carried out cannot have improved her fever. She then changed trains again to reach the big town nearest to us, crossing another zone border to the British Zone; once more waited many hours for a bus to the village which ran only at irregular intervals, there being sometimes breaks of several days at a time when diesel fuel ran out. It would have been a nightmare for a man in good health. What force must have been driving this frail sick creature to make the prospect of such a journey the better alternative—travelling conditions were well known—we none of us liked to contemplate and for her sake none of us asked questions; if Julie knew more than we heard on the night of her arrival, she said nothing. And I doubt if she knew, for what the girl mumbled in broken Russian meant nothing to Kerenyi or Julie.

However, with the unbeatable will of one who has an overriding purpose, Lali shook off in days an illness that would in normal times have involved three weeks in hospital. As she improved, the lines of her own appearance began to emerge from under the puffy, greyish pallor of half-starvation and she shed in half as many days ten years of age. I saw in reverse the process by which the very poor age, so that a woman of thirty looks fifty. This young woman, only just past twenty as I gathered, returned to her own age from a hag-like timelessness of ugliness and misery.

Each day Kerenyi and I trudged over the snowy woods. Over his remaining plaster he wore a pair of large wooden-soled rubber boots bartered in the village for Wilder's promised tyre. He must have suffered a good deal from the leg and his damaged arm but he gave no sign; a longing for action and the open air made him grasp the opportunity, for shooting was only possible when I was there.

The weather was of a lowering grey, our departures in the dark dawns of the turn of the year being not much darker than the days. But the snow held off, thanks to a wind down the north-south valley which the villagers told us would prevent snow as long as it blew. 'When it blows over the hills from the east, the snow will come again,' they said and told us strange stories of Saint Stephen's day and the *Percht* on the night of January 5th, an ancient devil-woman who captured the souls of unbaptised children and threatened the living with her disembowelling knife. That the heathen as well as the Church's versions of these legends still existed in their minds was oddly proved. Coming in one afternoon I chanced to look up at the saint's effigy over the back door and saw there a horseshoe which nobody in the house, as I found, had placed there. The heathen connection of that symbol goes very far back, to Odin's horse, and it must have been put there secretly in the night for owing to the treelessness of the house's surroundings it could not be approached during daylight without the stranger being seen. I supposed that someone thought a propitiation of the place or its owners to be needed, but Julie remembered vaguely that the horseshoe was connected in some way with Saint Stephen's legend. He was no longer identifiable, his outstretched hand with stones in it being broken off as well as his head, and neither Kerenyi nor myself knew that the effigy was his or that he gave his name to the original name of the house, Steffelsgut.

'We used to have a book here about those legends,' said Julie, frowning thoughtfully. 'I was fascinated by it as a girl—it had the strangest pictures. Probably those three men who came up from the village on Saint Stephen's day brought the horseshoe with them, d'you think? I wondered at the time, but that's a hiring and firing day hereabouts, now I think of it, and they offered to do any work I needed about the place . . . Odd, isn't it?'

'I don't much like the idea of people coming up here when you're alone,' said Kerenyi. 'We ought to get a dog.'

'There's no need to protect me,' Julie rejected him sharply. 'You don't understand these people; they won't touch me or anything of mine ever again. They adopt new situations into their old superstitions—don't you know that?'

'Just the same . . . ' I began, and decided not to finish the sentence. I saved it to say to Georgy later when we were alone, that the house was rather too near the border for my liking. To hide my change of mind, I suggested to Julie that she should mark her ownership by re-registering it in its old name. Somewhat to my surprise, she did not laugh at this idea, and during the evening meal she reverted to it, saying she would ask the priest what he thought of the idea, the next time she should speak to him. Kerenyi glanced up from his plate, startled at this remark, and I saw that neither religion nor superstition had belonged to his own view of his friend. To me, stranger as I was to their customs and their former lives, it was not surprising for I assumed that Julie belonged to the Catholic belief in reality as well as formally. But Georg did not comment and a moment later Julie rose and went to do something for her patient, leaving us alone except for the sick girl in the bed.

We spoke then of the border, and Georg said bitterly that for him to warn Julie of the danger of refugees who might be desperate would be to invite her instant refusal to take any measures of self-defence. I knew by then that this was true and was unhappily silent; and a moment later Julie returned and began to feed Lali.

Yet the nearness of an unattainable place just over those hills was part of that landscape long after the border was open again and long after the strangeness of the land was as familiar to me as the faces of friends. To this day it has a feeling of mystery to me, which lives behind its everyday reality. I see sometimes, awake or sleeping, the far mountains and the roll of country between us and them, the dark of forested stretches, and everywhere the deep, settled silence of the winter snows. Winter in those parts of Europe does not vary; it is a month-long fact of climate that makes easy a belief, or a still conscious disbelief, in ancient forces. That the sun may die does not seem impossible, and the snow has its own powers at once deadening, healing and secretly generative under the wide, trackless spaces where the only marks are the tiny threading lines of hares' jumps, of fox and badger leaving winter lairs. And I recapture the catching of breath at the deeper prints of deer suddenly seen, at which I would unsling my sporting rifle that Kerenyi was not supposed to use, and hand it quietly to him that his more certain marksmanship should secure a valuable prize.

The morning before I would have to return, we shot a small, wild boar, almost the whole flesh of which could be preserved and would provide Julie with meat for months; that gave me, townsman as I was, a feeling of something worth doing the value of which could not be challenged. Kerenyi shot him. I did not trust myself to get him at first shot and I felt such envy at his skill that I had to joke about it, saying his experience of killing was much greater than my own; with which he equably agreed. We dragged the carcase over three kilometres back to the house, leaving a smudgy brownish trail after us. The boar looked magnificent hanging from its trotters in the cold cellar, the dark blood still dripping into a stone pot from the disproportionately massive snout.

Upstairs, after cleaning ourselves up, we found the girl, for the first time recognisably a girl, sitting up in a chair by the stove wrapped in a blanket. A person now appeared, instead of an anonymous sick creature, with the memory of laughter in eyes set for gaiety and a mouth and round chin not formed for the dogged perseverance of her look. I felt as proud and possessive at the appearance of a human being from a wreck as if I had made her, myself.

XI

David, it seemed, was to stay with us until the end of February, and with egregious self-importance Colonel Manley was arranging this at David's request. I arrived back into an atmosphere more like a public relations office in the Mess than a military unit, with pompous messages going to and from London as to the essential importance of Captain Stephenson staying at his post for a few weeks in order to finish work only he was competent to do.

David himself now did no work at all; all his time was occupied between his private affairs and the complex arrangements for his staying on when friends in the Foreign Office—working out quite a different intrigue—were by this time making an equal show of wishing to engage his services at once. It was a quick course for me in social education. David's mother at one end was trying to carry out his request to pull as many wires as she could still hold for his immediate release, as he had wished when he was in London; Manley in Styria was furthering David's later wishes by keeping him, apparently for official reasons, where he was. As Wilder said, by the time David actually went to the Foreign Office he would seem a very important acquisition indeed. His file must already be as large as that of a man employed for roughly five years. And Colonel Manley did not hesitate to take up the suggestion made jokingly to him by David at dinner (he divided his dinners now equally between his courting and the necessity of keeping Manley interested) that he would have to request two officers to replace the so-needed Captain Stephenson. This, of course, in jest; but the jest was a useful one.

What the new employers must not suspect was that there was a personal reason for all this and it was only for that reason, as David himself pointed out, that he did not marry at once. He was listed in his new job as unmarried and it was possible that some ill-disposed person would remark upon the coincidence of his insisting, or getting his superiors to insist, on two months' extension of Army service and his arrival in London with a bride.

His candour, as always, was disarming and unnerving at the same time. Everything was represented as a great lark, but it now seemed incredible that nobody should challenge his assumption, his always tentative, throw-away assumption of helplessness, of the need for action by others which he knew, he said, he had no claim to, but people were so kind . . .

A fresh batch of repatriates arrived; there was much to do though nothing to compare with the pressure at the beginning of December. I shipped off the crazy 'Ukrainian', who turned out to be a Ruthenian Pole who had served the Gestapo as what the Germans call a 'man of confidence' which means a secret agent. In his place, besides the constant flow of returning soldiers, there were two Russian deserters; one of whom was of interest. He professed to be a Sergeant but was obviously of considerable technical education and by the unfairness of fate's workings his name, Torek, was already known to the world as one of a team of military technicians who had been 'persuading' German scientists to accept contracts to work in Russia. With the ignorance universal among Russians, he did not know that the abortive attempt to kidnap a physicist already engaged by the American Army was in newspapers on every bookstall of Europe and America. This case, forgotten years ago, was one of the many incidents that educated western countries in the methods and aims of the Russian government.

My tactic of interrogation, after a long discussion with Jack Morgenstern and Martin Johnson, was to pretend to believe Torek and, by implying his low status and lack of interest to us, to play upon his natural vanity. It was a difficult thing to do; but we were corporately determined to 'crack' this man, for the Americans were demanding him as their prisoner and we had a strong rivalry over him in which Manley backed us up. So important a renegade could only increase his own importance. Jack and Martin helped me and sat in on the interrogations but because of the language I did the actual questioning. Torek spoke some English, but it is psychologically important always to question a man in his own language for the use of that of the interrogator gives the man being questioned a tremendous advantage which is only to be justified as a trick to produce a feeling of superiority. In this case we wished to stimulate the man's conceit but without allowing him a feeling of being our superior. He cracked, in fact, over the language question, being unable any longer to overcome the desire to show us how highly educated he was. High technical proficiency does not, anywhere, presuppose anything about character, and 'experts' can be as childishly vain and venal as any shop assistant.

We had Torek, one morning, together with the other deserter who really was a simple soldier, in an interrogation room and it was clear that the device of pretending that he was on the same intellectual level as the peasant boy was succeeding. Jack signalled to me, as the technician began to fidget, interrupt and raise his voice, to break off the questioning. I bowed, somewhat reluctantly, to his vastly superior knowledge of human nature and called for the guard with a shrug and a glance at my watch as if this were really a most tiresome matter and I wished nothing more than to get to luncheon.

At the meal we naturally discussed the deserter, conversation on a matter so important to the Colonel's ambition being encouraged. Over this Russian, Manley showed the only interest in my society I was ever to be flattered by, and I got what I could out of the situation as long as it lasted. It may be that my enjoyment of this temporary popularity as well as the intense excitement of all three members of the interrogation team over the impending 'crack-up' of our victim made us blind to an incident which later assumed great significance. There is a sporting interest in such contests of will, especially where, as in this case, the object is at once of public import and of little human charm. He was too vain and self-important to be attractive, and at the same time these faults increased the pleasure of outwitting him. But while it is clear that our sporting attitude towards Torek was not particularly scrupulous it should not be thought that the term 'crack-up' means that he was reduced to either physical or nervous collapse; it was the usual term for the point at which a prisoner began to talk—not necessarily truthfully.

Wilder was about to go on his projected ski-ing leave with Veronica and Betty and asked us to telephone him when we got results, for we had made bets with him as to when and how this would occur.

'Don't forget, Jack,' he said—Jack was holding the stakes—'I get a bonus from David if the bastard turns out to be a Party member.'

'You've lost that already,' scoffed David, 'he wouldn't be a renegade if he were. I was betting on a certainty there!'

It was true that we had never, as far as we knew, had a Communist Party member through the pen; but then, we had never had a renegade of this type before.

'I'll call you myself,' promised Baxter, who was also betting on this detail. 'But be careful what you say on the telephone. I shall just say we have won, either the whole bet or the first part of it only. Understood?'

'Okay,' agreed Wilder. 'I almost wish I could put off going until the day after tomorrow.'

David being so wrapped up in his own concerns at that time, hardly entered into our excitement, confining his interest to the betting, but now it seemed he was struck with some new aspect of the interrogation and one that interested him greatly.

'Is this chap so important, then, that we have to take special security precautions in talking about him?' he asked Baxter curiously.

Baxter considered his reply. 'I hope you would never discuss an inmate of the pen on the telephone,' he then said, cautiously. 'But this man is, obviously, a special case.'

'But why?' persisted David. 'I haven't been following the case, so I don't understand what is so special about him.' As always when talking to Baxter his voice took on a slightly aggressive note for he cold not overlook or disarm what he knew to be the security man's dislike of himself; towards those with whom his charm did not work David felt a puzzled resentment.

'I'm not sure that I ought to tell you,' said Baxter, 'but unless I do, one or another of you may make some mistake out of ignorance.' The Mess servants now coming into the room, he waited until they finished and withdrew again before he went on. 'This is highly classified information, which if written would be Top Secret. Torek is not of himself very interesting to us or the Americans, but he may, if our identification of him is correct, have information of a number of things our American friends very much wish to know. That is why they have tried to take over his interrogation. He may know, in fact, what happened to several physicists who were in Germany and who disappeared. If they, or any of them, have gone to Russia they are probably working on projects—well, we needn't go into details—projects the Russians would give their collective ears to further. We can guess more or less what those are. Both HMG and the United States government attach the very greatest importance and urgency to discovering what Torek knows about these scientists and their present whereabouts. After the Canadian affair, we can take no chances.'

David said stubbornly, pushing at his lock of hair, 'I was under the impression the Russians were our Allies.'

Baxter considered this for a moment, a gloom of anxiety in his blunt face. 'So were we all, I suppose,' he said.

'Well in that case, why are we hiding things from them?' insisted David. 'It's our own fault if they resort to unconventional means of finding out what's going on. We should be sharing anything we know that can help them to combat a resurgence of Fascism.' There was something about this statement that had a repetitive air, as of a lesson learned by heart. But it was the style of statement David often made, in just that way, as if by rote, and not so much irritating as rather boring in its unreality. Baxter, however, seemed to take offence.

'Look here, Stephenson,' he said stiffly. 'I've been in the Service one way or another for twenty-four years and I am not likely to start questioning my superiors about my orders now. I have my instructions and I obey them without argument. And quite frankly, that's what I'd advise you to do as well.'

'Yes,' cried David, his colour rising with a hectic flush. 'That's just the trouble. Anything the Americans ask for is agreed to without argument. We're supposed to be a democracy aren't we? Then why don't we discuss things openly? Why all the secrecy?'

'Come, now, David,' said Martin Johnson peaceably, 'you are forgetting that only two years ago and less, the Americans were even more pro-Russian than we were. There must be some good reason for their change of attitude, don't you agree? A reason we may not completely know?'

'I dare say there is,' interrupted Baxter stolidly, 'but it isn't our job to ask for reasons. As long as we wear uniform our business is to give and accept orders; we give them to our inferiors and take them from our superiors. And that's all. Excuse me, will you, Sir?' He got up from the table, pulling down his battledress blouse with a sharp tug, and left the room, his well-polished boots making hard clicks on the bare, shiny floor.

'You shouldn't rag him the way you do, David,' said Manley. 'You know he's an oldfashioned policeman.' The Colonel was determined to ignore David's opinions, if they could be called that, and I agreed with him in that if in nothing else. 'You know you put it on thick just to annoy Baxter.'

'He is such a *silly* man,' said David in his new 'London' way of talking, and grinned at Manley, both accepting his view of the matter and drawing him into David's own view. He turned then to me. 'Can I sit in this evening, when you see this man again, Robert?'

I hesitated, frowning; I did not want distractions which would put me off my stroke as much as they would increase the renegade's notion of his importance.

'I tell you what, Inglis, we'll sit in the next room with the door just ajar, so that we can hear. I must admit, I'd like to be a witness, myself. We won't make a sound, so you won't be disturbed. How would that be?' Manley had never been a tithe as conciliatory to me before and when he put his wish as a request I could hardly object to it.

'Sir, you will be careful not to give a single sign of life?' Jack pressed him. And cunningly, 'We don't want him to slip out of our grasp and give our friends a chance to crow over us.' This was an argument exactly suited to its audience, and both Manley and David agreed eagerly to be as still as mice. And so it was agreed.

We broke up and I went to my room, with David following me. There was a telephone in the upstairs hall, and I heard him dial and ask for Agnes, with whom he had evidently intended to dine that evening.

'Darling, I have to be on duty tonight, after all,' he said. 'Listen, do something for me, will you, I can't get away and I don't want to make personal calls from here. You know how it is. I was going to telephone a friend in London tonight and he's expecting my call. Here's the number.' He dictated a number after a pause, presumably for Agnes to get a pencil. 'Ask for Johnny and tell him I'm on a rather important duty turn and will talk to him tomorrow. It's very important, tell him on no account to go out in the evening tomorrow until he's talked to me. Well, all right, then. Darling, how stuffy you are sometimes. Banks, Johnny Banks. Yes, that's all. But don't forget. He's making arrangements, important arrangements— for us.' He listened to the other end, and then, so suddenly it was obviously an interruption, he said, 'Darling, about that call tonight. I just remembered, I haven't put the call in—I meant to make a "service call" from the Club, but you'll manage it, won't you? But of course we can make "service calls" to people who aren't relatives! What an innocent you are!'

'Service calls' were cheap telephone calls to home for family members either for celebratory purposes or on occasions of emergency. It struck me forcibly that David was using his fiancée with as much skill as he did his mother and the Colonel. They continued talking, but I went downstairs then, back to the pen, where I had work to do. The guard said our renegade had been asking to see me urgently, but I told the man to give him no reply. He could wait a few hours. I called in at Jack's room on my way and told him our customer was getting restive; he was delighted and came to the door, rubbing his hands, and punched me lightly on the shoulder.

Until Tom put his head round the door several hours later I forgot entirely that he had been out to Julie's house to shoot that day and was due to bring Lali von Kasda back into the town with him. He had left late the night before, for an early start, and reported now that he had delivered his charge to the new reading room, where she was installed in the attic room prepared for her. She was, Tom said, bearing up, but was not yet up to much. I hardly noticed, I was so concentrated on my renegade.

Baxter, Jack and myself were going carefully over every scrap of information we had on the man we supposed him to be, and working out from these documents a series of questions. These must be so arranged in order and each one so formulated that they would leave the man in doubt for as long as possible as to how much we really knew. As I translated the agreed questions into Russian in note form, Jack and Baxter worked on the sequence. We kept interrupting each other to test out both the questions and their order, a demanding business in two languages. Presently Martin Johnson, having finished his own work for the day, came in to help us and by the time we went back to the Mess for dinner we had organised the coming interview in a way that should finish the business of establishing the man's identity that night.

Colonel Manley questioned us closely during dinner about our proposed tactics; we were quite the heroes of the hour and, as Manley said, his own demand for a Russian-speaker—myself—which had long been refused, had now magnificently justified itself. He wished, he said, to press the interrogation on as hard as possible, to find out while our man was still unsettled by the discovery of his real name and position as much as we could get about his recent activities. We agreed—that is, the team agreed—to push him as far as we were able, even if it meant an all-night sitting, which was, strictly speaking, forbidden. But Baxter objected when David, his eyes shining with his new excitement at the hunt, suggested we should imply a possible death penalty for kidnapping to soften him up; a possibility he could circumvent by turning 'King's Evidence'. Tom, who listened with interest but had professionally nothing to do with the interrogation, flinched at this idea.

Baxter, however, was more concerned with its practicability than its morality.

'He might know better,' he pointed out in that dry tone he used to David only, 'and then we should be discredited with him.'

I made a mental note that the idea was not a bad one, if very discreetly hinted at and not clearly expressed, and was eager to get back to my notes on the questions so that I could introduce such a hint somewhere. Between the urge to excel myself in so interesting a case and that dislike which most men feel for a renegade, even when he has come over to their own side, I felt none of Tom's scruples.

'I think the idea is a good one,' said Manley to Baxter, and turning to me, he suggested exactly what I had already silently determined to do. Baxter listened to my concurrence with—now—cautious agreement. It was David's proposal he disliked, not the idea as such. Manley glanced sideways at David over his oldfashioned glasses and I suddenly received the clear impression that they had been discussing the interrogation in some quite specific way between themselves while we were working on it. The thought glanced off my mind again at once under the pressure of more immediate concerns. I drank my coffee, impatient to be gone.

Presently we sent for our man. He quite bustled into the room, glancing round to find the one of us to whom he could talk his own language, while the guard was still stamping to attention and reporting delivery of his charge. This guard was in our plan and told the man to sit down and wait until we were ready; an old trick. Martin had his feet up on the desk in the interrogators' room and I lounged against the open connecting door behind which our subject waited. We talked for a few minutes of other things in casual undertones and then spent more time banging drawers and files shut and locking up for the night. During this stage-managing, Manley and David arrived and seated themselves behind the door where they were invisible from the next room. At last I turned to the door and said, as if bored with one more job to do, that we had better have a chat with our friend since we had sent for him—might as well . . . In the next half hour we raised his desire to have his importance recognised to boiling point by going stolidly through our prepared questions one by one as if in routine. Our last doubts that he was our man were soon removed, long before he broke out and announced it, by the times and places to which he admitted and the names he recognised.

I then dropped David's hint, by mentioning the existence of 'the final penalty' for kidnapping in some American states, the first time the Americans had been referred to. A flood of explanation resulted; he had not kidnapped anyone; the people he recruited were all eager to serve the Party and the homeland of socialism. One or two had been in secret sympathy with the USSR throughout the Nazi period; others discovered their sympathy when offered splendid contracts and all the facilities they could desire to do their jobs. Examples were mentioned. We were now well under way. The recording machine hummed softly from the signals office. Baxter hurried out to make sure they changed the recorders over promptly—it was known for gaps to appear in recordings which in those days were not as easy to handle as they now are. I made notes of names and references as we went along.

If he did not fear prosecution and punishment, I asked him, why did he assume a false name, rank and number on giving himself up? He admitted at once that he wanted to avoid the Americans; their methods were notoriously brutal as he had read in many books. I said that, coming from a member of the notorious SMERSH machine, this was a bold thing for him to say. Almost shocked, he asserted that he had never been enrolled in that apparatus, in spite of its having a foreign department; that was part of the internal security service of the USSR. He had always been an Army technician, only detailed since June the year before to this particular task on account of this specialised knowledge. I did not for a moment believe this, though I know now that it was quite possible for a man to work for one or another of the military and civil espionage or security organisations inside or outside Russia without knowing who issued his orders and gave him his commission. This man may just have been telling the truth and he was certainly very indignant at my accusations of lying. I accused him of avoiding the Americans and their zones in Germany and Austria because he knew he was liable to a serious criminal charge, quite apart from spying; he hoped, did he not, to elude their search by giving himself up to the British? He preferred the British, he said, because they were more civilised as all the world knew. It was quite clear he supposed that our relations with our American allies existed on the same basis of perfidy and suspicion as the Russians' with their allies. Why, then, had he defected at all? Because, he fell into my primitive trap, because he had failed in his task of getting the physicist so-and-so to Russia. I pretended to treat this as evidence that he did indeed try to kidnap the physicist by force knowing that he was already an American employee, but he vehemently denied this; the scientist turned out to be a Nazi, he said, and hated the Soviet Union and this began a long argument. He knew what awaited him for having failed to induce the man to serve his own masters.

This physicist was so important? I could hardly credit that . . . Here the man stumbled in his flood of talk. This he did not want to answer. He was no traitor to the Party and his country; he wanted solely to keep his head on his shoulders. The Party? I shrugged. Party members did not defect. His self-defence became passionate at this and he almost begged me to believe in his membership, quoting dates and numbers to convince me. Did I imagine a non-Party man would be entrusted with a task so crucially important as the abduction of so-and-so? So this man is of great importance? I countered.

Thus we struggled back and forth for hours. When he became mulish on one subject, I began on another, switching to and fro— we had agreed on signals for the various lists of questions between us in advance. I attacked him on the subject of the Americans again, pointing out that if he had no more reason to avoid them than a generalised preference for the British, how was it he reacted so swiftly to a mention of them in the first place—he was obviously lying and I knew for certain of his attempted kidnapping. It was in dozens of newspapers, already an international sensation!

I laid before him copies of the *Times* of several dates with long despatches on the case. He read slowly, unbelieving at first, then with a mixture of anxiety and excitement; pride at his notoriety and professional chagrin at his failure. This failure he felt bound to explain and did so at great length. He was divided between a curious, a most inappropriate, moralistic condemnation at my—our —having trapped him by pretending ignorance when we already knew much of his story, and the desire to excuse his failure. How could I so deceive him when he had put his confidence in me, that was unworthy; but I must understand that the difficulties of his task were far greater than his masters understood when they sent him off. He saw no contradiction in his attitude. Men need to construct for their actions some moral sanction, and I had often heard before arguments that covered acts of inhuman brutality and callousness far more heinous than his. This man's rationalisations were comparatively acceptable, that he served the needs of his country and the Party.

When he mentioned the Party he showed a kind of grief that appeared to be genuine and noticing this, I played on it until he explained at last that the very highest priority had been given to the capture of the physicist. Though knowledgeable, our man showed little theoretical understanding of the potentialities of the physicist's knowledge, as far as I could judge—he was himself rather a competent technician than a scientist and knew little of the larger issues involved. But he did know from the preparations of his own instructions that immense importance attached to his intended prize. He assured me that nothing so elaborate, so carefully planned and thought-out had been attempted before in his experience; the physicist was a key man and was to be taken to the Soviet Union at any cost. Only the merest chance intervened in the plans to persuade him, the chance of the scientist's young son waking up and starting to scream. A human mischance, as my man described it. Since his orders were to remove the physicist alive and well and on no account, including his own capture or death, was any harm to come to his objective, he could not use a weapon.

He could, however, although only just, escape, and this he did. In the dark snow-bound streets of the old university town he wandered for hours, terrified of pursuit and impeded by the weather; snow was not yet normally cleared from streets blocked as well by piled rubble from the bombs of the war. In the darkness he lost his way several times and during that night came to the conclusion that his only chance of survival lay in flight from his masters. His former jobs had gone easily; this was a combination of bad luck, the snow, the black darkness, the child screaming wildly in the overcrowded house which was immediately in an uproar. In his flight, he threw his equipment, weapon, the anaesthetic syringe, his disguise and the coat and hat for the physicist into the river from a bridge outside the town. His great good fortune in his misfortune was that in escaping he had at once taken the wrong turning and run away from the silent car waiting with his accomplices instead of towards it. In the weeks between that time and his surrender he crossed much of Germany and the whole of Austria, having decided that when he gave himself up, it should appear as if he came from the east and not the west.

It was now the middle of the night. Exhausted, we parted, and the recording machine was switched off. Manley and David at once joined us in the interrogators' room, our unshaven, haggard faces, the smoke-filled air and the stale ashtrays, the used coffee cups, giving us the ruffianly air of a gang of miscreants. The Colonel was urgent to have the transcript of the recordings, which only I could make. He must have them tomorrow—today, that was, to make his report. He would sign the report himself, he said. I was to record the translation in the interests of speed; an official transcript could be prepared afterwards for perfect accuracy.

Although such urgency was unique it did not seem strange, for the case itself was unique. It was not until half way through the dictated translation when I broke off for a few minutes and went to the signals office that I noticed that Manley had ordered two recording machines to be used. I could not see why two recordings were needed so urgently.

The dichotomy of our similar but contrary duties were not before this case so clearly posed to us; the majority of us either thought of the Russians as hostile—politically or morally based views of our own hostility—or simply accepted our orders as they came and so thought no more of them, and were not disturbed by it. But I knew that some of the men who had left-wing ideas were uneasy and needed explanations we were not permitted to give them. David's childish politics I did not take seriously, but I thought it unwise to leave the signals staff and some of the NCOs in a state of confusion. I told Baxter this and he listened thoughtfully. We had here, as I said, clearly taken sides, not only with the Americans against the Russians, but more confusingly, in protection of a German against the Russians—the physicist who was to have been captured, it was established by signals between us and American colleagues, was indeed a Nazi and a convinced one and the men knew this. I suggested cautiously that Sergeant Benson, who was universally liked and trusted by officers and men alike, should be asked to explain to the men, informally, enough of the outlines of what was at stake to settle their doubts about our ambiguity. I knew Baxter did not share my civilian view that the men were bound to think about their orders, but he was not at all the oldfashioned policeman type that it suited Manley to call him. He was not reactionary or authoritarian but simply a policeman, and he proved this by giving me a patient hearing and agreeing to talk it over with Sergeant Benson.

'What made you mention particularly the signals men?' he asked me. 'Simply that they must know more than the others?'

'Partly that,' I answered. 'Partly that I've heard them talking sometimes and I know they are leftish. Partly I remember something Kerenyi once said to me about the importance in modern war of including signals and transport staff in one's calculations and of having their entire loyalty and understanding. He was talking, in fact, of the July 20th Plot where at least part of the lower ranks bound to be involved were ignored. But it seemed to me there is something in what he said and we can learn from the mistakes of our enemies as well as of our friends.'

'It was part of Monty's secret of handling troops,' he said. 'I'll talk to Benson. Leave it with me, will you, Robert?'

'Good, of course,' I rose to leave him. 'I was only concerned to have said what was on my mind.'

'You were quite right, if a bit pedantic,' he said.

As I went away, David called me. A typewriter had been carried into Colonel Manley's office and he was typing the report with two fingers.

I noticed, idly, that not two, but three copies were being taken; and until I recalled the two recordings, assumed this was so that one copy could be sent to the Americans. It was against security rules for Top Secret reports like this one to be written with more than one carbon, the top going to the War Office and the sole copy remaining in our safe-keeping. But the second set of recording tapes had gone off that noon in a staff car which could be locked, instead of a jeep, and with two armed guards, to the nearest American command post that could accept charge of it.

David checked an obscure formulation in my oral translation and I left; but it seemed to me then a chancy way to write an important and secret report from a recorded voice, the typing of which is quite a skilled business. The constant playing-back would weaken the recording, I thought, but it was evidently Manley's direct order. And at least the door was kept shut so that passing men could not hear the scratchy record of my translation as it was stopped and started again. I wondered too why David had been chosen to write the report; pure favoritism I decided, for both Wilder and myself typed better than David and if my literary style leaves a good deal to be desired, at least I could be relied on not to misunderstand my own translation. In other words, I was piqued at being passed over. The official reason was that I had been working most of two nights and David could start fresh in the early morning, while I was to sleep late if I wished to. In fact, David himself suggested this method to the Colonel. It took him until dinner-time to finish, and he came into the anteroom, the papers, stamped in their official cover, or rather two covers, ready for Baxter. He was so cock-ahoop that he could not resist teasing the policeman.

'I suppose you know the old man is sending a personal report direct to the Foreign Office?' he asked in a casual drawl. Baxter looked up sharply and his stare became fixed. His colour rose and his eyes narrowed angrily. He controlled the anger and smiled.

'By your direct agency, I take it?' he said.

'As a matter of fact, yes,' answered David and lounged away to call for a drink. His fingers were covered with dark marks from the carbon papers and a struggle with the typewriter ribbon, about which I heard him next day complaining to a soldier clerk.

Baxter considered a moment. Then he got up without a word, leaving his drink, and went straight up to Manley's private room, where the Colonel was washing before dinner. What was there said, I do not know, but when Baxter came down a couple of minutes later, he fixed me with a look I should have been scared by if I had done something wrong, and said, very clearly.

'I want you to know that I am making a formal report on the news I just had from Captain Stephenson, Inglis. Be good enough to remember that if it should be necessary.'

It seemed to be a formal communication so I came to attention and said, 'Yes, Sir.' Tom coming in that moment, we were both glad to see him as a relief and although he glanced from one to the other of us he said nothing and everything seemed normal again.

Manley came in.

'Is Stephenson dining out *again?*' he asked, loudly, jovially, defensively. He looked around at our reserved faces with a gleam of oldfashioned suggestiveness in his smile, behind his glasses. It was Tom, who did not know what Baxter had just said to me, who answered with some neutral piece of civility.

'Ah, well, young love, you know!' cried Manley nervously and laughed in a way that again sounded suggestive. He rubbed his hands together and called over his shoulder for his usual pre-dinner whisky, his tone changing noticeably when he spoke to the Mess waiter. He was trying to be 'matey' with us. Evidently Baxter had been curt and definite in his comment on the dubious and incorrect methods used over the report. I felt very uncomfortable for I not only agreed with Baxter in a military sense, but felt a growing annoyance that I had myself been edged out of a chance of approval from my superiors for a job I had done myself, by two people who had contributed nothing to its achievement. Looking down at my drink to avoid Manley's challenging look, I noticed with relief that my watch was missing; I had not put it on again after taking a shower. I muttered some apology and ran back up to my room for it.

I waited there a few minutes, smoking a cigarette and staring abstractedly out of the window into the darkness. A shadowy outline of the garden trees could be seen in the dark patch made by my own head in the glass but it was so dark that almost nothing could be made out and I stood there musing, my mood slipping from its immediate resentment to a more distant comfort of having things to look forward to in my new friendships which would be unaffected by these temporary and unimportant intrigues. I could imagine telling this story, or the censored outlines of it, to Julie Homburg; as I constructed the scene she would laugh and shrug, saying scornfully that such methods, like those of theatrical feuds, usually defeated their own ends . . . In the next room I could hear David, moving hastily about in his usual state of lateness and disorganisation, as he got ready to go out.

But I could not lurk about up here much longer. I went out on to the landing, and at the same moment, David came out of his room. He was in his greatcoat, its collar turned up at the back in an unsoldierly fashion. With his ungloved hand he pushed a thick envelope into one coat pocket while with the right hand, already gloved, he closed his door. Seeing me, he gave me an abstracted smile, a sweet, mischievous, boyish grin. Nothing is more difficult than to describe the quality of a smile; David's had an effect of suddenness, changing the expression of his mouth instantly and giving his face its handsome look of great charm. The quick change gave the person to whom the smile was directed an impression that it was the sight of himself that changed a state of melancholy or irritation into well-being.

I smiled in return, expecting him to say something about the report, but he did not speak and we moved down the corridor to the head of the stairs together in silence. Downstairs, Jack's accented voice called to Martin Johnson that they would have to hurry with dinner—they must get back to Benda, who had been neglected for days.

'We want to get his case done with and get him off our hands, and above all, out of those cells downstairs. He's beginning to look like an underground plant, he's so pale.'

Other voices spoke, and someone laughed, but I felt an instant of trepidation and unease so strong that it was like guilt. I glanced at David. We had stopped, somehow, at the head of the stairs, and he too looked at me. The name of Benda flickered like an electric spark between David and myself and the little scene in the cellar was almost palpable; I could almost see the officer's cane, the crooked tie, the hurried breathing and the gleam of perspiration on his forehead in the cellar lights.

Involuntarily I looked at his hand, but of course, he was not carrying the cane—nobody ever did. But his gloved hand went, as if of its own volition, to his coat pocket and touched the envelope just visible above the opening, so that the pocket flap was pushed up untidily.

The memory of Benda jumped between us and connected instantly with something else, something that I could not place, but something that was wrong. Something I knew with certainty was not in order.

'Silly business, this about the report,' said David casually, smiling sideways at me to indicate that it was all Manley's doing, of course. We strolled down the stairs, side by side. 'You've come out of it very well, Robert. Terrific praises for your brains and tenacity—that's what the old boy said. It's a big coup, isn't it? That'll show the Americans they don't have everything their own way.'

He intended to go straight on out, but Manley's voice called from the anteroom and David came in after me.

'Yes, Sir?' he asked.

'The notes you made from the recordings while you were working on my report, David,' said the Colonel, heavily underlining the possessive adjective. 'Major Baxter has reminded me that they must be formally destroyed. We'd better go over and burn them, before you go out.'

'Oh, but Sir, I've already burned them. Major Baxter will find the ashes in the secret waste box. I even remembered to stir them round. Shall I come over with you to show you, Sir?'

'You're sure you destroyed everything?'

'Absolutely sure. And Sergeant Benson inspected the office after me before I locked up.'

'Oh, good. That's fine, then. Off you go now.'

We all said goodnight to David and that was all.

His reassurance that I was praised in the report which should have gone straight to our seniors in the War Office only and not to the Foreign Office confirmed my feeling that something was wrong. David was trying with those words to reassure me, even to bribe me into complaisance. My speechless dinner, behind Manley's monologue, was filled with almost distraught speculations.

It was obvious that the American intelligence people would be sent a direct recording and not a digest of the interrogation in the form of Manley's report; they were bound to have asked for that. In fact, I now remembered that Baxter had received and answered signals from the American unit concerned, just to that effect.

So the report made by David for Manley was an officious device to get the results of this important interrogation to London over my head—the interrogator normally made his own reports—where it would do both of them much good in the future, Manley with the War Office and David with the Foreign Office. Manley was perfectly entitled to take over the writing of a report if he wanted to do so, and success would annul the impropriety of giving the Foreign Office a direct copy instead of waiting for the War Office to do it. That aspect of the matter was in any case not my business, but Baxter's as a breach of security. I was sure Baxter would put in a protest, for what that was worth.

During dinner, too, Manley made a remark which betrayed the truth of David's claim to Baxter that the whole thing had been his own suggestion; I had not quite believed that at the time, knowing that David would say anything to annoy the policeman. But apparently, David did think of the idea himself, and needed to persuade Manley of its feasibility as Manley now, in the triumphant glow of a signal of congratulation from London, admitted.

'He's a brilliant young man that,' he said pompously to Baxter in a rather hectoring tone. 'He'll go far.'

'He certainly will,' agreed Jack in a tone suggesting with his usual oblique, cynical tolerance, just the view of the matter that Manley was concerned to have denied. Manley gave him a sharp look but decided not to pursue it and I saw a quick smile pass between Jack and Baxter at his silence.

After dinner, pursuing his policy of appeasement, Manley came back with the rest of us to the pen and continued the conversation. He spoke of the triumph we had collectively achieved, and assured me of the praise expressed in his report for my excellent interrogation of Torek. Even his presence in the interrogators' room in the evening was rare enough for the occasion to impress itself on my memory. And that he, like David, took the trouble to reassure me of my importance underlined the covert anxiety they evidently both felt at their ruse. But instead of pleasing me, he made my unease greater because that moment on the stairs with David when Benda's name was heard could not be fitted in with Manley's own perfectly obvious preoccupations. Was it only that David was aware of having used the Colonel's vanity to bypass my success and claim it for the two of them? Was this not very important breach of personal loyalty the only guilt he felt at the moment our eyes met and David touched the envelope showing above his coat pocket? David's nervousness then and its communication to me seemed stronger than was warranted, much stronger than anything Manley was now showing.

Manley leaned over the desk to pick up his cigarette packet and in doing so lost his balance slightly and righted himself by catching at the edge of the dark metal waste bin for secret waste.

Reminded by its clatter on the bare floor of the office, Manley turned to Baxter.

'You did come over the other evening to check that all the notes and draft papers were burned, I take it, Major? I forgot to ask you.'

'I came over after dinner and checked,' replied Baxter tightly. 'The bin was half full of burnt papers.'

Manley smirked with self-satisfaction, although he should himself have checked the detail, since it was his report.

'Give me a match, Inglis, will you?' Baxter said, I thought to change the subject. He pressed down the tobacco in his pipe and shook an empty matchbox.

'I've only got two left. Here, wait a moment.' I twisted a sheet of unused paper into a spill and lit it with one of the matches, handing it then to Baxter, who lit the pipe and dropped the twist of paper into the same waste bin, where it slowly burned out.

When they had gone, I picked up the spill of burnt paper from the bin and inspected it. Flakes of singed black ash fell off it. At the top I could still see the crown, not quite burnt, but at the other end, which was completely burned, the printer's marking and the official classification of the paper, which is a code of letters and numbers, was quite invisible to me though my eyesight is good. No doubt an expert could tell whether burnt papers had been written or typed on, or whether they were blank paper. I could not, and there was no reason for Baxter to have thought of doing so; he would just stir the ash about and accept the evidence. My puzzled thoughts continued to worry at the problem until I came back to David's telephone call to London. Did he ever call his friend Banks again—was Banks the name—as he told Agnes he would do? I was sure he had done so, and I knew that the papers Baxter found burned in the waste box were blank and the notes and third copy of Manley's report had found their way into that envelope in David's pocket and would soon be in the hands of the man in London named by David as Johnny Banks.

I pulled myself up. I knew nothing. I was inventing things. The look in David's eyes when he heard Benda mentioned was all I had to go on. The look in a man's eyes is not evidence; it was a subjective idea of my own and nothing more. The incident in the cellar was real enough; there I knew I had reason for suspicion. But that was a quite different affair even if the overtones of homosexuality were really as clear as they seemed to me.

That scene I could talk about to Jack Morgenstern; this I could mention to nobody. Impossible to speak of something so tenuous, something which, if it became known must result in a court martial. The envelope could have contained papers concerned with David's demobilisation from the Army, or with his forthcoming marriage. So could the London telephone call to Banks, as David himself told Agnes. Why was I so sure of the meaning of that moment on the stair head, of the reason for David touching the envelope in his pocket to reassure himself it was safe? I could find no answer, though the certainty of my perception at that moment remained with me.

Instead, I began to argue with myself. I was being fanciful. Even the moment at Benda's cell door was dubious, no more. Not enough to connect into evidence of criminal intentions on the man, even combined with Jack's observation of weals on Benda's back and shoulders—they could be self-inflicted. Jack's conversation with me on that subject was really nothing but a bit of gossip, only excusable by its privacy. And David's change of mind about Betty, his sudden preference for Agnes? There was a genuine change of heart, and any possible consequences to Betty after David's desertion of her were certainly not very scrupulous, but how much did any of us consider his responsibility in such a case? A few minutes' laughing conversation between David and Wilder in a bar which I could not hear was not enough to justify a belief that David was deliberately seeking information about the newly rich member of the party. I was allowing my wounded pride over Agnes to make me jealously determined to damage the successful suitor; that was at least as bad as anything I had seen David do.

Thus I took myself to task as a scandal-mongering old woman; my sensation of sureness which I knew was a genuine intuition, I called nothing but jealousy, unjustified by any strong feeling for Agnes. The moment on the stair was indignation fired from the same spark of hurt pride. Chronic mistrust of myself convinced me easily that my motive could only too well be a mean envy of a more charming, more talented rival. He was to get the kind of job I would give much to have, live the life I should like for myself, marry a girl who had seemed, briefly, to admire me. That was all.

XII

As far as I could I avoided going to the Officers' Club in town, or anywhere else I should have to meet David and Agnes. I had a good excuse, that my private studies had been neglected and I must catch up with them if I wanted to pass my examinations in the following summer. But the formal opening of the reading room and library was a function we were all officially requested to attend in the interests of winning the support of Austrians for democratic principles as exemplified by English literature and newspapers. I can see that a certain irony creeps into that statement; this is unfair for of all that was done in practical ways to convince the Austrian public of our good will, the opening of the doors closed since 1938 to the outer world through the printed word was greeted with the most enthusiasm. Though it is probable that the black market did, at that time, almost as much for our reputation by distributing urgently needed goods as official measures could; certainly it was almost universal.

Apart from the old people's party which was not so much policy as a genuflection towards Christian feeling, this was the first official intercourse between the defeated and the conquerors that I attended. I found the timidity of the worthies of the town humiliating to us as well as themselves and was ashamed of it; this was national egotism for their fearfulness of those in power was far more a memory from Nazi times and the short Russian occupation than any feeling about the British. After a few minutes of the ingratiation of a minor functionary, I made my escape and crossed to that corner of the room where the Austrian staff of the reading room were standing together in an unseen enclave of isolation. They were all dressed in the drabbest of shabby clothes. Even so, the change in Lali von Kasda was striking. Not only that she now ate regularly if frugally, it was clear, but she had a purpose in living for which she could see a prospect of success. After cutting short her thanks for having picked her up on the road that night, I asked after her son and at once her face was illuminated by a brilliance of devotion and she answered eagerly. She had heard from her mother and as soon as she could save the money for the journey she would go to the border of the American Zone where her mother would deliver him to her.

'It is only the endless goodness of yourself and Frau Homburg that I have to thank for this,' she said in careful English. 'She has already found a girl to take care of him and he will live at the house—you know I am registered there, don't you? I could not have him here, you see. It is so wonderful of her. And Frau Pohaisky is coming from Vienna to stay here. We shall be quite a little community, at the house.'

She stopped speaking and a change came over her face that gave her again a distant resemblance to that weary and suffering creature I first saw. 'If only my mother could leave,' she said with painful self-command, 'I could almost be happy.'

'I want to go to the house this weekend,' I told her. 'If you wish I can take you up.'

At that moment Agnes came up to ask for something and I turned to another of the employees.

'You are going to work in the library too?' I asked for something to say. She was a formidable, middle-aged woman, sallow and ravaged, with thin, black hair drawn back from her bony face of extreme plainness. I disliked her on sight; she was staring at the roomful of people being polite to each other with a savage look of contempt that seemed to me not only ill-judged in a new employee but singularly out of proportion.

She hardly glanced towards me as she replied, 'I do not like to speak German except when necessary.' I had addressed her in what I assumed was her language, but from her accent as well as her manner I saw I was mistaken.

'We can speak French if you prefer,' I said.

'You think my English is not good enough?' she said haughtily.

I offered her a cigarette, which she took with her left hand, and I noticed that her right hung down stiffly by her side.

'Thank you,' she said grudgingly. 'But I have nowhere to put my glass.'

I moved back so that she could put her wine glass—we were offered wine to drink, for Army supplies were not allowed to be served to Austrians—on the nearest book shelf.

'You don't come from here, then?' I asked in French, despite her remark.

'Good God, no,' she said violently in a good French accent. Then, in explanation, 'I am a Pole!' And for the next ten minutes she lectured me, with hardly a pause to draw breath, on the iniquities of the Austrians. I was glad I had suggested French.

To stem the flood I asked—not a wise choice perhaps—how she came to be so far from her home, and she told me she had been in the Warsaw Home Army and was on the run from August 1944 until the British entered Graz.

'Every man's hand was against me,' she said with grim satisfaction. 'The blood-stained Russians and the blood-stained Germans alike.' The Old Testament phrase was appropriate to her vengeful anger.

Driven ever further by the iron brooms of war she finished up in a small town I had never heard of, Mauterndorf, beyond the mountains of Lower Tauern and just beyond the furthest point the Red Army reached. Her description of the peasants there reminded me of Julie and the villagers.

I felt a glow of pleasure and anticipation in the thought that I should see Julie in a day or so.

'Why do you smile?' asked the Polish woman with quick suspicion. 'It was no joke, I can assure you of that.' Then she paused and seemed to consider that perhaps she was being unwise to expose her hostility so openly for she had no idea who I might be. 'But I have to admit that bad as they were they weren't a tenth as frightful as our Polish peasants in eastern Poland. My family came from Vilna and the people about there are hardly human. *They* would have killed me!' She glanced at me sharply. 'I look like a gypsy.'

Wilder was making gestures at me and I excused myself.

'Thanks for rescuing me,' I said. 'What is it?'

'Who's your Yiddisher momma?' he said in his ribald way. 'I've picked up that nice little Austrian piece and we're going to the "Parrot" but she won't go without you. You will come, won't you?'

'All right,' I agreed, and he gave me his laughing look of understanding. 'But you know, that Polish woman isn't Jewish.'

'Isn't she? She looks it. How do you know anyway?'

'I don't know—I just recognise it. But where is Veronica?'

'I rang up and she's coming on. Thought I was two-timing her, did you? You are the primmest chap, Robert. You'd make a smashing lawyer.' The little stab of anxiety I felt at his invitation to Lali was not caused by primness, but I did not disabuse him.

The *'Papagei'* was a little black-market restaurant and bar found by Wilder, or rather which had found him, for he supplied it with black-market liquor. I was unsurprised to see one of the Club waiters coming out as we went in. There was an Out of Bounds sign on the closed door for which, I knew, the owner had paid a heavy bribe. The place was, in fact, not on the Out of Bounds list but he liked to be exclusive. I had gone there several times in the last weeks in order to avoid the Club when I felt like eating out of the Mess.

Veronica was already there with Betty and Tom. I had not seen Betty for weeks and I saw now, as we sat down, that she had taken on a brittle, angry gaiety which made me again sorry for her. She still did not look well, and was wearing too much make-up.

I made the introductions, saying, 'This is Lady Veronica Masters, Miss Teacher, Major Wallingham; Captain Wilder, you know —Fräulein von Kasda.'

'Von Kasda? Are you a relative of Ferdinand von Kasda?' asked Veronica at once.

'My brother or my father?' asked Lali. 'They were both Ferdinand.'

'It would be your father. My brother knew him, years ago.'

All was well, which relieved me. Betty, taking her cue from her elders and social betters, was pleasant to Lali when she had to speak to her, a great concession to what was called a 'bit of frat' by Englishwomen in the occupied countries.

We had not been there more than half an hour when a group took a table on the other side of the half-dark room among whom I recognised, to my surprise, the Polish woman from the Library.

Wilder nodded at one of the men, a tough-looking blond with a facial scar and a broken nose.

'Who are they?' asked Betty. 'They don't look like Austrians.'

'Poles,' said Wilder briefly, 'from the DP camp.' It was clear he did not wish to discuss them and I could guess why. The DPs were more active than Austrian shop-people in the black market for they enjoyed a privileged position, being victims of Nazism. If black-marketing had been all they were involved in I have no doubt they would have done nothing but good. But, unfortunately, they were active in other and less useful ways. Presently the group was joined by a fresh arrival. I would hardly have noticed him but I saw Lali's attention riveted on him and that made me look carefully. The lighting, as usual in those days in civilian restaurants, was subdued, and this man was one of those who merge into background so completely that he can be seen many times without leaving much memory of face or figure. It was his company that made him noticeable and I don't quite know how I became aware that he was as much a stranger in that place as Lali von Kasda. He got up several times during his meal and went out, to the hall, the bar or the lavatory. The third time he went by I looked up and followed him with my gaze to see where he went; he glanced over his shoulder and saw me watching him. As he came back, he called to his companions so that all could hear, in German, 'I managed to reach them at last.'

'Good, so now we know he has been telephoning,' I said. He made me uneasy.

'He has not been telephoning,' said Lali in a low voice. 'He is watching us.' She was frightened. 'He is a Russian, not a Pole.'

'How can you possibly tell?' Betty challenged her, a little scornfully.

Lali looked at her, a speculative look as if she were a generation older than Betty and understood her every thought before it was known to the thinker. In fact she was, I think, several years younger. She did not answer the question, and it passed unnoticed in the general chatter about ski-ing. Wilder was full of his new scheme for opening ski-hotels for Allied troops.

'Get things going again,' he expressed it. 'This country is a paradise. We have to make ski-ing into a sport for everybody, not only a luxury for the rich playboys; there's a mint of money in it.'

'It's wonderful,' agreed Betty enthusiastically. 'I fell about all over the place, but you don't mind, it doesn't hurt. I'm going again as soon as I have leave.'

'It hurts all right if you're going fast,' said Veronica laughing. 'You can break half the bones in your body. Like hunting, the better you are the more dangerous it is.'

Tom wanted to know, shyly, if he could take it up. He hated to mention his injuries, but he was clearly interested. Veronica assured him that he could and they all argued us into going with them the next time they went ski-ing.

I drove Lali back to her lodging on the top floor over the library, which now had its display window lighted. There was a photograph of the King, another of the Commander in Chief, Austria, over a signed message hoping for ever-improving relations between the British and the Austrians, and—more interesting—a spread of the London newspapers which even at that hour a group was minutely studying, translating the English words from mouth to mouth. We sat in the car watching the group.

'Perhaps we shall become friends,' Lali said sadly, knowing what was in the C-in-C's message and knowing what the actual state of affairs was.

'Not yet,' I said, 'it's too soon. But even this official hypocrisy is better than nothing. Tell me, are you sure that chap in the restaurant was a Russian?'

'Of course,' she said, surprised at my going back to the incident. 'You must know I have lived with them since the end of the war. Of course he is.' She stopped, puzzled as to how to express herself. 'Didn't you feel yourself that he didn't belong there? He normally wears uniform, I'm sure.'

'And you think he was watching us—us particularly?'

'Well—that I can't be sure of. You see, I am very nervous of them and I may have been imagining something that was not there.'

'You mean yourself? You thought he was watching you?'

'I don't know,' she said uneasily. 'I am always afraid of that.'

'I don't think it was you,' I said slowly, 'but if anything happens, anything at all, let me know at once. Will you?'

Two days later, coming out of the Mess entrance gate I thought I saw a man like the one in the restaurant—as I have said, his face was not easy to bear in mind—in a parked car in the road. Civilian cars were not frequent at that time.

Feeling rather a fool, I told Baxter. He wanted to know what the man was like.

'Unnoticeable. Dusty complexion, colourless, dusty hair; neither light nor dark colouring but that thick-skinned brownish look with hair that goes very light in summer. Very broad set, short, walks with a sideways roll, something like a sailor. Guttural voice, low-pitched, strong Russian accent. I took him for a Pole since he was with a party of Poles; but an Austrian friend recognised the accent —or the type—before I did. He's a Russian, all right.'

'Hmm,' said Baxter. 'Better safe than sorry.'

An hour later there was a notice posted, asking all of us to cancel leave and any outings of more than an hour or so in duration until our technician was safely out of our hands. He was to be transported to London. I cursed my officiousness, for that put an end to my proposed weekend.

The next day Sergeant Benson reported a car of the same type and colour, the number of which he could not see, on the far side of the grounds. Baxter then asked me not to leave the grounds at all, saying it would be almost as bad if I were touched as for the technician to be recaptured by his former comrades.

'If they know Torek is here, they may know you are his interrogator,' he said, frowning rather grimly past my head.

'Didn't you say something about going shooting this weekend? Don't do any telephoning to cancel, will you? Someone might notice. Can't be too careful.'

'It will be more noticed if I don't go and don't let them know,' I argued. He looked at me and raised his eyebrows.

'I'll get a message to the patrol unit,' he said. Then slowly, 'What concerns me is how they knew—if they do know.'

'Picked up the trail somewhere on his trek?'

'Probably. But we've had a whole series of wrong-number telephone calls in the last day or so. That's always a bad sign.'

He had made me really nervous now.

'I'll sleep over in the interrogators' room for a day or so, if you like,' I volunteered. The mere thought that anything could happen to this man while I was in charge of him, or at any rate more in charge than anybody else, made me feel that profound dread of disciplinary action that everyone who has been in the Army will understand—the fear of a court of enquiry.

'Can't you speed up his removal to London?' I asked. 'There's not much more we can ask him, as you know. It's all technical stuff we have no expertise in, now.'

'It's the weather. The RAF people can't take their Mosquitos off until the snow stops. The forecasts have been at "storm" for days and it shows no sign of abating.'

'That will account for my not arriving for the weekend too,' I pointed out. 'Don't get in touch with the border people, it's better not, and I can make my excuse afterwards. I hadn't considered the weather.'

Between my concern about my charge and my disappointment

at not going to Julie's house with Lali I was still not really thinking about Baxter's problem, and when he replied to my remark referring to what was on his mind, I did not at once know what he meant.

'You're right,' he said, crumpling up his square, stolid face with a comical effect. 'The correct thing to do is to move him from here so unexpectedly that anybody interested is caught off guard. We have to get him out of here without anybody knowing.' He picked up his scrambler telephone and then put it back. 'Go and find Sergeant Benson, will you, and ask him to get me the RAF station commander on this line at once, himself, and tell him to say nothing to anybody about the call. If I get it myself at the switchboard somebody will notice.' Then, thinking of everything in his slow, thorough way, 'Is Benson on duty now?' I looked at my watch as I rose to go, and nodded.

The Sergeant-Major was up in the attics, discussing a problem of the rebuilding operations. Some boarding delivered for the new window shutters was flimsy and unweathered so that it would warp. To my horror I saw that the attics were swarming with local carpenters and workmen from the timber merchant's. But I said nothing, gave my message quickly to Benson and returned to tell Baxter of my discovery.

He called Benson in on the house line.

'Escort the local workmen to the gates and allow no one except members of this unit into the pen until I give you leave,' he said brusquely. 'Be quick, and then report back here.'

Benson's square face was a study in dismay.

'Don't blame yourself, Sergeant. I ought to have told you before. Don't speak of it to any of the men.'

'Which order do I carry out first, Major Baxter?'

'Get rid of these men first, then put the call in.'

Baxter got up from his swivel chair and moved to a window, the outside panes of which were drifted half way up with snow. He could watch the little group of civilians in their weather-proof frieze coats as they went out of the gates, which were locked after them.

'Pity,' he said under his breath. 'They are bound to gossip. Security is the bloodiest business. One never does think of everything. Now, listen, Inglis. I am going to bully the RAF commander into taking off tonight, weather or no weather. While I'm on the scrambler to him, you go and case the joint. Don't let anyone at all approach my door while I am speaking. Look at the duty roster and give everybody but the guards the evening off. Tell the guard inside the pen he must deal with any telephone calls tonight himself. Understood? The other guards, except the man on the gate, must patrol the grounds until I give the word, from dusk on. Make sure that they know there's to be no slacking in the guard room, even if it snows again. They are to move about the whole time. When you've done that, go and find out who will be in Mess this evening, so that we can keep an eye on them. No interrogations or report-writing tonight—pass the word but don't say why. Tell them I've seen a suspicious character hanging around again.'

At this moment the scrambler telephone began to ring on his desk and Baxter waved me away.

We went to bed at the normal time after an uncomfortable evening spent checking on the guard detail. Colonel Manley was amused at Baxter's caution, but suspected nothing more than caution. At three the policeman opened my door carefully and I joined him, shrugging into my top coat as I went.

Benson was downstairs, muffled up to the eyes, and carrying side-arms. We crept out of the silent house like thieves, every sound magnified by the quiet. Our prisoner was clearly terrified at being woken at that hour; no doubt such a visitation seemed even more sinister to him with his background than it was.

'Silence,' I adjured him ferociously. 'Make a sound and I'll clobber you. Come on, get dressed.' I reached behind me for the outer clothing held by Benson, who was watching the cell door. The only other occupied cell was Benda's and he woke up and called out a question, which remained unanswered. We all paused in our silent activity, but no one else stirred. Nobody heard him or us. When our man was dressed, Benson went up to make sure the door to the garages was clear and we ran hastily across the open space of garden as soon as the patrolling guard disappeared round the corner of the pen. Baxter was forced to wrap the chain by which he was hand-cuffed to Torek in his scarf, for it clinked every time either of them moved. We pushed the heavy car up to the gates between us, Benson and I, and then settled ourselves, I holding a Sten gun at the ready while Benson opened the gates and came back to get into the driver's seat. The motor sounded like a clap of thunder to our strained ears, but before a guard could appear at the noise Benson had pulled the gates shut and returned to the car, and we were off.

'You see how easy it could be?' muttered Baxter. 'So much for Manley's jokes about my exaggerated fears.'

It was terrifyingly easy, and as risky as it was easy. If anything went wrong with the car, we were done for. Benson had spent the evening going over everything that could go wrong with his own hands, but the unreliability of the internal combustion engine was never more real to me than on that night drive. It took almost an hour to reach the RAF station, where the Commander himself awaited us with the pilot and one signals Sergeant. Even the navigator, waiting in the outer office, had not been briefed. As we escorted our prisoner to the frail aircraft which looked too small to be real, we felt like the last men left alive. Even the pilot, who looked hardly twenty, failed to produce the usual jokes of his perilous trade but kept stealing suspicious looks at the man he was to transport.

'We've cleared the runway as much as we could, but it's dicey. You sure you can get off, Bunny?' asked the station commander.

'Piece of cake, old boy,' replied the juvenile squadron-leader automatically, but he did not look as if he believed his own words. 'It's the passenger I don't care much for.'

'He's too scared to give you any trouble,' Baxter assured him.

'I wish I'd put myself down for this trip,' said the Wing Commander after the two of them were closed in the Mosquito. He said something more but his words were swallowed by the roar of the starting engines. The machine moved away from us, taxiing in a turn, incredibly light and defenceless. A few moments later it rocketed up into the wind, already far away on the flat, empty expanse of airfield.

'Jesus Christ,' muttered the station commander, and even in that cold he was sweating. But the aircraft miraculously stayed in the wild air, seeming to balance itself like a bird in the air currents. Its winking lights fled away from us and I suddenly thought of Kerenyi's words about his departure by air from the doomed fortress of Stalingrad.

That was the last I saw of the renegade Torek, but not the last I heard of him for he became as notorious as Gouzenko or Klaus Fuchs.

There was not much Manley could do to Baxter, for the security officer was in complete control of security arrangements and was within his rights—since the action had succeeded. What might have happened to him and to me if it had gone wrong was verbally explored by Manley with minute detail over and over again. We were only saved by the arrival, within a day or so of each other, of the two replacements for David Stephenson; in front of the newcomers Manley refrained from talking about what was, from his point of view, a reduction of his own prestige. A few days after that David left for his new profession.

I thought beforehand with resentment of this double replacement for an officer who did almost nothing; but in fact, it was a blessing. I was, with Johnson and Morgenstern, much relieved of overwork. And, once Manley's nagging was stopped by the new arrivals, there was the relief of having achieved a success in the first important job entrusted to me quite on my own, and the even greater relief of having got rid of my dangerous charge safely on to other shoulders.

From the distance of time, this adventure may appear to be rather ludicrous. But it was very much part of the post war situation and serious enough at the time. Then, the all-pervading presence of suspicion, hate and conspiracy was a dominant factor of life. Popularisation, the refraction of constant repetition in fiction, has removed the reality of that atmosphere into a never-never world almost impossible to dismantle. The world slid into a state of universal plotting in which Russian xenophobia and mania for conspiracy were forced on the western countries whether they wanted to be involved or not. No doubt the other three Allies would have been engaged in just as much underground activity, as they later were. But then the need for information was almost entirely on the eastern side; it was the west and especially the Americans who had knowledge the Russian government needed and not the other way about.

The extraordinary sentimentalisation of international affairs which has bedevilled politics since the need arose to gain co-operation from a mass of ignorant voters in all western countries introduced a new condition into all administration. It was the same condition Kerenyi defined to me as the necessity to engage the loyalty of signals staff in the July 20th Plot.

Every typist could become a saboteuse in a thousand jobs, unimportant in themselves but involving some small portion of knowledge, of the sight of half-understood papers. And every clerk and mechanic believed, through the flatteries of vote-seeking politicians, that a cursory reading of newspapers which themselves knew little gave him the right and insight to make up his own mind about political questions of which he knew exactly nothing.

The profound sentimentalisation was responsible, too, for the almost adoring admiration of the Russians among millions of simple people, who are by no means confined to the half-educated. The misty recognition that it was the Russians who had won the war and the idealisation of the terrible sufferings of the Russian people since 1917 made them appear heroes of a titanic struggle when they were really the unconsulted victims of a fierce mistake of history. A profound misconception—again based on unremitting propaganda —that Lenin and Stalin not only knew what they were doing, but were doing what was necessary and right has robbed the Russian people of the pity they deserve from civilised nations and replaced it by an idiotic praise for what the Russians themselves hate and fear, the brutalisation and denaturing of their own people.

Under this profound misconception, thousands of deluded Frenchmen, Italians, British and Americans wanted at that time to help the heroic struggle, as they thought of it. Their delusion was fed by propaganda for democracy by politicians who equated ignorance with the sound judgment of the plain man. Their belief in their own competence to make judgments based on propaganda themes led them, when they had the chance, to commit crimes, as much against civilisation as against the laws of their countries. They were then condemned as traitors by the same people who had formed their delusions.

At the time I am writing of, this absurd and sad state of affairs was still publicly unknown and the manifold conspiracies of spies and their pay-masters were more numerous than ever before in history. This was no increase of perfidy, but the consequence of mechanisation in modern history, warfare and administration. Since the Russians were then the active seekers after secrets, the effect on western society was to push it over the course of years towards the obscurantist conspiratorialism of Russian society, rather than to draw Russian society nearer to the modern world; and for this we must blame ourselves as a society. Especially in England the matted undergrowth of class differences added other motives for disloyalty; not least in that large class of state servants bred for a great Empire who saw their world of influence shrinking and themselves becoming over-numerous, for in England itself real power still lay in the hands of a small group and the administrators felt themselves, with justice, to be merely faithful servants and not holders of power.

My own suspicions of David Stephenson may now appear tenuous but they were then part of a miasma of half-understood fears which saturated the moral atmosphere of Europe.

XIII

Though it was by now the beginning of March there was no sign in Styria that winter would ever loosen its grip; God seemed to be adding his wrath to the efforts of men to kill each other and unknown numbers of children and old people died from the illnesses of undernourishment, their death certificates reading 'heart attack' or 'influenza'. The benefits of an old and stable organisation and the stability afforded by the presence of the western Allies saved Austria from the fate of less fortunate communities, but things were very bad.

Tom and myself were by no means the only serving officers to feel responsibility for this suffering; all over the areas occupied by the Americans, French and British great efforts were made by the victors to relieve the worst of the famine in their own districts, often against the criticisms of those at home who could have no idea of the state of central Europe and who hugged the vengeful spirit left by a disastrous war without victory.

It was very common in those days to hear the military talking on the one hand with pretended brutality of Krauts and natives, and on the other, supplying those natives they personally knew with food, clothing and the means of barter. In other words I joined the black market and used Wilder's excellent if illicit business ventures to provide food, by the sale of our privileged supplies to his shadowy contacts, for Lali von Kasda; and since she proved to have a stubborn pride in the matter, to the other staff of the library. Those business affairs were complicated and Wilder himself became more and more taken up with them so that the rest of us did his work in return for his outside duties, as we called them.

And if there is much of food in these pages, it is because to eat was the dominant, and for millions the only, preoccupation of that time.

Both Tom Wallingham and I disliked the 'fiddling', as it was called, but Captains in the Army are not munificently paid and since we gave away our profits, we may perhaps be forgiven even by the righteous who have never lacked for anything. We both drew the line at the misuse of public property and I believe in this we were in the minority. The only occasion this rule was broken was when Tom used some official petrol to drive Lali, on the excuse of visiting an American friend of his, to the bridge over the Enns river which was the zone border, in order to save her the terrible train journey again.

I was on duty and could not go with Tom, but was to pick up Lali and the newly arrived son later and drive them to Julie's house. I was rather apprehensive than excited; the existence of the boy now became real to me and I was not sure I cared for the idea. When Tom came into the interrogators' room he was exhausted after driving since before dawn, but he looked as well so grim and withdrawn that I hardly recognised him.

'Has something gone wrong?' I asked sharply.

'Wrong?' He scowled. 'No, everything is just splendid.' The savage tone of sarcasm was so unlike him, indeed I had never before heard anything like it from him, that I felt a frightful drop inside me and the thought that something had happened to Lali made me unable to speak for a moment. When he saw my expression, his own face changed instantly back to something more like his normal self.

'I'm sorry,' he said quickly. 'Don't get flapped, there's nothing gone wrong. Except . . .' He turned away and flung himself on to one of the hard chairs, his sheepskin coat bunching about him, and sank his head for a moment in his hands.

'Oh, God, what a world,' he said violently to the bare floor.

'Tell me,' I said, 'quickly, Tom.'

'You know Lali's mother has some senior officer or other in her house? Well, they watch her, of course, in spite of the supposed free movement rules. She was evidently afraid to attract any attention and stayed on the far side of the bridge—have you ever seen it? It's a wooden temporary bridge, not very wide; you can easily see across. She was all muffled up, of course. I could hardly see her face. She stood by that little sentry hut where the Russian control stands— poor devil, it's not his fault and he was obviously chilled to the bone himself. The American Sergeant on our side said they'd had a bit of trouble yesterday and it was better for Lali not to cross the bridge unless she really must. So there she was, trying to shout messages. Finally the American took her to the middle of the bridge and the Russki came up to them. She speaks a bit of Russian, fortunately, but I can tell you I was bloody scared for a minute or two. Then the sentry went back and spoke to Lali's mother and brought the child over to Lali in his arms. I could do nothing because I didn't get a pass for the zone border—the arrangement was that Countess von Kasda was to come over with the child. But this bit of trouble yesterday—I didn't discover what it was, by the way, the Sergeant was very cagey—made everybody jumpy and trigger-happy. There was this Russian peasant boy, only a kid himself, carrying the little boy and some stamped card thing. He was obviously scared stiff and if his own Sergeant had been there I doubt if we'd have got the child at all. We beat it as fast as we could before anyone changed their minds. Poor Lali was shaking so that she could hardly walk, and once I got her into the car, she broke down. She didn't exchange a single word with her mother, not a word . . . They called to each other but you couldn't hear, what with a couple of trucks running their motors, and the wind.'

We sat for some time, saying nothing.

'I'd better telephone the library and get somebody to go up to Lali,' I said at last. 'She won't be fit to go on tonight after this.'

I picked up the receiver and got the Polish woman, by chance, and asked her to go up to the top floor and speak to Lali, tell her I would come early for her and make sure she had everything she needed. This she ungraciously agreed to do. But her harshness did not go all the way through the weave, for Lali told me afterwards that she stayed for two hours and prepared a meal for the two of them and the child.

I wanted badly to drive into the town myself, but I knew discretion was the better part of ardour. I could only do my own cause a disservice by being present at such a moment. I was, after all, a representative of the forces between whose wheels human beings were ground as if they were inanimate matter. Instead, Tom and I locked up the official cupboards, checked the keys to the cells, looked in the secret waste bin and reported to the Corporal of the guard. We then went over to the house next door through the garden fence as always, and ordered triple whiskies which made the Mess servant, Wilson, raise his eyebrows at us.

'I wonder why we called this place the pen,' said Tom suddenly, after the second drink. 'As if the inmates were animals.'

'It's very unusual,' answered Martin Johnson pedantically. 'All the interrogation centres I knew until I came here were called cages.'

'So they are. You know, I'd never noticed that,' I said.

'Cage sounds even worse,' said Tom.

'Perhaps it is something to do with Indian Army practices?' suggested Jack Morgenstern. 'The place was set up by Colonel Manley, as I recall, and I dare say their terms are different.'

We didn't know the answer, any of us. We were just talking.

When I picked up Lali and the child the next morning she said nothing at all to me of the events of the day before. She knew, of course, that Tom would tell me, but probably felt herself unable to talk of it without weeping. She was very quiet, and looked tired, as she must be after a long journey in that weather. And I said nothing either; our friendship was based on an agreed discretion, and though my own wishes had gone a long way past the repetition of evenings spent at the 'Papagei' in the company of others, I was still uncertain both of her feelings and of how far I wanted to venture into a situation hedged by many difficulties. Not only the existence of Lali's son, who gave her responsibilities unusual for a girl of twenty, but her own stubborn independence and reserve made me cautious. I was also aware of a whole circle of protective guardians now gathered about her, foremost among them Julie herself. My experience with girls had been constant, but casual. As Wilder so truly said speaking of David Stephenson and Agnes, I didn't know much about decent girls; and perhaps my upbringing by uncompromising feminists gave me a further inhibition of respect.

The pallid, puffy child with his unhealthy, soft fat seemed on the face of it more likely to be an added burden to Lali than a reward for much effort. He wailed and 'grizzled' from time to time as we drove, for the most part in silence. She seemed to be out of the habit of being maternal and held the boy awkwardly, as if not quite knowing what to do with him. Her own looks had so greatly improved in the last weeks that the contrast with the sickly child was striking. He seemed to me to be small for his age, though fat, and showed little desire to escape his mother's grasp and make a nuisance of himself in the car as a normal child of that age should.

Half-way up the lane, we had to draw over and stop to let a big sledge pass us, sliding down the packed snow surface, the horse slipping constantly and turning up its head to pull on the bit, foam flecking its mouth.

'Poor creature,' said Lali, watching the straining beast with a knowledgeable look.

Starting the engine again I knew at once that we were stuck. A back wheel turned in a soft patch and the car slewed impotently sideways as the near wheel's chains caught and the off wheel spun uselessly.

'Blast,' I said, trying not to pull the steering in my nervousness. Tom had taught me how to deal with skids but I was still pretty amateurish as a driver.

'There's nothing to put under the wheels?' Lali asked. 'It will be better to run backwards, perhaps. Or shall I get out and look for some branches?'

Once I reversed there was nothing to do but creep backwards down to the join with the road. From there, in the driving mirror, I could see the hunched figure of the sledge driver with his hooded head turned towards us and was sure he was laughing at us. If he had known how near I was to losing control of the car he would have been as scared as I was, only a few metres below us on the lane.

'Let's have a hot drink at the inn,' I suggested, 'before we try again.'

The surly woman with a cast in one eye agreed to heat up what she called coffee for us; I ordered slivovitz. The patrol Corporal was not there and the woman refused us milk for the child. I began most heartily to share Julie's attitude to the local peasants. They all seemed to have some deformity of body or mind.

'At least it is warm in here,' said Lali in English, looking after the woman as she went. She was chafing the child's red little hands with a worried air. He stopped crying, interested by the change of scene no doubt.

'Listen,' she said suddenly, 'may I ask you about that nice Major Baxter I had to go and see? Or is that not allowed, to ask questions?'

'I think it probably isn't allowed, but ask me anyway.'

'He wanted to know how I knew the man we saw the evening after the library opened was a Russian. And if he was, why he should be with Poles. The Poles hate the Russians, he said, and Malczewska is a nationalist Pole.' Malczewska was the Polish woman who worked with her in the reading room.

'Bribery, I imagine. I don't know, in fact. But I suppose the Poles in the DP camp are interested in the black market so they need good relations with the Russians. Wouldn't that be it?' I knew this was not the strict truth, for the Polish DPs and the Russians earned money slipping people through on what was then called the black railway, an activity that would get a Russian shot if caught.

'I suppose so,' she agreed slowly. 'But I couldn't understand from Major Baxter's questions whether he thought the Russian was interested in me, or not. That was what I wanted to ask you . . . ?'

'He wasn't concerned with you,' I said cautiously. 'I can't tell you what he was interested in—that's secret. But I do know it is nothing to do with you.' I indicated the child she held on her lap. 'He wouldn't be here if they wanted you for anything, would he?'

The woman now came in from the kitchen and brought a bowl such as the peasants use to drink their milky coffee 'ersatz' and another with warm, bluish, skimmed milk. She said grudgingly, in thick dialect, what this favour would cost as she put the two bowls down, together with a plate with a thick piece of dark bread on it. Lali began to break the bread into the bowl of milk, mashing it with a spoon into a pulp for the child.

'He's always hungry,' she said with pride, as she fed him.

'If you hold him in your left arm, you'll manage better,' I pointed out. With a startled look at my face, she changed the child round and indeed it was easier that way. I reached her a handkerchief to deal with his splutters. He did seem very hungry.

'When did you last feed him? Here give him to me. You're making an awful mess of it. You're as bad as Kerenyi with your hands.'

She placed the child on my knee so that she could give both hands to feeding him, and he seemed quite indifferent to the change to a stranger, which struck me again as unnatural.

'Kerenyi,' she said thoughtfully, spooning mashed bread and milk into the child's mouth, 'he is a very strange man. Do you know him well?'

'Since he returned from Russia,' I said, holding the boy's hand to prevent him interfering with the spoon. 'But didn't you know him?'

'No, he never came to my home,' she said. 'Julie did, with my brother, twice. You know about that, though.'

'I know nothing really,' I answered. 'I'm always afraid to ask questions.' I drank, holding the glass well away and turning my head, then breathing hard to stop myself choking on the vicious spirit. 'This stuff is fierce.'

She sniffed at the glass.

'It's stronger than we make at home. I remember clearly the first time Julie came. I was very young then. I thought my brother Nando was just hopelessly in love with her, but it didn't occur to me that she was with him. I suppose because she was so famous.' She stopped feeding the child to stare in front of her, holding up the scratched tin spoon. 'I was terribly embarrassed. I asked her about a lovely brooch she put on—she was dressing—and she said her husband had designed it. He'd disappeared, but we didn't know she was hiding him in her apartment then. We didn't know that until much later.'

'Hiding him? Her husband?' I stammered. So that was the meaning of the unheard questions that morning when the pump froze, and Julie's rage with Kerenyi. No wonder he never mentioned it again, not even when we were alone.

'But surely you know that? She hid him the whole time, from March 1938 up to the end. Then he was killed, the same day that Julie was injured, right at the end. That was how Julie came to be in hospital because only a day or two after Vienna was taken, the Red Army cultural department was looking for all the theatre people to get the theatres opened again. That's how they found her, but her husband was dead.'

'So that was . . . I'd heard them talking, Julie and Kerenyi. And she told us a long story one night, about her difficulties with the Allies. But the key to the story, I didn't know. The only time I heard her really speak of it—right at the first when Georg was just released—she was in such a rage with him that I never even thought of trying to find out anything after that.'

'No,' said Lali, as if it were something perfectly natural and everyday. 'She never speaks of it. There's something stops her speaking of it.' The child gave a wail of disappointment and she began again to push the food into his mouth.

I felt stunned at what she so calmly told me.

'Listen,' I said, 'Let's get this straight. Are you telling me that Frau Homburg—Julia Homburg—had her husband there in Vienna with her right through the war?' She nodded, as if this were taken for granted. 'And that people, other people, knew about it?'

'I don't think anybody actually knew,' she said judicially, 'though, yes, Kerenyi did. But some people knew there was something. And in time, you see, they began to know what it was. That is how Frau Pohaisky says it was. Nando knew there was something secret. He used to go all quiet when anybody asked him questions. Neighbours of ours. People were curious about her, being an actress, and they knew she and Nando were very close. Everybody knew that.'

'But that must mean he was . . . '

'Jewish? Oh, yes. He was a Socialist as well. That was almost as dangerous, then, I think.'

'Good God,' I said. 'Good God in Heaven!' I began to try to remember everything said by myself and by her. Had I said anything unforgivable? For I knew that my not knowing could not affect the way she would feel about anything I said.

'You are upset,' she said in a small, anxious tone so that I turned to look directly at her—we were sitting side by side—not understanding why this should either surprise or worry her. I had a most strange feeling, as if I had never seen her before and yet she was very familiar, far more familiar than we really were, even intimate. She had a round face, brown eyes whose natural look was merry although I had never seen her merry. I felt as if I were seeing through her present aspect to what she had previously looked like and been like. Not that she any longer seemed ill; it was not a matter, as it was the first evening she sat up after her fever, of seeing what her features might be; it was rather that the stoical and stubborn grief and acceptance in her fell away for an instant, so that the indefinable shape and manner were there of an untried young girl of good family.

'I thought you knew,' she then said. I shook my head, still staring into her face and seeing, as it were, through the changedness of that almost visible young girl, the presence of an infinitely multiplied series of unthinkable pressures, inescapable facts, duties, circumstances, leading logically from one to another so that in a short space of time quite incommensurate with its results a whole world of people was changed forever.

From a dead, shadowy figure behind Julia Homburg to the small child before my eyes, I jumped at one bound to the knowledge of something of crucial importance to the life of the girl beside me as something I could no longer choose to avoid if I wished. I was in love with Lali, and if in that moment of shock there was little of the erotic in this admission, I did at once feel the essential egotism of the male, that he must come first. And this, I already knew, I could not achieve. The child, the last man of her family, would always come first and for his life I and everyone like me, must remain a foreigner who could only remove him from the world to which he was destined. Under my steady, and to her, potentially menacing look, she began to tremble and shift inwardly about to find some way out from a situation the beginnings of which she could see in my eyes and which to her recently meant only danger. Seeing the nervousness tauten her lips and eyes, I forced myself to look away, and reverted, to account for my manner, to our conversation's subject.

'What must it have been like? Shut up, for years, with somebody who could never go out, never do anything for himself, never be seen, never spoken of. Like a sort of doubled solitary confinement for life . . .'

She accepted with visible relief the implied explanation of my long, silent consideration of her: that I was not seeing her at all.

'When Kerenyi talked about it, I wondered then which of the two of them it must have been worse for,' she said.

'You knew this, then, before Kerenyi talked about it to you?'

'Oh, yes, for some time now. Frau Pohaisky came to see her husband, you see. He's been living with us for years, since he was released from Dachau. Frau Pohaisky was in a camp at the end too; she was arrested after the plot against Hitler.'

'This friend, Frau Pohaisky, was involved in the plot, too, then?'

'Oh, no, she has nothing to do with politics,' she said, her head bent sideways to see the child's face as she wiped his mouth while he beat on the dirty bare wood of the table with the bent spoon he had captured. 'She was just arrested. Lots of people were at that time. She never did discover why . . . something she said, probably. She lives with Julie now, in the apartment in Vienna where it all happened. A month or so after she was released her own place was requisitioned by the Americans, as soon as they arrived. And there's an actor there too, whose house got burned down—I forget his name. It's awfully hard to find anywhere to live, in Vienna. And she could take care of Julie a bit, too . . .'

'But Julie must have been quite recovered by then?'

'Yes, she was working again by then. But she could never look after the household herself, Julie.' The idea seemed to amuse Lali and she forgot her nervousness of me.

'I heard Frau Pohaisky mentioned, but I thought she was some kind of housekeeper.'

'Oh, no,' she said, sounding shocked. 'But you'll see. She's wonderfully good and terribly competent. I'm a bit scared of her—she's so religious . . .' Lali was now wrapping up the boy again, in his shawl, and I called the woman, to pay her.

'I'll pay for the milk, Robert,' said Lali. She insisted and I understood why, but it depressed me. I was being warned off and I knew it.

It seemed colder than ever outside and there was no beauty left in the winter; it had lasted too long and was now only to be endured.

XIV

In my prolonged absence, as it felt to me, much had changed in the
house. It seemed now to be full of people; before, its emptiness
enclosed Julie and Kerenyi in a not unhappy loneliness and we all had
a feeling of imposing ourselves, of camping out in its once used and
filled spaces. But in the last five or six weeks a variety of furniture had
found its way into the empty rooms, some clearly makeshift and
some that looked as if it might belong there; Julie had not wasted
the advantages provided by the sale of game and the guilty con-
sciences of the local people and had, as she recounted, bought up a
number of 'quite nice old things' from goodness knows where.
There were large and heavy painted chests and cupboards of local
peasant provenance, chairs with roughly carved-out backs and un-
shaped seats at the enormously weighty dining table remaining
from the original furniture, a big and tall object that would be
called a dresser in England, and several beds with their coverings.
In all, one could now recognise a house being lived in, acquisitions
which, though not what the house had once been used to, as it were,
were still by no means unworthy of its rustic dignity.

There was a middle-aged woman with an ascetic look dealing,
with that indefinable competence of firm handling, with foodstuffs
in the kitchen which is the sign of the good housewife that Julie
herself so conspicuously lacked. We should now eat, it was clear, for
pleasure as well as mere nourishment.

In the large effulgence of a bronze lamp drawn down low over the
long kitchen table, now almost white with scrubbing, this woman
looked up and recognised Lali with a smile of joy that broke
through an habitual self-restraint.

'Ah, dearest child, at last!' she cried, abandoning at once something she was kneading and coming forward to embrace Lali and
the child without touching them with her floury hands, by clasping
them both together between her outstretched arms and her body.
And, stepping back a little, 'How much better you look. And
Nando got over the border all right!'

A peasant girl now appeared from the cellar door, carrying something heavy, and stood there, considering with her mistrustful eyes wide open the child who was to be her charge. Julie heard the voices and came in with that air of quickness without haste which was her own special way of moving and the place was alive with greetings, exclamations, questions and laughter. I joined Kerenyi who leaned, slightly lop-sided, against the door frame of the small living room, watching the greetings, and hit him lightly on his good shoulder.

'How's the leg, you old bandit?'

'Fine. The doctor in town, a regular old drunken Army surgeon, by the way, says it will always be a bit shorter than the other. Come in here—I want to talk to you.'

'I thought you'd been posted,' he said as we sat down in the warm room smelling of wood-fire. 'Until your friend from the border patrol stopped by and said you'd be here this weekend.'

'We had a big crisis. I'll tell you about it some time—it's still high security, now. Why didn't you let me know you'd been in the town?'

'There's only one bus a day in each direction, you know, and I had to do everything about my papers in that time. But I've got skis now, so as long as the snow lasts I can move easily. That's what I wanted to say, before we all became sociable and the place is filled with chattering women-folk.' This last, in that particular tone he always used when saying exactly what he did not mean, a trick of his innate cantankerousness that must often have caused trouble for him. 'The first thing I did on the skis was to get down to the DP camp to have a look at the two Hungarian chaps—you remember?'

This camp was about as far from the house in a northerly direction, as the town was in a south-westerly, and being over hilly country, excellent for a ski-ing tour.

'Sure. How are they doing?'

'One means to go home; the other chap wants to stay here. Dreadful place, that camp. But I won't go into that. The point is, the whole place was alive with talk about your little outfit; and when you consider that the inmates are fairly strictly divided—or rather they divide themselves—into their native units so that Hungarians don't mix much with Poles or Russians and so on, you'll see that means a hot story.

'They say that a high-ranking Red Army officer was over here from Horn in Lower Austria where their headquarters are, or one of them, picking up information among the men who operate the black railway, about somebody in the pen. He'd got through to this district from somewhere in Germany, I gathered, and given himself up to you people. The railway is mostly operated by Poles, as I suppose you know.'

I said uneasily, 'I know about this Georg.' It was indeed only a confirmation of other evidences, slight in themselves but conclusive together, that Baxter had already collected about the unnoticeable man with the civilian car.

'Yes, I imagine you do. But what I think I ought to tell you in case you don't know it, is the hot tip in the camp that the original leak to the Russians came from *inside* the pen. It may just be gossip. I give it to you for what it's worth. I wanted to tell you this, in case you may be in any personal danger, you or Wallingham. That's the only thing that concerns me.'

'I believe the danger is over now. But thank you.' He said no more, and neither did I. I wondered if Baxter had heard that piece of gossip in his enquiries. I supposed, rather miserably, I should have to mention it to him on my return.

'You ought not to be straining your leg ski-ing.' I changed the subject. 'You can't be fit for it.'

'The longer I do nothing, the less fit I shall be,' he replied and then we were joined by the women and Julie introduced me to Frau Pohaisky.

The crowding impressions and sensations were enough to make me almost dizzy during that evening. The yellow lamp-light was now much stronger and steadier, and I could see that, among many other things, the regiment of Frau Pohaisky saw to it that lamps were now kept clean. The upper cone of the stove had been freshly whitewashed and there was no sign of dust or disorder to be seen, except that the windows were still undomestically curtainless so that we reflected ourselves in the luminous shadows outside the immediate circle of the lamp, through the double panes and against the outer shutters. Our little community was enlarged by other figures dimly refracted, double-edged, wavering with the uneven old glass; so that it seemed to me that the purpose of window curtains was not only to shut out the outside world but to keep out the other side of reflection, our own shadows, the beings that were ourselves. Ghosts, in fact.

What Kerenyi told me brought back with a fresh urgency and uncertainty all my doubts where David was concerned. Yet, if Torek had been betrayed to his countrymen, what more likely than that he was recognised by a companion in the group of illicit emigrants and newly displaced persons which he joined at a middle point in his trek eastwards, where their path southwards crossed his? And when he left their company again to defect to the British, what more obvious than that one of them remarked his absence and talked of it? These illicit travelers were in a state of continuous fear and suspicion of each other and of the Poles and Russians who passed them from hand to hand on their journey. In every camp and every civilian boarding-house or inn at which they slept overnight or met their contacts for the next stage of their flight they were threatened not only by agents from their now Communist homelands, but by the police of the western Allies who tried to control the traffic without necessarily wanting to put a stop to it, as well as by the Austrian police who wanted to prevent the refugees staying in the country.

Yet Kerenyi's words ran through my head over and over again. Someone in the pen. Torek was safe in custody in London, I told myself. Even if my suspicions were now supported by this objective evidence, all danger was safely over thanks to Baxter's quick determination. And, above all, it was not my business. Nearly five years in the Army had taught me never to volunteer, and most certainly not to volunteer advice to my superior officers. I would report the rumour and that ended my own responsibility.

Self-doubting under the bright overflow of talk and gesture, I was intensely aware of Julie in a dress of dark crimson, the only brilliant colour in the room, which glowed as she moved and glowed again in the murky depths of the windows. Two months now away from her own work and immersed in a totally different kind of activity, she was rested and renewed through and through and beginning to be somewhat irritably curious and 'jumpy' about what might be going on in Vienna and in the theatre.

Her beauty was completely realised, not young, not old certainly, but worked out, as it were, to its full nobility and charged with the contents of her life like a bowl brimming over its lip with a dark, vivid wine. To describe her face would be pointless, since its harmonies of skin and hair colouring, the way the hair grew off her broad forehead, the very large and lively eyes, the rather wide and mobile mouth, were only details of a unity of the whole person. The face was only part of something that depended just as much on her long, muscular and elegant hands, on the exact relation between the size of head and length of throat; on her tall presence and above all, on the voice with its own brilliance and intensity that would have given a mysterious meaning to an enquiry as to the price of sugar. She was beautiful then in a way that convention requires, but too in a depth that was for me the formulation of that deep-end perception of physical beauty which I have mentioned before. Watching her now, my feelings culminated in a sense of the unity and sacred nature of all beauty, connecting backwards in my mind to the night snowscape of the pen gardens under the winter moon with its gleam on the distant mountains through the black tracing of twigs and branches.

The fulfilled beauty of the grown woman illuminated Lali as being of near-childish simplicity, her really countrified pleasantness of face and person being demonstrated as positively downright against the integrated complexity of Julia Homburg. The heat of the stove gave her a high colour and her eyes shone when she laughed with that merriness that was her real character. The achievement of getting the child 'out' as the saying then went was great enough to create a genuine happiness for us all, almost like the joy of a birth. What Lali told me in the inn about Julie and what I already knew of the circumstances of all their lives only intensified the happiness and contrasted it with the forebodings of my thoughts about David which recurred constantly to my mind in the midst of all our talk. In spite of this, perhaps sharpened by it, I was aware that this was an occasion when the ease of communication was worth all the pains of living between languages and between the cultures borne by languages.

We did not stay up late, however, for the women were living lives of hard work and Kerenyi and I wanted to start out shooting very early. I continued the evening into my sleep where Lali and Julie became interchangeable and were the objects of erotic dreaming. I awoke at Kerenyi's shake at my shoulder in the dark morning with an intense feeling of anticipation.

We had a good day in spite of a bag disappointingly small; I let a fine deer get away by a clear miss that involved me in a good deal of teasing. Georg's arm was much improved and he could now bend it almost normally, other muscles having apparently begun to develop to assume the work of what was withered. It was bleak weather and in the afternoon—Frau Pohaisky provided us with thick sandwiches of bread and dripping—it began to snow with sullen persistence in a driving wind. By the time we reached the house again a blizzard was blowing.

'I hope it blows itself out in the night,' grumbled Georg as we trapped round the corner of the entrance arch and into the courtyard. 'There is Tom's car. He'll have to stay the night.'

'He bought himself a sleeping bag, just in case,' I agreed. 'I say, what's that jeep doing there?' There was a winterised jeep, ungainly looking with its tarpaulin and perspex super-structure to keep out the weather, standing in the court on the far side of Tom's splendid but battered Mercedes.

I hope there's enough to eat was my only thought. As we came to the door I was surprised to see that the jeep carried American plates.

Margarete Pohaisky was at the door before we opened it, our house-shoes in one hand, ready to pull at Georg's boots. I could pull mine off with the help of the split stone set outside the door for that purpose, but between injured leg and injured arm, he needed help.

'I'm glad you are back,' she said without ceremony. 'We're going to have a tremendous scene, I'm afraid.' She jerked a sharp chin at the standing jeep in the dusk. 'As you see, we have company.' What struck me at the moment was that, flatteringly, she included me with them and not with what she clearly thought of as opponents, if not enemies. I knew, of course, that there was a not negligible sense in which I ought to identify myself with whomever the newcomers were; it was one of the many and constant conflicts I was at that time struggling with. For I did not, in any natural way, identify myself with Allies come, we quickly discovered, to have a reckoning; on the contrary, I was on the 'other' side.

But not alone. The tall and serious American and his British colleague were accompanied by two friends of Julia Homburg's whom I now saw for the first time after having heard a good deal of them in the way of anecdotes from Julia herself.

They were introduced as Hansi Ostrovsky and Willy Mundel and were, the former middle-aged, and the latter almost elderly, colleagues of Julie's from the theatre in Vienna. They were on intimate terms with her and with Georg, who was greeted by both of them with an almost emotional affection that would have made them suspect in London, but was quite natural to this more demonstrative society.

'Back from the dead . . . my dear Georgy, I can't tell you how wonderful it is to see you.' The speaker, Ostrovsky, was a slight greying and dessicated man with a long face and hair cut droopy and long—or rather not cut—at sides and back, and bald on top. Mundel was large and broad, a face of unusual mobility as if made of some malleable mass like putty but of a rosy and healthy colour, in itself enough of a novelty at that time to be noticeable. He put his arms round Kerenyi and rubbed his grey head against Georg's without saying anything. For several minutes the three were so occupied in catching up on an absence of years that I turned to the other two arrivals and introduced myself to their shut faces. There was at once the atmosphere that they were keyed up for some purpose. Their implicit insistence on superiority, on dominating the situation, was most clearly at odds with their status of guests who were, that was already clear, not going to be able to leave that night. An essentially comical situation which they seemed to feel defensively as threatening to their dignity.

Since I was hostile to them both I must make it clear that these two men were both 'decent chaps' who wanted, quite genuinely, to clear up a question of right and wrong. The fundament of my attitude was that I denied them the competence to decide between right and wrong while they, albeit nervously—but only because of the social dilemma posed by the inclement weather—were quite sure of their right and even their duty, to judge; and of their competence to do so.

The American named himself as Colton Barber, a foreign correspondent of a great newspaper in New York, and the Englishman, his colleague of a news agency in London. I myself, it was at once obvious, was an anomaly to both of them and they could not, in any sense, place me. And Barber's name warned me, if Frau Pohaisky had not already done so, for I knew of his attack on Julie.

After our introductions in English, the Englishman presenting himself as John O'Leary (in spite of which name he certainly was English, and not Irish), we all spoke German throughout. This was dictated by Frau Pohaisky's speaking no English and by Julie's English being shaky at best. Something in the manner of both of the journalists made it clear that the use of German was a concession on their part, a detail which added a further note of dependence and incongruity to their being snowed up with the household.

'You seem to know all these people very well,' commented my countryman. I thought this an impertinence but it belonged to that time that such implications could be spoken without the speaker finding it improper; why should I not know them? I almost asked but smiled vaguely instead.

'You must have had quite a drive down here?' I suggested to them both.

'Only this last stretch,' Barber answered. 'We lost our way once but this is the only really uncleared stretch of road. Though God knows how we'll ever get out again.' He gave an anxious glance towards the windows, and at that moment the tall form of Kerenyi was outlined in the dark snowy expanse, a cloak of some kind over his shoulders making him shapeless as he went round the house closing the shutters from the inside. He would normally have carried out this daily task before removing his boots, but the jeep outside had brought him in out of curiosity. I hoped he had thought to pull on the heavy clogs that stood always ready for such short exits by the outer door; he really was not fit, in spite of his determination, to take the liberties with his health that he constantly forced on himself. I now knew from his medical papers that it was only will-power that allowed his exertions, for his heart was affected by his privations. I don't know whether he knew that himself.

Tom appeared from the cellars where I knew he had been packing away the stores we bought together before I came; sugar and flour, tins, such details as pepper and salt. Seeds for the spring, if, as sometimes seemed superstitiously unlikely, that season should ever come again. We had insisted that the original relationship of one-sided gifts must stop in the interests of equality, and that the stores we brought were payment for the shooting rights. Tom had thought of that refinement of friendship.

I introduced him by his title, which warned him at once that something was 'up' and that I had already taken my own position. He was, thus, a guarantee of enormous respectability that I was glad to be able to produce. How much of my immediate attitude was due to jealousy of a threat to my own position of original friend I am still not able to say; a good deal of it probably.

As if he knew what Tom had been doing, Barber now said to Julie, busy with the table, that he and his colleague had brought their own stores with them.

'They will not be needed,' she said pleasantly. 'We have plenty, thank God, for our guests.'

'But I feel we ought to contribute. I mean, the weather and all that . . .'

She straightened from leaning over to set our knives and forks and stood for a second still, looking at him.

'It won't be the first time you have accepted my hospitality, Mr Barber,' she said lightly, and went out to the kitchen. It was a declaration of war.

'Have you been here before, Colly?' I asked O'Leary quickly, suspecting some disingenuity as journalists do.

'No never. She means years ago, in Vienna. Before.'

The new servant now came in with a tray of coarse glasses, including the tumblers brought from the Mess, and an unlabelled bottle of local slivovitz. Kerenyi followed, and opened the bottle. We all accepted drinks. The food we were shortly to eat smelled delicious from the kitchen. We were constrained and uneasy, exchanging small remarks, opponents met in a neutral place to discuss our differences between an arbitrator—but the arbitrator here was one of the parties.

I went out to the kitchen to find Lali, who had spent the day on the tiresome task of getting the child's small stock of clothing into some kind of order and making a list of what he most urgently needed, which was almost everything, for where he came from there was literally nothing to be bought.

She looked up from feeding him as I came in.

'He's beginning to feed himself,' said Frau Pohaisky. The boy was backward for his age, as well as unnaturally quiet, but he smiled widely at me and crowed, stammering his syllables. I sat down beside them and ruffled his fair hair.

'Let him try to do it himself,' I said. 'You mustn't baby him.'

'He wastes the food so,' she objected, 'gets it everywhere but in his mouth.' She had the awkward, bothered air that came over her when she dealt with her son; he was so immensely valuable that she was almost afraid of him. But I was more comfortable in the kitchen.

'The supper smells wonderful,' I looked up at Frau Pohaisky, who was just, as it happened, looking at me, with a considering air. Lali too glanced up at her, and when she saw the look, a slow blush rose into her face. The room was suddenly charged with feeling.

During supper I waited for one of the strangers to begin. We talked of Vienna, but the theatre was not mentioned. Ostrovsky and Mundel did most of the talking; the former was nervous and it was obvious that he knew why the two journalists had come so far, while with Mundel it was hard to tell what he thought except that he was amused in a scornful way. He talked with Julie for some time about a visit she once made to his house east of Vienna, in which he apparently lived throughout the war; from his voice and manner I could see he was an actor and could not work out his position with the others for while his comments brought out that he had not worked for years until recently going back to Vienna, it was also clear that he and Julie were very old and familiar friends who had some mutual understanding.

It was when Frau Pohaisky asked him about 'home' that I realised that this was the actor mentioned by Lali who now shared Julie's apartment with herself and the older woman.

Supper was over but we still sat round the table, wine before us, smoking. Ostrovsky spoke abruptly into the waiting silence.

'When are you coming back, Julie? We miss you more and more.'

Julie waited, smiling thoughtfully, before she answered, and I saw Kerenyi and Mundel exchange quick glances as if at the arrival of something they had confidently expected.

'I'm not sure I am coming back,' said Julie calmly. 'Someone has to stay here to care for Nando. I am thinking of approaching the Graz theatre.'

'Nando?' said Ostrovsky sharply, with a sound of shock.

'The child,' explained Julie and gave him a look of tolerant understanding which showed me that Ostrovsky was evidently known to be tactless.

'Oh,' he said helplessly, a sound of apology and self-condemnation.

Frau Pohaisky moved quickly as if to speak and then held her peace; she was not going to help them if Julie wanted to be obstructive. Kerenyi, who might also have said that he would in any case remain here, sat back smiling to himself, and leaning, it was now a habit, a little sideways.

'But we need you; and sooner or later, you will have to clear your name from these absurd charges against you. It's all a misunderstanding; you know that yourself.'

'Yes,' said Julie peaceably, 'a misunderstanding so deep that there is no way of arguing about it, even if I wished to. It is said, and you allow it to be said without denying it, that I compromised with the Nazi government. That is quite true. What you might add, but do not, is the reason for my compromising.'

'The whole atmosphere in Vienna makes it impossible, you know that, Julie. The only one who can defend you is yourself. Then you would find backing enough, as you know quite well. But as long as you refuse to speak, nobody can do anything convincing.' Hans-Joachim Ostrovsky leaned forward towards Julie, speaking pleadingly, but, I felt, objectively, as if arguing not a personal affair but a matter of state—as I afterwards discovered it was to him.

'Hansi is right there, Julie,' intervened Mundel thoughtfully. 'I can't say I agree with his way of putting the matter, but one does have to take the fact of occupation into account and it really is hopeless just now to expect to be able to behave like a free agent.' He turned his heavily folded face to Kerenyi and went on. 'Why don't you say something, Georgy, something that will persuade Julie to tell these two—who want to be our friends—what really happened? You are, after all, the only one, I take it, who absolutely knows what happened aside from Julie herself.'

'Yes, I know why Julie compromised with the Nazis,' Georgy agreed. He paused, frowning downwards to consider how to put what he wanted to say and then glanced at Julie with a deeply examining look to which she replied with a wide stare, her lips parted as if to speak. But she said nothing, waiting for him to make up his own mind.

We shuffled in the silence uncomfortably, we men at the table; the two other women watched Julie's face. Then Kerenyi reached for his glass and spoke seriously, as if making an announcement of import.

'No. If I defend my old friend—really, my oldest *surviving* friend—I imply that there could be something to defend her about. I have done enough interfering in my life. I don't quite understand what Julie feels about this, but if she refuses to speak it would be a piece of crass impertinence for me to say anything. Nobody has the right to judge her actions except those who have been in the same position.'

Julie released a long sigh and relaxed against the back of her straight chair as if she had feared to get another, and wrong, answer.

'But the theatre!' cried Ostrovsky. 'We need her. We want to save her, to resolve this monstrous misunderstanding. She ought to be working; the audience demands her and can't understand why she is not there for them.'

'The audience that hissed me?' asked Julie softly.

'That was a momentary outbreak of idiocy; you know that, Julie.'

'For me it was decisive,' she said, pressing her lips together and narrowing her eyes, as if assessing again the moment in the theatre. 'That was the mob once again. Before, they yelled for Hitler—then for the Allies when they came. They would have yelled in the interim for the Russians too, but the Russians themselves ended that chance. When the press was manipulated against me for reasons that had nothing to do with myself, they yelled against *me*. Good, I accept the verdict of the public.' She turned her head, smiling sarcastically at Mundel.

'And you are wrong, Willy. I am a free agent, for the first time in my life. Before I was not free and was forced to do what was expected of me. Now I make up my own mind.' She included the two journalists in her unfriendly smile. 'Don't you see that I am in fact accepting your view of the world? You say everybody is responsible and must make up his own mind or be condemned as an accomplice of dictatorship; that is just what I have done.'

'But this is different,' said O'Leary, genuinely astonished. 'We are not dictating to anyone—we are democratic.'

'Exactly, and so am I; I have judged for myself and made up my mind.'

'Yes, now you decide not to play. Then, you went on playing for the Nazis, in spite of their demanding that you should divorce your husband. Then you agreed to that outrage—yes, outrage—but now you don't care to act any more under Allied control!'

Barber was almost shouting in his anger. 'You can't blame people if they draw their own conclusions from your attitudes then and now!'

'I don't blame you,' she said almost kindly, as if to a child, but with an undertone of contempt. '*You* don't know what you are talking about, but the Viennese public does. They know what it is like to live under a tyranny and they should have taken my part. But as soon as the word was given, they turned on me.'

'Would somebody explain to me just what appeared in the newspapers?' I knew from Julie, but I wanted to hear their version.

Mundel answered me. 'The story about Julie's divorce appeared in Barber's paper, after the Americans in Vienna had been attacked in the pro-Communist press for protecting—allegedly protecting—former Nazis. The report was, of course, picked up by the Vienna papers and there was quite a storm—for two days. It is already forgotten.'

'In other words,' said Georg, 'Julie's story was used to refute Communist propaganda against the western allies by suggesting that the Russians were also protecting former Nazis—Julia Homburg in this case.'

'I hardly had much choice in April 1945,' pointed out Julie.

'They know that, of course. Your case just happened to be handy, that is all,' explained Mundel patiently.

'I know that, Willy; even my political ignorance can see that. But what none of you seems to grasp is, that is just the point. In order to answer a Communist ploy I am attacked although even the attackers, let alone the public, know there is more to the story than they mention. The public, stupid and mean-spirited as it is, believe what they read and look no further, consider no further; they simply turn on me like a pack of dogs.'

'They're sorry now!' cried Ostrovsky. 'The demand for your rehabilitation is growing every day. The outcry in the first place was really only the expression of frustration and misery that people have no outlet for.'

'I don't need to be rehabilitated. On the contrary, I want a public apology.'

'We shall get nowhere like this,' said Mundel shaking his head.

'Did you expect to get anywhere?' asked Georg.

'I thought we could reach a rational compromise, yes, or I would not have come. I hoped that Julie would explain herself to Barber and O'Leary so that they could set the record straight and she could honourably return to her own life.'

Georg laughed a sharp bark of anger. 'If you thought that, you don't know how newspapers work. They will never retract a story unless they are forced by threats of legal action, which in this case are impossible. Even if either of these gentlemen would agree to it.'

'He's quite right there,' agreed O'Leary with cynical frankness. 'I should hate to try to sell a row-back like that to my people.'

'Then why did you come?' cried Mundel, now irritable.

O'Leary hesitated, a certain embarrassment which did him credit showed in his thin, cockney face. 'Since we're all being so outspoken, I'll tell the truth,' he said. 'I was curious.'

To my surprise, Julia laughed, a sincere sound of amusement and not theatrical, not for effect.

'That's a perfectly human reaction,' she said. 'That I'm used to.'

Mundel addressed O'Leary and Barber, talking round his cigarette, which was of the black, coarse, rank tobacco he smoked all the time; he was also the only one of the circle who continually drank from his glass and refilled it as it emptied.

'What Julie is really saying, in her own way, is that you—all of you—ought to use the same standards for yourselves as you demand from us. You did, both of you, imply when you suggested this journey to Ostrovsky and myself that you would and could arrange for Julie to be rehabilitated in the eyes of the public if she would only explain to you how everything happened, so that you were honestly convinced. Now you say something quite different. It's just the same with the larger political argument. You won't admit that you have no more control than we had then over what your politicians do—mainly for internal political reasons in your own countries—in international politics. The sell-out at Yalta was—I believe that is now universally agreed—against your own national interests, since neither England nor the USA can wish Europe to be Communist. For the sake of unity in the Allied camp even Churchill's doubts were overruled, as we heard at the time from the Propaganda Ministry—and disbelieved—as we did everything that came from that quarter. But it seems now that not everything Goebbels put his stamp on was lies.

'I am convinced that you will have to fight the Red Army in the next years if you are to hold even those areas of central Europe you do still, rather uncertainly, hold. I don't believe you will fight. You will be edged out after "free" elections have brought in Communist governments in west and south Germany and here in Austria. The 1945 elections here left the Russians in absolutely no doubt as to what happens in genuinely free elections, and they will certainly not anywhere rely again on undoctored voting. You may be quite sure of that. You refuse to admit this, at any rate to us; I have no doubt you admit it amongst yourselves, but to us, the enemy, you stick to your insincere attitudes. Why, then, should Julie take anything you say seriously, since she has lived through the entire disaster and knows far more about it than you ever can?'

'Let's take your first point first,' said O'Leary. 'I don't agree with you altogether about the Russians, but I've seen enough like everyone in the occupied countries since the end of the war to admit that there is a great danger. I remember Berlin while the Potsdam Conference was on and the situation was much more obvious and public there than in Vienna. But what you say about our changing our tune—Barber and me—after we arrived here is not true. You misunderstood us. Neither of us told you we could put the record straight with our *own* public, no matter how convincing Frau Homburg might be—which, by the way, she has not been. What we meant and what we can still do, is set the record straight with the Viennese press.'

'You mean you can manipulate the press in the occupied countries but are not free to tell the truth at home?' said Kerenyi brutally.

'Again, you are twisting facts,' protested Barber, leaning forward over the table to emphasize his words by waving his hands. 'So far nothing has been said that convinces me I was unfair to Frau Homburg in my original despatch. But it's true, there has been a good deal of outcry in Vienna about Julia Homburg's unexplained disappearance from the city. The local Viennese press reports that she was suspected of Nazi sympathies because of her divorce were not taken very seriously after the first shock of their impact; few people, outside the audience in the theatre the night of the scene that so angered and upset Frau Homburg, knew it had happened. The public has lost a favourite player without understanding why. I can't speak for the British authorities in Vienna on the Control Council, but I do know that the Americans there would be glad to have the matter cleared up by means of publishing Frau Homburg's own account of her story.'

'You're saying what I said before in other words. You can manipulate the licensed newspapers in Vienna but have no intention of admitting a mistake in your own country.'

'I haven't yet admitted to a mistake, and unless Frau Homburg changes her attitude, I don't see any prospect of doing so. My story stands that a divorce was arranged at the behest of the Nazi administration of the theatre and that Frau Homburg went on appearing after the request was made to her and she had agreed to it. It seems to me that the fact that her divorced husband was actually there—if it is a fact—only makes that worse.'

'Since Julie will not defend herself, I shall say nothing about that statement, except that it exposes your total lack of comprehension of what it is like to live in a totalitarian state. All I have to say about your remarks is this: you don't admit to a mistake, yet you are prepared to correct this mistake in Vienna. Why?'

'Because the Communist newspapers have taken the case up,' interrupted O'Leary, before Barber could collect his wits to answer. '*The Osterreichische Zeitung, Volksstimme* and *Abend* all carried articles in the last weeks alleging victimisation of Frau Homburg by the western partners in the Control Council, because she accepted Russian help immediately after the end of hostilities.'

'Since she was unconscious and expected to die when she was taken to the hospital, she hardly had any say in her treatment.'

This from Ostrovsky, with resentful gloom, as one who sticks to what is right in spite of being ill-treated.

Kerenyi began to laugh to himself.

'It seems to me you have given us a complete justification of Julie's argument against you,' he said. 'You now admit that you are here to persuade Frau Homburg to return to her theatre simply because you once again need to reply to Communist propaganda. Although you refuse to admit that you were mistaken in originally condemning her unheard.'

'We are trying to give her a hearing now!' cried Barber, intensely irritated with an apparently sincere lack of understanding.

'A private hearing for purely political reasons. You could—or the Control Council members could, rather—instruct the licensed press in Vienna to back-pedal on the original story without your having been convinced you had overlooked some important facts in your own account.'

'They will probably do that in any case,' admitted Barber. 'But I wanted to get to the bottom of the story, myself.'

'You could do that without tormenting Julie with things she would rather forget,' said Lali, suddenly breaking a long silence.

'You could ask the other people in her house, for instance. The caretaker, the other tenants.'

'I wanted her own story,' he insisted stubbornly.

'And she refuses to behave like the defeated citizen of an occupied enemy country now, just as she refused to behave like a good citizen of the Nazi regime then. It appears to me that Julie is, in fact, the only consistent person among us.' Kerenyi sat back and lit a cigarette, still with that air of laughing to himself.

'That's one way of putting it. One could say, on the other hand, that she is arrogant and egotistical!' Barber had now lost his temper. He turned on O'Leary in the same breath and accused him of letting him, Barber, down by bringing the Communist press into the argument.

'Julie always was arrogant and an egotist,' said Mundel. 'Most artists are.'

'Look here, Barber, I'm beginning to agree with these people,' argued O'Leary, flushing hotly at Barber's reproach. 'I thought you wanted to get at the facts. The articles in the Commie papers are just as much part of the facts as the details of Frau Homburg's divorce.'

Kerenyi went out of the room and came back after a few minutes with a bottle of yellowish liquid, uncorked, and a large book. He proceeded to offer us spirits, which spread a strong smell like rotting apricots through the smoke-filled room, and after drinking himself and shaking his head at the glass, he opened the book and began to search in it for something. I could see it was an old edition of a dictionary of quotations; I wondered where he found it.

'This stuff is a disgrace,' he said, drinking again, 'nothing like Barack at all. Yes, here it is.' He found what he was looking for in the index and now turned to the indicated page and read out the quotation attributed to Stephen Decatur, about 'our country, right or wrong.'

'I thought it was an American who said that,' he confirmed with satisfaction, 'and it still seems to be true. Which makes it all the odder that an American should not understand when other people take the same view.' He drank again; I felt sure he was screwing his courage up and my impression was correct. 'Now I am going to tell you something very personal, instead of what Julie will *not* tell you. During the early part of the war I was living with a distant relative of Julie's by marriage.' I was struck once again with the care he took never actually to mention Julie's husband. 'The girl was Jewish; therefore I could not legally marry her. I could have gone to Hungary and recovered my Hungarian citizenship. Then I could have married her. I did not do that because I was too much concerned with more immediate affairs. Not affairs of much moment—my somewhat restricted work, literary criticism and a translation, which, by the way, I never finished. In the autumn of 1941 the transportations to Poland began again. This girl was rounded up by the purest chance and disappeared from the face of the earth. I have no doubt now that I ought to have tried to go away, though whether I could have saved her, of course, I don't know. I was too concerned with what Julie would call abstracts to undertake such a difficult project; it was the girl who died, however. Later, as you know, I suppose, I had something to do with the conspiracy against Hitler's life. Now I am a certified anti-Nazi and have already received an offer to return to Vienna as editor of a new literary weekly to be licensed in the French sector. I refused that offer and I am now very glad I did. Julie is right—she always ignored abstract ideas and stuck to personal loyalties. By that means you end up disliked by all sides, and the world being what it is, that seems to me a good state to be in. I wish for various reasons, including Julie's own future, that she would defend her actions during the war; but she was obviously right in what she did.' He stood up, looking down at Ostrovsky's bent head.

'Come along, Hansi,' he said. 'Admit that Julie was right and we'll go off into the kitchen and get royally drunk on this filthy imitation Barack.'

To my surprise, Ostrovsky rose to his feet, rather carefully as if he felt ill and weak, which he certainly appeared to be.

'Yes,' he said slowly, 'Julie was and is right.' There was a grim scraping of chairs as the two men pushed their way out of the circle round the table. Julie put her head on her hand. Everyone was silent.

After a few moments, I followed them out and found Tom there too, sitting sideways to the long kitchen table, rubbing stoically at his boots with saddle soap.

'I knew I wouldn't understand a word,' he said, 'so there didn't seem much point in my staying. I hope nobody minded?'

'The thing that annoys me,' I said at last, as Georgy gave us drinks, 'is that besides upsetting Julie they have spoiled our weekend. They and the snowstorm, that is.'

Presently Lali joined us, having been up to look at the boy. 'Margarete has gone to bed. Is it all right if I sit with you? They are still arguing in there, it bothers me.'

We talked in English because of Tom, and that made it easier to keep to the slow chat of pleasant people. There was a feeling of waiting for something. Every now and then a burst of loud voices from the inner room let us know how intensely they did argue, there within. It was perhaps an hour later that we heard Julie's voice clearly, as she unlatched the door.

'Then, if you are so sure of your rightness, why do you insist on my admitting it? No outsider has to endorse what is clearly right. In insisting, you admit that you are unsure . . . Can't you see that?'

She opened the door, and stood in the frame of it, looking away from us into the inner room. O'Leary's voice said, almost shouted, something thickly.

'We can't possibly stay here, after this,' said Barber, and came into the kitchen, past Julie, who continued to stand in the doorway. 'We must drive on, to the next village.'

'You can't do that,' Tom said sensibly, 'the lane is snowed up. You can't possibly drive down.'

'Of course, we can,' cried O'Leary and staggered. They had drunk too much. 'Jeeps go anywhere!'

'You'll drive over the border by mistake,' warned Georg. 'We're only a step from the border here, you know. And the Yugoslavs shoot on sight, and shoot to kill.'

'Don't worry,' said Tom equably, 'they'll never get into the lane.'

I went to the outer door and looked outside. To my horror I saw that the snow had stopped; there was a treacherous appearance of calm outside. All the world was wrapped in a thickness of peaceful white that covered sound, sight and distance.

'Look here,' I said, 'it really is much more dangerous than you know. Do be sensible and stay here until morning.'

Barber was pulling on his heavy coat.

'I know what I'm doing,' he said angrily. 'I can't stay here another minute.'

'You're crazy,' I replied with fury now, 'and be good enough to close the door after you. It's quite hard enough to keep the house warm without you letting the night in.' He had thrown open the outer door with a theatrical gesture. O'Leary rushed out, staggered a moment as the cold hit him, and then bent his head and ran towards the standing jeep, through the covering of new snow.

'Look, they're mad,' cried Ostrovsky. 'We must stop them.'

'How?' asked Julie from the inner door.

'But do they know the way?' asked Lali.

Kerenyi, Tom and I looked at each other, and Tom shrugged his shoulders.

'They're big boys now,' he said and I wondered where he had picked up the Americanism.

'Of course, they'll be all right,' agreed Kerenyi.

I glanced down at my watch. It was not late—we had eaten early—it was just ten o'clock. The men of the patrol would still be up in the village pub. What did not occur to me was that they really could miss the lane. We listened while the jeep engine roared sullenly, waiting for it to stall at the slope up to the entrance arch. But the top snow was thick and soft enough for the chains to catch, they roared up, we heard them change gears, and gradually the noise died away.

'Damn it, they've made it,' said Tom with reluctant admiration. Then, 'We ought to have stopped them, though.'

'Yes, but how?' said Julie again.

'I'm rather glad they went,' yawned Lali. 'They were disturbing.'

None of us thought much of it; we were relieved in fact and much concerned with arranging beds for Ostrovsky and Mundel. Afterwards, Tom and I agreed that since we two knew what jeeps were capable of, we ought to have stopped the two drunken reporters, if necessary, by force. But that was afterwards.

XV

'I wouldn't try to persuade Julie of that, if I were you,' said Lali with a comically rueful expression which I knew mocked my solemnity. 'She's quite made up her mind about her attitude and is still determined to get a public admission that she was not a Nazi. I was there when Georgy tried to talk her out of it. You should have heard her.'

Two weeks later we were still talking of the visit of the two journalists and the reason for it. We discussed that at least as much as we speculated on what happened to them when they rushed out of the house 'like King Lear in a jeep', as Lali put it, 'into the storm'. We sat in the 'Papagei' at a corner table, and our dinners there had now become occasions for two; Tom and Wilder and the other two women had tacitly ceased coming with us or I had ceased suggesting it, but nothing had been said between Lali and myself about any reason for this change.

'I suppose if Georgy can't persuade her, I haven't much hope,' I agreed. 'But I do feel she wants to go back to work, don't you? It seems such a waste—and really, this stupid deadlock could go on for ages.'

'Oh, I agree with you and Georgy. But I don't see what we can do. And it would be fatal to let Julie think we weren't behind her.' Lali looked across the room, her hazel eyes suddenly serious. 'She's been so awfully alone for years and years. She loves having a family. I mean, I know how she feels because I always had a family around me until I came here, so I know how awful it is to be without that feeling of being protected by—by people caring about you.'

I stared at her little hand lying on the table where she played with a fork while speaking, and imagined taking it in my own hand but did not dare. Her confidence in me was still so fragile that I had to be very, very careful.

'People do care about you,' I said in an embarrassed undertone which sounded more emotional than I meant it to.

'Yes, friends. But it's not the same.'

'In a way, you have more family now than you had before,' I argued stubbornly, not wanting to admit that I could not, potentially, replace her security for her. 'You only had your mother before, since you never see your sisters and . . .' conscious of blundering, I stopped.

'And I have no husband, and no brother, you mean?' I had not at all meant that but I was used now to her refusal to listen to any approach towards intimacy between us. 'Actually, you know, to go back to Julie—I think you'd have more chance of persuading her than Georgy. She won't listen to anything he says—haven't you noticed? But I can't see what you can *do*. Something has to happen —words are no use.'

'It's awfully sad about Georgy,' I said. 'I think he's very unhappy, don't you?'

'I'm afraid he is. He must have been in love with her for years without really knowing it. But . . .' She stopped, her rounded face changed in an instant, to a look of desperation and she gripped the fork convulsively. 'You don't understand about Julie. She just can't —can't love anybody or be close to anybody. Everything has been spoiled by the things that happened. Nando just disappearing—I mean my brother Nando—and her husband and the Germans and the Russians and . . . everything got so dirty, somehow.'

'What was Nando like?' I asked to bridge the silence, help her.

'He was very good-looking in his own way. Tall, bonny, always amusing and kind.' She glanced sharply at me sideways, defending her brother. 'People thought he was unserious, and he was, but it's just people like that who are nice to live with. I mean, he didn't do much, it's true, but he never did any harm either. I'm glad in a way, that he doesn't know . . . ' It was clear that now, as often before, she was not speaking only of what she appeared to say but of other women than Julie and other men than Nando; her own boy who had disappeared, herself.

'But life has to go on . . . '

'Yes,' she said softly. 'I feel that, but Julie suffered far more than I did and she just can't get over it.'

'Do you feel that?' I asked and stammered before I could go on. 'You feel that you could get over it?'

She dropped the fork and faced me and I saw her eyes were full of tears.

'I'm afraid I have got over it. I feel I ought not to, but it's all become misty—past. If Nando weren't there, I would hardly believe it any more.'

'Don't blame yourself,' I begged. 'It would be terrible if you were frozen, like Julie. Not that Julie is cold or hard,' I added hastily.

'I believe you're in love with Julie,' she said, with a return to her teasing smile which had an aspect of relief at not having to be serious.

'Perhaps I am, in a way,' I said, and now touched the fingers curled on the tablecloth. 'I've got you and her and the house and Georgy all mixed up in a sort of muddle of love and I hardly know which is which.'

'That's the funniest declaration of love I ever heard of,' she said and laughed a little unsteadily. 'Which of us d'you think you'll decide on?'

'All together,' I said and now held her look with a new determination.

'But of course, that all depends on you, doesn't it? I mean, without you it wouldn't all hold together, my poor muddle.'

'I think you've been lonely, too, haven't you?'

'I didn't know it until recently,' I said truthfully.

I looked up at a step near us and saw Wilder approaching the table.

'Oh, damn,' I muttered and Lali followed my look.

'We never have any private place to go,' she complained with a sudden note of irritation that made me foolishly happy.

'I'm sorry to interrupt, Robert,' Wilder greeted us by nodding and sat down when Lali asked him to. 'I thought I'd better come over straight away. There's been a 'phone call for you in the Mess from the border patrol people. They've got a couple of men there who are asking for you—Americans or something. I didn't quite grasp what this Corporal was carrying on about, but he seemed quite excited. Said they'd been put over the Yugoslav border by a bunch of Balkan bandits, as he called them. Tom told me to tell the patrol Corporal that either you or he would be over in the morning. Does that make sense to you?'

'Those journalists!' cried Lali, with a startled laugh. 'They did cross the border by accident, then!'

'I was afraid of that all the time,' I agreed. 'I thought it was odd we didn't hear from Vienna when they got back—but, of course, you never know with journalists, so I wasn't sure.'

'If they crossed the border, they're lucky to be alive. The Yugoslavs don't seem to like unexpected visitors,' Wilder said, and I explained to him, without going into details, what had happened a fortnight and more before.

'They must be a bit cracked' was his verdict on the temerity of the two unfortunate journalists. 'I remember the weekend you were away and it was a real stinker, a blizzard like in a film.'

'It's my day off tomorrow,' said Lali. 'Can I come with you, Robert?'

'If I go, of course.' I was delighted at the suggestion. 'But I have to get permission first, from Colonel Manley.'

'Oh, the old boy will agree. He sniffed a bit of publicity for himself at once,' Wilder assured us with his own kind of hilarity at the follies of human nature.

'Publicity?' I said surprised. 'I don't quite get . . . ?'

'No, you wouldn't think of it,' he said with affectionate scorn at my ignorance. 'But from a newspaper point of view it's a big story, and these two will certainly make the most of it. I bet you anything old Manley tells you to bring them back to the Mess for dinner.'

In fact, Manley thought of something more public than an invitation to dinner and arranged for the two stragglers to be accommodated at the Club Hotel in the town for which privilege they would normally require a military permit. Otherwise, Wilder's diagnosis of the Colonel's attitude was correct and I was positively enjoined to get off early the following day to find out what this extraordinary telephone call was all about, as he put it. Indeed, it was clear from the curiosity and disguised envy of Manley's manner when I returned to the Mess that evening that he was astonished and irritated that anything so interesting should have happened to me and I believe he would have suggested coming with me to the border patrol if such a self-invitation had not been beneath his touchy dignity.

'I suppose the Corporal asked for you because you happen to have been at the patrol post,' he said, and I realised that he supposed the telephone call to be a quasi-official one to the unit which dealt with repatriates in the district. Since Colonel Manley never showed the slightest interest in what I did with my leaves and weekends off, he did not know about the house or Julie Homburg, of whom he would not have heard in any case. Neither Tom nor

Wilder, and quite certainly not myself, mentioned our good fortune, out of that secrecy that grows on soldiers in their desire to get away from military life and to keep to themselves any private source of comfort they have the luck to discover. I doubt if he even knew that we went shooting when we went off for a day or so.

At the time I was more interested in the prospect of having Lali's company for a whole day than in either Colonel Manley or the two journalists and their adventures, because Lali said, as I stopped the car outside the reading room and was about to alight to open her door, that I should please kiss her good night. Once or twice before I had touched her cheek with my lips on parting from her but that was always treated as accident. These were real kisses, more real than anything I ever knew. I should soon be twenty-four but nearly five years with the Army ensured a large gap in my adult life, a gap not of sexual experience but of feeling. I had often suspected that there was a difference; all that poetry and literature could not have been inspired by the recurring and urgent need to release a physical pressure. I knew now that the wonderful feeling of anticipation I woke with the day after I took Lali and her son out to Julie's house was about to be realised. And it was of these moments I was thinking as Manley talked to me.

The drive to the border was easy this time, for after a short, sharp thaw which cleared the caked snow from the roads, the weather was again frosty and clear. It was a brilliant morning and Lali, now equipped with boots and proper woollens and top coat, for which she insisted on paying herself from her slender wages, matched the day with her gaiety. Stimulated by the current of excitement between us, and inspired by some stories of mine about the Yugoslavs in Trieste, she spun a fantastic version of the recent adventures of the two journalists, imitating the Slav accents of the captors and the American and cockney voices of the captives, so that we were shouting with laughter in the car as we sped along. The reality turned out to be as comic, though perhaps not so immediately funny, as Lali's version.

'Colonel Manley phoned that you'd left,' the Corporal greeted me. 'You've been very quick, Sir.'

'Yes, the road is quite clear now. Where are your two guests, Corporal?'

I went through the entrance and turned towards the public side of the tavern.

'Oh, they're on our side,' said the Corporal, sounding shocked, 'being Allied personnel.' I took no notice of that and Lali went in before me into the patrol Mess room.

'Inglis!' O'Leary almost shouted in his relief. 'Your Colonel said you were on the way. He wants us to come back with you and he's arranged for us to be put up in the transit hotel for a couple of days. Damn decent of him.' Like the Corporal, he ignored Lali.

'Haven't you managed to get a shave?' I asked with some distaste. They both looked like shipwrecked mariners, giving an impression of being half frozen although it was, as usual, well heated in that room. They clearly had not shaved since they left the house a fortnight before, and Barber had lost his heavy fur-lined overcoat. They both wore completely inadequate light shoes of the typically Serbian kind made of plaited strips of leather on a hardened thin leather sole. It was clear that 'partisans' now wore their stout snow-boots as well as Barber's coat.

Barber sat with his back towards the door and turned only slowly, as if uninterested in our arrival. O'Leary gave him a quick look and said, 'Barber's been ill.' He certainly looked ill; I was shocked at his languid, plaintive face, which was both puffy and haggard.

'It was the food,' he said and, on seeing Lali, rose with the good manners of the well-brought-up American. 'Oh, good morning, Ma'am.' He looked from her to me with a puzzled frown, trying to place her. I gained a quick impression of his being shocked like a man who has just been under fire. He seemed almost stunned.

'Can you ask for some coffee for us all, Corporal?' I said, unwinding my scarf. Lali was taking off her heavy outer coat and I hung it up for her with my own.

'I've laid on lunch,' the Corporal answered me, with his normal manner of managing everything, and sure enough, a few moments later the cross-eyed woman entered and began to lay a table with a clean cloth in one of the high-backed booths under his critical eye.

'It was good of you . . . ' Barber began, stumbling over the words. Then he stopped and looked about him as if trying to recall what he wanted to say.

'You'll be all right,' O'Leary assured him, like a nurse with a fractious patient, and frowned with a kind of weary disgust. 'He's never had to rough it before, and it was pretty rough.' He leaned towards me and said under his breath, evidently thinking Lali could not hear, 'Dysentery, you know!'

That, however, was not what was worrying him, I was sure.

We sat down at the now covered table with a curious embarrassment which for the first few moments I attributed to the presence of
a woman. But glances of questioning and a sideways jerk of the
head from the Corporal, encouraging me to ask questions, confirmed that he too had noticed the constraint and failed to discover
its cause; for the predictable mood of the returned prisoners would
have been relief at their escape, and gratitude to us for our prompt
hospitality.

'Tell me what happened,' I said to O'Leary since Barber made
no further attempts to speak.

He thought for a little, deciding how to put it.

'The jeep got stuck in a snowdrift about half an hour after we
left you all. They found us in the morning, half frozen, as soon as it
got light, and, of course, arrested us. We've lost the jeep—there'll be
trouble over that.'

'You must have been on the wrong road,' said the Corporal. 'If
you ask me, you were lucky to be found after you'd broken down. If
you'd still been moving, they'd have shot you for sure. They always
do, even sometimes over this side of the border.'

He turned to me puzzled, and uneasy. 'What beats me, is how
they ever got up there without one of us seeing them. We reckon to
warn every vehicle, but nobody saw them.'

'They took us to Zagreb,' said Barber suddenly.

Glasses of beer were now being set on the table by the waitress
and Barber at once clutched his glass in both hands as if afraid it
might be taken away from him, and began to drink greedily. He
seemed so much demoralised that I feared they must have been
physically ill treated. When the food came, typically Army fare of
stewed beef with carrots and potatoes, he behaved in the same way.
O'Leary, who appeared much more normal except for the lack of
any pleasure at his release, was uninterested in the food, saying
that they had eaten a large breakfast only an hour or so before,
having slept late. But Lali and I tackled it with appetite, for we
started early and were hungry.

'Well, go on,' I urged impatiently. 'You've told us nothing yet.'

'There's nothing to tell,' replied O'Leary sharply. 'We were in
jail and filthy it was, too, the whole time and then they suddenly
pushed us into an old truck and brought us back up here.' He
looked at Barber, a look I can only call furtive, as if afraid of
contradiction. 'We didn't know where they were taking us, of course,

until we looked out and saw the British uniforms. They prodded us in the back with their machine pistols and we walked over. They obviously knew where the patrol could be found because the timing was perfect. The patrol jeep was just arriving as they unloaded us.'

'Well, we have a sort of routine. We know we'll always see a patrol of theirs just there at that time of the afternoon—just before dark. They sort of check on us and we on them, see?'

'It's quite a long way from Zagreb here,' I said.

'We were in the truck all day,' agreed O'Leary gloomily. 'And damned uncomfortable it was. I'm black and blue from the rattling about.'

I knew as everyone did that the Yugoslav 'partisans' were still in a highly excitable state of mind, constantly fearing foreign intervention to upset their new control of their country. The Corporal, naturally, liked to exaggerate the difficulties of his job, in which the single patrol units were often left alone for days on end, but although I did not quite believe all his hints of wild shooting, I still found the treatment of unwanted foreigners by the fierce ex-partisan soldiers rather less drastic than might have been expected. O'Leary's meagre account gave no grounds for their intimidated and unhappy manner. I was evidently learning from my experience as an interrogator and I shared the obvious reservations of the Corporal; Barber and O'Leary were not telling us everything and this was quite contrary to my expectation. Usually men who have escaped danger like to brag of it. I looked at the Corporal and he understood me and rose at once.

'You want to see the others, while you're here, Sir?'

We went out and crossed the middle passage into the public side of the inn.

'I don't like it, Sir,' he said at once, bluntly, when the door was closed. 'We took no notice last night because they were so tired, and chilled through and hungry. But I hope there's nothing wrong, because we'll get it in the neck when our Lieutenant comes. I had to signal him on the blower that they were here, you see. He speaks a bit of the lingo and the locals will all be talking their heads off.'

'Yes, of course, you had to report it,' I said, surprised at his even considering not doing so.

'Well, we don't report every little incident, not always,' he said. 'We don't want trouble, any more than they do, really—see?' He jerked his head, indicating the Yugoslavs, I supposed.

Lali put her head round the door and announced her intention of going to speak to the man who supplied milk and butter up at the house.

'Put your coat on,' I said. 'It's very cold.'

'I don't see what could be wrong, you know,' I went on to the Corporal as she disappeared again. 'They aren't military personnel, they don't know anything. Or what exactly did you have in mind?'

'I don't know quite. Just their funny attitude, I suppose. Like they weren't too pleased to be back—or pleased with themselves, either, if it comes to that.'

'I think they've had a terrific scare,' I said, 'probably it's just that.'

'Well then you'd think they'd be delighted to have got away, wouldn't you?'

'You would,' I agreed, 'but they may not have come round yet. Mr Barber—that's the American—seems rather ill, too.'

'Oh, squits,' he said disparagingly. 'I wouldn't call that ill . . .'

We turned as the door opened and Lali came in again.

'You've been awfully quick,' I said, surprised. 'Didn't you find anyone at home?'

'Yes, I met Golubovitch in the square,' she replied in German, 'I have to speak to you, Robert.'

'Could you leave us alone, for a minute, Corporal?' I asked, and he nodded at once and went out, no doubt assuming that we had some business to discuss of a financial nature.

'Listen,' she said excitedly. 'There's a whole group of the local people talking like mad about these two. Some of the people here speak Slovenian, as you know. They say they heard these two on the radio, telling how wonderful Tito is and how Socialism is the future of the world. They spoke in English, they say, and it was translated sentence by sentence. That's to prove it was authentic . . .'

'Good God. It can't be true! Wait a moment, I'll get my coat and come with you.'

The peasants were already dispersed by the time we came out, but we went to Golubovitch's little house across the square and found his wife there, who confirmed her husband's story. The family were of the Slav minority of the district and often listened to the radio from Ljubljana and Zagreb. This detail, certainly unknown to Barber and O'Leary, exposed the cause of their unease before they had crossed even the first hurdle of their obvious intention to say nothing of this incident, which, at the same time, explained their release. They had been bribed with the promise of a prompt return over the border.

'Now what *are* we going to do?' asked Lali as we walked back across the square. She began to laugh in spite of herself. 'It's even worse than anything I invented!'

'I shall have to tackle them. How can they have thought they could get away with such a daft scheme? It was bound to come out.' At that moment I found it anything but funny.

I was both angry and embarrassed at such a humiliating dilemma for Barber and O'Leary. Although I supposed it was not a crime, unless they'd been fools enough to attack their own governments, since they were neither of them under military orders. 'You'd have thought they would hold out for more than a few days,' I complained bitterly.

'They were frightened.' Lali excused them. 'I dare say neither of them has ever been really scared before.'

'You'd better stay in the other room,' I said gloomily. My day out with Lali was not turning out quite the jaunt I had imagined. I opened the door to the military room, and saw that the Corporal was back there. It was so painfully unpleasant that I knew I must get it over with at once.

'How did you ever think you could get away with such a crazy thing?' I demanded, as I crossed to them, sitting idly by the table with the dishes still on it and smoking the Corporal's cigarette ration. 'The story is all over the village. Don't you know half these people speak Slovenian and Serbo-Croat?'

O'Leary stared up at me, his mouth slightly open with shock at my rude attack.

'What d'you mean?' he said aggressively. 'You don't believe what these peasants say, for God's sake?'

'You know perfectly well what I mean, You agreed to speak on Zagreb radio when they promised to let you go. It's true, isn't it?'

'Well, what if it is? We aren't soldiers.'

'They threatened to shoot us,' said Barber, lifting a heavy head and speaking in an almost awed tone. 'Shoot us as spies!'

'Well you shouldn't have crossed the border,' I shouted furiously. 'We warned you you'd have trouble!'

'We couldn't stay there after—after the things that were said,' he muttered.

'They are nothing to what will be said now,' I countered. 'What d'you think Frau Homburg will say to you now, you self-righteous, stupid clots? All your fine talk about resisting the wicked Nazis, and democracy and Lord knows what—and the first moment the pressure is on you, you crack up like—like . . .' I could think of nothing suitable to compare them with.

'That's what I told O'Leary,' Barber confessed simply. 'I said we ought to face the music, but he's afraid of losing his job.'

'I suppose you aren't?' jeered O'Leary savagely. 'Well, I've had it, that's quite clear.'

'I shall tell the truth, as I wanted to all along,' said Barber regaining his self-confidence in a way that was ludicrously out of place, and yet his crumpled dignity was preferable to O'Leary's pusillanimity. 'I shall request my editor to publish the facts as they happened. And I shall apologise publicly to Frau Homburg in the paper.'

'They'll never publish!'

'Oh, I think they will,' Barber almost smiled. 'It's a terrific story, I guess.'

'You newspapermen really are the most appalling cynics,' I said and sat down, not knowing whether to laugh or rage at him. I don't think he knew at all what I meant. It seemed at once the right and expedient thing to do, and he was quite satisfied with his intention. Indeed, I think he was relieved. Certainly he became much more cheerful and his invalid air lessened at once, to my astonishment. O'Leary stared at his colleague with intent concentration and it was clear that he too was now working out how best he could rescue the situation, or even procure some advantage from it.

'After all, they were our Allies in the war,' he muttered, half under his breath. Suddenly, the Corporal, an unsurprised witness of this scene, began to laugh aloud.

'If you can get away with that line in London,' I said, 'you can get away with anything.'

'There's a lot of sympathy for the Yugoslavs in Britain,' O'Leary countered with preposterous seriousness.

'I dare say, but that has nothing to do with it. You'll be in trouble anyway for contributing to Communist propaganda.'

But I was being naïve and they were right. By the time we reached the hotel they were confidently working out the best way to put over their more or less true story. They even had the impudence to ask me to dine with them in the Club but I had better things to do and left them to the company of a half-terrified and half-delighted Colonel Manley. I have not the least doubt that by the next day when their colleagues arrived with photographers from Vienna to interview them, they believed altogether in the correctness of their actions and had probably forgotten that they ever tried to hide them.

I dropped Lali off outside the reading room on our return because she would have been obliged to wait in the car outside the Club Hotel while I took in the two guests. And then I went back and up the steep stairs to the top floor where Lali had her lonely room.

It was the first time I visited her there. The room was neat, plain, half-empty, with only a woven rag rug on the bare boards. In a cracked pottery jar stood a bunch of fir twigs with cones, beside three unframed photographs. Her mother, a young man who so resembled Lali and that I knew must be her dead brother and the child; the last a small picture taken in recent weeks of a round little head that might have been any small child and even to its mother can hardly have been more than an act of piety in absence. She could only visit Nando every third or fourth week when her turn for a free weekend came round. I was looking for a fourth face, but did not find it.

There was no direct heating in the room, but the main house chimney warmed it from one wall, distempered with a deplorable rolled-on pattern of leaves and birds.

'You see, we have somewhere private to go, after all,' I said as I laid down my cap and gloves.

For an instant there was a return of fear in her eyes, but I made no attempt to approach more nearly and after a little silence she smiled rather waveringly and said we could have a glass of wine for she had managed to afford a modest bottle. This was said tentatively, shyly, and she looked away from me.

'We have to sit over by that wall,' she added hastily. 'I put the table there because that's the warm side. Be careful, though, the table is a bit rickety.'

I uncorked the bottle. The wine was rather thin and sour. We touched the thick glasses together as a toast.

'Were you saving the bottle for this occasion?' I asked.

She looked at me defensively, but returned my smile.

'Yes, I was,' she answered simply. Presently, she added, 'I wish Julie and Georgy were here too.'

'I'm very glad they aren't.'

'I only meant—I'd like them to be happy . . . too.'

Much later, when it was time for me to return to the Mess, she returned to Julie.

'Do you think Mr Barber meant what he said about having an apology to Julie printed in his newspaper?'

'He does at the moment, but I wouldn't rely on it,' I said.

'If he did mean it, Julie would go back to Vienna,' she said, watching me to see if I would mind this. I said nothing for I had not considered this eventuality. But it was too unlikely a chance to count on.

'I shall be glad with all my heart if it comes off. So long as you don't go with her.'

INTERIM

It did come off. The two journalists may not have known about Slav minorities in southern Austria but they knew their trade. The brief time between that evening and the following noon when a shower of news and radio reporters descended on the town was not wasted. They worked the 'story' over so neatly that it looked as if they deliberately chose to save their lives in order to get back to civilisation and tell the world of the danger of Communism. Colonel Manley had his picture in all the London popular papers after being seen for several hours being polite to a swarm of photographers who drank the Club bar dry at his expense—a point I think he only understood afterwards. Only after the swarm roared off again towards Vienna did the two heroes shave off their half-grown beards and abandon their Serb footwear. The day following O'Leary went back to his office in Vienna and we never saw him again. Barber was flown back to New York and there wrote his series of articles on the threat of totalitarianism, beginning with the promised self-accusations and the story of Julia Homburg as the misunderstood opponent of tyranny, which made Julie's name a nine-day wonder in the United States.

It was a hilarious incident. A pity I was too much engaged elsewhere to appreciate it as it deserved.

For in quite another way the seriousness of life dissolved into pre-spring in the slashing rains and sleet of truly appalling weather which washed away the weight of the winter and its terrible events long before the sun began to shine with weak astonishment at its own survival. The world wallowed in the slush and mud of thaw, the rain poured down in torrents; great winds blew, hallooing like Homeric laughter in the night.

I was wildly in love and my love was answered with, at first, hesitant and unpractised ardour and then with increasingly delicate and involved intuition; intuition not less physical than spiritual. My own varied experience prepared me ill for the truth of loving and I think I may count it to my credit that I recognised this. It would be impossible to write directly of such matters about my own wife and the mother of my children, even supposing I wished to do so; moreover, those who know about love will understand me and those who have never had that supreme good fortune would know no more after the most detailed and uninhibited descriptions. For the validity of loving is in its total privacy; only sex can be discussed.

Weeks passed in a daze, and I have no doubt that Wilder's customers sowed the vegetable and salad seeds he had imported, from the Mother Superior of the Old People's Home down to the ugly old man near the border. I was as unconscious of the changing season for some time as I was of my duties. I must have carried them out, I suppose, for I do not recall more acerbity on Colonel Manley's part than I was used to. The weather I did notice, for it confined us much to Lali's little bare room in the evenings, which was just as it should be, and the rest of life was lived in the constant anticipation of being in that room again. From outside came news of floods and bridges collapsing, cows carried away, tree trunks obstructing roads; I found it hard to understand why anyone should worry about such matters, for reality was the inward flood of joy and discovery that seems so ridiculous when one is not oneself being carried along in it.

The most moving thing about our deepening communion was that gradually, almost unnoticeably, spiritual barriers were dismantled for me alone in Lali which perforce were constructed in the course of the eighteen months she spent in a state of constant, daily danger of being forced brutally and with hatred into being used as an object. It was clear that nothing of the terrible kind of savagery we heard all too much of ever happened, for Lali herself, and later her mother, even joked about their tricks and ruses of evasion in which they used both their Russian General and the child's constant presence as protectors instead of allowing themselves to be used. And if such things ever had happened, they would never have spoken of the subject at all. But the strain and the wariness left in her a kind of emotional lassitude that she never quite lost and which is often to be felt in girls who grew up in that time and in those places. And slowly it dawned on me that if I—Robert Inglis—was worthy of such gifts, then I needed to prove myself to no one further and to feel myself nobody's inferior. So that in my liberating Lali, she liberated me.

But one morning I awoke with a sense of some new anticipation. Hard to place for a moment—what was it? Ah, we were to drive up to the house today for a long weekend. That was it; for four whole days we should not be separated in the day-time or at night. I jumped from my hard Army bed, crossed the room to close the open window and felt, astonished, that the air flowing in over me was not cold for the first time since I arrived at the pen the previous autumn. The air was warm, the sun rode freely in soft blue and the clouds were no longer purple threats of snow or the tatters of storm; they were light round puffs of nothing. On the tree nearest to my window I saw the twigs minutely clear, no longer tight in self-defence but covered all over in buds already showing green, and as I leaned out I saw that the bushes of the garden were in first leaf and the trodden, sodden grass showed a fresh brilliance. From far and near a million birds called each other; it was the miraculous cliché of spring, and the cat from the Mess kitchen crept through the rank grass on its secret search for prey.

The eastern lane showed its polished yellow bones of rock where a few days before it had been a torrent while the ditches were still brimming with cloudy water which ran, here and there, over the track where tangles of brush wood hindered its direct passage.

'It's the first time we've actually seen this track,' I said. 'D'you remember the first time?'

'No, nothing. I came to in the house at some moment—I don't know how long after you got me there.'

'Really, nothing—not the snow and me calling to you?'

She shook her head. 'I seem to recall getting off a bus and asking somebody the way. That's all . . .'

'Good,' I said, 'I'm glad you can't remember.'

'What?' she cried, pretending disappointment. 'You don't want me to remember the motorised knight rescuing the forlorn maiden —well, not quite maiden?'

'You were forlorn, all right. You'd have a fit if you could see now what you looked like then.'

'There you are, you see! You do resent my not remembering your noble deed.'

'You needn't sound so self-satisfied. At the time all I thought of was whether I should ever get the car started again. I'd only been taught to drive a few weeks before.'

'It's not obvious now. You seem to drive very well. But then, I find you altogether a rather competent person.'

I shot her a quick glance to make sure what she meant by that, and we both began to laugh at everything and nothing.

Georgy was standing in the courtyard talking to the new man who was to take care of the farming. He waved and limped over to us as I swerved the car into its usual place. Even before we were well clear of the doors, he knew.

'As you see,' he waved an arm still rather awkward, at the elder bush by the arch already veiled in green, 'spring has arrived at last.'

That was all that was said and more was not needed. Once in the house and away from the man's eyes, Lali put her arms round his neck and kissed him and then Nando, towing his nursemaid and followed by Margarete Pohaisky, came rushing out of the inner room. The obvious point occurred to me for the first time that we should in some ways be far less private here than we were when we could be together only in the evenings. But it was not so; in silent conspiracy it was agreed that we were lovers entitled to sit next to each other at meals, go off together in the streaming, bursting country in our rubber boots, and sleep supposedly in adjoining rooms. They must, I suppose, have taken it for granted that Lali would marry me long before I could do so. For that was the only subject on which we did not agree. If either of us feared disapproval from Frau Pohaisky, and I think we were both a little apprenhensive of her, we were mistaken. The only part of our world now missing was Julie, who had gone back to the greater world. From thence came almost daily scrawled missives—one could hardly call them letters—telling of the results of Colton Barber's publicity thunder-clap, the proposal of a lecture tour (refused) and several films (being considered) as well as dozens of instructions about the house, land, Nando and how Georgy was to keep the accounts. Nando figured largely in these notes, for the legal question of his known but unprovable parentage was being tackled with Julie's characteristic energy by the simple means of naming him as her heir.

With her native sense and far-sightedness Julie must have recognised that Lali in her essential soundness was bound to marry in the near future and was determined that Nando should never become anyone other than Ferdinand von Kasda.

As soon as Lali was together with her son again, a subtle change began to form between us, and I was forced to recognise clearly what in the last weeks I quite easily forgot. No matter how much in love we were, no matter how impossible it might become for either of us to disentangle ourselves from what was of its nature a permanent relationship, the fact of my foreignness came between Lali and her inherited family duty. Once again, I did not quite belong and I remembered vividly the occasion in the village tavern when I felt the foreboding that I should never come first with Lali.

It was not that Nando made possessive claims, or even that Lali seemed to do so; it was simply his existence which was opposed to my own. The boy himself belonged happily to everyone; always used to his grandmother as well as Lali, he transferred a diffused affection between the absent Julie, his real mother and Margarete Pohaisky, who did most in the way of bringing him up. Like most normal children made backward by privation, he made a sudden jump from a baby to a small boy as soon as he was properly fed. He ran about and chattered incessantly, rambling on in long narratives in which his grandmother and Julie—whom he always called by her name—were mixed up with Frau Pohaisky, Georgy, the man about the farm and, increasingly, myself. I was, I knew, included in his happy affection. I returned it—he now was an enchanting child with his mother's merry eyes and natural clearness and straightness. But the problem presented by him was not removed and could not be removed.

On Sunday afternoon he came into the living room—it was necessary to conserve fuel so that we used that room still for both sitting and eating—rubbing the sleep out of his eyes after his nap. He climbed at once on to Georgy's long, thin thigh and Georgy began to bounce him in the German version of 'Ride a cock horse to Banbury Cross', I chimed in with the English words and this, naturally, fascinated the child. He seemed to notice then for the first time that I was quite differently dressed from Georgy, who always wore the close-fitting knee breeches of rough-side leather, stout dark woollen stockings and a short thick jacket of black and dark green which were like those worn by all the men of the district, including the farm hand. They were familiar; Nando knew no others. Except my uniform.

'Why does Robert wear different clothes?' he asked, stopping his bouncing suddenly, so that he almost fell off his sinewy perch.

'Because Robert is a soldier,' answered Kerenyi, 'like all your family have always been.'

'Well, you're not a soldier, then. You don't wear those clothes.'
Naturally, Nando did not yet understand the word 'family'.

'Not now, but I was for a time,' said Georgy and began again to bounce his knee, while Nando turned his head to survey my battledress.

'Did you wear Robert's clothes, then, when you were a soldier?'

'Out of the mouths of babes and sucklings,' said Margarete Pohaisky under her breath. Lali gave her a sharp look, seeing for the first time that the older woman perfectly understood the situation thus expressed. There was a silence long enough to be noticeable.

'Something like them,' agreed Georgy cheerfully. 'A bit different.'

It is not to be supposed that Nando spoke as clearly as this but because he was always with adults he never did speak in baby-talk and his words were recognisably the same ones we used ourselves.

'Talk some more like that,' he said imperiously to me. 'Like you did before.'

Instead of using English, I replied in French. Nando shouted with laughter.

'How interesting; he doesn't recognize that it's a different language,' said Georgy quietly.

'He will soon, now,' I said and heard that my voice sounded bitter.

'I shall go and make coffee,' Frau Pohaisky rose and laid down her sewing—her hands were never idle for a moment. 'Real coffee.' She turned at the door and added deliberately, 'Which we owe to you, Robert.'

'Nanny Pohaisky goes to say her prayers in Church,' announced Nando. He was still concerned with clothing, for Frau Pohaisky wore different clothes on Sunday. 'I don't yet. I'm not old enough. I say mine by my bed.'

'Oh, Nando!' said Lali helplessly, but instead of laughing she began to cry. She got up quickly and left the room and something stopped me following her.

'Of course,' said Georgy calmly, as Frau Pohaisky came in with the coffee cups and went out again, 'of course, you could transfer to a job—a posting, I mean—that would take you to Vienna and keep you here for some time.'

He set down the child and began without haste to set out the cups and saucers from the tray onto the table by our places.

'With your languages,' he said. 'And you speak Russian, too.'

'I've never heard you *hint*, before,' I said savagely.

'Yes,' he replied equably, 'I shouldn't interfere.'

'Matter of fact, it's a first-class idea. Why didn't I think of it? God, I could use a drink.'

'So could I. Let's have a quick Barack. I've got some of the real stuff from over the border.'

He limped over to a cupboard and withdrew a bottle of Hungarian apricot *Schnapps* and two little glasses.

'I didn't think of it, in fact, myself,' he disclaimed, as he poured out drinks. 'Julie did. I got this from my DPs. Julie is bloody good at solving other people's problems. It's only our own she can't get to terms with.'

'Why does Mummy cry like that?' asked Nando, but nobody answered him and to distract his attention I began to tickle the big tabby behind his ear so that she began to purr loudly. Nando always liked that.

'Shall I go and tell Mummy coffee is ready?' he asked Frau Pohaisky as she put down the coffee pot. And after a few minutes they came back together.

'I've often meant to ask you, Robert,' began Frau Pohaisky serenely, 'how did you come to speak Russian? It's a rather unusual accomplishment.'

I explained how it came about and found myself telling them how my parents went again to Russia for two years in 1936 and how I visited them there at the invitation—that was then the only way of arranging such a visit—of the British Ambassador, for a summer holiday from school.

'It was a big air-conditioning plant my father installed. But the contract was never finished. There was some fearful row about people interfering and my father threw up the contract. I suppose it was something to do with the Purges which were then in full spate. They paid him, though. I remember him saying that he would never have been offered the contract at all if it weren't that no Russian engineer could carry out the work at that time.'

'So you've actually seen Russia?' Frau Pohaisky said as if I'd been on the planet Mars. 'Tell us what it was like.'

'That was the summer of '38 and though it was summer, it was simply dreadful. Unless you've seen it you can't imagine such a primitive poverty. I was fifteen then and I don't suppose I understood half of what I saw, but it was enough. I've always felt a deep pity for the ordinary Russian people ever since. They were so sad, so sullen, so terrified of everybody and everything. It was immeasurably sad and frightening. I suppose I've never got over the impression it left on me and I was out of myself with joy when my father said they were coming back to England with me instead of staying on the last three months of his contract. All the equipment was installed by then and just the actual switching-on, as it were, unfinished.'

'I expect the NKVD badgered him into terminating the contract so that he wouldn't know the final dispositions. They probably thought he was going to blow the whole thing up with a time fuse after he'd left.' This from Georgy.

'It's entirely possible. In fact, he suspected as much himself. They were certainly as obstructive over everything as they possibly could be. They even tried to keep me inside the Embassy buildings in Moscow and it took my mother a fortnight to get permission for me to visit them. They lived like prisoners themselves in a house walled off outside the town—it was called Ordjhonikidze at first, but they changed the name while my father was there. None of us could leave the house without an escort and, you know, this wasn't a military installation or anything, but a food-storage plant. I've no doubt it was copied a hundred times from my father's designs in other places.'

'It's almost incredible that they allowed either your mother or you to go there,' said Lali. 'They are unbelievably suspicious.'

'It was in the original contract, you see, and that was signed in 1935. Before the Purges began.'

'Imagine it taking two years to instal an air-conditioning plant,' said Frau Pohaisky wonderingly.

'Well, the whole complex of buildings was being built at the same time, of course,' I explained. 'Even so, it took for ever. All the machinery and electrical installations that came from England took months to reach the place. And they'd been so thoroughly searched on the way, over and over again, that half the electrical stuff had to be repaired before it could be installed. It was all pulled about by people who didn't understand it. Naturally my father's protests at the interferences were ground for further suspicion. He must have been one of the last foreign engineers ever to work in the USSR.'

'Until recently,' said Georgy. 'I read in the papers that they are recruiting people again now.' He looked slyly at me under his brows. 'What was the name of that terrible old Nazi they tried to kidnap in Göttingen?'

'Professor Emden,' I said. 'He's an authority on solid fuels for aeronautics.'

'That's the chap. You know, Robert, if you feel like doing me a favour some time, you could get me a subscription to the *Times*. I miss the foreign press, here.'

Lali and I looked at each other guiltily.

'How awful that we never thought of it ourselves,' she said, raising her hand to her mouth. 'And it's so easy for me to arrange!'

'It would be two days old if not three, before the post got it here,' I pointed out.

'My dear boy, I've been out of date since 1938, so three days isn't going to make much difference.' He laughed suddenly. 'That's not quite true—I did see some foreign stuff during the war.'

'Let us not talk about the war, Herr Doctor,' said Frau Pohaisky.

'No indeed. Let's talk about the future.' He began at once to discuss the plans for the farm and reafforestation to replace the felled timber. We knew as little as Kerenyi did of the practical side of this, but the planning and accounting work were interesting. We studied the surveys and plans and made suggestions which he noted for the next visit of the builder.

'Of course, he'll turn them all down,' he said. 'I've learned that much about builders, already.'

'I'm amazed that you can get anything done,' I said.

'Oh, yes, so long as you stay away from the authorities you can get things done. And Julie has pots of money, you know. It's all been piling up for the last year or so when one could buy nothing worth having.'

'But this can't take up all your time, Georgy,' said Lali. 'You must start your own work again, too.'

He did not answer for a moment and I looked to see why. He was scowling down at his bony hands in a way that I recognised.

'I am, in a way,' he said at last. 'I've got the manuscript—the galleys, rather—of Franz Wedeker's book from Zurich and I've started on writing and expanding it.'

'Franz Wedeker?' I asked, remembering something vaguely about a manuscript in Zurich. 'Who is he?'

He stared at me, astounded at my ignorance, but it was Frau Pohaisky who answered.

'Franz Wedeker was Julie's husband.'

'Oh!' I said shocked and startled. 'I'd never heard his name.'

'Julie wants it done,' said Kerenyi quietly. 'And I can do that for her.'

'Is there much work to do on it?'

'A good deal, yes. He was cut off from the outside world, you see. And though a serious political thinker, he was no writer.'

'I think it's a wonderful thing for you to do,' said Lali softly. 'It will be a monument to him.'

He looked up at her with loving attention.

'I see you understand,' he said.

And in a way that I cannot explain, I understood that our future inside this small community could be left to resolve itself. It was no use trying to force the issue, and could only do harm. I must wait patiently until Lali herself fitted myself and Nando together; and although nothing had happened, I felt hopeful that this would come about.

It was days later, when we were eating one evening in the 'Papagei', that Lali brought up the subject of my unusual upbringing again.

'You see,' she said, 'it doesn't seem strange to us to speak several languages, though I'm not at all clever myself with them. So I didn't quite understand why you always seem so defensive on the subject. But when you talked about going to Russia and all that, I suddenly understood—because the English girls in the reading room always seem to resent anyone who can speak German properly. I don't mean us, you know, we don't count; but if some British officer comes in who can really speak to the Austrian staff in German, then they get cross. I suppose, if that is usual in England, you must have had a bad time at school . . . ?'

I thought of my horrible schooldays, peopled by an infinite series of Colonel Manleys, small and large, and grinned suddenly at her—though my schooldays never before struck me as funny.

'It was awful. They called me Russki. Even though I was quite good at games, I never lived it down. I must say, the Army was a great relief, after school.'

'I'm glad you never did any fighting, though,' she said.

'So am I—now I know what it was like—my languages saved me from killing people, anyway. And, after all, what was it all about . . . ? The world is in a worse mess now than it was then, and Europe ruined . . . England ruined, too.'

The unhappy, puzzled look began to gather in her eyes with which she always reacted to any talk of the war, and I quickly changed the subject.

'I had a letter from Julie today—a proper letter, not like her usual ones with no beginning and no end.'

'So had I! Was it the same thing—to ask you to go to Vienna in June?'

'She's asked you too? Wonderful—we can go together.'

Lali gave me a sideways smile.

'Julie's up to something,' she said in English.

'Of course. She wants us to admire her before the end of the season. It will be great fun. I've never seen her act.'

'I have, twice. During the war.'

'Why do you think she has something up her sleeve—apart from your signing all those papers about Nando, I mean?'

'I don't know . . . I just got the impression . . .'

'It just comes right. I have to go and take my exams at the beginning of June, and then I'm due for leave when I get back here. You know, I've never seen Vienna.'

'I don't know it very well myself, only for visits. But it will be nice to be in a position to show *you* something new.'

'Speaking of something new,' I said, 'let's get out of here before Wilder or somebody comes in and wastes the evening for us.'

'Where do you have to go to take your exams?' She asked as we waited for the bill to be brought. 'I shall hate you being away for two whole weeks.'

'A place called the School of Slavonic Studies. And another academy, part of the Staff College.'

'Why does Wilder tease you about being a lawyer? You're not going to take law exams, after all?'

'It's an English joke. He means I'm too stuffy about rules and regulations.'

'Hm. Certainly nobody could accuse Wilder of being that!'

Lali said this with such an odd little prim air that we both began to laugh, and laughed all the way back to her room through the warm spring evening.

Oddly enough, I did not have to propose myself for a posting to Vienna in a different branch of the service. It was suggested to me while I was in England for the examinations and I knew that in the quiet way the English do things, it was already known that I possessed attachments in Austria.

Vienna itself was quite a shock. I expected it to be in a state of devastation, like all the major towns of Germany itself. But it was the most beautiful city I had ever seen and I think I should still have found it lovely even if I were not there for the first time with Lali and with the prospect of Julie's company. There was, naturally, a good deal of destruction visible. But the identity of the city was not destroyed; it had survived. Its unity was at once to be felt, artificially divided though it was.

Going through London I bought some new equipment, Tom having been good enough to send me to his tailor and to warn that immensely serious personage of my coming. So on the evening I first went with Lali to the Burgtheater, I think I looked a credit to the service and to her. True I was still a little nervous of my Sam Browne belt in case it might creak—a dreadful military solecism —but I had taken the solemn advice of Tom's tailor and bought one second-hand which he happened to have by him; it was as highly polished and soundless as Tom's own.

The great house on the Ring which became afterwards so familiar was then not yet rebuilt. The company played at a former vaudeville theatre and though the professionals made fun of the Ronacher, it will always have a reflection of glamour for me. The play was a new production of Oscar Wilde's *The Importance of Being Earnest,* which is unnecessarily renamed in German *Bunbury.* Unnecessary because the joke on the name of Earnest comes off just as well in German as in English; but puns are not considered the thing in the German language, perhaps because it is not well-formed for them, as English is. It was a brilliantly lavish production; at that time theatrical productions tended to be particularly luxurious, in order to comfort the public, perhaps, for the everyday world outside. I thought the handsome actor who played *Earnest* was somewhat wooden and did not understand the real humour of the part, but Julie was a dream of enchanting fun; Wilde would have chosen her himself. Somehow she was even more accomplished than I expected—it is an almost universal trait of human nature, which I shared, that we never believe our nearest and dearest can really be talented. Unless, of course, we first know them in their professional habitat, but I first met Julie in an exceedingly private role. The audience was enthusiastic, the players enjoying themselves and their success. Among the public were a number of other Allied officers from all four occupation forces; two senior RAF officers, a box full of stout Russians with their wives in velvet splendour, two handsome Frenchmen and several Americans. In spite of the uniforms, there was no 'occupied' atmosphere; love of the theatre, the excellence of the play and what I afterwards discovered to be a typical Viennese liking for foreigners, whether in uniform or not, made it a success. In the interval we stood with minute glasses of rather poor Vermouth and listened to the Russians discussing the performance in the bar, unaware that they were understood. They kept their heads together and greeted nobody, careful not to expose themselves to each other as approving of their surroundings; but their comments on the play and the actors gave them unconsciously away. They were clearly adoring it all. The only thing I did not enjoy was the proximity of the two French officers, who were far too handsome to be up to any good and kept shooting flirtatious glances at Lali. She, I was reassured to see, did not quite know how to deal with their smiles and murmured compliments made as if to each other and not to be overheard and she gave away her understanding of them by blushing. However, I had the last word, for a liveried attendant came up to us, asked my name and gave me a message from Frau Homburg that we should await the rest of our supper party in the restaurant; of course, Julie knew how this public accolade would delight me and I was able to bear the remaining minutes of the interval with equanimity.

Walking away with Lali in front of me under the now silent envy of the two Frenchmen, I felt myself to be the most fortunate man in the world; and indeed it would be hard to find anyone luckier than I was then. We were both still very young, and having both been cut off by the war from a normal youth, in some ways still childish. We were in a state of mutual adoration; and though the results of my examinations were not yet officially published, I knew I had done quite well and that I could expect a posting with greater responsibilities and higher rank to be the quick consequence. This argued well for our future together. Finally, I found myself for the first time in my life among people who seemed not to find me odd; and, moreover people whose attainments made it impossible to

231

underestimate their judgment. Accompanied by a charming girl and publicly singled out for friendship by one of the most beautiful and distinguished women in a city famous for the looks of its women, I could hardly be blamed if I felt pretty pleased with myself.

The supper party to which we repaired at a small and expensive restaurant nearby cut me down to size. We went round there, innocently, afoot—at a time when an Allied officer of any influence at all did not move in the evening without a large car with a driver —and from the air of the man who opened the door I saw that I was obviously a very low fellow indeed if I could not command transport. In the street we were bound to behave formally but as soon as the door closed behind us we joined hands and as Lali gave up her modest jacket, we were even about to catch up on an abstinence of several hours by exchanging a quick kiss. At this inopportune moment I came under the contemptuous surveillance of a head-waiter who could have competed with Tom's tailor in London for solemnity and who would certainly have intimidated Tom himself. His look said clearly that the sort of people he nowadays had to deal with . . . and addressed Lali to her astonishment as Countess. Unused to anything of the kind from her usual companions in the reading room, Lali began a small chuckle of amusement but soon gave up that idea under his raised eyebrows. Completely deflated, the Herr Keptin was in effect ordered to take his place at Frau Homburg's table in an almost empty room in which it was clear that to be so early was almost as bad as spitting on the floor.

'How d'you think he knew who I am?' Lali whispered and nervously accepted a cigarette. Of course, this dignitary of a waiter was bending over us already, offering us an aperitif; he was much too well trained to interfere with my lighting Lali's cigarette. I felt like demanding slivovitz out of sheer nervous hysteria, but afraid of humiliating Lali I suggested sherry and a whole tray of different kinds of this wine was at once produced, all of them bearing the official overstamp of British Army stores—sherry being an almost exclusively English drink.

'Perhaps Julie told them who the guests would be? No, hardly. I don't know.' I came to know this man well later and to admire his quality; he would have made a perfect regimental Sergeant-Major. And he told me once that he recognised Lali immediately from her resemblance to Ferdinand von Kasda.

It seemed hours before the rest of the party appeared from their changing and *démaquillages;* in fact about fifteen minutes, and then within a few minutes the tables were all filled up and the late evening meal was in full swing with waiters and fat waitresses running about and everyone chattering. At the next table to ours was a staggeringly pretty blonde with a good-looking American Colonel.

At our table were Julie herself, the actor who played 'Earnest' and his quiet, non-professional wife, Ostrovsky and a young girl who proved to be a protégée of Ostrovsky's. As soon as Lali was among her own people, whom she did not know well except for Julie, she recovered herself completely and in a few minutes was exchanging the complicated jokes bandied about by the rest of the company as if she sat there every evening. This multi-lingual joking, in which languages were played with like coloured baubles, exchanged with bewildering suddenness so that the point of the banter was always in the change from one language to another, was initially an intimidating experience. At first I did not trust myself to join in, but presently intervened with a remark in Italian which in its own language is slightly improper but in the equivalent French or German not; to my relief and pleasure this was greeted with a shout of laughter and I gradually forgot my shyness. Presently the beautiful blonde announced that she intended to play Somerset Maugham's *Jane* at a commercial theatre during the next season; did everyone not agree with this idea? Elliott—with a wave of her brilliantly red-nailed hand at her companion—was against it. Instantly, as if a switch had been turned, the whole company was deep in a professional argument, entirely serious and formidably expert.

Presently Julie, on my left, turned to me and asked me, with the abrupt change of manner which any mention of Kerenyi always caused in her, how Georgy was.

'He wouldn't come up to Vienna with you two, I notice,' she said almost irritably.

'I think he's pretty busy on the book,' I excused the absent Georgy.

'Ah, yes, that's what he says!' She changed the subject again and wanted to know about my fortnight in England and how the examinations went. I replied that I was hopeful of success and taking time by the forelock, added that it might, if I were proved right, mean a remove to Vienna. Both Julie on one side and Lali on the other stopped and stared at me with a pause noticeable in the babble of talk.

'A move,' said Lali at last in a small voice.

'But what about Lali?' asked Julie with her usual directness.

'Well,' I said slowly, pushing my wine glass to and fro in a pattern on the gleaming table linen, 'we shall have to see about that, shan't we?'

'You might have told me in private,' protested Lali in an undertone.

Julie glanced at her quickly, understanding at once why I chose the moment I did. We had, quite suddenly, reached the point of no return and just because we all recognised this fact, we began to talk of other things.

I noticed only later that it was the mention of Georgy that brought the subject of our own private life into the open, and was struck anew at the mysterious way human beings communicate with each other.

BOOK TWO
1950-1951

I

The door of my office opened a crack and the clerk put in his head.

'There's a lady to see you, Major. Shall I ask her to make an appointment?'

I had not the least idea who this might be, but gave my table the quick inspection which had become second nature in the last years. There was, however, nothing compromising in view.

'Ask her to come in. I'm not busy.'

He too gave the routine glance round the room, noting that the map case and files were closed, opened the door and admitted the guest. I was astonished to see Agnes—Agnes Stephenson she had been for several years then.

At first sight she seemed just the same, very quiet and modest, slightly uncertain in manner, an uncertainty that matched oddly with her unassailable good breeding and her atmosphere of goodness. She was carefully and fashionably dressed; I noticed that as an innovation and an improvement on her former rather provincial and tentative taste in clothes and makeup. Marriage had sharpened my perceptions, not only I hope, in matters of feminine style.

'I heard you'd had a son,' she said, after we had exchanged the usual greeting. 'Congratulations.'

'And you a son and a daughter, so congratulations for you too. How are you all?'

'We're all in splendid form,' said Agnes, and hesitated. 'The thing is, we're going to be here—posted to Vienna. You're the person I thought of first.'

She had never been a good dissembler and it was not only that I knew that this statement could not possibly be true that convinced me she was untruthful. Her innate truthfulness was the fundament of her character rather than one trait of it, so that insincerity was instantly noticeable in her as something acquired.

'We'd better start straight away being perfectly open,' she said laughing. Something she could not formerly have said for it would not occur to her to be anything else. 'David is hoping you'll be able to introduce us to some nice people, amusing people. He's already decided that the Embassy is hopelessly dull and stuffy after Washington.'

'Fine. Let's start right off by having dinner tomorrow. Just a minute. I'll check.' I picked up the telephone and dialled my own number.

'Lali? You remember Agnes Macdonald who gave you your first job in the library? She's here in the office! They've been posted to Vienna. Can we have them to dinner tomorrow? Or shall we take them out?'

I heard Lali call to the cook and then she said to me, 'Of course. Shall I get somebody else? Or just us?'

'Oh, yes, get somebody else, if you can find somebody at such short notice. You're sure it's all right?'

'It's lovely; but why shouldn't it be? He's quite recovered days ago.'

'He' was our son Sebastian, now just eighteen months old and just getting over a bad cold. He was the pride of my life and even more than that, the guarantee of permanence. Since his birth the slight, unspoken, but always to be felt opposition to our marriage from Lali's mother had disappeared. Sebastian did not, and we did not want him to, take first place before Lali's older son, but though his name was Inglis and not von Kasda he was equally Lali's child and the intense family loyalties of her clan accepted him and therefore me. The fact that Lali's mother was alone in her struggle to maintain their property, which coloured our attitude to her with guilt, only made this relief and happiness the greater. Nando remained the heir for the Kasdas, and we were now entitled to our personal life as well. It solved the main part of a thorny problem which at one time threatened to make us unhappy; the problem remained, but acquired a balancing stability.

Fortunately we were unable to find other guests for that evening; there chanced to be a first night at the Opera. Because David telephoned in the afternoon to propose that they should bring with them an American couple from Washington who happened to be visiting the city for the first time.

Lorraine and Wendell Boyd were southerners and though this

238

evening was my only acquaintance with them I remember their names because they called each other Lorry and Wen and insisted on us doing likewise. The names were not the only odd thing about the evening.

Lali had never met David and I noticed at once that he was concerned to be gallant with her.

'I've heard a lot about you,' he said, sitting down beside her on the sofa with his champagne tilting in its glass towards her. We were celebrating the reunion.

Lali smiled past him at Agnes, very slender and smart in a full-skirted black dress from Paris.

'What have you been saying about me? That I was a bad librarian?'

'Oh, not from Agnes,' disclaimed David. 'She never tells me anything about people. No, I hear you know absolutely everybody worth knowing in Vienna. All the singers and actors and artists and writers. Everybody.'

'Do we know everybody, Robert?' asked my wife. 'I suppose we do, in a way.'

'Everybody would obviously want to know you, just as we do now that we've met you,' said David before I could reply.

'I feel as if I'd known you for ages, because of knowing Agnes. She was almost the first foreigner I knew after I left the zone. Except for Robert and Tom Wallingham.'

'I say, d'you still see old Tom?' David glanced up at me in surprise.

'Of course,' I said, 'we're meeting him next week in the country. He's coming over to get some shooting.'

'What a funny old boy he was,' David shook his head and his lock of hair slipped over his forehead just as it always did.

'But Tom is not old,' objected Lali seriously. Lorry Boyd had meanwhile asked a question about the 'zone' and Lali turned sideways to her on her right. 'My home is in the Russian Zone, in Lower Austria, but I left there at the end of 1946. That's what we always mean when we say the zone, here.'

'You mean you lived under the Russians?' breathed Lorry, apparently awestruck. 'But of course you got out as soon as you could?' I recognised in her manner the type of Americans, then very familiar, with a wildly romantic, demonic view of the Russians, but Lali either did not understand this or did not want to.

'I left because of my son,' she said, 'but my mother is still living there.'

'How terrible!'

'Our house is there, you see,' explained Lali, 'It belongs to my eldest son and if my mother left he would probably lose it.'

The Boyds exchanged looks which said clearly that this was not a sufficient ground for remaining; like many people who have never been threatened with the loss of their property they took the possessions of other people lightly.

'Did you say you were going to the country next week?' Wen politely changed the subject. 'That's a great pity. We hoped Mrs Inglis would have time to show us something of Vienna, while we're here.'

'What a shame,' I agreed, pouring out more wine. I went over to ring for a fresh bottle. 'But we have already made all sorts of arrangements with other people, so I'm afraid we have to go.'

I resented Lali being treated, as she often was by visitors, as a guide and interpreter, but was so used to the attitude that I could dispose of it almost without noticing it by now. Just the same, until we were called to the table Lali was kept busy recommending the things and places the Boyds must see, since she could not escort them.

Sightseeing clearly bored David, and when we went into the dining room he took the opportunity to stop the talk of it.

'This is a bad business in Korea,' he said directly to me, across Lorry Boyd.

'Why, David,' she said reproachfully, 'that's no way to talk. You all know our forces had to drive up to the Yalu, why we just had to.'

'No, no,' he said, 'you've misunderstood me. I didn't mean the drive to the Yalu. Of course, we had to go on up there. I meant the Chinese intervention.'

I noticed he had acquired what I believe is called a midAtlantic turn of phrase if not accent, in Washington.

'The Chinese?' asked Wen sharply. Forgotten now, this was a moment of terror for the world in November 1950; the threat from China was just then becoming a reality. The presence of Chinese 'volunteers' had been announced in the Peking press but it was by no means common knowledge and certainly not in Europe.

'But even if they do come in, MacArthur can deal with them.'

'Come in!' said David with an effect of derision. 'Why, they're in. And what's more, they are driving back the United Nations —that is, the Americans—and the Roks on both fronts. You know, of course, that the command is divided by the range of hills? Well, on both sides we're retreating. Have been for days now.'

'I guess you've been had for a sucker, David,' said Wen. 'That just can't be true.' His southern accent was so cosy and his confidence so solid that his charming drawl carried complete conviction. 'Ah'll back our MacArthur against them little, yellow—ah— men. And where'd you hear that stuff, anyway? There's been nothing in the news about all that.'

David hesitated, just as Agnes had done the day before. The announcement from Peking was mentioned by Reuter but I had not seen it in any newspaper, neither had it appeared in the monitoring reports that came into the office every day; from a news point of view it was still an uncomfirmed boast and from my professional point of view, a secret because I knew of the reports of the Commander in Chief made to the Joint Chiefs of Staff in Washington. So, apparently, did David—or was his news really nothing but the single Reuter message—which was true but there was no way David could yet know that it was true.

'I expect David means a story sent from Peking a few days ago,' I said, I hoped smoothly. 'But I haven't seen any confirmation of it. The *Times* did not carry the story. I'm sure of that, because we've all been reading the news from Korea, naturally.'

'I got it from a very firm source,' said David, now stubborn in the face of what I meant as a way out for him but which he took as opposition. He emptied his glass and looked quickly at Agnes across the table and then at Lorry, whose face had taken on the same seriousness she read in her husband's frown. Raising his voice, David went on, 'You must be able to confirm it, Robert; in your job you hear everything—don't you?'

'My dear chap, I'm only a collating clerk for the British staff in the Allied Control Commission here. What would I hear of the Far East? I answer conundrums for my chief about the occupation of Austria, nothing more. You overestimate me, flatteringly enough.'

The housekeeper was pouring out more wine and my spirits sank when David eagerly picked up his glass as soon as she filled it, and emptied it in one drink without even pausing between gulps.

'May I?' he said quickly, and held out his glass again. Lali asked the servant to put the bottle on the table; I had not thought to warn her beforehand—in fact I had forgotten it myself—that David tended to drink too much. The woman now brought out a silver coaster and Lorry Boyd seized on the chance.

'How lovely! I want to get some when we go through London.'

'They were a wedding present,' Lali co-operated without knowing what was wrong. The two Americans, naturally, were not pleased at the suggestion that their national hero was retreating.

The conversation was of silver and antiques for some time and David was quiet, wearing his sulky look, and drinking steadily at least twice as much as the rest of us. While we were debating whether it was better to make a stop in Dublin to buy glass and get the advantage of the lower prices, or whether the higher London prices were compensated for by greater choice and variety. Considering the implications of David's comments, I decided he was simply rather childishly claiming as inside information what was only a snippet of news available to everyone who saw the news agency tapes.

As we moved into the other room again to drink our coffee, Boyd asked me in an undertone whether we could not hear the wireless news; he was evidently still disturbed about the matter. It was too late for the news, but a moment later Kerenyi was announced. He frequently called late in the evening, being very much attached to Lali and the children. As soon as he was introduced, I asked him if there were any fresh news. But there was nothing new and although he had seen the agency message days before, he confirmed me in my opinion that the press in Europe was treating it as unreliable and ignoring it until it should be backed up by some less dubious source than Peking.

'If it is true, and I'm afraid it may be,' he said cautiously, 'there is clearly a news shut-down from Korea and Tokyo until the situation is clear.' This I took to be the responsible view of a serious journalist, knowing in any case that it was indeed so. So I cheered up the Boyds by explaining that Kerenyi certainly knew what he was talking about and there was no need to worry for the moment. They were too glad of the reassurance to notice that it was a false one which took the matter no further.

David was staring at Kerenyi with the puzzled anxiety of a man still just sober enough to know he has drank too much.

'Surely I recognise you from somewhere, don't I?' he asked. He had, I was sure, no intention of sounding uncivil, but a certain note of condescension entered his voice and that made Agnes look across at him with a little shake of her head—not for the first time that evening. But he did not see her.

Georgy replied that he had no recollection of having ever met David before, but they had in fact met and I reminded Kerenyi of it.

'Of course,' cried David, 'before I left the Army—I remember you now. You're the chap who was involved in the Hitler plot!'

This had to be explained to the Boyds, who were much interested though I could see that Georg was bored by their naïve admiration and disclaimed, as he always did, both his own influence in that historical event and its political importance.

'What is more interesting,' he said as soon as he could 'is that *Thoughts on the Control of Power* is to come out in New York and London. Julie phoned me today.' Julie had been in New York again for six weeks on business.

'Oh, Georgy, how wonderful,' both Lali and I cried out together. She embraced him joyfully; her eyes filled with generous tears of joy.

'It can hardly sell, we know that,' Georg said. 'But Julie is overjoyed. It's been a long, hard fight to get recognition for it.'

'I'm sure this is very good news,' David was flippant. 'But what book is it?'

Lali explained. 'It was originally written by an old friend of Georg's who died in the war. The manuscript was smuggled out to Zurich. After the war the Russians made difficulties about its publication. Georg rewrote and expanded it under his own name to circumvent the occupation ban on the original. It came out in Geneva over a year ago—the very same day that Sebastian was born. It's dedicated to him.'

The book was in fact dedicated 'To a Child About to Be Born,' for it was printed before we knew whether our child was a boy or a girl.

'But isn't that plagiarism?' asked David, jealous of attention going elsewhere and pretending to be puzzled.

'Oh, David!' protested Agnes, flushing to her eyes with shame. Lali made a quick movement and opened her lips to speak angrily, but I caught her hand to prevent her. Kerenyi was quite able to take care of himself.

He allowed the silence to develop for a moment before he answered.

'It was a question of getting recognition for important ideas,' he said quietly. 'I couldn't allow my personal pride to stand in the way of their being published. That would have been to continue myself the injustice done to my friend in his life—and in his death.'

Only Lali and myself knew just what Georg meant by this, but it was said in a tone of authority that allowed no question. David said nothing more; yet he had touched, as if by an instinct for cruelty, for just what would most wound, on Kerenyi's fear of appearing to adopt Franz Wedeker's strange prestige for himself. Kerenyi had the moral courage to face that fear in himself and we knew how he struggled with his longing to reject responsibility before he could bring himself to raise his friend a monument in a fashion so open to just such mean-spirited criticism.

'It's a very interesting title,' said Wen rather solemnly. 'I shall most certainly order it straight away. In fact, Lorry, it occurs to me I may be able to help your book, Mr Kerenyi. I mean your friend's book.' He beamed with the pleasure of being helpful as well as relief at being back with business considerations he could understand and I suddenly liked him immensely for that delicacy of 'your friend's book.'

'I'm not in the publishing business myself but I have friends who are, and I believe I may be able to influence a choice for the Political Literature Society of America which would certainly be a great help for you.'

'But, my dear Mr Boyd, you have not yet read the book,' objected Kerenyi gently. 'You may find you do not at all agree with its ideas.'

'Sir,' replied Boyd with perfect dignity, 'if this book had to be smuggled away from the Nazis and is currently condemned by the Russians, it can only be a democratic book.'

'That is very true,' said Georg, succeeding in not smiling. 'And what is more, it is well done—the ideas are not mine but the writing is and I write well. Better than the original author, who was academic and a thinker rather than aesthetic and a writer.'

With all due form they exchanged cards. David, climbing quickly, as he might have said himself with his new Americanisms of speech, on to the bandwagon now that it could be seen to be a sturdy vehicle, congratulated Kerenyi.

'We shall see. Let us hope so. I am sure Mr Boyd will do what he can,' Kerenyi was slightly pompous in his central European way.

'Oh, he certainly can do what he promises,' cried David. 'He's a very influential man indeed. How glad I am we proposed bringing you and Lorry, Wen!' David laughed happily, turning to Agnes, who glowed with pleasure at what might have been a disaster turning out so well. Only Lali raised her eyebrows at the credit thus claimed, and only I saw her, I think.

The evening was indeed righted, and all was amity over the whiskies and sodas so that my fears of future embarrassments for us in either introducing the Stephensons to our friends or in having to evade doing so quite faded. David had learned a good deal in his three years in Washington. When the conversation touched for a moment on the danger of war, his voice did rise but he managed to keep his concern for peace within the bounds of a perfectly respectable desire for restraint by all the powers concerned and only once emphasized a fear of American militarism which was then felt by many people but not often expressed openly. I noticed that when he mentioned the longing of the Russian people for a stable peace in that context, Agnes moved slightly and David slipped quickly off the direction of his remark to a corollary that this longing was, after all, universal. Whether consciously or not, I saw, they had worked out a system of tiny signals by which his neurotic prepossessions were kept under control. And I was very glad of this, not only for reasons of social and personal convenience, but genuinely for Agnes, too. I did not realise then that this very feeling of relief and pleasure was a sign of the strong current of anxiety that Agnes brought with her. But I did notice that there was evidently a level of alcohol intake at which David's subconscious desire for strife could be controlled and, as it were, stabilized.

'What else did Julie say?' Lali reverted to the transatlantic conversation. 'When will she be back? She seems to have been away for about a year!'

'Yes, it does seem a long time,' said Georgy, 'but not as long as when she was making *Anna*.'

This, again, needed to be explained to the other guests, who were all entranced at the idea of a friend we spoke of so intimately being a famous figure in the world of Hollywood, if only of that one film. The new film of *Anna Karenina* was a sensation of the previous season and when they were reminded the Boyds and the

245

Stephensons recalled too the newspaper series in Colton Barber's paper which had given Julia Homburg the spate of publicity that resulted in the film offer being made to her.

'How wonderful for you to know Julia Homburg!' cried Lorry Boyd enviously. 'I would just love to make her acquaintance. I thought she was perfect in that movie. Such a shame she never made any others—but perhaps she's going to?'

'I don't think so,' said Lali dubiously. 'I don't think she got on very well in Hollywood.'

'She never did like film-making,' said Georgy. 'I remember before the war how she tried to avoid it if she could and always teased Hella because she liked the cameras.'

'Oh, Georgy, speaking of Hella. We saw her last night in the Russian comedy. It's simply terrible. How could she be such a fool as to agree to it?'

'She didn't quite agree,' said Georgy judiciously. 'The possible actors drew lots for the cast and she was unlucky, she and the rest.'

'I wonder she didn't manage to get out of her part,' Lali laughed. 'She's usually so clever at getting what she wants!'

'Hella Schneider now has made quite a number of films.' I turned to Mrs Boyd. 'I'm afraid we are very rudely talking about people you don't know.'

'Why no, I'm just fascinated.' She opened her eyes wide. 'If only we could stay and meet them all!'

'What Russian comedy is that?' David sounded interested and a little offended, both at not knowing what the conversation was about and at a Russian play being criticised.

'It's rather interesting. I don't quite agree with Lali,' answered Georgy. 'But to understand what Lali means—you'll discover it for yourselves naturally—you have to know that all the Allies like to persuade the big theatres to put on translations of their own plays. It's easy enough with the British and French—they have such large theatrical repertoires, after all. But the public doesn't seem to like Russian stuff much except for the classics, and neither do the actors.'

'The Americans aren't much better off,' I said slyly, 'look at the flop when *Porgy and Bess* was played here . . .'

'Oh, well, Gershwin . . . But the play we're speaking of is rather fun, I thought. It's about a group of Party activists who are in

246

Moscow to induce one of the Ministries to arrange some action they need in their own district. They all live in the same hotel room, taking it in turns to sleep in the beds, and they have the most complicated and amusing time trying to get in to see some big-wig or other. The play never states what it is they want done, or which Ministry, or where they come from. It's all a quite good idea. Only unfortunately, the central idea is just the thing that we all find funny about the Russians—their inefficiency—how telephone calls never get through, and cables never arrive and trains are held up. I believe it was considered very daring in Moscow.'

'But I can't understand the Russians wanting to put it on. You know, at first the house was half empty every night and now it's full every night of people making fun of the Russians. Especially them all sleeping together in the same beds and queuing up to wash, women and men together. And the scene where the hero is screaming on the telephone in a hurry to get through because he won't get any food at the canteen in five minutes more . . . of course, the public treats it as anti-Russian propaganda.'

'It ought not to be allowed,' said David, getting angry.

I laughed. 'It's a lot better than the production of *Boris Goudounov*. That was really a disaster. The critics slaughtered it. The bass, being Russian, had trouble with co-ordination since the rest of the cast sang in German. And you couldn't see a thing on the stage. It was pitch dark. The public called it *The Dark Continent* and seats had to be filled with free tickets. In the end it became a joke and the audience laughed during the death of Boris every night it was on.'

'You're being dreadfully unfair, Robert,' said Lali, unable to prevent herself laughing at my account, which, as she knew, was quite accurate. 'You don't mention the marvellous production of *Eugene Onegin*. That was so lovely, I cried!'

'Is it still on?' asked David eagerly. 'I've never seen it.'

'Yes, *Onegin* is splendid,' I agreed, 'but that was a Viennese production, and belongs to the nineteenth century. It's not modern Russian.'

'Neither is *Boris*,' Georgy pointed out.

'Well, *Boris* is one of their national monuments. And it was a Russian-directed production.'

'I see you are just as anti-Russian as ever, Robert.' David only just succeeded in sounding pleasant.

'Oh, Robert is an old reactionary, we're all agreed on that,' Georgy said. 'But it is true that the Russians are rather detached from our theatrical notions and some of their ideas seem old-fashioned and cumbersome when one sees them here.'

'It sounds odd to hear the Russians labelled as traditionalist,' said Agnes gently, wanting to soften the exchange while still agreeing with her husband.

'Theatrically, they are very much traditionalists,' Georgy on his own subject, became didactic. To prove his point he reverted to a guest tour of the Moscow Arts company, of which he saw every performance, and in the more familiar conflict between the central European and western views of theatre, the controversial subject of laughing at the Russians, which I should never have allowed to arise, was forgotten. In a slight embarrassment at Georgy's seriousness, which they did not understand, our other guests were united harmoniously.

The Boyds left before David and Agnes, and it was not until we were seeing these latter to the door that David reverted again to his—or, as he maintained, my—neurotic attitude to the Russians.

'I can see, Robert, that you have very much adopted the central European view of the Soviet Union. But, I'll tell you something that you couldn't learn here—you'd have to go to Washington to find it out. And that is, Europeans are so fascinated by the Russians that they ignore the real and present danger of war. That danger comes from Washington, where they have no idea of the realities of war and are not afraid of it, as the Russians are. The Russians have done their expanding and I, for one, don't blame them for it, considering what they suffered. But the Americans are just starting to expand, and it would horrify you to hear the talk in Washington. They believe they are going to rule the world.'

This was a perfectly reasonable point of view which I heard not for the first time. If David had not at dinner spoken of matters that I was pretty sure he could not have lawful cognisance of, I should have been quite convinced by it.

My regular leave of ten days began next morning, but I went into the office, having left some unfinished business there. I checked too with the political intelligence people, privately called the Wild Boys. There was one man there I trusted and he could discretely find out how many people on the staff, in the Control Commission and in the Embassy—at this time there was much overlapping of competencies—*ought* at this time to know about General MacArthur's two reports to the American Chiefs of Staff and how many did in fact know. The messages about those reports were still marked with the highest level of 'classification' that exists. The secrecy grade that is usually referred to, not entirely in jest, as 'burn before reading'. I knew there had been no security leak from my map-room which was almost a one-man business in which my own clerk never even knew such papers came in and out of the office. They were brought in locked bags to which there was only one key and that never left the man in charge of the papers. I read them in this man's presence and he then took them away again. The only reason I was not obliged to go to his office to read such things when I needed to be informed of them was that they sometimes entailed map alterations and I kept the maps.

There was no reason why my request for a security report should cause any remark; it was frequently done as a matter of routine on all kinds of subjects and without warning. I often received such checks myself without knowing what they were about.

The crucial point of this matter, I had better explain, was its timing. A few days later the whole world knew of the Chinese intervention in Korea but at this moment the fact and the discussions about it were entirely an American staff secret of which my knowledge was gained by quite illicit means.

In spite of packing for all four of us, Lali found time that morning to send out cards for an introductory party for the Stephensons to which all our Viennese friends were invited. We then piled ourselves and the nursemaid into the car with the feeling of having deserved our holiday, and set off for Julie's house in Styria.

II

As I must have already made clear, I am of an unexcitable and phlegmatic nature; the great exception to this was always my feeling for Julia Homburg. Initial admiration had deepened long since to an affection tinged almost with awe; the unbridgeable differences of station and attainment and perhaps the difference in age made this feeling a love without physical being but it was love nonetheless attended by all the possessiveness and jealousy usual to an attachment of this platonic nature. Theoretically, I am aware that she is a woman with faults and failings like other human beings but for me her person and character are beyond ordinary judgments and when, as sometimes happened, Lali and Julie clashed over the upbringing of Nando, admiration and glee mingled with trepidation that my gentle Lali should dare to oppose her beloved and formidable friend and Nando's legal guardian.

I met her train, which was late. The maid seen from the distance, bags in her hands, turning her head and calling impatiently for a porter, told me where their compartment was and I hurried down the platform, through the crowd. The moment Julie descended a porter appeared. She did nothing, seeming not to notice the pushing throng or the noise, but stood looking round for me, her tall presence in splendid furs creating at once a space about her by that unselfconsciousness and concentration on the matter in hand that made people call her arrogant. I had not seen her for nearly two months and though she had only left the transatlantic aeroplane twenty-four hours before she did not seem tired.

'Ah, Robert,' she kissed my cheek quietly but still glancing about her as if she expected to see someone besides myself. 'How is the house? Are you settled in? Isn't it nice that we could all get away . . . we've brought the new curtain stuff.' She was wearing a rather full hat of the same furs as her coat and I made a comment on it, as we went down the platform, the porter almost running behind us with his trolley, nagged by the housekeeper as he went.

'I can't wait to get home. Yes, the hat's fun, isn't it. We got the idea from the *Anna* film. In fact, it's the same hat. I have so much to talk about—all sorts of things. Oh, Robert, you've changed cars. Well, it's very grand but I rather liked that old thing you had before. What is it called? Oh, yes I've heard of it.'

'A man was leaving to go home and wanted to get rid of it. He'd have to pay a huge tax on it in England so I got it cheap.' The car was in fact an elderly Rolls and I was very proud of it; we could never have afforded it except under privileged occupation conditions. It suited Julie as if it were made for her.

'It is certainly a lot more comfortable than the old car,' she said as we drove off. 'Isn't it, Frau Lisl?' turning to the housekeeper in the back seat, who was smoothing her hand respectfully over the leather and polished woodwork.

'Such luxury,' murmured Frau Lisl.

'But the coat isn't the same as in *Anna,* is it?' I asked Julie, wheedling a compliment from her.

'How you notice things!' she smiled with affectionate indulgence, giving me what she knew I wanted with that compliance that covered a profound but kind indifference.

'How are the two boys, Herr Doktor?' It was an unspoken agreement that I was never addressed by my military title, just as I never now appeared in Julie's presence in uniform. She had a particular dislike of uniforms, not only those of the occupying powers which I noticed when I first knew her but simply of uniforms.

'They are in wonderful form, thank you, Frau Lisl. Nando is roaring about all the time, being a jet fighter pilot.'

'Yes, Nando is one of the things we must talk about. And I want you to back me up, Robert, that he ought to have a tutor. The nursery school is useless, I'm quite sure. He must start to work before he goes to primary school or we shall never get him into the Theresianum.'

She knew as well as I did that Lali was reluctant to force Nando to work, loving his beguiling idleness. And she knew, too, that this lazy, charming nature worried me in the boy so that I was bound to be her ally.

'We shall see how Lali feels about it,' I said uneasily. She gave me a quick glance.

'It's only natural for a mother to spoil her children, and quite right,' she agreed, 'but that's what the rest of the family is there for;

to balance the spoiling.'

We had put off this discussion before but I could see that this time Julie was determined. She was ambitious for the boy and cared as much as his mother and grandmother for the place of his family in the world. She put into words exactly what I divined in her thoughts.

'The world gets more competitive all the time, and family influence is no longer enough to assure Nando of his rightful place; he has to earn it, too. You know, Robert, those months in America taught me that, more than I ever knew it before. Not that I would want Nando to be like that—concerned with nothing but money, or even concerned with money at all. But the von Kasdas are all born relying on a framework that is simply no longer there.'

We turned now into the hill lane towards the house, and I thought of the first times I had driven up there, bringing first Kerenyi and then Lali to its promise of safety and shelter. Now there was only an early scattering of snow over the hills, brindling the fields; the stand of tall pines to the left on a sudden rise where the Slovenian border ran were black against the pale brilliance of the sunny sky, not yet wearing their winter dress that made them look like a great hang of silver foxes.

'The border,' said Julie, remembering too. 'Did I tell you—I saw Barber in New York, Robert? Poor man, he has still not forgiven himself. That was a strange business!'

'I read his stuff sometimes. He is almost pathologically anti-Communist. Too much so, I find. I don't agree with this demonology that is so fashionable nowadays. It obscures the real question, it seems to me.'

'He's a fanatical nature, you know. I remember him in the Nazi time; he was just as passionate, and without really understanding what it was about even then.'

'He's very fortunate that he doesn't have to understand,' I said disingenuously remembering the second occasion I met Barber, and no doubt my voice sounded cold or resentful for she glanced at me sideways. We had never told anyone but Kerenyi the whole of that incident.

'That's a rather profound remark,' she said, but thoughtfully, not laughing at my seriousness as she sometimes did. 'And that, you see, is the really generous and good thing about that kind of American; they fight the danger without really having been forced to know what it means. Even when they go too far, as I agree Barber does perhaps, and this Senator Taft. But one has to remember that and be grateful.'

Thank God I turned the car carefully into the awkward turn under the gateway; for as I did so a streak of bright colour in a scarlet jersey, Nando, shot across the car's path, arms spread wide, banshee wail audible, being a jet. I jammed the brakes full on and the big motor stopped almost instantly in its track. We all shot forward, Julie bruising her instinctively raised hand and me my ribs against the wheel. Poor Frau Lisl tumbled down between the seats. I was for a second in a towering rage. Flinging open my door, I shouted at the terrified child who had stopped in flight, his eyes tight shut in fear.

'I'll paddle your backside for that,' I yelled in English. 'You know you're not allowed to play in the courtyard!'

I descended and almost staggered with a sudden sensation of weakness and sickness; if I had been driving with the usual swoop down into the courtyard I must inevitably have injured him seriously.

'Daddy!' he wailed and flung himself at me for shelter perhaps as much against my own rage as in realisation of his danger. He burst into tears and I gripped him convulsively, the sensation of his strong little body filling me, as it always did, with the mixture of passionate love, jealousy and irritation with his indiscipline which caused so much trouble.

'You've hurt your Aunt Julie,' I scolded and I could hear my voice shaking. 'And just look at poor Frau Lisl.'

Lali ran out, hearing the uproar and for a moment all was confusion, everyone grasping at the boy, not knowing whether to cuff or kiss him and in the end doing both at once. This fuss slid over into excited greetings and demands for news as we moved into the house and the farm man took the boot keys off me to get out Julie's bags. I could see that Julie was still looking for another presence, but she did not ask where Georgy was.

The kitchen looked very different nowadays, with white paint, a new tiled floor, modern equipment and a big gas range as well as the old coal fire. The lighting was changed to electricity the year before, but the current was not powerful enough to be relied upon for cooking. Besides, as Julie said, gas was cheaper and she had her moments of frugality in small things, just as she would not consent to have the coal range taken out for the sake of space. Who knew, bad times might come again?

She stood in the large kitchen, quite still and her stillness could be more meaningful than many women's activity.

'It's here I think of as home, when I'm away,' she said. 'I shall never forget it as it was when I first saw it again, after the war.'

'We ought to have taken some photographs before it was renovated,' I said. 'We shall forget.'

'I don't think I shall ever forget,' she said softly. As she spoke I relived for an instant the moment when she lit the lamp so that I saw her face and she saw my uniform and became for a moment hostile. She glanced about her restlessly now, and Lali said that Georgy was out shooting with Tom, answering Julie's unspoken question as women do when they are intimate with each other.

'Where is Sebastian?' asked Julie, not commenting on this, and moving towards the living room door. 'Yes, and I dreamed of this room, too while I was in New York. Odd, I never dream of Vienna, only of here.' As she picked up Sebastian and kissed him and he crowed with pleasure, she jerked her chin with a characteristic gesture at Lali. 'You know what I dreamed? Of you, when you were ill, but it wasn't really you, it was Ruth Wedliceny, as she was then when she lived here early in the war. I don't believe in all this psychology stuff, but that dream was a sort of revelation. D'you know how I mean, Robert? As if Ruth were replaced by Lali . . .' She set down the child abstractedly and slipped her coat off her shoulders on to a chair, pushing her hat off her head carelessly with a backwards movement of the hand. 'I remember it quite clearly. I woke up, wondering if Ruth haunted this place—but she wouldn't. If she haunts anywhere, it must be Georgy's old flat . . . When I awoke, the bedroom was terribly overheated and I suppose that's what made me dream so vividly. I remember the feeling of the oppressive heat and airlessness and then I thought, quite clearly to myself—but we saved Lali. Then I fell asleep again.'

'It's very unusual to remember a dream so clearly,' I said, uneasily. She had never before on any hearing mentioned Georgy's lost girl.

'I didn't remember it at once. But I remembered I'd dreamt something important and made an effort to get it back, and it gradually came back. It was uncanny.'

'It is uncanny,' said Lali, and shivered a little. 'You know,

Georgy told me once, just when Sebastian was born, that after Ruth disappeared . . . but perhaps he told you . . . ?'

'No, he hasn't mentioned Ruth by name since—when? Yes, since 1944. That was the last time he was in Vienna before he was captured.'

'He told me that for years he had the feeling that the child lived on inside him; that gave me such a strange feeling. Perhaps we all do live in each other?'

Nando had crept into the open doorway and stood watching us with his own characteristic expression of assessing how far he could venture with us, and particularly with me, after his escapade. There was nothing of calculation in this look; paradoxically, it was of an extraordinary innocence and sweetness, indeed it was normally comical. Yet grown-up for a child of six.

I was determined to teach him a lesson and not let him get away with such dangerous follies just because Julie's return made discipline seem inappropriate.

'Go upstairs, Nando,' I said, trying to sound stern. 'I shall come and talk to you presently.'

'Are you really going to beat him, Robert?' asked Julie when the child was gone after a look at his mother of imploring unbelief that she should thus abandon him to his fate.

'I shall have to,' I said. 'It's awful, but we have to establish some sort of rule of law. The child does just as he likes and that wouldn't matter so much if he had the least sense of self-preservation.'

'Oh, but Robert . . . !' wailed Lali helplessly. 'Don't hit him in cold blood. He will be frightened. You should have walloped him at once . . .'

'Or send him to bed with no supper,' suggested Julie. 'Though that is such a very calculated punishment—my father used to punish me with bed without supper, and for the silliest things.'

'I think that's crueller than hitting him,' I said, 'and what's more you know quite well Frau Lisl or Maria will feed him in secret.'

I was angry again now with the boy for introducing this atmosphere of anxiety into Julie's return, to which I so much looked forward that I was secretly overjoyed when Georgy said casually that morning that he should go shooting after all, instead of going to Graz with me. Graz was a town he much disliked, but that was not the only reason he put off seeing Julie for an hour or so more. I knew he found it easier to greet her in private.

'You must understand my position,' I said now and heard the note of priggishness I so much disliked in myself creep into my voice. 'Out of fear of being hard on Nando because I'm his step-father, I enforce no discipline at all. He's not a biddable child and if he is not to have a bad time at school, he has to learn what is expected of him. I hate punishing him—you both know that —because I'm always afraid of making him dislike me. But, young as he is, I feel sometimes that he knows that instinctively. That's very bad, you know . . .'

'You're quite right, I know,' said Lali miserably. 'But go and get it over, and then we can forget it.'

As I left the room, feeling as if I were going to be beaten myself, I could hear Julie's voice taking the opportunity of suggesting to Lali that the boy needed a tutor. It was typical of her to grasp such a good opening and I found myself on the stairs thinking that if she weren't so wonderful she would be a managing woman.

It's true, the old saying that beating children hurts the beater more than the punished. The little wretch was laughing two min-utes later but I felt like a criminal. However, by the time Kerenyi and Tom returned from shooting with a hare, a pheasant and two fat rabbits, we were all recovered and Julie was creeping on all fours on the living room floor—we still used the small back room although the house was long since fully furnished again—mooing at Sebastian alternately with being a witch while the two children squealed with joy and fear.

'You're an old cow-witch,' yelled Nando, flying at her and then jumping away again as she again turned into a witch with an in-stantaneous trick of mimicry that one could never analyse no matter how often one saw it. 'Julie-witch, Julie-witch . . .' He stopped in the middle of the chant and listened, with his head on one side. 'They're back!' he cried and rushed out to the kitchen. She made a final moo at Sebastian and then rose to her feet, picking him up quickly and covering his flushed, little, round face with kisses and blowing in a special secret kiss she had for him on the back of his neck, which made him delirious with pleasure.

As she set him back on the floor, crowing and bubbling, I had the sudden impression that she was nervous, more than expectant, almost apprehensive. She pulled her belt straight and pushed her long, ringless hands through her untidy hair; as the door reopened

—Nando had slammed it—I heard her catch her breath. I did not want to see this and moved towards the kitchen saying something about inspecting their bag.

Kerenyi was in the doorway; his eyes on Julie, he did not see me. I knew that she was looking at him with that same expression and what had always been unthinkable was suddenly an accomplished fact. He said nothing but I heard her whisper something breathlessly and another glimpse of his eyes confirmed my intrusion as I went out.

I have no idea what I said but there must have been something in my voice for Lali shot me a look when I spoke to Tom and a moment later Sebastian, being abandoned by us all, gave a bawl of rage. Lali turned at once, but gave me a second look and then called to Maria, who was doing something at the sink, to fetch Sebastian. When Maria came back she was flushed and giggling and she nudged Frau Lisl with a murmured remark in dialect as she took the child through towards the main stairs.

'What a day!' said Lali. 'I'll come down and help you with that, Tom.'

She took him away, and I was grateful to her, because she was not jealous of my jealousy, and I knew she understood in her own way. In a few minutes I was able to be truly glad for them not to be alone after so many years, and not to be tormenting each other as they had since Georg's return. Now that it was out in the open I knew that we had always known it; the past made it seem impossible, but it was always there and I myself would not have been startled if we had not all been upset over Nando's narrow escape that morning.

'But why so suddenly?' demanded Lali at dinner. 'You've been quarrelling for years in a way that made it perfectly obvious to everybody but yourselves, and now you suddenly make up your minds.'

'The second separation, I suppose,' said Julie, laughing. 'I felt awful when I left for New York and I felt then that things couldn't go on much longer as they were. And when I came back in that dreadful plane, I was panicky in case he didn't feel the same.'

'You must have been making yourself panicky then,' said Georg, 'You knew quite well how I felt. *I've* known for years—I can even tell you when I knew.'

'When?' she said, and flushed as if she knew the answer.

'In Poland, during the war. I can see you remember as well as I do.'

'Well, I think it's wonderful, the things everybody knows without knowing.' Tom raised his glass to Julie. 'And, come to think of it, I must have known something too, ordering this case of champagne as I did.'

'And now that's enough about us,' said Georgy. 'Tell us all your news from the new world.'

'You know all about the book . . . what comes next? I suppose, Colton Barber. He wrote me a note and we dined together. He is coming for three months soon, for what he calls a swing through eastern Europe, but is still waiting for some of the visas.'

'That will be a depressing job,' said Georg.

'The Belgrade government is making difficulties about letting him go there, but Barber said they will give in in the end because the State Department has taken the matter up for him.'

'I don't quite understand why Yugoslavia should hesitate,' I said. 'He backs them up in his paper against the Russians.'

'Perhaps because of the way he strayed over the border that time,' suggested Georg.

Julie laughed at me. 'How you dislike poor Barber, Robert. He's really a very nice, sincere man.'

'I don't dislike him. But I do distrust this messianic, this almost mystic, attitude about the satellite countries. It's dangerous to talk about liberating eastern Europe. And with the war in Korea in such a worrying state it really almost amounts to warmongering.'

'Don't you think it is the war in Korea that has sharpened all these passions?' asked Kerenyi.

'Well, yes, I think so, and that's what I mean in fact. The situation in Europe as well as in the Far East is so chancy, I think responsible newspapers ought to be as careful as diplomats.'

'If Barber were here he would say you are compromising,' Kerenyi laughed, remembering the night Barber was in the house.

'No, Georgy, he wouldn't say that any more,' Julie shook her head. 'He's changed in that way, if in no other. He talked for hours about the time he spent in a Communist prison. He called it the turning point in his life, and I do honestly think he behaved so honourably when he got out that we ought to respect him for it. After all, my difficulties in Vienna could have dragged on for years if Barber hadn't made such a handsome recantation of the harm he did me—and made his paper print it. And I don't think it was easy for him, from the way he spoke of it.'

'I don't suppose it was easy to persuade his editor, no,' said Georg a little grimly. 'But he certainly owed you that apology and explanation. And, of course, it was a highly dramatic story. A first-class, thrilling personal confession, from a newspaper point of view.'

'I didn't read it,' said Tom. 'Tell me about it.'

'It was a whole series about the dangers of totalitarianism. But the first one was the one. A terrific self-accusation of how he judged others but when he was only a day or so under the pressure Julia Homburg lived under for years, he gave in to save his skin. What a terrible thing tyranny is and how only the strongest characters can resist it. And so on. That story, a full page headed "I Accuse Myself" was a world sensation. It was translanted all over the place, and Julie got thousands of letters and offers and gifts.'

'An oil millionaire in Texas wanted to marry me, and they wanted to make a film of the whole story. I refused, of course, but that was how I came to get the offer to play *Anna Karenina* in Hollywood.' Julie shook her head, laughing at the memory.

As we were making ready for bed and already yawning, Lali remembered about the Stephensons.

'I like her better than him, but they're both nice,' she said to Julie, 'and he's so keen on getting to know people. So do come, won't you darling? It won't be a vast party—I know you hate them —and it's supper, not cocktails.'

'Of course I'll come, little one,' Julie agreed with that easygoing kindness which, like her forgiveness of Barber, was the outcome of a deep indifference to almost everything in the world. Mundel—long since become a friend and occasional drinking companion—once told me that even the exile from the theatre when I first knew her was more the product of weariness of spirit and loss of belief in her work than a genuine rebellion of anger.

'I thought you didn't like him much, Lali. I felt rather I was forcing them on you but we don't have to do any more than this one party. After that, it's up to them.'

'Oh yes, I quite like him, he's rather sweet. He gave me a protective feeling.' She laughed at their smiles of teasing affection. 'You know how I love to take care of people perfectly able to take care of themselves.'

'You're a good girl,' said Tom, 'a really good girl.'

'Ah, you!' she said. 'I really do have to take care of you. Why don't you come back to Vienna with us and come to the party? It's only a day or so more away from your old farm.'

'I might do that, I haven't seen Stephenson since he was demobilised.'

'He's changed,' I said, and wondered at the slight doubt in Tom's look.

'Has he?' asked Kerenyi, doubt in his voice too.

'You do recall him, then?' I said unwisely. I had, of course, never discussed David Stephenson with Tom, and was annoyed with myself now for saying what could imply not only that I'd discussed him with Kerenyi—which I had not—but what sounded like a confirmation that David needed to change.

'I remembered him when I thought back,' said Georg. 'I find I often have a vagueness about things and people at that time. I suppose I was a bit dotty.'

'You were a wreck,' said Tom with the candour of an old friend. 'But you've improved lately, I think. You'll beat me at fishing yet.' Kerenyi had twice been to Ireland to stay with Tom.

'When you beat him at chess, he'll catch a bigger salmon than you!' cried Julie. Her English had enormously improved, or recovered itself, in the last year or so. This happened to most people who mixed at all with *die Okkupanten;* but Julie had a strong and charming accent with a flavour of French in it, French being her real second language.

'Well—chess! I can't keep up with you intellectuals at chess . . .'

'And speaking of fishing,' said Julie, plucking scornfully at the frayed cuff of Tom's filthy, old tweed jacket, 'I hope you've all brought a decent set of clothes with you? You know we have to go to Church on Sunday?'

'Of course,' I assured her. 'Lali's even brought a hat and Tom is going to wear a coronet, aren't you, Tom?'

'Certainly. It's in my room, wrapped in a bandanna handkerchief.'

With that inward look I had often seen while she was pregnant, Lali was listening, her head on one side.

'I think I hear 'Bastian. I'll go on up.'

I yawned, feeling the wine pleasantly. 'I'll come with you. Early start tomorrow, you boozers, remember . . .'

Both Tom and Kerenyi could drink half the night and be as

fresh as ever at five-thirty but I, somewhat to my chagrin, needed my sleep.

The next day was wonderful, a real 'Steffelsgut day', as we said. The dark November sky, swagging low with huge clouds like great bunches of purple grapes, was moved constantly by a strong, wayward wind. It was not cold; there was quick squalls of rain and every bush and tree was sharply outlined and double-real. We were out all day and Lali—she could never shoot because of her horror of hurting anything living—brought the children out for a bundled-up picnic lunch in the sold-off Army Land Rover used for a farm station wagon. She wore a pair of jodhpurs and this reminded Julie of a new plan.

'I've decided I will buy a couple of horses, after all. The money people say I can afford to keep another man here.' The farm land was worked by a married couple, rarely seen, the woman taking care of the house during its long emptinesses.

'Julie, how wonderful! Can I come to the sales with you?'

'With me?' said Julie laughing at Lali's eagerness. 'You'll have to go alone to the sales! I mean to push it all onto you. It's time Nando started to know one end of a pony from the other.'

'I say,' interrupted Tom, understanding, apparently by second sight that they spoke of horses. 'Come to my place, Lali. My neighbours breed and I'm sure you'd get a bargain. They fly bloodstock all over the place nowadays, and if you get a young stallion you can breed a bit. It's really an investment; you could make some splendid foals, cross-bred with the Arab strains you have here and if things improve a bit, with the Hungarian stock, which I believe is badly in need of blood strains.'

'The Hungarians,' objected Julie blankly. 'We can't even get over the border.'

'You'd be surprised,' said Tom, now in his element, 'the things that horses do to closed frontiers. My neighbours sold two mares to a Russian State Farm last year—wait a minute and I'll recall the name . . .'

'Look here, Julie, I believe Tom's got a good idea,' Kerenyi put in. 'We could certainly cover costs and perhaps make up some of the expense of this place. It's pure luxury as it is, you know.'

'You're right there,' Julie sounded rueful. 'With the new timber, I used up all my share of the farming; really the only advantage of keeping it—financially I mean, is the tax rebates it gets me.'

'Don't the forestry people help with the cost of the timbering, Julie?' I asked. 'I thought they did, where the trees are a real need?'

'No,' she said. 'My total income is too high, it seems. I believe I'm supposed to get some war damage credit or something but, naturally, that won't be regulated for twenty years yet. Young Pohaisky says the coalition can't agree, so the law hasn't even got to the Allied Commission yet, for approval.'

We descended now from the Land Rover and Nando was pulling at my belt to persuade me to show him the bag. Unlike his mother, he had a boyish, bloodthirsty streak. The two of us moved across to the other side of a spindleberry bush, and I thought for the thousandth time on seeing one of the lovely things, that was what the burning bush in the Bible was like. The others were talking again about horses, and Kerenyi said something in answer to a question about business from Julie that all that could be left until after they were married.

The wind at that moment blustered and the soft brilliance of spindleberries on arid twigs from which the last dry leaves flew, blurred my vision of Georg and Julie behind it.

She said, in that clear, challenging voice so impossible to describe, 'Married? But, my dear, we aren't going to be married! We don't have to go in for all that formality, you and I.'

'Of course we're going to be married,' he said brusquely.

The mittened hand slipped out of mine, and the constant habit of attention to children reasserted itself. Nando put out his arms as if to embrace the bush that ranged well above his head, his head uptilted to take its beauty in, and I saw his shining eyes, so like his mother's, dreamy and wide.

'D'you think it's the bush in that story Mummy read to me?' he asked in an awed voice. His recollection of the children's Bible story at bedtime was so in tune with my own more direct knowledge of the myth that I was moved by our sharing so intimate an experience; I was always conscious that he was not my son and it seemed a strange and happy omen that we should both have this thought.

'I think it must be the same. Though I don't know if this kind of bush grows there where the Bible story was. But something very like it, you know?'

'Is it different there?' he asked, lifting his serious eyes, so rarely serious, not able to grasp that the desert land of the Levant could be other than his own familiar landscape of grass, of the urbane and elegant greys of Vienna, or distant peaks with that snow he was still not aware of remembering. 'I'm sure it *is* the same tree,' he said firmly. It was the vision that made a thousand medieval religious paintings of Bethlehem in the form of European villages; and, of course, it was in a sense right that this burning bush in the dark, clear day of almost winter was and must have been for time out of mind, for millions the burning bush. I stopped myself in time from trying to explain everything; he was showing me, not me him, the process of absorption of knowledge, the apprehension of ancient transmitted thought and insight which is carried on from generation to generation. I was oppressed with the deep responsibility of the elder who is just wise enough to know he is not necessarily the wiser.

'We mustn't quarrel,' said Julie, later in the small living room, 'so Robert, you stay and hold the balance. Because we clearly have to have this question out.'

Kerenyi gave his bark of laughter that meant some appreciation of absurdity that was never amusement; amused, he laughed quite differently—with the children, for instance. I was mending a children's toy, a decrepit and mangy white dog of Nando's, by now become Sebastian's favourite bedmate which by some strange chance of nursery unlogic had been dragged out of doors where it got under a farm implement. Frau Lisl found a curved carpet needle but was not allowed to mend the thing; I must do that with a stout linen thread and some fresh sawdust baked in the oven to kill at least some of the germs.

'Darling, doesn't it occur to you that Robert would rather not be the umpire in this discussion?'

'Of course it occurs to me,' she said with her calm stringency. 'But I haven't waited most of my life to get a real family so that they can get out of the nasty bits. I'd have waited for Lali but I know in advance that she would side with you and take no notice of rational argument.'

'Rational argument being what you want done?'

'Of course.'

'You're quite wrong, too, if you think Robert will inevitably be on your side. Robert is for convention and tradition, even when they don't happen to suit his own wishes . . . aren't you, Robert?' He shot me his secretive, 'clever' look so that I was obliged to laugh.

'I'm for maintaining the framework of living, yes,' I admitted. 'But I really don't see—in your case—much reason for formalising your relationship. I hope you don't mind me saying what I really think—since you have dragged me into your private life?'

'There you are, Georgy—just what I said!'

'Wait a bit. I haven't finished.' But as if she guessed she waved me silent.

'And what about domestic arrangements?' he asked. 'I am not, I suppose, a very domestic animal, but I think it might be rather interesting to live—actually live—with Julie.'

'Well, why not? The apartment is huge. It's already been re-arranged so that two other people live there—why not three?'

'Mundel and Frau Pohaisky were brought in by the chances of war and occupation. Partly for mutual protection, partly to keep the housing authorities quiet. It is not an arrangement that can last for ever.'

'I certainly can't ask them to go,' said Julie.

'There won't be any need to. Things have settled down now. The Pohaisky apartment is still requisitioned, so Margarete is entitled to a small flat of her own and she can easily get one. In fact I rather think she could get her own apartment back, since fortunately the Yanks have it. When we announce our approaching marriage, they will both make other arrangements. It's as simple as that.'

'Margarete has been very good to me. I can't condemn her to loneliness now—she's getting on, you know.'

'Margarete Pohaisky knows more people than I do. If it comes to that, she even has a husband.'

'You know he will never leave the von Kasda place again. He's a total cripple.'

'Frau Pohaisky is a genuine problem, Georgy,' I interjected. 'But, wait . . .' I stopped what I was about to say and busied myself with the problem of eyes. 'I shall have to get another needle for these things.'

'There's sewing stuff in the drawer there,' said Julie, knowing I was hedging. 'What were you going to suggest?' she added suspiciously. She picked up one of the yellow and black glass eyes and examined the back. 'Yes, they've got little holes through, just like buttons.' She rose—we were sitting at the centre table where the lamp stood—and went over to the side table to find me a needle fine enough for the eyes.

'How's this one?' she asked, bending over me, and passing her hand in front of me to pick up one of the glass buttons. 'Robert, let Frau Lisl do it—it's a finicky job for you, and Sebastian need not know.'

'I don't mind doing it,' I said. She put her hand for a moment on my bent shoulder. I could feel its slight but noticeable tremor and was intensely aware that they were not talking about what was really in their minds. I suspected her of touching me deliberately so that I should know how deeply disturbed she was. 'And Sebastian might guess; then he would feel I couldn't be bothered. You know how children are . . .'

Julie skirted the table, touched the stove to feel its warmth and glanced with her quick frown at the closed door to the kitchen. She did not sit down at once, but gripped the back of her chair, staring at the door.

'They are keeping away so that we can talk in peace,' she said as if angry, giving the last word an almost savage tone.

'Rubbish,' I said to the still grubby plush, feeling through it for the hole of the button with the fresh needle. 'Both Tom and Lali have a lot to do. It's his turn to clean the guns.'

Kerenyi rose too, pushing back his chair harshly over the wide and uneven wooden planks of the floor, nowadays kept smoothly polished. He took Julie by the shoulders and turned her to face him, looking down into her reluctant face with narrowed eyes so that he looked more like a judge assessing a witness than a lover persuading his mistress.

'You can't live with the past for ever,' he said quietly, with suppressed force. 'Or not, at least, with the past and me too. You are making me feel like a cannibal as I never did over the book. We belong together—because of the past as much as anything else.' She made a sharp confused movement and he let her go. 'If you would think about it, you would understand that I'm right,' he said bitterly, 'but you won't think about it.'

He turned away from Julie and went with his slightly halting gait to the far door. His face reminded me of its look when he was first in this house, of bitter shame and anger.

'We shall waste the last sweetness of our lives. Just as we've wasted the last four years.' He went out and left the heavy door swinging. It creaked on its hinges and the subdued clatter of table silver could be heard as someone laid the table in the dining room.

'No, Georgy! Wait!' She started forward to follow him, and then stopped, staring in front of her at nothing, the sharp frown between her brows.

'It's hard for him,' she said to me, 'he can't . . .'

'I think you mean, you can't,' I answered. It was the first time I had ever wanted to hurt her or dreamed I could do so. But I loved Georgy too, and it hurt me for him that she shamed his manhood in some way that I, without having lived in their past, could not put a finger on. Because to me she was perfect, I wanted her to be perfect and behave with perfect understanding and magnanimity. 'You humiliate him; you've known him so long and yet you hardly know him at all.'

And the strange thing is, she knew this.

'What do you mean?' she cried angrily, and stopped short. 'I can't. I can't.' She turned on me. 'You don't understand. We should quarrel all the time.'

'Big news,' I said crudely. 'Well, I think that's the best I can do with poor old Neddy.'

'He is ghastly, isn't he?' She picked the horrid object up, deformed and crooked, patchy from washing, one eye higher than the other so that the edge of the plush showed raw underneath it. 'A monster!'

She half turned and gave me a considering look.

On the way to the door, she remembered her manners, saying rather breathlessly, 'It's all right if I take it up to Sebastian, is it? Listen Robert, I do want—I do want nothing to happen to them like it happened to us.'

'Yes. If only we could control things. But even your innocent American has discovered that we can't.'

She came slowly back towards me, holding the grotesque toy in front of her, somehow awkwardly.

'You sound so bitter,' she said doubtfully. 'And I don't mean about the state of the world, either.'

Though it was now clear there was more to be said, I did not get up, but with a perhaps not very pleasant sensation of, for once, being more in command of a situation than Julie was, remained seated while she stood before me.

'My feelings are rather mixed,' I said slowly, 'and that makes me

feel even more strongly than I might otherwise do, that you ought
—yes, ought—to think about this situation. I just can "guess" how
hard it is for you. But there are other things. The children, for
instance. Naturally, you and Georgy won't live your lives only for
the family, but consider how bad it will be in a few years' time for
Nando, to know that his Julie-witch lives . . . You see what I mean?
The world is in a quite bad enough state without us adding our bit
of disorder to it . . .'

She was staring at me with the sharp frown between her brows as
if she were trying to see into me—which I suppose she was. But she
said nothing and at last I went on.

'You know how I feel about you—and Georgy. That doesn't give
me the right to interfere, but Nando does. I felt today, while he was
talking about the spindleberry bush, that for the first time we really
understood each other. I am conscious—very conscious—that it was
I who needed to overcome something, not Nando. He's perfectly
prepared to trust me, his little faults are the faults of goodness,
openness—there isn't a scrap of meanness in him.'

'Well, go on!' she said impatiently, after a long wait.

'What I'm trying to say is that after I'd made the effort and
overcome my inhibition, or jealousy or whatever it was, there was a
marvellous feeling of—liberty.' The sewing things and scraps were
now all gathered together; I was busy doing that. I got up to go to
the stove to burn the oddments. Julie put a hand on my arm and
for a slow moment we stared nakedly into each other's eyes.

'Of course, in reality I'm less free even than I was before. But I
don't feel less free.'

'There's a great difference in the two situations,' she said
tersely. 'A very great difference. You don't know what you are
talking about.'

'I know that,' I said. 'But the barrier you put up is no longer
real—you're holding it up deliberately.'

'Oh!' she cried, 'why do I have to live with such brutal oafs!
You're impossible!' She left the room quickly, almost running, and
slammed the door behind her so that it could be heard all over the
house.

III

From myself and Tom the habit had been adopted of drinks before dinner but we no longer took them from the kitchen cupboard in coarse tumblers. A painted low cupboard in the hall contained the bottles, decanters and glasses and the draught from the front door was deflected by a heavy leather screen that we decided, when Lali and I found it a year before, looked vaguely Spanish. The locally carved staircase, its low treads now polished like all the floors, and a red and black Afghan were reflected in a stained old pier glass. Tom said with satisfaction every time he was there that this was gracious living, an expression he was oddly fond of; better than drinking in his own farm kitchen, as he said.

In those days there were still purchases to be made of things whose origins were better not enquired into. Just as the property of Julie's mother and stepfather was scattered to all the winds of heaven, so the possessions of other families came into our hands by way of exchange. Sometimes things of great value were to be bought cheap in country towns, and there were stories of people who went back to towns near their homes and rebought their own property. This had not happened to Julie, possibly because she never lived long in that house before the war, and would hardly have recognised any of its furnishings except a picture or two, or the candelabrum she remembered.

I think we all felt satisfaction in having cobbled something together which acquired value not only from us and our usage, but from adopting homeless objects and giving them a place, just as we supposed that others did for the stuff looted from here, and from a thousand houses like the von Kasdas', which I had never seen.

I stood, leaning one elbow on the lowest support of the banister, and drinking Barack with Georg, who sat on the bottom step. We heard Tom's voice and I found the courage to speak to him before Tom came in.

'Don't push her, Georg. She's coming round. I'm sure.'

He gave me his shrewd look, upwards and sideways, through the smoke of his cigarette.

'If she is, it's only because I'm pushing her,' he said dryly. He got up with an exaggerated groan from his uncomfortable seat to give Tom a drink. The groan was for my benefit; Georg was taking up copies of English conventions such as pretending that men never talk of private matters.

'About those horses,' he said, handing Tom whisky and water. 'I've thought of a difficulty. How can we know there will be a riding public, so to speak? Perhaps it's finished for ever?'

'Oh, surely not,' Tom was both amused and shocked. 'You're such a townsman, Georg. I'm sure Lali would never have such a notion.'

'Lots of people will be just as keen as Lali herself is,' I pointed out.

'And the Lippizaner—no sign of their fame fading.'

'Yes, but the Spanish horses are a show-piece; their popularity may be partly artificial—tourist stuff.'

'You just don't understand about bloodstock,' Tom shook his head. 'Of course, we have to go into the whole thing in a business-like fashion at both ends. But there's no doubt at all that good horseflesh has kept and will keep its value.'

'But here,' persisted Georg, 'who knows what may happen? The Russians—if the Americans withdraw from here over this war in Korea?'

I looked up the shadowed stairway to make sure Lali was not on her way down. 'If you're thinking of what Stephenson said the other evening, I wouldn't take him too seriously, Georgy. He was painting things blacker than they are—he always did have a tendency to do that; the Americans aren't going to pull out of Europe. Think of Berlin.'

'I suppose you are right, but a lot of sensible men in Vienna are worried that the Americans will have their hands too full to worry much about us for the next year or so.'

'The investment of prestige and money is now too great for any part of Europe to be given up. Berlin can't be held if even a kilometre is lost, and the Americans know that.'

'I suppose we all underestimate the huge size of the American economy,' said Georg thoughtfully. 'Let's hope it's as immense as they are always boasting.'

'Tell me about the Stephensons,' suggested Tom, who became as uneasy as Lali did at any talk approaching the political. 'How is Agnes?'

'She seemed well—and I thought, happy. They have two children, did you know?'

'I'm glad of that. He needed something to steady him down. He was a bit wild, like my brother.' Tom looked at Kerenyi. 'Did you know Stephenson, Georg? I can't recall.'

'Very slightly,' said Georg. 'But from what I saw of your brother I wouldn't have said there was much resemblance.'

'Oh, the old boy was a madcap as a youngster,' said Tom uncomfortably. 'He ran away to sea when he was sixteen. Hated Eton, you know.'

I could not help noticing how false we all became as soon as we spoke of David Stephenson, for no apparent reason. Even Georg, perhaps because of the memory of David's insulting remark to him, was stiff and frowned thoughtfully into his glass as if he considered something in it that worried him, almost like a man trying to decide whether he should mention something embarrassing.

This came strongly home to me when Julie came down with Lali, for here was a situation which might well have oppressed or embarrassed each of our circle for one or another reason; yet our mutual consciousness of a serious threat to our peace of mind was not accompanied by any of the rather vulgar insincerity with which we spoke of David and Agnes. Why, for instance, had I gratuitously said I thought Agnes happy? I was quite sure in fact that she was not and could not be happy. And I was equally sure that Tom, the most truthful of men, saw no resemblance between David and his elder brother.

There was, as always, much to talk about that need not touch on painful realities, and Julie, Kerenyi and Tom were all practiced in the gentle art of avoiding their own unhappiness. We could even speak of tomorrow's Mass, which was to include the dedication of a bronze plaque to the memory of Julie's mother and step-father; we spoke of this without jokes but also without bitterness. Julie's long anger with the local people seemed almost suddenly to have burned itself out, and she spoke of them with indifference as having, some of them, wished to contribute to the cost of the bronze; she refused these contributions, suggesting they should go instead to the local hospital. Her indifference was in striking contrast with the still ferocious contempt and mockery she showed when speaking of the same people to me only a few weeks before on some trivial matter of business in which their normal, stupid slyness had been demonstrated.

'They can't help it,' she said slowly, 'and people can't be changed. It's just the same in the theatre. We are hopelessly out of date and only just beginning to adopt new plays, specially new, foreign plays. Which we then proceed to ruin by using our old techniques on them.'

'But you've never been an advocate of naturalism for everything, have you, Julie?' Lali wanted to know.

'Not for everything, no. Not for Goethe, not for much of Shakespeare, though some of the work done on the comedies in England during the war and since is good and interesting in a very naturalist way. What is that theatre called, Georgy, the one that sent us a guest group?'

'I expect you mean the Old Vic, don't you? Though it's a man at the Memorial Theatre at Stratford who is doing much of the work I think you mean.'

'Yes, Old Vic; I knew it was a funny name, but I couldn't remember what. I don't know if I quite go as far as that man from Stratford—he seemed to me to make the poetry secondary to all that business when I saw his production of *As You Like It* in Munich last year. But I should like to see a lot more "ordinariness" in some Greek productions, for instance. I wanted to get a series of Aeschylus; *Suppliants, The Persians* and *Prometheus* for the next season—I mean, for 1951—approved. Then follow with the *Oresteia* the next year. But just the very people took up the idea with enthusiasm whom I knew would storm about, ranting and howling and losing the hieratic, priestly feeling and the sense of the actions. So I dropped the whole campaign for a year or so.'

She looked across the table at Georgy with a quick smile of complicity. 'I know you think I should have persisted. But you were so busy with the book then, I knew I couldn't expect much press support against the Old Gang of the critics. And how right I was —just remember that awful bawling and banging production of Sartre's *Huis Clos*. A total disaster. And all the greybeard critics here and in Germany praised it!'

'The public certainly showed more sense of theatre than the critics, there,' I said.

'They sometimes do, fortunately.'

'We could take up the campaign publicly next spring,' suggested Georg thoughtfully. 'I've been asked to speak at the Theatre Critics' Seminar at Salzburg, so that it could seem as if I had the Festival in mind in the first instance . . . how would that be for tactics . . . ?'

'Mm—we must give it some thought; it needs careful planning, but Salzburg is not a bad idea. The discussion—or dispute—would be removed from the local atmosphere to an international stage. Of course, you'd be very unpopular. Half Vienna would start screaming about disloyalty and treachery in allowing foreigners to interfere in our tradition, and all that stuff.'

'That would surely be an advantage. Vienna is so provincial since the war, so cut off from the modern world—and not only in the theatre.'

Julie narrowed her eyes to view the prospect. 'I should be pretty unpopular, too. But then, my views are not unknown. But I'd be accused of putting you up to it.'

'With justice,' I pointed out. 'You are putting him up to it.'

She shot me a sharp look, and I thought that this time I was really going to be rebuked with asperity. Lali interrupted, however, and if Julie did mean to pay me out for my 'brutality' while we were alone, she changed her mind.

'You haven't much to lose, Julie. You have a good many enemies in any case.'

'The penalty of being proved in the right,' said Georgy. 'You were a bit too completely in the right a couple of years ago, when you came back to Vienna . . .'

'Hmm,' she said pretending to be rueful, 'you're right there, Lali.'

'It wouldn't be the first time we've engaged in a little intrigue together,' said Georgy, who clearly liked the idea. 'You know, I think I'll write something about it. The need for new techniques with new playwrights—that sort of thing.'

He meant an article in the rather high-brow monthly he now edited.

'No, no, that would really set the cat among the pigeons,' laughed Julie. 'We have to work this out with great care. I think Salzburg is a much better backdrop. There it won't be immediately obvious that we've plotted together . . .'

'But why should it not be obvious?' asked Lali softly. She turned, then, sideways, and began to talk to Tom about the idea of his coming to Vienna for a few days. For some time both Julie and Georg said nothing, but during the rest of the evening a change began to take place in the atmosphere between them as if their professional intimacy were widening its scope into their private lives.

Nothing more was said during the following days, about marriage between Julie and Kerenyi. This is not to say that nothing happened; on the contrary, after the discussion about co-operation between Kerenyi and Julie over theatre politics—a co-operation which went back to before the war and was far from being a new idea—the feeling between them began noticeably to change and mainly from Julie's side. Several times I caught her watching Georg with that considering look she gave me when she took Sebastian's toy dog from me. Then the sharp frown would appear between her brows and she would give her shoulders a little shake. It was not designed, the way she did it; it was simply that the physical expression of feeling was her business in life and she could not help it coming into her own private life any more than I could help always thinking of security or Georg seeing all things as printed words.

I wondered often how, since the barrier to the past was still so high and strong, she could have encouraged Georg to work on her husband's book. At some time they must surely have found it unavoidable to mention him directly? I was sure, however, that her husband never had been mentioned between them since that morning after Kerenyi was freed from the pen, and that, had Julie been present when the Stephensons and the Boyds dined with us, Georgy would not then have defended himself by explaining his actions but would have allowed the matter to pass in silence. In him too there was a high barrier, and I knew enough to know that the memory of the girl transported in 1941 was for him a grim comment on his whole conduct during the war—outwardly so honourable—and a chief cause of his respect for Julie's silence.

Those days, or rather those evenings, for we were all together only in the evenings, were not strained and certainly not unhappy. A pervasion of the house began. The ghosts were exorcised and a new spirit came to join us, a spirit long constrained and prisoned, the release of a possible happiness; an ease from a desperate control on Georg's part and an inward stillness on hers. I do not know, of course, when they became lovers in the usual sense of the term. But I did know that for years—I should have known it from my own nature even if it had not been almost palpable in Georg because we knew each other from the start so well and without speech—his

273

celibacy was a torment to him. Clearly, one could not love a woman like Julia Homburg and content oneself with anything less.

So a lovely gaiety spread among us, gradually and surely, which would never be without its fierce struggles; they were both too demanding and proud for peace.

The wind raged round the house over the weekend; on Monday afternoon I was sorry when it suddenly dropped for I liked to remember the storm piping, pulling and buffeting the house when I first knew it, and to feel now the security and soundness of the walls and shutters that kept it out. The weather changed to a still, bright frost, with rime stiffening in whiteness trees, grasses and bushes so that the children were in a wonderland of their own height in the garden and fields, every twig and blade and withered flower on its stalk iced and outlined, and the trees above them clattering their branches together mysteriously in a thin breeze that never reached to the ground.

Since the shock with the car, Nando had not been a jet pilot, but he now found a new measure for his adventurousness; Tom taught him to skate on the little duckpond, smelly in summer but now rapturously frozen clean. The child would shoot down the slope on to the ice with wild whoops of terror and joy and we had a lot of trouble preventing the muffled bundle of Sebastian trying to emulate him. Naturally, Nando had to skate alone as soon as he could balance himself, and persuaded Maria to strap on his skates while we were out shooting; equally naturally it ended in a cut forehead and swollen nose.

'What on earth have you done to your face?' Tom asked sternly when he saw the boy.

The child replied in his quaint, precise English. 'I fell on my nose. Tom, will you show me that turn again tomorrow? I can't get it right.'

'I don't know that your mother will let me do that,' said Tom, looking round at Lali. 'You promised me you wouldn't go on the ice alone.'

'But I didn't go alone, Maria went with me. She did go away again, after a bit, because she got so cold, but I didn't *go* alone.'

'But how did you fall on your face? You should fall on your bottom!'

'Well, the slope's a bit bumby. I tipped over. It did hurt!'

'You mean bumpy,' I said. 'What are we to do with you, you

little horror? You're supposed to skate on ice, not run down the slope on your skates.'

'The slope is icy too,' he pointed out logically, 'and it's such a funny feeling.'

'It must have felt very funny when you bumped your head!' said Julie. She turned the child's head up with her hand curved under his chin, the better to see the damage. 'It's quite a cut.'

'It looks worse than it is,' said Lali. 'The iodine makes it discoloured.' She sighed. 'You'll all just have to get used to him being a von Kasda. He'll never be like you and Georgy, Robert. He's not going to have any brains at all, none of our chaps ever have. He'll always be doing things like this.'

'I didn't cry a bit,' offered Nando, as if that were a mitigation of his naughtiness, which it was.

Julie laughed outright and said in French so that he could not understand her, 'He has plenty of brains it seems to me.'

'I mean book-brains,' explained Lali. 'I think he's going to be a farmer. He talks about staying here and not wanting to go back.'

'He could do worse,' said Georgy, coming in and hearing the last of the remark.

'I smell a plot,' said Julie, and to Tom, 'You're encouraging him not to want to go to school.'

'We've never even mentioned school,' Tom denied it cheerfully. 'But I think his mother's right; he'll never make a scholar. He's going to be a countryman, aren't you Nando?'

'What's a countryman?' asked Nando. 'Can Sebastian be one too?'

'He really is going to be bilingual,' said Julie with satisfaction. 'What do you think, Georgy? Should we leave him to go his own way—you've never said.'

Kerenyi watched the boy's brilliant, smiling, bold eyes for a moment. He too spoke in French so that Nando should not understand him.

'He has more charm even than his uncle and it doesn't matter what you do with him, you won't change him an iota.'

This was part of the running discussion that we constantly returned to. Georg had not before mentioned the older Nando in Julie's presence, but nobody except Lali seemed to notice this; the older Nando, like other shadows, was gone, and could be safely spoken of.

'Well, yes, but Nando did have to go to the University,' objected Lali, changing as we all did, our points of view from day to day on the intractable subject of our responsibility. 'I don't know!' she sighed again. 'I get cross with you all when you keep on at the child; on the other hand he is terribly wilful . . .'

Lali, like the others, perhaps like myself, and I was conscious of it for the first time, was now living here and in the present. Her ghosts too, shadows I had not even faces for, were fading enough for her to live gradually away from them; that process began after Sebastian's birth. Perhaps it was that we were all here and now, in our own beings and not as administrators of the past, but living towards the future. That was what gave the house its new atmosphere. Not that the past was forgotten, still less rejected; the worst and best of it could never be that. But it was adopted into the present and became part of living.

Not, either, that the discussion about whether or not Nando should be induced to take life seriously stopped; on the contrary it came up again that evening and for that matter it comes up to this day and is still not solved. It was and is, however, discussed in terms of the living Nando; both his father, Otto, and his uncle Nando ceased to be silent agents in the question.

All that, if I have at all succeeded in explaining myself, gave me a great deal to fight for when a hazard to our lives showed itself; which, very soon after this holiday, happened.

IV

The house we lived in the Eighth District of Vienna was the property of Maris Pantic, an actress disbarred for several years from playing because she had lived, during the war, with the Nazi Party administrator of the state theatres. Though it was requisitioned the rent was not small and our landlady lived very well from it, with the aid of film small parts. It was a pretty house, damaged by a bomb in the garden that ruined a group of syringa trees, and after Kerenyi suggested it should be taken by us, we arranged for repairs to be done so that the property was almost as good as new. I believe Maris Pantic was an old friend of his, but I did not care much for her; she seemed to me sly and under her ingratiating, self-pitying manner I felt a hardness almost like cruelty. Julie would defend her, saying she should not have been penalised; she had done less harm than others who were still as respectable for good society as they ever were.

'She always did live on men,' she said once, 'but it's typical of the self-righteousness that soaks everything nowadays that her sex life is what is punished.' And out of her cantankerous sense of justice, she would invite Maris when she had guests, and force her on people who would rather have shown a belated but genuine dislike of the Nazis, or perhaps the Germans, by showing coldness at any rate after their total defeat. I say sense of justice, but I know I always find the best motives for what Julie does; and what more strongly moved her was a scorn for both Maris and the respectable philistines, which it amused her to show by kindness on the one hand and by flouting hypocrisy on the other.

So we usually asked our landlady when we gave a big party, and she duly accepted an invitation to supper to meet the Stephensons. We were twenty people and I congratulated the Stephensons in my own mind on having the chance to meet a group it would take them months to acquaint themselves with without our help. If, indeed they were likely ever to meet some of them socially, for a number of

277

our friends, first and foremost Julie herself, by no means mixed with any of the Allied powers by choice. This attitude was by now almost reversed from that of the immediate postwar period, when for a great variety of reasons, including naked need, the western Allies were sought as friends, lovers, protectors, advisers and the operators—last but perhaps not least—of the black market. By the autumn of 1950 members of the Allied forces or Control Administration were accepted, or not, for themselves by anyone whose acquaintance was worth having.

Through Lali and our friendship with Julia Homburg and Kerenyi and through them with a wide acquaintance of theatre people and journalists, I was in a favoured position for a mere Major; and for a man without name or fortune in a society almost as class-conscious as England this position was already, only five years after the end of the war, almost unique. I was sought after by Anglo-American fellow-officers and colleagues much my superior in rank, and envied by them. It is clear that I was and am proud of this social success, so that I may as well admit to pride; not pride in the success itself, which was entirely due to Lali, but to the advantage I was able to enjoy in having access to it. For no one knew better than myself that I could have been married to a princess and still not have been accepted if I were not liked for myself, and only fools or failures underestimate the power of society.

Our main rooms were decorated in pale and dark greens, English colours that matched very well the late-eighteenth-century house; and that evening all the flowers, in splendid arrangements, were white. The big candelabra, the serving dishes and a large oval flower bowl on the supper table were the property of an impoverished princely house, silver we hired for parties on the condition of never mentioning to whom it belonged. Unlike the Nazis and the Russians we neither stole nor forced the sale of objects we coveted, but simply enjoyed them while we had the chance. Lali was used from birth to such lovely things but to me they were a never-failing source of conscious pleasure; the only part of our household surviving from Lali's own family possessions was the table silver, saved from looting by lying buried for over eighteen months and then being brought piecemeal to us in Vienna by Countess von Kasda.

We had picked an evening when the theatre programme finished early so that Julie, who was playing, would not need to rush.

Georgy arrived first, bringing with him the latest issue of his monthly periodical, which appeared that morning. It contained an article, unsigned, but written as everyone knew by himself, attacking the coalition government for corruption. Maris followed him in a few minutes and then Hella Schneider direct from her performance and magnificently dressed, with her American Colonel, and we all discussed this article, standing, in a most un-Austrian fashion, with drinks in our hands by the big window overlooking the garden.

'I've always thought you very foolish for attacking the government all the time, Georgy, and I still think so,' said Hella with an air of scorn she often showed to Georg, because she looked upon his unconcern with money as failure. 'But I must admit, this is quite witty and you make some good points.'

'You read it, Hella?' Georgy sounded surprised, and by his smile he showed he did not believe this.

'Elliott read it aloud to me while I was dressing,' she said. 'Though I suppose you think me incapable of understanding your subtleties?'

'My dear Hella, I am sure you have no reason to say that. You know I believe you to be capable—of anything. And it was written, after all, for the public . . .'

'Just the same, you will never get a really good job if you go on telling everyone of any influence in Vienna that they are crooks and fools.'

'It gives me a great deal of satisfaction, though,' he said, and looked past Hella and the tall, handsome Colonel towards the entrance of the room which stood wide open to the stairs. The house was so built that the main rooms were on the mezzanine, reached by a pretty rococo staircase with a wrought-iron rail; this was one of the most attractive features of our home. Georgy's quick ears had picked up the sounds of the outer door and steps on the stairs. But it was not Julie, but Mundel with Hansi Ostrovsky. The guests of honour were still not there; and I glanced quickly at my watch. There were several guests they needed to know about before conversation became general and if they were much later the whole company would be assembled before they arrived.

That is what, in fact, happened, and even the new American Ambassador and the second man at our own Embassy were already standing chatting over second or third drinks before the Stephensons appeared.

When Agnes almost ran into the room they were nearly three-quarters of an hour late. She was wearing a dress of some thin, papery silk, of a silver grey colour which rustled charmingly, but her look could only be described as distraught and she was out of breath.

'I'm so desperately sorry,' she gasped twisting her hands on her bag in an agony of embarrassment, 'but the car broke down. It's too terrible . . .'

Just as the manner of his wife was clearly due to something more than consciousness of a social mishap, so David's manner as he strolled in after her was obviously carefully planned. He was enjoying himself and drawled something about never again buying a British car. He smiled rather languidly round the circle of faces turned towards them as I began to introduce them, nodding to those he already knew and reaching a slack hand to those he met for the first time with the air of a man who goes through a ridiculous procedure to please inferiors, though he knew perfectly well that all Europeans shake hands in greeting. When we reached the newly arrived American Ambassador, the old man wagged his massive head and coughed.

'Young man,' he said mock-sternly, 'you seem to have picked up bad habits in Washington. Your wife is quite out of breath. Aren't you ashamed to make a pretty lady run like that?'

'No, Sir,' said David pertly, 'Agnes makes herself run. I wouldn't dare.'

'Hmm,' grunted the Ambassador, coughing again, and showing now that he did not intend a joke. He turned to Julie and continued his conversation with her, interrupted by the entry of the Stephensons, about a film. As soon as the round of introductions was complete, David returned to the old Ambassador and broke into their talk about the white Russian director of the film.

'Malikovsky directed *Anna Karenina,* didn't he?' he said, one hand in a trousers pocket and a cigarette in his mouth. 'You were awfully good in that.'

'Thank you,' said Julie dryly, and that was all. She had, as the saying goes, at once taken against him.

'But I think he's done enough Tolstoy—don't you, Sir? I should think he'd want to do some modern Russian things.'

'He'd have trouble putting that idea over in Hollywood right now,' commented the old man in a tone almost as dry as Julie's. 'The atmosphere there is hardly permissive to Soviet subjects.'

'Ye-es, that's true,' he agreed. 'Almost everyone in the States at the moment is quite drearily conformist and bigoted . . .'

'Did you not enjoy this movie of *The Cossacks,* then?' asked Maris Pantic, standing with them in a gauzy black dress. Her English was poor and she disliked having to speak it, but wanted to continue talking about this film, in which she had taken a small part 'on location' in Spain.

'Oh, I haven't seen it. I never go to movies.'

'How do you know this famous lady was good, then, in *Anna?*' asked the diplomat, bowing towards Julie.

'Ah, that was different. The Austrian Ambassador—such a dear little man—gave a special party for it and asked us all to a private showing.'

'That dear little man,' intervened Kerenyi, since it was clear that Julie did not mean to answer, 'spent the war in Buchenwald and is one of the most distinguished Hellenists in Europe. But, Excellency, I should like you to meet an old friend of ours. Jochen Thorn: you may have seen him recently as Peer Gynt? But he doesn't speak English, I'm afraid.'

The old man, in rough-hewn German, began to question the actor about the expert makeup needed to create a resemblance between himself and the young boy who played Peer Gynt as a lad. David's gambit was going all wrong, and at a party not my own I should have enjoyed his predicament. These were the most distinguished of the guests and he wished to talk to them, but he was unable to prevent himself treating them with a pretended indifference that could only make them ignore him.

We were now called to supper. There were four round tables of five persons each. Lali believed in odd numbers as making for better talk than couples and liked to mix all kinds of people. David was seated with Hella Schneider and Hans-Joachim Ostrovsky, the American Ambassadress and my own chief. We were in no doubt at all that Hella had taken the trouble to inform herself as to who was invited with her before she answered Lali's card, for she mixed almost entirely in American circles. So that she was delighted with this opportunity to see the new Ambassadress so quickly and put herself out to be her most charming, and when Hella wished to charm she could seduce the birds from the trees.

Julie, with the Ambassador, Hella's Colonel and the publisher of a 'black' Catholic newspaper, sat with a young actress just returned from a guest tour in Germany. Diagonally to their table we placed an elderly Countess notoriously a member of the Socialist Party, so that she and the pious Catholic could argue, we hoped, fruitfully. I was next to this lady as umpire in case the argument became too fruitful for comfort, with Agnes on my other hand while Kerenyi and Willy Mundel completed our table. Jochen Thorn with Maris and First Secretary of the British Embassy sat with Lali and Tom, whom we had succeeded in persuading to come back to Vienna with us. We were so placed in the spacious room that we could talk from table to table, and yet have room to get up and serve ourselves from the supper table laid out in the neighbouring room, a pretty oval that was our usual dining room.

During the soup it became clear that Agnes was not fitting into this multilingual and informal company, for although her French was adequate she spoke no German. But people go to parties to enjoy themselves and it is a hard law that who does not keep up is left behind; the better the company the more rigorously the law works and this company was a signal proof of Lali's system of mixing guests. The talk could hardly have been more amusing and although there was nothing that need exclude Agnes, still she did not include herself, and a notable area of silence that exuded suppressed anxiety surrounded her.

We were milling about the long serving table, picking out delicacies for each other when the hired butler brought me a card; Mr Colton H. Barber had just arrived and would esteem it an honour to be allowed to join us, in the stilted way of well-brought-up Americans.

I raised my eyebrows at Lali and she shook her head, not knowing what I meant.

'My goodness, Lali, I forgot to tell you!' cried Julie, picking up a slice of cold turkey between two spoons and standing with it high in the air like a conductor poising his baton. 'I had a telegram from Barber today and told Frau Lisl to give him your address if he arrived.'

'What fun,' said Lali and went to bring him in. 'I do so love people just to turn up . . .' We could hear her at the head of the stairs as she greeted the newcomer. 'But don't be silly—it's wonderful that you came before we'd eaten up everything like a herd of locusts . . . no, herd is wrong, but it doesn't matter. You must be cold from that horrible ride in from the airport. Have a proper drink before you eat?' There was a murmur from Barber and Lali laughed. 'What's the matter with your clothes? They look perfectly all right to me. If you wore a bow-tie instead of that sincere black one you'd look as if you had a dinner jacket on, all black and white as you are like a magpie.'

'You are really being too kind,' said Barber hanging devotedly over her and advancing behind her to the table. 'But no drink, thank you, if I may just join straight in with the food? I'm as hungry as a wolf.'

There was a chatter of greetings, for Barber knew almost everyone and oddly enough this belated and quite unexpected arrival showed up David's childish ploy in a most unhappy fashion, for here Barber came, from the other side of the world, uninvited, and fitted himself in without the least fuss. He moved a chair next to Lali and had clearly decided to fall respectfully in love with her, a compliment he conveyed with the greatest delicacy.

Only the Stephensons were not with us, Agnes in a state of abstracted nervous tension and David resolved on being outside the company. By his manner of condescension and casualness and a trick of conveying surprised amusement at the surroundings, the food, the wine, he implied a scornful comment on us for having given him this party he so greatly desired. Although his career, like that of all diplomats, depended to a great extent on his getting on with his superiors, he could be heard arguing gracelessly with the Ambassadress—a woman old enough to be his mother—and sometimes loudly enough to be audible over the general chatter and laughter. Possibly he did not know who she was, the late arrival of the Stephensons having made any explanation of the guests impossible. But he certainly knew the identity of my chief, for on being introduced David reminded him of a lifelong friendship with his own father and recalled the last occasion on which they had met, at his father's funeral; even in the way he accepted greetings for his mother, David conveyed the impression that he found such claiming of intimacy an impertinence rather than the compliment it actually was. I could hear him as he talked to his table companions, changing the subject as soon as one was begun and asserting his own opinions aggressively without making any oblique effort to discover others' views before he did so.

Every time he raised his voice Agnes winced, directing her attention almost entirely to the table David sat at, until I began to feel annoyed with her for showing her feelings. This is an injustice often visited on the marriage partners of neurotics, for she knew what I did not—that David was determined upon making a scene. I thought for a moment, feeling her tremor beside me, of Betty Teacher's tears on the evening David made up his mind to marry Agnes, and not for the first time recognised that we all ally ourselves with people who feed our own inner needs. In David's case, the need of paranoiacs to bully those who are devoted to them. But sorry as I was for David's wife, I felt her failure to control a situation which can hardly have been new to her—that of David's drinking too much before going to a party with strangers—as partly her own fault. Under the quick conversation, I thought briefly of our children and wondered whether Agnes was as little able to control her domestic life as her public one, and if so what kind of bewildered nervous strain David's children must live under.

My Marxist neighbour was discussing a well-known professor of psychiatry with the Catholic newspaper owner, and having found one of the few subjects on which their views, for quite different reasons, coincided, they were vying with each other in denigration of this eminent doctor.

'Of course, theoretically Malibran is brilliant, but one can really only judge doctors by results, and can he prove that he ever had a cure? I really doubt it . . .'

'But he's credited with dozens of cures,' objected Mundel.

'That's just it,' said the Catholic quickly before his 'red' vis-a-vis could answer. 'But where his patients recover, I'm sure it's because of purely medical treatment—having a long rest, sleeping properly, keeping a healthy diet and getting away from domestic problems.'

'And by the striking devotion of the nursing staff,' added the feminist swiftly.

'I should think the patients in his clinic work out their own cures as much as anything,' suggested Julie. 'Talking to each other, you know?'

'Probably they get cured by the salutary shock of seeing other patients who have really collapsed into psycho-neurosis or psychosis,' said Kerenyi cynically. 'I'm certain it would cure me.'

'Oh, really, Georgy!' I objected into the general laughter. 'The sight of seriously deranged people would make them worse out of sheer terror . . .'

'Not at all. Half of the neurotics I know are not really ill at all. They are frightened egotists and suffer from lack of self-discipline and worrying about themselves too much.'

'Now, wait a moment!' cried Mundel. 'That's possible if you confine the argument to the milder neuroses. But you can't believe that real mental diseases can be touched by such hit-and-miss chances as conversation and taking a hold on themselves. I mean, schizophrenia and such illnesses.'

'Well, one thing's sure. It can't be touched either by a process of self-analysis brewed in the claustrophobic emotionalism of nineteenth-century domestic life.'

'Georgy's off again on his hobby-horse,' said Julie and we all laughed again.

'No, but seriously—why should an inversion of petty-bourgeois puritanism be able to cure a neurasthenic whose nerves were shattered by—let's say—the tank battles of the last war?'

'There's a point of view that would say a man who failed to stand modern warfare was saner than his fellows rather than less sane,' I said.

Georgy threw back his head and shouted with enjoyment.

'Well then, only the deserter is truly sane! He rescues himself from an insane situation by fleeing from it.'

'Not a proposition ever likely to recommend itself to established medicine!'

The Catholic publisher disapproved of our levity, and shook his head seriously. He disapproved too of Georgy's views editorially, but his enjoyment of the argument forced him to agree with his rival.

'The point about rejection of middle-class puritanism is a good one. In particular that sexual repression is always a bad thing—that seems to me quite untenable. Even if one agrees that, for instance, an obsession with money has sexual roots, still human society would be impossible without such controls as are supposed to cause neuroses . . .'

'Not only men but the higher animals sacrifice sexual appetites to other needs, such as security and defence,' my socialist neighbour began didactically. I lost the remainder of her words, listening to David's voice which made some remark about Hella Schneider's husband and glancing across I could see that he indicated the

285

Colonel.

'But Elliott is not my husband,' answered Hella, and with a charming air of sadness, 'I am a widow.'

As a matter of fact, as everyone present knew, the reason Hella did not marry her very rich American admirer was that the death of her husband, an SS-General of police, could not be legally established. She made it sound, however, not only that David had said something impermissible but that he had reminded her of grief. I saw him push the hair off his forehead and turn at once to my chief, who, like the Colonel, was in uniform, and at once began to speak of some mutual acquaintance of theirs in London. David was nothing if not quick-witted and he recognised that in Hella he met a more than equal dueller.

'That's the thing that always seems unreal to me,' said Agnes speaking quickly for the first time, and rather more loudly than was necessary. 'I mean, the first thing ambitious people are willing to sacrifice is personal happiness. I've often noticed it with diplomats . . .' she trailed off, aware of sounding personal, but everyone waited politely, so she was forced to continue. 'Not only diplomats, of course, but people whose careers depend on being—what's the word I mean—conventional . . . doctors, politicians . . . you know?'

'How true,' approved my other neighbour, 'and moreover, people who allow themselves sexual licence are often neurotic in spite of it.'

'Or because of it,' said Georgy.

'Oh, but General,' interrupted Hella's voice enthusiastically, 'I can't agree with you about Paris. I had the most wonderful time there last spring.' She had cut David out of the conversation again and had all my chief's attention.

I rose with my 'red' Countess to go to the supper table again, and Julie joined us there. As the other woman went round the table, Julie spoke in an undertone.

'What a very odd man, this friend of yours.'

I looked at her quickly and saw she meant, as always, more than she said.

'I felt I had to do something,' I said. 'In fact, they almost asked us to give this party. I knew him in the Army, you know, at the time I first met you and Georgy.'

'But you never brought him with you to my house. He's not a particular friend, is he?'

'Not really, no. But why?'

The other seeker after sweetmeats found what she wanted and left us alone, but Julie did not raise her voice from its murmur which no one else could hear.

'I recognise a type. He reminds me of people I knew—before. Be a little careful.' Several more people came to select desserts and we drifted back to our places, carrying plates. I could hear David again, and this time he spoke of war criminals and I heard the name of Benda, who was then in Landsberg prison in Bavaria, under sentence of death. David had already found time to discover that Benda's execution was constantly postponed on one legal ground or another, and by discussing this with my chief he deliberately forced the subject on the American Ambassadress as if it were her personal responsibility that the American authorities had not yet hanged Benda. I felt an inward jolt of premonition; Julie, inevitably, was right. I now understood Agnes' nervousness for he clearly meant to make trouble.

'The fact is, we don't know anything about human nature,' said Mundel. 'And all the psychological theories are much too personal and narrow—even superficial. I think they actually prevent the growth of knowledge by being so neat and satisfying on the surface.'

'It's extraordinary how we all agree in damning modern psychology.' I laughed, having to make a conscious effort to sound amused. 'Perhaps we are just bored with it, and want something new?'

'You mean the whole thing was a medical fad?' Georgy asked as he pushed back his chair. 'Or that we treat serious matters as a parlour game? Can I bring you some fruit, Mrs Stephenson?' Agnes rose with him and went to the next room to choose.

I could hear Tom's voice, level and comforting, talking of fishing with the first secretary and Maris, who flattered them with her questioning. It was all right. We were all much too civilised for David to succeed in making a scene.

'I only meant that we are being perhaps rather foolishly pragmatic about the popularisation of a kind of medicine we don't really know anything about,' I replied in a few minutes' time when they returned to the table.

'Pragmatic?' said Georgy with his bark of laughter. 'What else can one be when speaking of human nature?'

By the time we rose to leave our tables for coffee, David was obviously drunk. He swayed as he stood up, almost knocking into Hella, whose Colonel moved watchfully closer. David's face was pale, the features in some indescribable way blurred in their lines and the forehead damp over which the lock of fair hair fell. There was something almost sinister in the way, and I remembered it from four years before in the pen, that his whole face seemed to change when his compulsion—whatever it really was—made him drink heavily; he looked both older and younger, like an old child or a child already marked by profligate experience.

His face as it now was reminded me of children seen in the horrible novels of the Alexandrine slums. And like those children, he was both disgusting and piteous, irreclamable. The thought went through my mind, as I waited for the others to go through the doors before me, that he must never come into contact with Sebastian or Nando.

Standing with a coffee cup in his hand, he made an effort visible at any rate to me, who knew him, to control his intoxication; but not so that he could behave himself. He was deciding with whom he should pick his quarrel.

The obvious person was Hella Schneider, whose record during the war made her vulnerable, as he probably already knew; but she had shown him how formidably able she was to take care of herself. Typically, he would not directly attack a man; I watched his eyes slide over the company and pick on Maris Pantic. He might just as well have picked on Julie, who had none of Hella's visible hardness but perhaps his instinct warned him there. Or perhaps, simply, Maris was for a moment left alone. Brandy glass in hand, David lounged over to Maris.

'Tell me about everyone,' he said, bending over her tiny form with an almost caressing air. 'You must know simply everyone. It's such a curious feeling for me, you know, and I haven't got used to it yet . . .'

'What is curious?' prompted Maris, smiling up at him with her forlorn air of bearing up gallantly under a cruel fate, and offering him her own brand of sexy unhappiness. She certainly thought he was flirting with her and was flattered for he was years younger than herself. Her deep, quavering voice was particularly attractive with its foreign accent and David bent still nearer, enjoying immensely the prospect of teasing someone so suited in her overt femininity to serve his repressed dislike of women.

'The feeling I have since I came here . . . but I'd better not say it. It occurs to me that it's awfully tactless.'

She shook her head, disclaiming offence in advance, awaiting some slightly improper compliment.

'Well, if you promise not to mind? I mean, the feeling of wondering all the time what the people I'm talking to were doing—let's say, six years ago. I mean, everyone I meet seems to have been resisting Hitler—we all know that, like Dr Kerenyi over there.' He said Georg's name and title with a negligent insolence that cast doubt on the genuineness of the degree as of the person. 'But I can't help wondering—I expect you don't understand that, though?'

The knife slid in so smoothly that for a moment Maris did not know she was stabbed. Her reaction was so slow that a noticeable pause ensued.

'In the theatre, you know,' she then said uncertainly, 'we don't much concern ourselves with politics.'

'No, I suppose not. It's easier not to, isn't it? Not you, naturally, but Mr Thorn over there, now . . . He's a German, isn't he? D'you think he was always as humorous and polite as he is this evening? Was he always an actor, or did he do other things in the war? One can't help wondering, you know . . .'

'He was always an actor, oh, yes,' she said, wondering at his notion that anyone could just become an actor in the middle of his life. 'I've known him since 1941, I think it was, when he came here.'

'Ah then, I imagine he's in the clear. He could never have been in the SS?'

'Of course not, he's not at all the type,' murmured Maris, 'but don't you think we should go and talk to your wife? She seems to be alone.'

'Agnes doesn't speak German,' replied David with sudden brusqueness and while Maris was actually pointing out that they were speaking English, he went on, now loudly.

'But these cultured actors must have given performances for the troops, even for the SS, didn't they? Or so I've heard . . . though they were resisting inwardly, they supported the regime that far?'

He did not see that Julie had risen and come up behind him; most of the women were seated and the men moved about among them.

'Thorn?' she asked in her clear voice. 'Yes he did play at least once for the SS. In Poland, I know.' Suddenly her voice cut like a whiplash so that Georgy turned round from his own conversation at the sound. 'I was there, too.'

'Oh, but I heard that you were *very* anti-Nazi . . . I mean, isn't it true that you hid . . .'

'I was in Poland on the same tour for the troop theatres as Jochen Thorn,' Julie interrupted. 'And it was hideous—hideously uncomfortable, too. We both took care never to go on one of those trips again.'

'Took care not to know? Yes, how understandable. So you stayed here, after that, and just played for men on leave, you mean?'

'At that time, I still believed that the public needed the theatre —entertainment, you would call it—even more in bad times than in good. So, I suppose, did we all.'

'You feel differently now, then? A triumph of democracy!'

She surveyed him with an implication of disinterest in some oddity of nature that was far less theatrical than David's own manner.

'I don't think I've learned much about democracy in the last few years,' she said, smiling, 'it's just a matter of experience.'

As the waiter offered David more brandy, which he accepted, both Julie and Maris turned away and I thought with relief that David's scene had after all ended without much hurt. Indeed, half the company heard nothing of it. He turned to Barber, who was discussing the Korean war with the Ambassador, and I moved away as well, sure that David was in good hands.

At that time it was a subject on which everybody argued themselves hoarse, and when a few minutes later I heard their voices raised I thought nothing of it. It was Agnes who came up to me and spoke softly, pulling with a trembling hand at my arm.

'Robert, you must separate them. Quickly!'

I crossed the large room, to hear David accusing the two Americans wildly of being about to use atomic bombs on the Chinese.

'You'll keep clear of the Russians because they, thank God, have the bomb too. But it's quite safe to slaughter millions of Chinese peasants for having the impudence to help the North Koreans!'

'I say, let's not go too far,' I said. 'This is not a debating society. Let's control ourselves.'

David threw back his head, laughing loudly. The lock of hair tossed on his brow and fell back again and he brushed at it impatiently with his hand, holding the brandy glass.

'Dear Robert, always the little conformist, as long as it keeps you your job, eh, Robert? But you always were—seriously now—anti-Russian and pro-German, weren't you? I remember in the Army, how you cared for the war criminals with kid gloves . . .'

I was about to answer angrily, when the Ambassador spoke before me.

'Whatever the war criminals have done, they deserve a fair trial,' he said. 'And just remember, none of us has a completely clear conscience, though what you say about using the atom bomb in China is complete nonsense, as you very well know. But just remember the British and the Irish famines—for that matter we are not too proud ourselves of our record with the Indians . . .'

'Of course, you're Irish, Mr Sullivan!' David said, as Mrs Sullivan touched her husband's arm.

'Gently, John,' she said. 'Don't get excited. You know it's bad for you.'

'I'm not excited, dear,' his voice changed when he spoke to his wife, but became brutal as he turned to David again.

'My grandparents were Irish. And my grandmother died of starvation. A million Irish died of starvation in those years, Mr Stephenson. That was one in nine of the population of Ireland. While Britain was richer than any nation had ever been before. And just across a little piece of water you can almost see over, but nobody took much notice. I guess you British didn't even know, did you? It's easier not to know, as you were saying yourself, a few minutes ago . . .'

'I guess maybe people really didn't know,' suggested the pacific Barber. 'We forget how slow and patchy news was in those days.'

Our intervention succeeded for a space, for when the old Ambassador spoke again his voice was quiet with the certainty of the power of his own position and the power of the nation he represented.

'You need not distress yourself, Mr Stephenson, the atomic bomb won't be dropped north of the Yalu or anywhere else.' It was the recovery, by an effort, of urbanity, but it could have sounded like a slightly rallying condescension, as I suppose to David it did. The senior, pretending for social reasons to take a somewhat impertinent junior seriously. I would myself, with that perhaps extreme caution

David had mentioned just now, have avoided giving him another chance or the assembled company another shock, and have changed the subject. But then I am not an Ambassador, nor an Irishman; and perhaps the old man did not quite assess the amount of alcohol David was consuming.

'We are all glad to have your reassurance, Sir,' he said, bowing slightly with an obviously overdone deference. 'But on the other hand, it is hard to forget that the Americans have in fact dropped atomic bombs—twice already.'

'A much larger number of times altogether, to be pedantic,' said the second British diplomat, jokingly. It is extraordinary how often diplomats, who are by profession supposed to be tactfully aware of undercurrents in situations and conversation, allow such moments to develop instead of turning them into innocuous channels. David's colleague meant to bridge a return to casual talk, but his flippant tone was very slightly misjudged, emphasised. The Ambassador took it as support of David's allegation, and with that consciousness of supreme power which burdens the Americans in their relations with less powerful nations, and which is perhaps exacerbated by history when dealing with the British, was goaded by the tone as much as the substance of the remark.

'Do I have to remind you—I seem to be doing that this evening —that the British were as much involved as the Americans in the dropping of those two bombs?'

'I at any rate absolutely dissociate myself from that decision,' said David stiffly and went pale once again, but this time with a genuine sense of outrage, it seemed to me. 'The dropping of the second bomb, on Nagasaki, was a monstrous crime.'

The last two words were difficult to pronounce for a man as drunk as David was, and he seemed aware that he slurred them. His face twisted with fury at having failed in a moment that should have been dignified, and for an instant I felt a return of my old sympathy for him.

'You do, do you?' The Ambassador positively growled with uncontrollable irritation that came from an unadmitted bad conscience—for David was referring to the second bomb being of a different 'mixture' and the suspicion widely held that it was dropped for purely experimental reasons—as well as from awareness of having allowed himself to be trapped in a ridiculous position. 'Yet an hour ago you subscribed to the idea of collective guilt

—when it concerned others!'

'I was a junior officer in the Army,' cried David, beside himself. 'What control did I have over governments? Still less over my superior officers! How could it be any responsibility of mine?'

'Well now, responsibility—that's a vexed question,' began Barber, hoping once again to retreat into theories and ignore the realities and antagonisms of the argument.

'According to your own admission, we are all responsible,' almost shouted the Ambassador, and would have gone on, but a frightening change came over his face which appeared to darken in colour and to go blank and rigid, while he held his short and massive frame quite still with strain. He stood, breathing heavily and listening, as it were, to something inside himself. The whole group stared and I held my breath but after a moment he blinked slowly and allowed his wife to take him by the arm and lead him to a chair in which he sat down heavily and closed his eyes.

'I guess I did get a little excited, Nell,' he said after a long moment.

'Can I do anything?' I asked anxiously, while Barber hovered with a handkerchief held out. Mrs Sullivan shook her head, and after a little while the Ambassador opened his eyes.

'I'm all right, my boy,' he said. 'Or I will be in a minute.'

Tom and the man from our embassy came up now to David and inveigled him away into the oval dining room, which had been cleared. The waiters and our housekeeper flitted to and fro, offering whisky and soda, fruit juice and Vichy water. Slowly the chatter rose again and after a decent interval the Sullivans took their leave. The old man pressed my hand.

'A very good party, Robert,' he said and patted my arm reassuringly. Immediately afterwards Hella and her Colonel left, and a few minutes later the other English diplomat. I expected the rest of the guests to follow them, but because they had been the object of the original attack on Maris, they stayed to prove themselves not affected by it and were concerned to cover the whole matter with swift talk and laughter. My chief took the diplomat's place with Tom, watching David. An appearance of complete normality returned and you would have said it was a most successful party. But I knew the story would be all over Vienna the next morning, and I knew too that for that reason alone the Ambassador could not possibly ignore what had happened.

It was mild for November and the heating a little too effective, so I opened one of the long windows to the garden. Lali sat with Hansi Ostrovsky and Mundel, explaining something to Agnes, in spite of her inattention.

I watched Julie as she moved over to the window and stood there gazing out at the dark; she lifted her face to the damp air, deep in some memory, and Kerenyi joined her there. They stood together without touching or looking round at each other, Georgy with his hands in his pockets.

'Do you remember the first time we ever stood here?' she asked him. 'It was June then, and the nightingales sang.'

'I remember. It seems a long time ago.'

'It is a long time. Ten years.'

'Can it be? And no nightingales, now.'

She moved her head and gave him a smile that turned my heart over.

'I don't need the nightingales,' she said. She put out a long, ringless hand then, and he took it without looking down, seeming to know without seeing, what she did. After a moment Kerenyi put up her hand against his heart and then kissed it and they stood there for a long time without words. They were altogether a silent pair at that time; they had little need for speech perhaps, having exchanged so many words in their time to so little comfort.

Presently Agnes excused herself and went into the other room, to suggest it was time to leave. Gradually the guests were going, until Lali and I were left talking quietly with Julie and Georgy. After several minutes Agnes came back, shaking her head resignedly at Lali. Her eyes wandered over the room and the people in it as if she hardly recognised them, so that I asked myself if she had taken something to still her nerves. A hopeless indifference underlay the distress and anxiety of her eyes, and a physical change seemed to come over her face as if the muscular structure were loosened so that one could see in a woman still young where the lines would later be.

My chief appeared at the open doors, and jerked his head backwards whence he came.

'I think the ladies had better leave,' he said quickly, 'I'm afraid he's going to be sick.' He caught sight of Agnes and added, as if he had forgotten her until then, 'I will drive Mrs Stephenson home.'

Agnes moved forward to intervene, but Julie touched her hand and prevented her.

'Let the men manage,' she said in German, forgetting that Agnes did not understand her. 'I can't leave Lali until . . .'

'I can't go without David,' cried Agnes, answering my chief almost indignantly. She was now almost in tears of humiliation, at the sight of our faces, stiff with embarrassment and resentment. The use of the blunt words that her husband might actually vomit with drunkenness, as well as the source from which they came were so incongruous, so incredibly out of place, that we all stood there looking at her, unable to act.

'I'm most terribly sorry,' said my chief absurdly, 'I didn't mean to sound offensive . . .' The sight of a Lieutenant-General with three rows of campaign ribbons on his tunic and all the authority of his age and rank lost in a situation that he can only have experienced before as a junior officer at Mess nights twenty-five years before was the last straw of the ludicrous.

My God, I thought, this is the end of me.

It was at this moment that David reappeared, clutching high up at the frame of the double doors, his face deadly pale and dark shadows under his haunted eyes. How could I ever have thought that any normal relationship, any relationship at all, was possible with this man? It was now so clearly impossible that I felt bewilderment at my own error of judgment; I thought the last few years had taught me too much for such things to happen to me, but evidently not. Yet a few weeks ago he seemed—not normal, he could hardly be that—but so much more aware of the dangers of his own temperament and so conscious of his dependence on his wife that I believed him safe. Safe enough to expose myself and my closest friends to this clownish exhibition.

Behind David stood Tom, watchful; he too, good friend, had been drinking heavily to keep his ward company as the only way to control him. But Tom could drink a barrel dry without showing any more outward sign than a heightened colour. David maundered something half under his breath, turned towards Tom and lost his footing, lurching heavily and almost unbalancing him for he fell against Tom's bad side, which was never strong.

'Tom, you're drunk, you old bastard,' he cried loudly, swayed back again to the door frame and held on to it, instantly forgetting what he was saying and trying to recall it. His eyes went round the silent group before him; we were all in that state of helplessness when no amount of experience or manners can tell what to do for the object of concern is totally unpredictable. As David's eyes flickered over his wife's face an expression of extreme malice came into them, like a child determined to behave badly to its mother. He moved towards me and swayed forward, hand unsteadily out.

'What very grand parties you do give, Robert,' he said thickly. 'Too grand for me . . . But the women like it, and we must give the women what they want! Your wife, now, she's an ambitious girl, anyone can see that . . . she keeps you up to it, I'll bet!' He laughed loudly, the laugh ending in a gulp.

Tom was still behind him; I ignored David's words and took his cold, damp hand to say goodnight since he seemed to expect that, glancing quickly over his shoulder to Tom. He saw the look, inevitably. Unable to decide between anger at being taken care of and satisfaction at upsetting everyone, David swayed before me for a moment, waving his hand in the air.

'Yes, she's a pretty little thing, your little woman. I bet the Russians had a good time with her, eh, Tom?'

'Hold your tongue,' said Tom sharply. 'You're going too far.'

'Ah-ha!' A loud, triumphant shout. 'Caught you on the raw there, did I?' He sniggered. 'And you such a virtuous chap, too. But, Robert, I was won-wondering just the other day, what it feels like to marry a girl who's been through the Russians' hands—I mean, when you hate them so—must be a funny feeling sometimes—e-eh?'

In the stunned silence I heard Agnes wail.

'Oh, God, no!'

I didn't know I was going to hit him until I did. The blow connected, too, though very clumsily. His head snapped back, teeth clicked loudly and he fell full length. A shot of pure agony ran through my hand and arm and cleared the red mist from behind my eyes. David gave a howl of pain and I saw dimly that his left arm was doubled back under him. Kerenyi and Tom hauled him roughly to his feet and my chief drew the women out of the room. Agnes had her hands over her face and leaned on the wall.

'We ought to beat you black and blue,' said Kerenyi through his teeth. 'You nasty little scoundrel.'

'He's not worth beating. Don't soil your hands on him,' grunted Tom, hanging on to the raving David, who howled and wept, clutching at his dislocated arm. 'Pity it wasn't your neck. Shut up, for God's sake! You'll have the whole neighbourhood about our ears.'

'A doctor,' howled David, blubbering and snivelling, 'get me a doctor!'

'We shall have to get a doctor, I'm afraid,' I said slowly, staring at my hand which was already swelling and misshapen.

'Yes, we shall,' said my boss, coming in again. He stared from David to me. 'A scandal,' he said grimly. 'There'll be a scandal.' Then, to Tom, 'Can you two control him? I'll call the duty doctor and then take the women home. We must get Frau Homburg and Mrs Stephenson out of this, at any rate.'

I heard him telephoning in the hall downstairs. A few moments later the front door closed. I sat down, feeling sick with pain. But it was David who vomited. Lali, thank heaven, had disappeared. He was half unconscious by the time the doctor came; we heard his jeep in the silent street and Tom went down to let him in.

When he touched my hand I felt myself go faint.

'There's something broken, I'm afraid. You'll both have to come to the clinic. I'll get the ambulance.' To Tom he said coldly, 'What happened?'

Tom muttered some nonsense, I hardly heard what. He wanted to come with me, but I said he should rather stay in the house in case Lali needed something. The ambulance was only a few minutes in arriving, and I asked Tom to go up and tell Lali I would get back as soon as I could.

'If you can keep him in the clinic until tomorrow it would be a good thing,' I said to the doctor, indicating David.

'You're more likely to have to stay there,' he replied curtly. 'You'll have to have that hand X-rayed and plastered.'

A small cross-bone at the base of the thumb was broken, and I wore plaster for nearly three months. But it needed only one day of that period for the story to be all over the city. When I arrived at my office the day after next there was a message from the powers that be. The American Ambassador, as luck would have it, dined with our Ambassador the day after the disaster and complained of Stephenson's behaviour. The medical report on the 'accident' closed the circle; I gathered that the lines to London were hot with angry and conflicting messages for two days and within a week, without anyone seeing him again, David Stephenson was posted.

It was a week after that, when I was already used to the plaster on my hand, that I got another message; there was to be an official, but highly confidential, enquiry. I was to fly at once to London. Anything else was hardly possible; it was only wishful thinking that allowed me to hope David's influential friends could extend their protection far enough to embrace complaints from foreign Ambassadors.

Far worse than all the official results of this evening, however, was its effect on Lali. It was not in her nature to 'take it out' on me for Stephenson's insults, but the very fact that our lives continued apparently just as before the incident took away all my content and much of my own self-confidence, grown so greatly in the last year or so. Even, or rather especially, in the moments when we were most intimate I could feel the lack of her real being. Only once or twice did I, coming into the house, hear the children and Lali laughing together as they formerly laughed so much, but when I came into the room, while the children remained normally gay Lali herself changed at once, subtly and against her own will. I could feel her striving for our inner harmony and companionship. The knowledge that she made these efforts was as painful to me as the sensation of her fear that I believed secretly what Stephenson had said. For I knew that about such things as he spoke of in his drunken rage there was a total conspiracy of silence among all but the most abandoned and corrupt. Thus we could never speak of David's words and I knew that this silence must in a very short time so undermine our relationship that it would—perhaps quite slowly and the more agonisingly—starve to death. Within the first few days I could feel in myself the weakening of impulse, the creeping of inhibition into what was an almost perfect relationship, that must shrivel it gradually. For if I had always apprehended the emptiness of substitutes for love before I ever knew love, how little likely was I going to be able to maintain such an empty relationship after four years of a union grown into flower from such unpromising beginnings, and flowering the more marvellously for its initial hesitations? I knew too that it was only a matter of time before this shrivelling of our inner life must be felt by the children, and wreck first the confidence won at such patient cost between myself and my step-son, and then affect unconsciously Sebastian himself. From there it would spread to the delicate balance of my deep feeling for Julia Homburg. I knew enough of masculine nature to be aware that it was my happiness with Lali that kept that most delicate, subtle and tender mirror-image of love within the boundaries of what I could permit myself and of what Julie would permit. For she would know immediately if that feeling changed.

So in the space of five weeks, David Stephenson threatened the whole fabric of my life; from its professional basis inwards to its innermost core. And I now knew him well enough to believe that if he could know this, it would give him satisfaction.

V

'It's the same lady that came once before to the office,' whispered my clerk conspiratorially, and my heart sank. Agnes was, with one exception, the last person in the world I wanted to have to talk to.

She came in carrying a couple of small parcels done up in that fancy taping used by fashionable confectioners. Farewell presents I supposed. I was as concerned to look at her parcels and handbag, gloves and the rest, as she to keep her gaze on my tidied desk. Having put everything down on the chair she would normally have sat upon, she stared at the chair helplessly for a moment and then wandered off across the room to the barred window which looked out on the supremely uninteresting view of an inside courtyard of the big barracks block behind Schönbrunn Palace built for the SS garrison of Vienna in the war. This seemed to depress her still more and she sighed aloud. I was embarrassed too by an absurd feeling that she should look somehow changed, but she looked normal except for that wandering eye. It was almost a week ago, after all.

But surely the form her life had taken must show some outward sign? I knew by now from office talk that the scene the other night was not unique by any means. 'A man in the Embassy' who had come here six months before the Stephensons, from the Consulate General in New York, and who knew them and their Washington sojourn, had tales of similar performances, none of which had involved, however, persons highly enough placed to affect David's career directly. I was sure David himself looked upon the results of his scene as a piece of pure bad luck, if not deliberate malice on my part; I ought to have warned him, as he said to a mutual acquaintance. Typically he did not mention the new American Ambassador in his complaints except to describe him as a pathetic old has-been, for he could have taken him into consideration without any hint from me.

'We're flying to Bangkok tomorrow,' said Agnes abruptly. 'My mother came today to take the children back with her.' Her voice shook as she spoke of her mother, and I could imagine the un-comprehending questions of a manse widow to such a startling change of plans.

'Have you the right clothes for Bangkok?' I could think of nothing better to say.

'Not really, but Washington was fairly hot and we shall have to manage for a few months.' Then, very quietly, 'I've been asked not to go to London, you see.'

Quasi-officially exiled, then. Or did his friends simply think it wise to keep David out of sight for a time until his escapade was forgotten?

'I felt I must come—to—apologise to both of you. But I just couldn't face Lali. After her generosity . . .' She stopped and I recognised, in spite of my anger—and my hand still hurt—that what Agnes felt she must say was indeed of a most delicate nature. What David actually said and about whom was so far not part of the gossip as to why I had hit him. Now she looked straight at me. 'I want you to know that I shall never repeat it—not for his sake, either. And neither will he, I'm sure. Quite sure.'

I returned her look; no matter how tragic her own position tied to this man, I was not prepared to pretend I had forgiven David.

'No. He won't repeat that story; it makes him look too black-guardly.'

Her lips and brows twitched painfully but she said nothing, only stared at my hand in plaster.

'He'll find another story,' I said. 'One that makes me look ridiculous.'

She caught breath to protest, but again said nothing. Then she moved a couple of steps towards her parcels and bag.

'Of course I can't expect you to feel any different,' she said distressfully. 'I just thought I might be able to talk to you. I tried to talk to Tom Wallingham, but he just patted my hand and said not to upset myself.'

We were both still standing, I behind the desk, she in the middle of the empty space, half turned to the window which provided a target for her eyes. After that straight look, she kept switching her gaze from me to the window, but did not catch my eyes directly. I was dimly aware that there was something else she wanted to say; she really did want to talk to me. A thread of something intimidating, almost menacing, entered the atmosphere.

'What is it?' I asked, hearing my own voice as strained.

'Did David ever come to see you here?' she asked, apparently inconsequently. 'Here in your office?'

'No. There has hardly been time, has there?'

'Of course, you were away after you had us to dinner, until . . .'

Her eyes wandered past me again, she drew breath in that small gasp as before, to say something she could not bring out. Like a cold touch I felt sweat on my forehead that had not been there an instant before.

'Why do you ask that?' Out of habit I kept my voice down; no need for the clerk to hear, although this room had a padded inside door with an automatic spring lock which made it very difficult for anyone to eavesdrop. I heard myself say very slowly, 'Are you trying to warn me?' In an instant I saw her coming here, twice, as a monstrous breach of security on my part and as—what?—on hers. How did she know even where my office was, a stranger to Vienna and our official apparatus there? Of course, she could get in easily enough, even to places as barred as my office. She was on the Diplomatic List, she was a lady, obviously wealthy, absolutely *comme il faut*. She had come instead of David, and at his request I was now certain, and she was telling me so.

Her gaze now went to the big map cupboards on two walls, and came back again to me.

'I don't know what to do,' she said. She was not a clever woman and found it difficult to say things that could possibly appear to mean other things.

'I would suggest a doctor if I thought he would go to one.'

'Yes. Somebody else suggested that, too,' she said helplessly. 'But he won't. He doesn't know that he can't take drink like other people. And afterwards he forgets what happened.'

'I should think Bangkok is a pretty poor place for doctors,' I said, 'but perhaps you could, if there is a decent one there, get him to come to see you socially, so that David'—I had to force myself to say the name and she saw that—'could get used to him, d'you see . . . ?'

'If only his friends didn't encourage him!' she cried. 'And I have to drink with him when he's in that mood, or he goes off on his own. I'm afraid . . .' A long silence. 'I'm afraid something will happen one day—one night, I mean.' If the other evening did not count as 'something', what must she already have experienced with him?

'Aren't there some pills you can give him? What are they called; pacifiers or something?'

'Tranquillisers, you mean. I've tried but they make him worse if he takes a drink on top. And I can't tell him it's not just aspirin or he wouldn't take it. *I* take them, sometimes when he goes out alone. They give one a strange feeling of indifference; it's rather pleasant.'

'A pity it's Bangkok; I believe the climate is bad and if one can believe Conrad and Somerset Maugham, people all drink a lot out there.'

'It was the only place there was a vacancy of the right sort,' she said. 'Anywhere else would have meant a lot of reshuffling and that would cause more talk.'

'He is very lucky to have friends to take so much trouble for him—and make themselves responsible.'

'Responsible?' she breathed. 'Ah, if you knew!' She clutched her hands together for a moment so that the knuckles went white. The thought of whoever was responsible brought something back to her mind. 'I think—I heard a hint from Johnny Banks in the FO—that there was another report from here, before this one. Did you know about that?'

'Banks?' I said, 'that name sounds familiar. . . . Do I know him?'

'I don't think so, he's always in London. David has known him for years. They were at the University together, I think. But why . . . ?'

'The name reminded me of something. I'm not sure what. But you said another enquiry—is it possible? You've only been here— what?—five weeks?'

'Yes,' she admitted miserably, 'perhaps it isn't true, but David did say something about being asked a lot of questions.' She picked up her oddments. 'I really must go. I'm holding up your work.'

It dawned on me that those questions were the result of my own security check. I had a strong impulse to tell her, insanely, that I should have to report this conversation too, but recovered myself in time. I took her to the door, exchanging goodbyes, and asked the clerk to see her out.

After she was gone I sat for a long time at my desk, staring straight before me, saying over and over in my mind that I must think. Then I telephoned my boss and asked if I could see him tomorrow, early and alone.

'Change them all?' he said, and passed a bony hand over his

thin, sharply precise face. 'There will be another enquiry, as like as not. You realise that?'

'It is a nuisance. I can see that you would blame me for this. But, on the other hand, we could perhaps congratulate ourselves on catching the evil—if it is an evil—so early on . . . ?'

'But all the codes,' he groaned. 'All the locks!'

'I just don't think it's safe,' I said. 'I may be wrong, fanciful. But I feel my responsibility. Better safe than sorry, as you might say.'

'We could report it as a result simply of this recent, deplorable affair. Simply precautionary. How would that look, d'you think?'

'I see you too think it may be necessary.'

'I think you don't get excited. You're a steady sort of chap, Robert, and I'm inclined to trust you.' I was glad he used my name, which he had not done that morning up to then.

'It's a thousand pounds to a litre of Heuriger, Mrs Stephenson simply asked somebody in the Embassy where she could find me, without any reference openly or in her own mind, to my job. And somebody just told her. If it is not so, I am sure she is unconscious of what she may be being used for. But, for my part, I don't think we should risk even such a tiny chance. There was something about the whole interview that made me—suspicious.'

'What? How? You'll be asked in London, you know.'

'I don't know. I don't want to embroider it, invent what was not there. Sometimes one just has feelings, and that's as far as I'll go.'

'But we—you—have no evidence,' he complained. 'All these frail threads of nothing; the remarks about the Chinese and so on. Are you sure there is nothing else? Something you just vaguely remember, perhaps? I'd feel better if you could place this "feeling".'

'He sometimes seemed odd, in the Army,' I admitted, 'but it's only a suspicion. I'm afraid one that looks unworthy, but there it is.'

'I don't call it unworthy,'' he grumbled, 'but other people may. You know that? You're sure you haven't forgotten something definite from your Army days together? Anything at all?'

'Nothing concrete, no. Only impressions. It's just—I think he is unsound and that's the truth.'

'He certainly is that. But the mere conviction won't get you far with the enquiry people. Does Lali know why you are going to London, by the way?'

'No. It isn't the first time I've been there officially and she must think it is just one of those policy conferences I've been to before.'

'I mean, if you've told her anything I'd better know; I'm bound to see her.'

'We haven't discussed it at all.' I scowled at the blotter. 'I haven't told her any complicated stories—lies—if that is what you mean.'

'No, it's always better not to lie,' he said seriously. 'And don't worry. I've backed you up to the hilt in my own report. They can hardly discount that.'

'That's good of you,' I said.

'No. Self-interest. You're my chap and my judgment is to be judged. By the way . . . I quoted what was said, in my report. So that they don't have to ask you that. But I did not name the person of whom the remarks were made. There were several ladies present . . . you see?'

'Thank you.'

'Again, no. There must not be the faintest feeling left that you or anyone connected with you is in the slightest . . . vulnerable.' There was silence. 'What a business. The damage people like that cause completely innocent bystanders.'

The confidential enquiry was to be held to discuss David Stephenson's misconduct; I was merely one of the witnesses in a list of incidents going back two years to a police complaint that a British diplomat drove while drunk to the public danger somewhere in Michigan. Having refused to give his name, the matter had somehow been smudged into vagueness, though it was known that he was David Stephenson. But I could hardly have felt less confidence if my own behaviour were to be criticised.

It was an unpleasant flight with high winds; I did not sleep much in the dreary hotel room in a London still, apparently, devoted to austerity. At five minutes to ten I presented myself; the first person I saw in the dark waiting room I was taken to was Colonel Manley in civilian clothes. I greeted him and he replied with stiff coldness.

'Still in uniform, I see,' he said, sniffing slightly.

'Not as a rule, but I was told to appear in service dress.'

'Tell me,' he said, coming closer and overcoming his distaste for me in the interests of inside information, 'what is this all about, eh? These people tell one nothing; treat one like a lackey.' These people were the Foreign Office personnel branch. 'It would be useful to know what I'm supposed to say, don't you know. Not that I have anything to hide, and in any case I'm out of their jurisdiction, and the Army's too for that matter. Just that one doesn't care for this kind of hole and corner affair much.' He managed to convey that I would be, naturally, more at home in a hole or corner than himself.

'I know no more than you,' I said. 'Just obeying orders.'

At this moment a tall, thin man came through the room and was about to disappear through the far door, when he turned back, smiling pleasantly.

'Shan't be long,' he said. 'By the way, you won't discuss this little matter between you, will you? Against the rules, you know.'

'What does he take me for?' Manley wanted furiously to know. 'That's just what I mean about the way they treat one.'

I opened my *Times* and began to read. After a few minutes, Manley strode over to the window. Then he came back to the chair next to mine.

'Funny there is nobody else here. Do you suppose we can be the only people called?'

'Surely not,' I said. 'I expect they take us a couple at a time. And not all the—all the people they want to hear from will be in London. I dare say they have a lot of paperwork to deal with.'

'Paper work? Affidavits, you mean? Look here, just how serious is this business? What's it all about?'

'I wish I knew,' I said. 'The news from Korea is pretty bad.' I shook out the pages of the paper and began again to read. Or seemed to read. I was thinking of some of the people who might be in this room, and would not be. I was here because of the incident in my house, but Manley must take it that I was present as an officer from the pen and must be wondering why others of us were not here. Perhaps he did not even know that it was Stephenson he was to be questioned about? I began, in spite of myself, to feel sorry for him and even amused.

'I wish I'd brought a newspaper with me,' he grumbled resentfully. 'How much longer am I to be kept waiting like my own office boy, I'd like to know.'

I was about to ask him what kind of an office his was, when the thin man put his well-groomed head round the door.

'Mr Manley?' he said. 'Will you come in, please?'

As the door began to close behind them I could hear Manley

explaining that his retirement colonelcy was a substantive regular Army rank.

After a little over twenty minutes, the same man called me in. Manley was no longer present; they must have shown him out by another way.

It was very informal. Apart from the thin man, an elderly stenotypist in a purple hand-knitted jumper, an extremely handsome man who looked like the popular notion of a diplomat, and a third man by the desk. His chair, like the others in the room, was pushed sideways so that it was not easy to tell if he was conducting the enquiry. But his 'presence' told me he was the senior here. A heavy visage with deeply folded skin of saturnine darkness; hair streaked in black and grey, thick shoulders hunched in a voluminous and untidy jacket and a crooked dark tie. The black eyes with liverish whites were hooded with heavy, overlarge lids. I had never seen eyes like them.

The thin man said politely, 'Do sit down, won't you? This is Major Robert Inglis of the Allied Control Commission in Austria, stationed in Vienna. I'll go from left to right with the names, Brakespeare, Tulliver, Mrs Barry and myself, Bobkins.'

'Good morning, Mrs Barry. Good morning, gentlemen,' I muttered.

'We have your life history here, Major, so we may start at once with the incident at your house, may we not?' To my surprise it was the stenographer who spoke and it took me a moment to grasp that she was asking me if I wanted to say anything before they began.

'Certainly,' I said, and cleared my throat.

'If I may,' began Brakespeare, bending his elegant form forward. He twinkled with all the kindness of a man whom everybody likes and admires. 'I feel we ought to say, before we ask you anything at all, that we do realise that this is a painful business for you, Major Inglis. You have, after all, known David Stephenson for some years and are a—perhaps not an old friend, but an established one. Is that correct? Now, you must not feel that anything you say here will be used against Stephenson as the police are supposed to say, and don't. We just want to get at the facts and this little discussion is entirely confidential. You saw Mr Manley in the waiting room, of course, and he has told us how highly he thought of Stephenson when he was in the Army.' A tiny break in the smooth flow: Manley had said something less flattering about myself? 'Now perhaps you would tell us to start with just what happened at your dinner party in Vienna?'

'Supper party,' I corrected. 'After the theatre, quite late.'

'Oh,' he said, softly agreeable at being corrected. 'Well, if it matters.'

'It could matter,' I answered, 'because the Stephensons were the only guests who had not been occupied the whole evening up to the party.'

'You mean?' This was Bobkins.

'I had the impression when they arrived that Agnes—Mrs Stephenson—was flustered, and that he was bored and had been drinking.'

The heavy man sighed and said nothing.

'I don't want to give an impression that Stephenson was drunk. I only mean it is a long time to wait for one's evening meal if one is not at the Opera or some other entertainment. They were late, and we went in to eat a few minutes after their arrival.'

'How many minutes?' asked Brakespeare.

'Perhaps ten. Just long enough for the introductions—except for my wife and myself all the guests were strangers to the Stephensons —oh, apart from one man they had met a few weeks before.'

'Could I have a list of the guests, please?' asked Mrs Barry, her pencil stopping. 'Afterwards, I mean. Unless . . . ?' She moved her head to question the others.

'Probably the guests are not important to the—ah—incident,' opined Brakespeare.

'Not even the American Ambassador to Vienna?' Tulliver spoke for the first time in a voice that matched his appearance, grating like the sound pebbles pulled by the tide. He was definitely the senior present.

'Ah, of course,' Brakespeare deferred.

'I don't know that the guests, apart from Mr and Mrs Sullivan and my own chief, come much into the incident—as personalities, I mean. Except that . . . some of them are well known in Vienna and even abroad, and the affair was bound to be a good deal talked of for that reason.'

'And the remarks made by Stephenson would hardly have been so offensive had there not been Viennese ladies present,' mentioned Tulliver, emphasising the adjective slightly.

'I understand that Stephenson could be heard above the general talk during—ah—supper, arguing with Mrs Sullivan and your own superior officer?'

'Unfortunately, yes,' I answered Bobkins, wondering who had told him that. 'I was afraid he did not know to whom he was talking. But his late arrival prevented me telling him . . .'

'And did he continue to argue after supper?'

'After a little while he began a discussion with an actress, Frau Pantic, which was not entirely pleasant. She was tactful, however, and the matter passed off. Though not without Mr Sullivan's intervention.'

'What exactly was said then? Do you remember?'

I recounted as well as I could the first argument and Sullivan's remarks about Ireland and the famine.

'You made it sound much less forceful in your first description, Inglis,' interrupted Tulliver. 'Try not to *bagatelliser,* or we shan't understand what actually happened.'

'I'm sorry. If I must tell the plain truth it was most painful and, I think, deliberate. I tried to pull Stephenson up, but he resented that and it only made matters worse. But he was completely staggered by Mr Sullivan's anger.' I stopped, not quite remembering how things had gone. 'Then a friend, Tom Wallingham, who has know him as long as I have, took Stephenson off into a side room and kept him occupied for a time.'

'You said deliberate?' said Brakespeare. 'Surely not quite that?'

'I had that impression. There was a feeling of strain before the remarks were made about Nazis.'

'Ah, strain, yes, we've heard that. Stephenson has been very overworked, we gather. In Washington. You too, then, had the impression he was under a strain? Or overstrained, perhaps?'

Here Tulliver underlined a typed remark on a paper that lay before him, and then pushed it over to Mrs Barry, who copied it into her record. I have very good eyesight and I saw the sentence. It read "two months' leave on quitting Washington". Brakespeare glanced at the paper as if interrupted in what he was saying and went on with pleasant patience. 'You were about to say?'

'Strain, yes, but I don't quite know how to express it, it was just a feeling of tension in him. He always felt very strongly about the Nazis and their crimes.'

'And felt, one gathers, that you do not feel strongly enough? I mean no criticism of you, but it—that feeling—may have irritated

309

him?'

I was grateful to Brakespeare.

'Exactly. You see, he was only a few weeks there. He did not quite understand that several years have passed since he was dealing with repatriated soldiers; some of whom were . . . were Nazis.' The unwelcome thought of Benda made me stumble slightly and it caused, I was sure, a bad impression. 'Some were criminals, horrible people. But he did not have time to understand that the situation then and now is much more complicated than it seems on the surface; he was always a little emotional on the subject and though he wanted very much to enjoy Viennese society I don't think he quite took into account that he would have to overcome his perhaps rather generalised prejudice.'

'So you think he may have felt, perhaps, resentment, at Mr Sullivan? Or even that he was being asked to prevaricate on a moral issue?'

'He may have done. Mr Sullivan was very sharp.'

'Irish name,' murmured Bobkins.

'Did *you* feel any surprise at Mr Sullivan's reproof?' Brakespeare was kindness itself.

'I was startled, yes. He seemed so angry. I mean, I hadn't thought before of how Irish people must think of that time; he mentioned the death of his grandmother, you know. But from his point of view, one has to admit that there is some objective truth in what he said.'

'You agreed with him, then?'

'Agreed? No, I was startled by a reversal of what I had always taken for granted. But certainly, I was struck by his argument.'

'You didn't feel he had gone too far? It was an English party, after all?'

'It was not like that at the time. Stephenson had gone a good deal too far in his remarks to Frau Pantic and the old boy—I'm sorry, Mr Sullivan . . .'

'Very objective of you,' approved Brakespeare. 'And our transatlantic friends are always chivalrous to women.'

'Not only the Americans,' murmured Bobkins, amused. 'Major Inglis broke his hand.'

'Yes. Let's get to that bit,' said Tulliver.

'Fortunately most of the guests had left. Stephenson made improper remarks about the behaviour of the Russians towards the

Austrian population.' I glanced at Mrs Barry to excuse this pompous circumvention; her head was bent and she strewed her hieroglyphs with incredible speed.

'And you lost your temper?' I couldn't see why Brakespeare seemed so pleased, unless it was to be able to blame me.

'Yes.'

'Why?'

'There were still three women present, including his own wife, who was most upset.'

'His wife, your wife and . . . ?'

'Julia Homburg.'

Mrs Barry's head came up. '*Anna Karenina?*' she asked.

'Exactly.'

'Dear me,' said Tulliver, 'worser and worser. How much appeared in the papers?'

'The papers? Why, nothing,' I said, shocked.

'Thank God for that, anyway.'

'D'you *know* her, then?' asked Bobkins. 'Julia Homburg?'

'She is a close friend, and the guardian of my stepson.'

'That was the only good film I've seen, except for Westerns, since the old French films went off.' Tulliver sounded almost wistful. 'Why doesn't Julia Homburg make more?'

'I believe—she does not talk business much—the Hollywood company refused to allow her a say in the rest of the cast. They wanted to pair her with some pretty boy or other in a farrago about the July 20th Plot. Or so she told us, but she loves to make up wild stories about her months in Hollywood. I think it's really that she doesn't care about films.'

The atmosphere had noticeably changed and I thanked Julie for her help, in my mind. There was now a rustling at the door and then a knock. A young woman put a ruffled head round the door and said, 'Tea, Sir?'

'Thanks, yes. You too, Inglis?'

'I'd like a cup, thank you.' The tea was disgusting, half milk and very sweet. Everyone in the room lit cigarettes, and I did too.

'Now, where were we?' Brakespeare began again, pushing away his cup and saucer, which stood on the desk. Mrs Barry glanced at his movement and I saw her raise her eyebrows; evidently the gesture of pushing his cup towards the middle of the desk constituted a slight liberty in this strange hierarchy. His lips were already parted for his next words, but Tulliver spoke without haste.

'I think I'd like to go back a bit in time. Did Stephenson come to your unit in Styria after or before your own arrival?'

I had to think back for a moment.

'He was there when I arrived.'

'That was your first meeting, then?'

'Yes. Everyone there was strange to me.'

'Didn't we get all this from the Honourable Thomas Wallingham? And that other man—what was his name?' Brakespeare was light in tone. 'As well as Manley.'

'Johnson,' said Mrs Barry.

'Yes, we did,' agreed Tulliver coolly. 'Now, Inglis, try to remember—I know it's a long time ago—the course of events over Torek in 1947. You recall his interrogation, of course. It must have been a great sensation, at the time. How much did Stephenson help with his interrogation?'

'With the interrogation?' I needed no time to remember the answer to that question. 'He did not help at all. He speaks no Russian, as far as I know; certainly none then.'

'The interrogation was entirely carried out in Russian, then?'

'Entirely. If I may explain, we agreed on a strategy, as it were . . .'

'No explanation needed.'

I was silent, not understanding.

Brakespeare came in again, softly. 'So that you were, in effect, the only man who understood exactly what was happening over Torek?'

'I suppose—at the time—I was, but it was . . .'

'Mr Manley says he and Stephenson assisted,' offered Bobkins.

'On one occasion they were in the next room, listening without being seen.'

'And without understanding anything of what they heard? An odd thing for them to do, wasn't it?' Brakespeare, again.

'As Mr Tulliver said, it was a great sensation for us at the time. We were all excited and even made bets. On the outcome, you know.'

'Yes, Mr Baxter mentioned them.'

What else, I wondered, had Baxter said.

'Mr Baxter put in a report at that time, I suppose you know?'

'He told me he meant to do so.'

'Do you know what happened to his report?'

I stared, disoriented. 'What happened? Why, it went to his superior officer, I take it.'

'You did not see a copy of it?' This was Tulliver again, in a musing voice. 'You know which report we are speaking of?'

'I am thinking of the one Baxter made when he was told that Colonel Manely had sent reports direct both to the War Office and the Foreign Office.'

'That's right. But you didn't see it?'

'Well—of course not.'

'I thought Baxter might have shown it to you, since you were so much involved . . .' Tulliver sounded almost humble.

'Not with the security aspect. And both Major Baxter and Colonel Manley were my superior officers. Baxter was stiffly correct about such things.'

'Yet he told you he meant to protest about Manley's private reporting?' murmured Brakespeare.

'I believe he wanted a witness to the fact; but he certainly did not show me the report and I never heard another word about it, that I recall.'

'A pity,' said Tulliver softly.

Silence. Then I said, trying not to sound worried. 'I hope I'm not giving you stupid answers, but I am quite at sea.'

'I suppose you are,' said Tulliver and shifted his bulk with a little grunt, to lean forward on his elbows. 'I will, however, enlighten you, as is only fair, but what I am about to say is Topper than Top Secret. You understand?'

'Yes,' I said with an inward tremor.

'Baxter's report cannot be found. And unfortunately both his immediate superior and the archives chap of that time are not available to give us information.'

I stared.

'What a perfectly extraordinary thing,' I stammered.

'Oh, papers do go astray sometimes,' said Brakespeare rather quickly. 'But it's bad luck that one of these men was killed in a car crash and the other emigrated to Canada and we can't trace him.'

'Can't Major—Mr—Baxter help?'

'Certainly,' said Tulliver. 'It was a very short report, he says. Simply giving notice that a breach of security in a matter of international importance and great secrecy had occurred, in that a private report had been sent to official but unauthorised persons, and that he wished to be formally relieved of his responsibility in the matter.'

'He did not get a reply?'

'Yes, but a signal only, saying not to worry, all was well. That signal we have.'

'Or any rate a signal to that effect on the correct date,' said Brakespeare, 'but of course it could refer to anything, anything at all.'

Tulliver leaned back in his chair and rubbed an elbow.

'That desk is hard,' he observed. His hooded eyes wandered across the room, vaguely, and lifted to consider the corner of the ceiling which was in shadow. It was altogether a rather dark room. I don't know what gave the impression that he was displeased, but I thought he was. Then he smiled directly at me and I saw he was not.

'Have we squeezed Major Inglis dry, do you think, eh?' He said to the room in general.

I rather expected one of them to remind him of the recent security check; but there was really no reason why they should be interested in that or even know about it and on thinking about it, I decided that they probably did not know of it. When I got back to my cold hotel room I wrote down as much as I could remember of the long conversation. I believe, by means of connecting one clearly recalled phrase with another, that I recapitulated it almost as it happened. Then, since it was well past any reasonable time for lunch, I went out to a Lyons Café nearby—the hotel was so uninviting that the steamy bustle of the teashop was attractive in its inimitable Englishness—and ordered tea and buttered crumpets, which were very good indeed. The only depressing thing about it was that the girl asked me if I wanted butter on the crumpets and when I replied, surprised, of course, said with sudden huffiness and a strong Irish accent that, well, most customers ordered marge, didn't they? I said, how could they? She frowned at me, leaning one hand on the tiled table top.

'Aren't you from here, then?' she asked.

'I've been away a long time,' I said.

'Ah. Abroad,' she said, relaxing into good temper. 'You a foreigner then?'

I said no but I thought she did not believe me. 'Foreigners always eat butter,' she remarked and, flicking a stain of tea from the shining surface of the table with her napkin, went away.

It worried me, absurdly, that I had heard nothing from Tom. Later he told me himself that he had been interviewed in Dublin on his return, and was not in London at all. But at the time it bothered me with a drain of confidence, as if my credibility were damaged by Tom not being there with his comforting ease. I told myself everything had gone very well; no questions at all indicated a failure on my part to report the minute incidents in the pen which I had determinedly forgotten and which in turn had led to my request for a security check over Stephenson's knowledge of the Chinese military intervention in Korea before it was public.

But I was still worried and uncertain for I had hardly understood the trend of their questions; obviously, I was not meant to, but I was struck forcibly with the inadequacy of any civilised process of getting at the truth of an event. I have heard men say as much after giving testimony in court cases.

In the hotel room, under the centre light that threw hard shadows, I studied my notes; they did not help me to understand what the enquiry board was getting at, but I suddenly remembered Kerenyi in the pen saying that one could question a man for weeks and not get the truth from him however much both parties wished to reach it. That ought to have been a comfort, but it was part of my bad conscience that it was not. I did nothing at the time over Benda, over that envelope, over the telephone call mentioning Banks, over the suspicions coming back when Stephenson seemed to know more than he could or should about American High Command reports from Korea. Now I was caught by my own attempts at fairness and caution and could not make a clean breast of it without risking my whole existence.

The next morning I went back to read through their transcript of what was said, and signed it. The reading was interesting. Not so much the transcript as an accompanying commentary on it. It was extraordinary how different the emphasis was; in the commentary there was a whole paragraph on my circumlocutory phrase 'Stephenson made improper remarks about the behavior of the Russians towards the Austrian population'. It did not seem at the time very important to me, though I felt surprise now that a further and more detailed account of what was actually said was not required of me. But, of course, my chief covered that in his report, I reminded myself. I was not alone in the room with the papers, but no member of the enquiry board was there. After I had sat there some time, pretending to reread them, but really thinking hard, Brakespeare came in to claim them back.

'How are you?' he seemed genuinely to want to know. 'Slept well, I hope. Hotels are vile nowadays.'

'You got this done awfully quickly,' I said, handing him the papers. 'How efficient you are here.'

I meant the enquiry board as a whole, but he replied with a pleased smile—that smile of a man whose eminence makes it seem necessary to pretend he cares about the approval of others.

'I'm a demon-fast worker when I have to be, yes.'

'You wrote the report, then? Sorry, I wouldn't have commented if I'd known. I thought Mrs Barry must have done it.'

'Oh, no, Mrs B is a stenographer. The transcript is her work, but I did up the notes myself. I'm just going over the street to take a small drink. Come with me, won't you?'

We crossed the wide roadway and cut down a side street, in which several other men were hastening, in dark suits of the wide-set, chalk-stripe then fashionable and mostly with hands in trouser pockets. It was a splendid, late Victorian bar room, all chased mirrors and dark wood. Even the barmaid, in spite of modern clothes, was in character.

'Gin and lemon,' said Brakespeare. 'You, Inglis?' I was flattered by his familiarity.

'The same for me,' I said though I did not care for gin. We drank standing. One of the dark-suited men came over to Brakespeare. He was tall, his clothes looked as if he had slept in them, and he slopped whisky round in a glass without ice. There was, then, no ice in London pubs.

The man nodded casually and spoke directly to Brakespeare with the most languid arrogance and the most strangled accent I think I ever heard.

'All going well, m'dear chap?'

Brakespeare gave me the smallest glance and replied that all was going very well.

'Be finished today, and I can get off for the weekend,' he added.

The man nodded as if he could hardly care less what Brakespeare did with his weekend, and Brakespeare was equally unconcerned with his interlocutor; his manner to this friend was markedly different from his charming, considerate air with me and I saw that this was because he was always kind to his inferiors and I was for him an inferior.

Lounging away, the languid man raised a long and dirty-nailed hand to someone else in greeting. Brakespeare thought of something and called after him.

'Johnny? Drop in my room this afternoon before you go, will you?'

'Ye-es, all right,' drawled Johnny and made slowly for the door.

'Heh, Banks!' called someone from a corner table, one of those little round tables with marble tops. 'Banks, you've left your change behind!'

It was as if a telescope had been adjusted into focus for me. Johnny Banks went on out of the door as if he did not hear. His drooping shoulders implied scornfully that the man who called out could bring the change back with him; he, Banks, could not be bothered to cross the saloon again to pick it up.

We gossipped for half an hour, about people Brakespeare knew in the Foreign Service who were then stationed in Vienna. Naturally, neither David Stephenson nor Johnny Banks was mentioned. But the telescope was now showing not vague masses, swooping abstract shapes and veils of mist; a clear view was formed of an ordered planetary in which the pattern was perfectly visible. It was not chance; there is no chance in human relations. It was the ordering of complex affairs by means which have stood the test of time, even if they operate slowly and are not understood. Because I was drawn, in 1947, into what was then probably the beginnings of a conspiracy, as an outsider and onlooker, I could now see the pattern down the barrel of a time-telescope. And this clear vision was conferred just because the conspirators had tried to use me, had included me—unwittingly—in their pattern. In a word, the conspirators had overreached themselves. I recognised the word: the name of Banks. I knew at last why David was literally driven to drink.

My return 'plane was not until the following day, Friday. So I had a little time to think. In the morning I telephoned and asked Tulliver if I might drop in to say goodbye. Until I was going down the corridor to his room—the enquiry board room—it did not occur to me that other people might be present. But I was lucky, he was alone. His voice on the telephone conveyed surprise, but he was cordial without condescension. He got up to greet me and I had suddenly the odd idea that he knew what I was going to say. I refused a chair and he shook his head, and strolled with me over to the window which showed a London prospect in November.

'How beautiful London is in this weather,' I said. 'The trees . . .'

He gave me a look from his veiled, strange eyes. 'Yes, old Sam Johnson was right,' he agreed.

'Sir John,' I said quickly. 'May I say something to you in complete confidence, just to you personally?' I had looked at the List to discover his title.

'I hope you will, my dear boy,' he said calmly in that harsh, dragging voice. It was just a completely conventional remark and reminded me not to dramatise myself.

'Something scurrilous and slanderous for which I have no evidence except a kind of accumulated set of vague memories I can't quite prove. And the habit of security . . .'

'Yes, your job,' he murmured. 'They teach you modern methods of security, I dare say. We, here, are deplorably out of date . . .'

'I don't want even to mention names, though you will know what I am thinking about.' He made no comment and I shut my hands into fists for a moment in my jacket pockets; this morning I was in civilian clothes. I plunged into an icy depth.

'There is a security leak and has been for some years, I believe. Not only the subject of your enquiry. Please don't ask me for any details; it is just a hunch. But I'm sure in my own mind.' There was no answer; I thought, he will never forgive this breach of good manners. 'I thought it my duty to tell you, even though . . .'

'My dear fellow,' he said quietly, 'for God's sake don't apologise. Can you not name one name?'

I looked away from the misty scene outside and saw his serious face in heavy folds of inherited authority; he was a very impressive man.

'I'm afraid to. It's so unjust.'

'Yes, that is always our trouble. I wouldn't want us to lose it, but sometimes . . . you know, a word in time . . . ?'

After a pause he added. 'It will never go outside this room —unless clear evidence turns up to support it.'

'Can I write something down?' I suggested. 'We can tear it up again at once. But I just can't get the words out.'

'What, burn the evidence in the ashtray?' he said with relieved schoolboy glee. 'Yes, let's do that. It makes it so authentic.'

I turned with him to the desk and he pushed over a telephone pad. I tore off the top slip before writing on it the two names.

'Why d'you do that?' he asked, pointing at the message pad.

'The impression underneath could be read,' I said, 'by experts.'

'Crumbs,' he muttered.

He read, tugging at his heavy eyebrow. Pointing, he said, 'That one I can conceive of. The other not.' The other was, of course, Brakespeare.

We really did burn the slip of paper in the ashtray, and mixed the ashes in with the cigar butts and ash.

On the aeroplane it occurred to me, besides all my thoughts of how different were the things we say, as it were officially, from what we really think or what moves us, that if Tulliver was not aware of an elementary precaution such as the under-impression of writing on a pad, known to every married woman who has ever had a lover, how little 'security' must mean in his profession.

It just went through my mind and I returned then to my personal worries, for which the last couple of days had been an almost welcome censor.

VI

It was the greatest luck in the world that the von Kasdas were titled, that Julie was famous enough for people all over the world to have heard at least of that one film. Otherwise there is not much doubt my head would have been forfeit. I understood enough by now of the way the world is managed to know that. There is a stern rule in worldly affairs that he who discloses some scandal is in the wrong; no matter how true the disclosure, how reluctant the witness, how great the discretion—the greater the truth the greater the libel. He who puts out a finger to touch the world of privilege must beware; above all, he who has ambitions to belong to the privileged. For years it will follow him, perhaps never spoken, but never forgotten: this was the man who got poor old David Stephenson into trouble.

I knew now that David Stephenson would wreck his life and the lives of all connected with him; he had the brand of a destroyer on him. And when the inevitable crash came it should not be said, or not with justice, that I knew something and had given no warning. Even after that time, I was sure, there would be many of those who knew the entire course of events who would secretly distrust me and think me disloyal.

But when the time came there would be blame. Official blame, to be put on anyone involved but not inside the protective circle, which must far outweigh any distrust of me at the time I took measures to protect myself from that future blame. That I was good at my job would not serve me; faithful servants can always be found.

The affair continued for weeks to cause extra work. Not only much technical change, but quiet, internal researches to discover how the Stephensons knew where I was to be found. These were in the hands of a confidant of my chief's in the Embassy itself, and by the slow chit-chat of office gossip there he did finally discover the perfectly innocent man who answered an apparently innocent question. These distasteful things were not done to penalise the man concerned, but simply to find out what happened, which is a fundamental law of security.

It was a relief to know that the whole thing was just what it seemed, not even an indiscretion, for obvious secrecy when dealing with such details is bad for security. But how Stephenson knew that I could be of interest to his friends—that we never did discover. Nor did we discover whether those friends suspected that the changes made in our arrangements were due to him; they need not have been for as chance would have it, a clerk in another department was sacked without notice about that time when the security police came upon traces of his contacts to the east. Security, as Baxter once said, is an endlessly difficult business; my own chief engaged a cook and she lived in his apartment for over a month before he realised that the lover she met on her days off was a Red Army Sergeant.

I was not personally concerned with the enquiries as to how Stephenson knew of my job, or of the then secret High Command documents from Korea a few weeks before our supper party. That concerned the special police and they combed and sifted for months until at least one thing was a certainty; that these two pieces of information did not come from anyone employed by us. The police had their own means of making sure I was uncompromised in either sense, that of indiscretion on my part or that of discovery from outside. An added difficulty was that all must be done without the knowledge, let alone the co-operation, of political intelligence, whom we, in inter-departmental, or rather inter-service, distrust, called the Wild Boys. For it was known that Banks was one of them, and could count on many friends in their ranks.

All this was distasteful and time-wasting, but as I have said, it was not the worst effect of David Stephenson's short stay in Vienna. Once or twice I surprised a look in my chief's eye as he talked to me of some service matter on duty as if he were considering whether I were not perhaps an unlucky chap to have in his vicinity; there was a hidden likeness in these looks to the sense of being an outsider that I brought back with me from London. As it was at home, so in the office, something was changed, without a word being said.

There were moments when I felt that if I had killed Stephenson it would not have been going too far; everything he touched was blighted. I began really to hate him, an emotion I never felt before or since against any human being. It was a feeling as distinct from my dislike of Manley, for instance, as the moon from blue cheese; a corroding passion. I began to understand why the Christian church insists that its children reject hatred. It is, like despair, a deadly sin. When I saw Lali's nervous, self-protective smile sometimes, I was frightened by the force of my own rage against Stephenson and the power of evil he carried in him.

For me, it was a good thing he left when he did. For him, too, I gathered; I heard he was doing excellent work and was a brilliantly capable public servant. The whole matter of his exit from the Vienna Embassy was dropped but I never believed for a moment, as others quite genuinely did, that he had, as they said, learned a sharp lesson—at our expense.

From the emphasis given my phrase about the cause of the fight in Brakespeare's notes, I could guess the trend the final report of the enquiry board was to take. David Stephenson, angered by the presence of former Nazis and equally by what he felt to be a permissive attitude towards occupation excesses—the phrase about the Russians would come in handy there in its ambiguity—and, having been overplied with drink by his host together with being in a state of nervous tiredness with a new job on his hands, had momentarily lost his head. I would appear of a vaguely authoritarian cast of mind, one of those who feel a strong attachment to power, any power. Since Brakespeare would decide what direct evidence should be quoted, I was pretty sure Mr Sullivan's remarks, equally with the direct quotation of what Stephenson said to cause the blow that dislocated his elbow—by his falling on it drunkenly—would be indirectly quoted in softened form.

The affair, had, for a time, another result. We were not as popular as formerly with the British Embassy and were thrown more than ever with our Austrian friends and relatives. There was no discrimination—it was just that people to whom such things happened were felt not to be quite easy as friends. The Stephensons being gone to the other side of the world, they escaped this change too, and my chief, who took the trouble to stay informed about them, reported that they were immensely popular in a post where personality counts for a great deal in the all-pervading boredom of diplomatic life, and that they gave hilarious parties. This latter he told me with an unspoken and unsmiling irony that comforted me a great deal; he at least was aware of the implications of the situation.

He also told me that Tulliver needed to be persuaded to sign the secret report on Stephenson's behaviour. That was just a piece of gossip from one of his many friends in London; but gossip I was glad to believe, for it confirmed my own guess as to the nature of the report.

'I've had a letter from Agnes Stephenson,' said Lali one evening as I came in. 'I thought we should never hear from her again; it's been months.' She said this with determined casualness.

'Damn Agnes Stephenson,' I said roundly. 'I'm surprised she has the nerve to write to you. Or that you ever expected to hear from her.'

'I'm sorry for her,' she said simply. Then, 'Do you want to read it?'

'I suppose so,' ungraciously I put out my hand. Then I heard the two boys calling me and put the letter down again.

'I haven't said goodnight to them. I won't be long.'

They were sitting up together in Nando's bed, and Nando was reading to Sebastian a simplified version of *Hänsel and Gretel,* a tale the gruesomeness of which never failed to please. I stood listening at the half-open door; of course, Nando knew at once that I was there, and his voice took on greater expression; he began to act the story with gestures learned, probably, from Julie. It was so innocent, the showing-off. They were so close to each other, the protective air of elder brother to whom the younger unconsciously plays up, so real, so human, that I felt sharp tears prick the back of my eyes. I waited until the end of the tale and enjoyed it as much as they did—or enjoyed them, perhaps. When I came in at last there were screams of surprise, wild tumblings, gales of laughter over nothing: There could not be anything fundamentally wrong with our lives or they would already have absorbed the wrongness of the atmosphere. Or would they? I did not know at what age children begin to know—not understand, but absorb—the feel of their emotional surroundings. Nando was over six and anything he felt would communicate itself to Sebastian, I thought; but there was no constraint or nervousness that I could feel.

'You must get back into bed now. You'll catch cold.'

'Oh, you worry so, Daddy,' cried Nando, climbing half up the rocking horse from its back legs. 'You're always worrying.' It was one of those big ones with a heavy stable base, which are not made now. Nando fell off as he climbed high enough to disturb the balance and rock the horse backward; at this expected collapse, more screams and laughter.

'Let me, let me,' yelled Sebastian, pulling at Nando's pyjama leg.

'No, you're too young, you'd hurt your head,' adjudicated Nando.

'Now who's worrying?' I cried scornfully.

'What's worrying?'' Sebastian rushed towards me. 'Throw me up! Come on, throw me up in the air!'

'You're too big, I can't.'

I struggled theatrically to lift him up and hold him over my head. He really was too big to be thrown in the air any more. I puffed and grunted as if his weight were too much for me, to their great delight.

Lali said from the door, 'You'll over-excite them—you always do.' But her voice did not sound cool as it had a few minutes before. 'They'll never get to sleep.'

'There you are,' I said to Nando. 'You hear what the Adjutant says. And you know I've always told you, you must never argue with the Adjutant.'

Sebastian wanted to know what an Adjutant was and Nando told him grandly that he would understand in good time. He turned to me, suddenly, for an instant.

'My first Daddy was an Adjutant, wasn't he?'

I heard Lali catch her breath.

'Georgy told me that,' he said proudly.

'Your first Daddy was a brave man and an Adjutant,' I agreed, very seriously. I wondered what legend we were planting, but I knew that legends must be planted. 'You must always do what he would have done.'

I was sitting on the edge of his bed now, and he leaned against my knee.

'What would he have done?' he wanted to know.

'He would be brave and truthful. And always stick to his own chaps, even if he knew they were being naughty.'

'I shall be very brave. But the other chaps will have to stick to me, I shan't bother with them.'

'You'll bother about them all right,' I said. 'We all do.'

'I'm going to climb Everest, all alone. Austrians all climb mountains.'

'Yes, you do that,' Lali advanced now into the room. 'But in the meantime you have to go to sleep or you won't grow up strong enough to climb mountains.'

When they were at last quiet, Lali offered me again the letter from Agnes.

'I don't really want to read it,' I protested.

'I think she's in terrible trouble. I have the feeling she needs . . . I don't know.' She frowned almost fretfully and hurried on. 'I don't know why I feel connected with her in some way. I can't explain it, but I do. She . . . she's so helpless, so much at his mercy. He's like the Nazis and the Russians, he doesn't care about anybody, he doesn't even know they exist. I feel as if I remember her from before.'

I took the letter then, and read it twice. It did breathe that atmosphere I had felt in Agnes the evening of the supper party, of a despairing indifference, as if it were so clear that she could do nothing she might as well not try. For some reason—nothing in the letter proposed such a thought—for some reason I wondered for the first time what their intimate life could be like.

'He's a sadist,' said Lali suddenly, with hatred. 'The way he spoke that night. He wanted to wound everybody, destroy everybody inside themselves.' Then very quietly, 'Julie has talked to me about it, several times. She knows about people.'

On the second reading I noticed that Agnes mentioned an old friend, retired from the Foreign Office, who had just arrived as salesman of a large group of British companies in the far east, and who was visiting them.

'Johnny Banks, a five-pound note to a bootlace,' I said aloud. 'Now there'll be trouble.'

'You—we—should never have had them here,' Lali cried, and burst into tears. 'He made me feel—we were so happy, before he came . . .' After a while I released her and she said more quietly. 'It's all very well, pretending nothing happened, but we can't let such people ruin us. If we have another baby; I mean, they'll notice.'

'Are we going to have another baby?' I asked her, a thread of expectancy rising in me.

'Well, I think we may,' she said defensively. 'Perhaps a girl?'

'A girl by all means,' I answered solemnly.

'Oh, you always make fun of me . . .'

'I'm not making fun. But it was you who said just now we ought to feel some sympathy for Agnes.'

'I do feel that, I do. But she could do something, too. She ought to leave him to make a mess of everything, on his own; think of the two children!'

Yes, I thought, the strongest, professional association in the world, stronger than any civil service or military circle of friends, stronger than the Vatican, stronger than any ties that men can make; the trades union of women who have children to care for. I was suddenly happy, for the first time since the autumn.

'They were such nice children,' said Lali grieving.

'They are safe in England, or rather in Scotland, with their grandmother,' I reminded her.

The idea of the children, at least, being away from Stephenson's baleful temperament cheered Lali up and she accepted her pre-dinner drink with a conspiratorial little smile I had not seen for a long time.

'I forgot,' she said, sipping, 'Julie rang up. That nice American will be back tomorrow from his swing through eastern Europe and she is having him to dinner. I hope you haven't made any appointments?'

'No. I haven't. How interesting; he will have lots of news.'

Colton Barber was one of the few newspapermen who at that time of Communist consolidation in eastern Europe was able to visit Hungary and Poland. He was granted, too, a visa for Prague but after being there only two days was suddenly informed that his permission was withdrawn and he must leave within a few hours. His paper received no replies at all to their requests for visas in Bucharest or in Sofia, but Barber spent several weeks in Yugoslavia and was altogether almost two months on his travels; a period as eventful for us as for him. His news, unlike ours, was communicable and he was full of his experiences, most of which he was obliged to save up in the form of notes for future, uncensored, use. We could hear his voice when we entered the hall, talking the technical details of their profession with Kerenyi. I glanced up at the sunburst clock as Frau Lisl took our coats, and noticed that its broken points and convex glass were at last repaired.

'Well we never expected to get into Rumania, and still less into Bulgaria,' he was saying, 'but I was pretty disappointed when I got chucked out of Prague. Somehow I thought the Czechs would have retained their civilised attitudes.'

'They didn't want you to see their *Gleichschaltung,*' said Georgy as they both rose. 'What's the English for that Robert?'

'There isn't any word for it, thank God,' I replied, 'though in some ways we could do with a little.'

Barber was making quite a business of kissing Lali's hand and settling her in her chair as Julie came in from the dining room, where she had been inspecting the table. She blew a kiss to Lali and then patted the side of my head as I kissed her hand, giving my fingers a quick pressure; I saw that she already knew our latest news and was delighted with it.

'So everything will be all right now,' she said as if to Barber, and meaning more than she said as she usually did. 'As you see, he got back safely.'

She waved towards the big desk, indicating that I should get drinks for us, always a job for Georgy or myself, for Julie pretended not to understand these new-fangled drinks, as she called them.

'Tell us about Hungary,' she went straight on. Her interest was personal, since part of her family came from Hungarian Transylvania, though the area of their home was by then Rumanian I believe—these frontiers which changed so frequently were unreal to me and I could never remember exactly how and when the changes had taken place.

'I wonder if any of your family still lives there?' Georgy asked. 'I remember thinking of your mother the night I was captured, near Oradea.'

'I've heard nothing of them for years,' she said dubiously. 'Not since about the middle of the war—but I don't think any of them could have left in time or I should have heard from them. They were mostly lawyers, you know, and I hardly think former lawyers can still be working . . . Well lawyers! In those parts, where half the the people are illiterate, a lawyer really as often as not means a letter-writer with an official title. Would they have lost their houses, d'you think, Barber?'

Barber shook his head in doubt. I hardly heard his reply, as he talked about land-reform and dispossession, for I drifted into a reverie of speculation as to what this room must have looked like during the war. The place was filled with a powerful, atmospheric sensation of the past, of people and events I never knew and that were never spoken of so that they were shadows without outlines but stronger than many past realities that are openly admitted to. The face of Franz Wedeker was familiar from newspaper pictures resurrected from archives at the time of Barber's famous self-accusation, and from the reviews of Georgy's book when Wedeker's history was several times recounted. So I could envisage the narrow, fine-drawn lines, large eyes with humorous corners, and an inquisitive sharpish nose contrasting against the brow of a scholar and a mouth so sensitive that it was hard to believe its owner could ever stand the years of captivity. I thought of him always as inhabiting this room, but I knew from Kerenyi that in fact he spent most of his imprisonment in a small room overlooking the courtyard and the back house, which was just then in process of rebuilding. Only the cellars survived a bomb in December 1944.

The place at the back of the apartment never became real to me or to Lali for we never saw it though I knew it was now used for storage again—its original function. What I could imagine was this room with its high casements to the street, tall bookcases of dark wood and the wide, flat writing table set diagonally so that anyone working at it could see sideways out of the windows and yet reach the nearest shelf where the usual reference books stood, yearbooks thirteen years out of date ranged alongside the shabby dictionaries of five languages. I knew this desk was now rarely used for its real purpose; only Julie's much-scribbled diary of appointments was always there, and it was used nowadays as a table on which at that moment a silver tray of drinks stood. Once it must have been covered with piled papers, the paraphernalia of a literary politician. Now, its real function as dead as its owner, it was an anachronism far too large for the slight use of one who never wrote anything more than a short note. It imposed its silent presence with a solid, rather ugly dignity and I thought, not the first time, that a woman as practical as Julie could have been expected to move it out of the room altogether. It must have been a daily reminder to her of things that I clearly remembered her saying when I first knew her, she never again wanted to think of. Was it a neurotic streak buried somewhere under that sanguine, energetic temperament that kept the desk there as a pious monument? That would fit the total silence that shrouded Franz Wedeker's person and death. Or was it, more simply, just the extreme conservatism of Viennese domesticity that allowed furnishings and arrangements to remain as they had always been and that never contemplated change unless forced to—of which the ancient, worn carpet was evidence?

Somehow I did not believe in the latter possibility; the desk had meaning for Julie, never mentioned and fading gradually into habit, but which retained a physical connection with herself that could be felt—the irreducible core of some part of her consciousness. She stood by it now, her head slightly tilted to one side and a bottle of Vermouth in her hand as she asked a silent question of Lali, who replied with a smiling nod. She gave the bottle then to Georgy and leaned forward over the flat top, resting both hands on the surface and craning her neck to see if there were still ice cubes in the bucket—a present from us.

As Julie stood quite still for a moment, I noticed with a slight shock that her long, delicately muscular and strong hands were embellished for the first time since I knew her. She wore not only a loose bracelet on her wrist, but on the ring finger an oldfashioned ring with a dark ruby in it. My invisible start—she noticed everything—directed her attention to her own hands; she looked down.

For an instant her hands quivered on the sullen gleam of the dark wood and then she put them behind her back with a hasty movement. Her eyes went wide with a blank gaze and her features showed that grief and anger I recalled as she looked at Lali for the first time after the war, ill, starved and exhausted. She moved quickly away from the desk, frowning the familiar sharp frown that made a line between her brows, and crossed to a tall, heavily ornamented vase that stood between two of the windows and still showed the hairlines of repairs. It held carnations with silvery pointed leaves and heads of several colours, hothouse flowers that did not suit the vase but were probably a gift from some admirer. She twitched the carnations into a new formation with brisk movements, frowning all the time and then dropped into a chair with a high back of shabby dark green velvet. As Georgy handed her her glass she glanced up at his eyes and spoke quietly.

'You're right. I shall put it in the storeroom.'

Barber stumbled for a moment, thinking himself interrupted, and then went on talking. I liked to think of Barber as naïve, but his perceptions were sharp and delicate for his friends.

'Oh, Budapest,' he said, his whole face darkening with a morose incredulity as he answered some questions of Georgy's. 'I'd hardly have known where I was if I didn't remember the sound of that queer language!' He scowled and emptied his glass quickly as if he needed the whisky. 'The police terror is much worse than Berlin in

'41 when I left because of Pearl Harbor. Both there and in Warsaw it's so secret that nobody ever mentions it; you hear and see nothing. Even to speak of the police is a state secret—I didn't even notice it until I went to Belgrade, where half the people I spoke to complained about the UDBA. I tried to persuade a man there that this proved they did not have anything like the police rule of Hungary and Poland, but naturally, he wouldn't believe me. It was weird, the way people stared in the street at a foreigner. But nobody speaks unless they are officially meant to.'

'Did they think you were an agent provocateur?' asked Lali fearfully.

'They must have done—or they were just scared of any stranger in western clothes. It's much worse in Warsaw than even Budapest, because there've been no western travellers there since 1939. And the ruins—God, the ruins . . . I was near to suicide in Warsaw.'

'But surely there are other journalists? Diplomats?'

'Not in Warsaw. And not in Prague and Budapest for the last year or so. The agencies keep local stringers, who are naturally under the control of the police. Diplomats are *never* seen, only their automobiles. I had to pass a double police cordon to get to a dinner party. One around the district—they all live in the same area—and one guarding the house itself. And they seem to know absolutely nothing about what goes on; they mix with each other, and that's that.'

'And the occupation?' asked Georg.

'You never see a Russian either, except I believe—I didn't—at formal ceremonial occasions like May 1st or May 8th, or national days.'

'But soldiers, I mean,' persisted Georg.

'Soldiers everywhere, yes, but not Russians, though they say all the senior officers in the Polish Army are Russians. The strangest thing about the atmosphere, when you do talk to anybody—officially, you understand, in his office—is that they all emphasise a sort of nationalism; the less real control they have over their own affairs, the more they talk about Magyar literature, and destruction of historical buildings in Warsaw by the SS, and so on. Even—or especially —when everybody knows the destruction in question, as in Budapest, was caused largely by the Russians.'

'That would hardly be true in Warsaw, though,' said Julie. 'I remember the inner town was much bombed even in 1942 or, rather, in 1939 but it was still in its ruined state, I mean.'

'Warsaw is almost totally wrecked. They showed me the plans for rebuilding the old city and I believe they mean to reconstruct it entirely. The ghetto area is quite flat and open. Nothing there, nothing at all. Not even ruins. I thought the poverty in Budapest was the end of everything—but Warsaw is infinitely worse. I guess Warsaw is what hell must be like.'

'But Hungary—it was always so rich,' wondered Lali. 'I remember my mother talking about the masses of food they had when Austria was starving after the First War . . .'

'Yes, but now the Russians are taking everything out of the country—you have no idea!'

'It's an extraordinary thing, when you think of it,' said Julie, 'that large parts of the country that really started all the whole horror have been protected from the worst of the consequences . . .'

'The Germans must occasionally get the advantage of their historical fate of being in the middle,' answered Georg with his bark of sardonic appreciation. 'Ourselves too.'

'I can't believe that people won't revolt,' I suggested. 'Not in Russia, perhaps, where they were always so poor; perhaps not either in Poland. But the more westernised countries surely, where they remember how things used to be?'

Barber shook his head. 'You don't understand what this police control means, Robert. A scowl in a breadline can get you a prison sentence! Jokes are forbidden in case they have double meanings. And it's getting much worse. The trial of Rajk last year won't be the last in any of these countries—you'll see.'

'You talk of nothing but politics,' said Julie. 'You're all as bad as the people in Hollywood said we central Europeans are! One man said to me there that the whole Nazi thing and the war were just one great bore, because nobody seemed to have any private worlds in that time. And, as he said, you can't really make books or films about people who have no private lives—there's just the old clichés about the jackboots.'

'How right he was, too,' agreed Barber, 'except they think in Hollywood that only Germans wear jackboots. But you can't really agree, surely, that you had no private life in those days . . . ?'

'None at all. There were secrets, but no privacy. I think back sometimes to before the war—it seems so rich and varied—though really there was a great deal of trouble. But private worlds survived.'

'This room seemed very much a private world when I first saw it,' said Barber, looking about him. 'But I must tell you, I do miss the old stove.'

'Yes, it was cosy, but the central heating is more practical, and after the bomb the stove never burned properly. Everytime it was repaired, something else went wrong!'

'There are private worlds now,' said Lali. 'The house for instance.'

'Yes, that's our hideout. And somehow, being so near the frontier makes it more precious—as if it could be overrun again . . .'

'I don't think you need worry about that frontier,' said Barber, 'since 1948 Yugoslav attitudes have changed a great deal. Of course, they blame the old Monarchy for everything, as they did before the war, but the Tito lot have their hands full. They won't start any trouble, believe me.'

'I wonder what Agram is like now?' surmised Georg, 'in a weird way it was rather gay in the war.'

'Well, they've had a bad time since the break. But there is no comparison with Poland or Hungary—as I told you, people actually complain about the police in Yugoslavia! And there are a couple of western newspapermen there. They grumble all the time, and life is not too comfortable even for dollar-earners. But I kept telling them how lucky they were, which didn't make me too popular . . .'

'I expect you to start telling us that!' Julie laughed at him.

'I guess I don't need to tell you . . . Kerenyi was in Russia, and you and Lali both lived through the end of the war.'

There was a moment of silence; something chilled the atmosphere and was instantly gone again. I longed for words to reassure Lali but found nothing that would not be too intimate. Here, in front of other people, I could have said something that could seem a generalisation; but inhibition shrank an always limited imagination to nothing. I could feel Julie's intent consciousness of us. We were finished by now with our meal, and she stood up, pushing back her chair.

'If you're all ready, let's have some coffee,' she suggested. As she went through the door into the living room, a narrow portal let into the dark panelling, she put an arm round Lali's waist. 'You're right, Barber, we *have* been very, very fortunate.'

Barber left the table after them, but went to one of the panels to peer at a dark, small painting hanging there.

'Is this the one you had repaired and reframed?' he asked in a tone of surprise. His voice clearly betrayed that he thought the picture hardly worth the trouble.

'That's the one, yes,' Julie sat down behind the coffee tray. 'It's my former father-in-law, did I tell you?'

'No, you didn't say that—that explains it.' Barber was relieved from the duty of tact.

She laughed. 'It is bad, isn't it? But I owed him something, and to repair his portrait was the best I could do. It was found down on a rubbish heap in the courtyard. Been there for weeks, but fortunately the weather was good. Then, I couldn't get it done for years —like the clock in the hall.'

Georgy pulled a chair up close to hers.

'I am useful for something, you see,' he said. 'I found you a restorer who would be bothered.'

She raised her eyebrows in pretended coolness. 'Who ever said you were not useful?' she asked, smiling. 'I'm not like Hella Schneider—I find you most useful for all sorts of things!'

Barber, with his rather charming affectation of devotion to Lali, brought her coffee and sat beside her.

'You four make me quite lonely,' he said. 'If I could just find a girl who came up to the two women I most admire, I'd get married myself.'

'You'll have a long way to search,' I said. Lali looked across and smiled in a way I had long missed, and I saw that without Julie doing anything, the whole trouble was resolved. How did she do it—what was said without words in her casual conversation, and how? They, she and Lali, were fortunate and the picture was rightly repaired in spite of its almost endearing badness; we were all comfortable together with each other again. I went back into the dining room to look closely at the portrait, which showed a middle-aged man with sharp, squinting eyes and a humourous mouth, wearing an oldfashioned stock-cravat. It was indeed very bad, and I understood Barber's surprise. Only, knowing Julie better than he did, I did not share it.

VII

Lali came in from the kitchen, with a glass of hot milk for herself, while I was shooting soda water into my usual late-night whisky from one of the oldfashioned syphons which were exchanged every week with great clatter and local gossip at the back door.

'It's odd, isn't it,' she carried on her thought aloud. 'Neither of them ever makes a gesture or says a word that you could call love-making. But they give off an intensely erotic feeling . . . don't you feel that?'

'I do indeed . . . so did Barber, evidently.'

'You—you're not jealous any more?' she asked tentatively. 'I wouldn't like to think it made you unhappy.'

'I've got over that. Nothing changed for us—and that's what I was afraid of,' I answered, a little disingenuously, a conventional dishonesty that Lali accepted with a smile.

'Of course nothing could change for us,' she agreed, with the same constructive dishonesty. 'Everything is cosy now . . . But I wonder sometimes what would have happened if Nando hadn't been killed . . . ?'

'I never knew him,' I said cautiously, 'So I can't visualise . . .'

'Perhaps it had to happen. I feel so strongly that Georgy and Julie must always have belonged to each other—quarrels and all. In spite of everything and everybody else. Don't you?'

'Hindsight,' I said, and leaned my cheek on her shining hair that always smelled so sweet and warm.

The telephone began to shrill, interrupting her reply. At this time of night it could only be something urgent, and I knew at once it was more trouble. My outward worries settled on me again in a second, and with them my distrust of my own judgment. Julia Homburg could scatter our private troubles with a few words of confident lovingness at just the moment when they could be resolved. But on me alone lay it to deal with my official world.

'What is it?' Lali asked fearfully, not meaning the telephone;

and I knew that my face betrayed anxiety, suspicion, even hatred which she had no means of understanding. For of course, I had not spoken to her about the other side of the scene with David; its results in the outside world or its causes.

'Maddening interruption,' I said and moved to answer the intruder. It was my chief's voice and he wanted to see me as soon as possible.

'Shall I come over now?' I offered.

'Won't your wife be upset?' His voice was hesitant, confirming my guess that it was bad news.

I muttered something, ungraciously. I could hardly say we had both been upset for two months.

'I'll come down to let you in. How long will you be? Ten minutes?'

'Make it fifteen. I have to get the car out.'

'You're not going to the office at this time of night?' asked Lali as I put the thing down.

'No, to his flat. I'll try not to be long.' I could see that resentment at my putting work before her wishes was as strong in her as her uncomprehending anxiety, and was again enraged against David Stephenson; if there were not this professional secrecy I could perhaps have overcome her own withdrawal from me weeks before. But she, naturally, could feel my caution and connected it with her own which came from an entirely different source. Yet, paradoxically, it made me happy too; she obviously wanted me not to go.

'I'm terribly sorry. I hope it won't be too long . . . I mean, not this evening, going out again, but . . .'

She followed me to the door of the room and held one wing of the door open for me.

'We must get back to living, like it was before . . . We shall, shan't we?'

'We shall,' I said, 'very soon. I promise you.'

'In time?' she insisted. 'Out of this—atmosphere?' She showed already the sleep-walking look of pregnancy and pressed a hand for a moment to her side.

'In plenty of time. Darling, don't worry. Try to trust me.'

'Ah,' she said quietly, 'if only it were enough to trust *you*. That's so easy.'

I was shifting gears at the lights into the Karlsplatz when it occurred to me that with 'before' Lali meant not before the scene with David, but before the catastrophe. She trusted me to bring back the world of her childish certainties; then I really did belong. Yes, before this child was born, I must rid us of all danger from the public world; we must leave a life where politics mattered for that of Julia Homburg, the world of private loyalties.

He lived in a modern block built just before the war, where everything was square, neat, well-lighted. It was not a bit like the muddled corridors, various stairways and irregular rooms of our own home, and still less like the old place in the country, but neither was it attractive in its space-saving smallness. I could see him standing outside the house door, with the keys in his hand as I turned into the square, hunching his shoulders against the cold.

The room was brilliantly lighted from a top lamp; there were no shadowy corners here, no indirectness; and everything in the room stood squarely, symmetrically. The only incongruity was a recording of Richard Strauss' 'Capriccio' playing already as we entered, and accompanying us throughout our conversation. For when the records were played through, he turned them and began again. Though he never went to the Opera or a concert, he was attached to some music which he used as another man might use a pipe. The long radio and gramophone cabinet almost filled one side of the room.

'Sit there,' he said pointing. 'That's for comfort rather than looks.' He always said the same things.

'It's the business about Stephenson,' he began with forced briskness. 'It's come up again.'

'Already?' I knew it, all the time.

His narrow, soldierly head came up with suddenness. He sat on the low sofa, feet together and long knees wide apart, so that he could contemplate with justified satisfaction his immaculate, hand-built boots emerging from the short gaiters of sharply creased battledress trousers. I, as always off duty, was wearing civilian clothes.

'You expected it then?'

'Of course; but so did you?'

'Yes. Certainly. But I thought it would be a year or so. The man's a wrong'un; it was bound to come, but—'

'Perhaps when Banks sacrificed his "career" I suppose the Centre must have thought all suspicions were stilled; but when he arrived out in Bangkok he was obviously still active.'

'How d'you know that? That Banks is out there?' He sounded so aggressive that for a moment I thought he suspected me. Then I saw from his astonished worried eyes, that he was adrift in a country that nothing had prepared him for. Between the lines, yes, he could deal with that situation and must often have done so; but never between loyalties.

'Lali received a letter today from Agnes Stephenson, mentioning an old friend who recently arrived out there. I knew who it must be, and I suppose Agnes meant me to know.'

'Yes, you said once before that she was trying to warn you—us.'

'Trying to save him, I would rather have said. By interfering with what he's doing.'

'You're so bloody subtle, Robert,' he grumbled. 'What d'you mean? That she wants him to get caught?'

'Get frightened enough to give up, I would guess.'

'He can't give up. He's made himself liable to a charge of treason.'

'The Centre could hardly touch him if he just stopped sending his reports. Or so Agnes would think, wouldn't she?'

'I suppose so,' he agreed dubiously. 'God, who knows how such people think?'

'Agnes is as sound as you are,' I said. 'You don't mind if I smoke?'

'Can she be? She married him after all. Must prove a certain leaning on her part towards . . . towards what, do I mean? A sort of cantankerousness or weakness? I don't know what the hell to think about anything any more, and that's the truth.'

'A leaning to protect the weak, yes,' I said slowly. 'That was clear from the first moment.'

'Of course, you were there,' he remembered. 'That's the sort of thing they'll want to ask you now. They are taking it seriously, at last, in London. It seems, the leaks go on. And now Banks is in Bangkok . . . you see?'

'I see that the cross roads has been reached. The stuff they have been getting from Banks, Stephenson and Brakespeare must be so important that the Centre is willing to take any risk. But they must think the team can get away with it, too . . .'

'Brakespeare,' he said. 'You harp on him, but there's not a shred of evidence, apparently. Of course, they don't tell simple soldiers like me—let alone you—what they're up to, but still, I do know

Brakespeare is in the clear. His background and record are lily-white.'

'So were Stephenson's.'

'Yes,' he said and his voice sounded grim. 'That's just it. Damn it, I knew the man's father at school.'

It would have been ludicrous to a stranger, hearing his sharp, Guards voice, quoting generations of confidence; but not to me.

'It won't do, you see.' I worked it out slowly as I spoke. 'If there is no other man working with Stephenson for the Centre, then their arrangements would have broken down when Banks left the Foreign Office. He was sacrificed, obviously, in order to reassure everybody that the whole insecurity was his and was now finished with. No other explanation fits all the facts as we know them. But evidently, too, the Special Branch did not accept the matter as closed, and continued to watch. And sure enough, the leakage continues.'

'It still does not prove it's Brakespeare who is passing stuff on from Stephenson or elsewhere. For one thing, the job Banks now has is with a group of manufacturing companies who do a lot of business with eastern countries. I mean, eastern, in both senses. That opens up a whole new vista of further trouble, don't you see? But it doesn't connect with Brakespeare, as far as I know. What I do know is, the suggestion you made in London was entirely rejected; they just don't believe you and they have no evidence. And this is not a matter of the Foreign Office personnel people, who might be protecting Brakespeare for some reason, whether perfidious or only stupid; this is the police, who are apparently sure there is nothing in your accusation against Brakespeare. You see, that moment in the public house—it was only a moment and rests solely on your own impression or opinion.'

I thought about this and there was a long pause filled with music.

'What you mean is, I am suspected myself of accusing Brakespeare for some reason of my own? Possibly even a treasonable reason?'

'No,' he said uneasily. 'No, that's not what *I* mean at all; but it may be what they mean. They want to interrogate you again, in fact.'

'But my story can't be shaken, Sir. Because it is true. That moment in the pub was completely unambiguous. I'd stake my life on it; and if they keep on at it, they will find the other man, the one who called out to Banks so that I heard his name. It was one of those crucial moments that seem like chance but are not chance at all. The use of Banks' name appears like a completely fortuitous circumstance only because we look at it from outside and far away. In fact, it was obvious that those same people used that pub constantly and all knew each other, so that any of their names could come up there at any time—or rather, at that time of day when they take a drink before lunch. D'you see what I mean? Certainly, the man who called out did not know who I was, and is probably a casual outsider anyway. But Brakespeare is—like Banks and Stephenson—of that extraordinary arrogant type who will take risks like inviting me to his local pub where all his friends and colleagues and accomplices go. He assumed, first, that I had never heard Banks' name and, second, that I was too dumb to connect anything in any case.'

'The type—the arrogance—yes, you have something there. But, of course, diplomats are notorious for just that sort of arrogance.'

'If we're going to be open with each other, you don't really believe that Stephenson is as guilty as it seems he is. Do you?'

He looked at me without answering while the records ran out and then got up to turn them. When he turned round from the record-player his face was bewildered and almost guilty.

'Believe?' he repeated. 'In a way, no, I can't believe it. I know it must be so. The evidence while he was here was conclusive. But I can't help wondering whether he is not being used as a front man for someone else. That Stephenson's son would do such a thing —you're quite right there—is absolutely incredible to me.' He waited but I said nothing and he went on at last. 'The scene in your house that evening, it could have been . . . perhaps he just drinks too much. The final report was very convincing, you know; and it admitted that Stephenson sometimes gets drunk. That would make him a good choice for a screen for someone else.'

'You've now seen the report, then?'

'I demanded a sight of it, before agreeing that you should be examined.'

'It seems to have convinced you, Sir,' I said, and a deep anxiety that was also a kind of grief, filled me.

'No,' he said slowly. 'It didn't convince me. Because I'm as sure of your integrity as I am of my own. But that's just it, man. If

Stephenson is corrupt, who on earth can anyone be sure of? I don't believe my own judgment any more. And in any case, I can't refuse to allow you to be interrogated. If Stephenson, Banks and even Brakespeare can come under suspicion, then we can too. Anyone can.'

'Yes. Mistrust spreads into everything and everyone.'

We sat without words for some time and the real content of this conversation became slowly concrete in our music-filled silence.

'I'm afraid I can't resign,' I said at last and I heard my voice dragging. 'That would amount to an admission of guilt. And I'm not guilty of anything except of seeing through Stephenson. Don't you see—Banks resigns and clears the London side of it up. Presumably he agreed to resign on grounds other than the true ones and there was a tacit agreement that he should not be prosecuted. If I can be forced to resign, that clears up the Vienna end and provides a possible culprit *on the military side as well*. Then the real traitors can go merrily on with their treason.'

'The question of your resigning your commission never entered my mind,' he said, 'though it may have entered other people's minds. The question is, whether I should retire myself. I'm over pensionable age, and I'll tell you frankly, I'm pretty sick of this atmosphere. I'm beginning to feel like that fellow who said one should cultivate one's garden and leave the world to go to hell in its own way.'

I did not look at him, even in that moment of shock I managed to keep my head enough to spare him my curious eyes.

'You see, I just don't feel competent to operate in this sort of affair. I feel as if, after a lifetime in the service, I'd been living in another world and things have been going on in the real world that are quite different from what I always thought. For instance, I've never talked like this before. Never. I'd have thought anybody who talked like this was cracked. And that's it, d'you see? Perhaps I am cracked. Or just an innocent bloody fool of a soldier, no use in the modern world.'

'And when this enquiry is over, as it will be, and the truth is out, I shall not renew my short-service commission. So the State loses two good servants as well as all the other damage.'

'I'm entitled to my retirement,' he said, almost angrily.

'Of course, Sir. I didn't mean . . . I was just thinking aloud.'

'The whole thing is a nightmare to me. I admit it. Probably I shouldn't have said all these things. Made a fool of myself, I shouldn't wonder. What I had to say was just that this policeman will be here next week.'

Of course, he was being disingenuous with himself; he talked because he had to talk to somebody and I was the only man involved enough for him to discuss it with.

'It will be the same man who has already questioned all your fellow-officers from Styria, from the pen. They tell me a man called Morgenstern—queer name—admits that he suspected Stephenson even then but didn't report it because it was based only on a personal dislike between them.'

'Morgenstern,' I said, 'I wonder what he's doing now?'

'He's in business and doing very well. Unlike your old friend Manley, who is apparently both rocky and dubious.'

'Manley said something about his office when I met him in London, but he didn't say what he did.'

'He's in public relations.' This was the only time in the whole conversation when either of us smiled.

'So the enquiry will go right back to the pen, to the first time I met Stephenson?' I thought of Benda and the cellar door; but I thought too of Julia Homburg's house and that gave me courage. Something must have changed in my manner, for he looked relieved.

'It'll be damned unpleasant, but it will turn out all right,' he said and clapped me on the shoulder when I left.

Yet as I walked away from the door, turning my back on him, I was visited by a sensation not felt for many years, but which belonged to my childhood; the feeling that the person behind one's back would be changed into someone or something else, if one turned round. But, of course, I did not turn round.

On the drive back from the Third to the Eighth District it dawned on me that my chief must have some much more powerful reason than dislike of the atmosphere with Stephenson, for him to decide to retire. I supposed then, and I still suppose, that David Stephenson must have looked him up when he came to Vienna, just as he looked me up. An old friend of his father's and in a senior position on the staff—of course he did. That my chief could have committed any indiscretion I did not believe, but that he felt a much deeper mistrust of himself than he expressed to me was clear. It might have comforted my own uncertainty to think that this upright and experienced soldier could also be undermined in his self-reliance by Stephenson's destructive nature. But, on the contrary, it deepened my own fear and hatred, for my chief was a pillar of that established order to which Brakespeare, Tulliver and Stephenson himself belonged, as his father did before him. That Stephenson could threaten my own career and my inner balance belonged to the nature of my between-worlds existence; but with my chief the whole fabric and construction of government and administration was undermined.

I was glad that Lali would be asleep so that I should have time to recover myself before morning. But Lali was not asleep; she came yawning to the bedroom door as I crept into the bathroom which lay between our room and the nursery.

'I've been trying to read Georgy's book,' she said in an undertone, 'but it's so difficult . . .'

'You should be fast asleep,' I admonished her, but a sensation of painful joy filled me which really only increased my worry.

'I wanted to wait for you,' she pretended to pout. 'Hush, you'll wake them.'

'It would take more than us whispering to wake them.'

She picked up my clothes as I dropped them on the chair and as I bent over to clean my teeth, she ran a finger softly down my spine.

'It's a pity men only show their backs when they're swimming. You've got such a nice back . . . when I went into pot Sebastian, they were so funny. All curled up together in Nando's bed, and Nando clutched him as if I was trying to take him away—Sebastian, I mean. You know, they are so alike, it's incredible how alike they are.'

'They really are brothers,' I brushed my hair and washed my hands and we turned to go. As Lali reached for the light switch I saw that her waistline was already softly thickening.

VIII

Somehow, that we were natural and happy again at home and in the release of long-denied emotion between our closest friends made the following ten days of interrogation and consultation in my official life appear the more anachronistic. As soon as the policeman, for that is what he was, introduced himself, he reminded me of Major Baxter. He was an ordinary reasonable fellow whom one could get along with in any normal circumstances, doing a necessary job with as little unpleasantness as was possible for himself and those he must interfere with. It was clear at once that I was not actively suspected by him of anything more than of not having told everything I knew. That this suspicion was justified I admitted and I told this man from the very start everything I could recall. I did not make up my mind to do this until the day after the conversation late at night in the curiously unattractive apartment of my chief.

Whether this conscious decision arose out of my personal life or out of the impression made on me by the loss of confidence in a man who had bought the right to his own authority over himself and others by a lifetime of service, I am not quite sure. The reunion of feeling between Lali and myself, the replacement of mutual consideration by unity, the refocusing of lovemaking with its inner meaning were so total, that the disharmony and unsoundness of my involvement with David Stephenson and everything connected with it formed a contrast stark enough to startle into consciousness a much less intuitive man even than I was. I felt that I must at any cost disinvolve myself from a complexity which, as I had already been warned, could rot my real life and that of my family; but the experience of the effects of corruption and bad faith on my chief widened this conviction into a certainty that I was unfitted for public life altogether. Other men may be able to divide their private lives from their public selves. They may, and I know they do, use one set of standards for business and another for personal

343

relations; very often a higher standard of scrupulousness in public than in private matters. I realised in those days that this was not possible for me.

My own job was a small and simple one. I was charged with the keeping of strategic and tactical maps which were a part of what is called in military jargon the Order of Battle. That these maps were of extreme secrecy is obvious, but my own concern was not with the information that caused me from time to time, on the instructions of my chief, to alter them and the dispositions marked on them. I knew nothing, or almost nothing, of the means by which such alterations became necessary. When additional secrets were confided to me, as in the case of the Chiefs of Staff consultations over the battles in Korea, it was because I could not do my work sensibly without knowing of them. They were, however, incidental to my work, which concerned in any case, only dispositions in central Europe. I was a cog, as the saying goes, in a large machine, but it was nevertheless not new to me to be approached as a possible source of secret information, both by our allies and, by more devious means, by our enemies. If I were not used to such approaches I could not have recognised the interest of the Stephensons in my work. As it was, my recognition came later than it ought to have done. But this stupidity, or trustfulness, on my part was my only dereliction of duty and was not even counted as such, for in fact it was the means of establishing proof against Stephenson.

It became clear in the first interview with the policeman from London that this was the official interest in myself; and far from it causing my ruin, it soon appeared that, if I wished, it could be the step to a permanent career. To have made enemies in the Foreign Service, I realised, was not to have closed avenues of advancement in other departments, but rather the contrary, because of unending interdepartmental rivalries. Only because I was still stationed abroad did the opinion of the Foreign Office appear to me so important. Before the policeman left Vienna again, it was made plain to me that by transferring from one department to another of the State service, and accepting an appointment at home, I could have an honorable and successful career in front of me.

I made no decision and none was either called for or was yet possible, for my commission still had a little while to run. The possibility was suggested to me in the way the English do such things, without anything definite being said. That was all. The policeman left again; my chief requested his return to his original regiment, which meant his retirement from active duty, and neither of these events caused any flutter in the small official world of Vienna. The first because it was known to so few people, and the second because it seemed perfectly natural since he came to the city nearly six years before with the first occupation contingents, and was ready to make way for a younger man.

Two days after the policeman left us—to report in London and to his colleagues in Bangkok through London—I received two visits.

I was to lunch with Barber and for that purpose arrived in the bar of the Bristol Hotel at one o'clock. My host was not yet there so I sat down with a drink and that morning's *Times,* just arrived. People sat about, went in and out, chatted and drank. There was the murmurous air of measured busyness usual in such places. I became aware that someone stood in front of me, and glanced up, expecting Barber's long form. It was a man I did not know; not tall but short, not short-cropped as to hair but rather with long strandy locks that reached his collar at the back, not American but English.

'Hello, Inglis,' he said with a sort of heartiness that did not match his casual appearance. 'Haven't seen you for an age. How goes it? Can I join you for a drink?' Here he looked at his wrist-watch, one of those that tell the date and can be worn under water. 'As a matter of fact, my man seems to be late. But he usually is . . .'

He seated himself and called for whisky and soda, which arrived immediately.

'Had a letter from David Stephenson yesterday,' he said, taking a first sip. 'Heard from him lately?'

'Not for some time,' I replied, still trying to remember who he was. 'How is he?'

'He's fine. Of course, in his sort of work, the strain on the nerves is always considerable. I know, being in the same sort of job.' He drank again and lit a cigarette, one of mine that lay on the table before us. 'It's only to old friends that one can mention such things, naturally. That's what makes it such a strain, doing these double jobs.'

'Head of Chancery at a smallish Embassy? I wouldn't have thought that such a strain.'

'Ah, you're cautious, I see, and quite right too. If only everybody

345

would mind their own business! But there are always people who think they know more than they do, and as some booby said, a little knowledge is a dangerous thing.'

'How is David's wife?' I asked, drinking too.

'Oh, she's in great form, I gather. She doesn't know, of course, that he's playing this double-double game. Men like David are heroes, really—don't you feel? Half the time they're suspected by their own people. Poor David feels that very much, I know.'

'I'm surprised at you speaking of it, then, to a complete stranger like myself.'

'You?' he said, shocked. 'My dear fellow, such an old friend and in the same business. He asked me, as a matter of fact, to remember him to you.'

'And you've done so,' I said pleasantly, 'and now, if you'll excuse me, I must go and meet my host, who has just gone to the bar.'

The incident was so ludicrous that if somebody had recounted it to me, I should not have believed it. When I paid my bill before going to the restaurant, there was a whisky and soda on it.

The second visit was not at all odd or unexpected, only unusual. My chief came into my office late in the afternoon, as I was thinking of finishing for the day. I did not expect to see him, for it was the day of the Allied Control Commission meeting, and normally he was 'on call' in his office while these regular meetings went on. We shall never know, I suppose, why the Russians did not walk out of the Austrian Control Commission, as they did in Berlin; in Germany almost all the four-power institutions were long since a matter of history. For whatever reasons, and they were certainly numerous and complex, the four-power meetings continued in Vienna until the peace treaty was signed, and though detailed control was by that time much slackened, the four-power machinery was maintained.

He came in and laid down his cap and gloves with his cane on the side table, and, for a moment bent over some papers lying there, which I was just about to lock up for the night. He turned abruptly, lifting his head in a habit he had, as if jerking the muscles against the tight collar of a dress tunic.

'Odd thing happened this afternoon,' he said. 'Chap came up to me as I was leaving the Control Commission and button-holed me. Horrible little brute, needed a haircut. Didn't catch his name. He said he was a friend of yours . . . ?'

'It sounds like the same man who approached me in the bar at the Bristol.'

'He had the bloody nerve to suggest I should go for a drink with him. Said he wanted to give me a message from Stephenson.'

'Then it was the same chap,' I nodded. 'What did he say then?'

'I told him in short order I was not aware of having the honour of his acquaintance and would he get to hell out of the building unless he could show me a pass—which I knew he didn't have.'

He stopped and glanced sideways at me, frowning.

'Stupid of me, wasn't it? I should have taken him home and let him talk. As it was, I was furious because there were a lot of people standing round—you know how it is after the meeting. I didn't think fast enough. Of course, he'd got himself in there somehow just because it was so public and yet not easy to get into—to give me the idea he was supposed to be hanging around. You see?'

'He probably did have a pass, at that,' I guessed thoughtfully.

'You think so? Anything's possible, I suppose. But one of the MPs heard me bark at him and moved him off. He went without any fuss. I could kick myself now, but all those Frenchmen and Yanks watching, they'd think I was in the black market, or something . . .'

'You haven't missed much,' I said, 'because he—or someone like him—came up to me at lunch today and started a rigmarole about Stephenson. Treated me like an old friend—I can't say I cared for it either, in public.'

'They must have heard about the special-branch man.'

'I suppose so. But what a way to go about it!'

'Well, in a bar—you can never hear what the man sitting next to your table says. Haven't you ever noticed that? It's quite a good place to pass messages. Did you ever see him before, this man?'

'No, did you?'

'No. But that doesn't prove much. I've always kept well away from that sort of spiv, whether on our side or the other.'

'But he was certainly British, don't you think?'

'Damned queer that he got close to you on the same day, though.'

'Stephenson's friends must feel that it is urgent to get the rumour around that all these suspicions are unfounded, and it's we who are the culprits, not him.'

'So long as they stop at passing rumours,' he said slowly. 'Look, Robert, I don't want to worry you unduly. I'm probably getting jumpy in my old age. But I think . . .'

'What, Sir?' I said, he waited so long.

'I think if I were you I'd get your family away for a few weeks. You can send them to the country, to that house of Frau Homburg's, can't you?'

I stared at his narrow face, at first unbelieving and then with a sensation of going cold; in fact, I had to prevent myself shivering.

'I'm alone, you see,' he said. 'There's nobody of mine here. And I'm probably imagining things in any case. At all events, don't take any unnecessary risks . . .'

I sat down, feeling behind me for my chair.

'Look here,' he said anxiously, 'no need to take this too seriously. I only mean . . .'

'Tom Wallingham will be there in a week or so,' I considered, 'and the farm people are always about. There's a new man for the stables, too.'

'Of course,' he remembered, 'you decided to buy some blood-stock. That fellow Kerenyi was being very amusing about it, I recall, months ago, when you first began to talk of it.'

'Yes, he thinks it all very funny, but in fact, it's a good invest-ment for Frau Homburg, and means the farm lands will be used instead of being a financial liability. That's what Tom is coming for, to bring over the first pair of Irish horses. They fly them now, you know.'

'Poor beasts!' he said.

'And there are a lot of workmen about, repairing the old stables.'

'Those boys of yours will be rich men some day,' he said. 'When they get back the other place as well.'

'If they ever do, yes.'

'Your wife is the sole heiress, isn't she?'

'In a way. Her sisters are married to German citizens, and they are formally disinherited, otherwise the place could be nationalised as former German property. They get up to such tricks—though not lately, it's true.'

'Germans are they? Well I'm damned!'

'They aren't in fact, either of them. One was a Slovenian and the other Czech, but they all found themselves in west Germany after the end of the war. Refugees—you know?'

'It's a shocking business, these old families,' he said, 'just the same at home, only we do it with death duties.' He picked up his cap and made to go.

'I'll do as you suggest,' I said, going with him to the door and opening it.

'Just a precaution.' He looked at me uneasily. 'I tell you, I shall be glad to be out of this atmosphere. Shropshire will seem like paradise. But, boring, I suppose.'

He would be knighted on retirement, I thought; and so he was and lives still in Shropshire, and that is why I have never mentioned his name.

IX

There were already signs of an early spring so that it was not difficult to persuade Lali that the country was the best place for the three of them. There were the stables, the horses, the coming baby. The drawback was that Nando would have to go to the village school for a few months, but he was to have a tutor in the afternoons after that summer, so a few more months of idleness would not do much harm—he took school with complete unseriousness in any case.

The house in the country would never be without some guest, some actor friend of Julie's, for several weeks a colleague of Georgy's who was in the final stage of writing a book, Julie herself for a day or so; there were always people about. Probably the fears were groundless, and certainly nothing further was heard of warnings or strange visits; as in real life it does happen, the whole incident was a left-over strand of unfinished business. Which is not to say that had my family been in the city, something could not have happened. No doubt my unwanted guest in the Bristol bar was identified somewhere and somehow, but I heard nothing more of it. Still it was better to be careful. Although for some years now there had been no kidnappings in Vienna, yet people did, even then, occasionally disappear and it was hard to know whether they were just the missing persons of any large town or something more sinister. I went to Styria almost every week-end, and collected two short leaves together to take a long holiday in the late summer when the baby would be born.

That was why Lali was not in Vienna on the day that Agnes Stephenson telephoned from the airport in the morning, just as I was leaving for the office.

It was June by then, June in all her brave beauty. The nightingales sang in the garden, returned as Julie once said, in spite of everything, to sing for us. I did not know, until the solitary summer in the house in the Eighth District, that nightingales sing in the daytime; but they do. They sang all the hours God sent. And the smashed syringe trees, with long new shoots, sprayed leaves and flowers through the older, broken, branches with a heady scent. Although I often longed for Lali and the children, I could think of them, too, in the peace of the deep country and yet enjoy, with the nostalgia of loneliness the solitude and quiet of the house in its side street. This was before Vienna was overrun by motor cars but their increase gave one already the desire to enjoy the city before it became a replica of all those other cities turned into motorised purgatories.

The voice on the telephone from Schwechat Airport was cool and hard with a quite different tone from the slight hesitancy I remembered; I thought I heard a note almost of bravado in it.

'I got a route where I could stop off here,' she said. 'On my way home. I have to talk to you. And it has to be today, I must go on tomorrow to London, because of the booking. So can I stay the night?'

I was expecting Julie and Kerenyi to an evening meal sent in by caterers, since I was alone in the house with a daily cleaning woman. But I could hardly refuse, and was in a hurry for the call was making me late. So I agreed and called up to the cleaner to prepare a room for a guest who would arrive within the hour, excused myself to Agnes and left hastily for the office. As I manoeuvred the car—one of those now beginning to fill the narrow roadways, as I was well aware—out of the garage down the street it occurred to me that I should leave a note to let Agnes know there would be other guests that evening and went back, by now out of temper, to do so.

I returned in the early evening to find the caterer's man laying the table and a note on the hall table explaining that Agnes was taking an exhausted traveller's sleep and would appear just before dinner. Since my main feeling was apprehension at having to see her at all, and a slight irritation that an evening with Julie and Kerenyi should be interrupted by such a controversial intruder, this news came as a relief. I retreated upstairs for an extended shower and changed into slacks and a light summer jacket. The waiter, who had been there often before, came in to ask what wine he should bring up and for permission to open a fresh bottle of whisky. I accepted his suggestion of a nice, long cool drink as he said in the English he was proud of, and sat by the bedroom window reading the paper and enjoying the last of a long day's sunshine. I waited with the usual delightful anticipation that attended on Julie's arrivals, for the doorbell to ring, under a very superficial interest in the news of the day before.

Fat Frau Spandela, in a gleaming fresh apron, was behaving, as she always did with the well-known Frau Homburg, as if Julie were at least a Cardinal in all his glory, bowing and rushing about in a great fuss because there was no coat to accept. In spite of the effect of hilarity this performance—the cleaner would not have let anyone else open the door for the world—always created, I knew at once that something was afoot. Both of them gave off a tremor of joyful nervousness that was by no means part of the normal manner of either. I had, in fact, hardly ever seen Julie nervous before.

'Aha!' I said, 'what have you two been up to?'

'I can see you've guessed,' Julie laughed.

'We finally did it. We're married!' and Georgy turned to Frau Spandela to repeat this news in German so that she at once burst into tears and rushed at Julie to kiss her hand and sob congratulations. She was only showing with her ridiculous excitement what we all felt, and we embraced each other with much emotion, none of us knowing whether to laugh or weep for joy.

'We had to go off secretly, you do understand? It was either that or half Vienna being there . . .'

'I must telephone Lali at once. My goodness she'll never forgive you! This calls for champagne . . . !'

'She knows, she knows . . . I telephoned yesterday!' We reached the drawing room and the whole thing must be gone through again with the waiter, who went pale with pride and pleasure when they both took his hand to thank him for his stammered good wishes.

'Champagne,' I cried, 'quickly, champagne!'

'Yes, yes, at once, I'll get it at once,' he ran off still shouting and we could hear him as he reappeared from the fortunately deep cellar with cool bottles, repeating to himself, *'Nein, so etwas, nein hast du so 'was gesehen . . .'*

At that time women's clothes were pretty and feminine and Julie wore a dress of rose and white Italian silk that made her, if possible, more beautiful than usual. She shook out her skirts, and pretended to curtsey and blushed like a girl when I told her so, and then Georgy caught her in his long arms and kissed her and in the midst of all this happy bustle and the loud pop of the first cork, a movement behind me reminded me of Agnes and there she stood in the doorway, staring at us.

She was wearing, oddly enough, and it must have been an un-remembered association in her mind, the same grey dress of thin, stiff silk that she wore for the catastrophic supper party, the autumn before. There was an instant of startled quiet, covered by the waiter offering glasses of champagne and hurrying back to his table for another glass, which Agnes accepted and set down untouched.

In the greetings and expressions of surprise at seeing her, the news was somehow not mentioned of the wedding; and after the first few minutes of suddenly awkward chat, it was clear that it would not be. I explained how Agnes came to be there, and the others asked after the children. David Stephenson was not men-tioned any more than the wedding, and possibly Agnes thought the occasion was some anniversary into which she had projected herself, and which out of tact it was better not to enquire about. Possibly and possibly not, for she seemed not to be much aware of her surroundings and did not even comment on the festive wine she was offered. Her face showed signs of more than one night's sleep lost in flight; she was much thinner and looked years older in the few months since I last saw her. There was no longer anything in her of the quiet, rather timid girl I knew in 1946; nothing either of her stillness, nor her trustingness. Even the air of being almost stiffly well-brought-up was gone, its place taken by a manner of unreal hardness. Such a change cannot really have taken place in some-thing over six months; but now it was openly and painfully on the surface. This was a woman already ageing, who had given up the attempt to hide her unhappiness.

I had found no opportunity to tell her who the expected guests were but though she was there, as she said on the telephone, ex-pressly to talk to me, she showed no sign of noticing the presence of people who might well have caused her embarrassment nor did she comment on Lali's absence. Clearly, she was more than used to odd situations; for to the former Agnes and to the wife of a man in a profession noted for its formality, the situation might well have seemed odd. Or was it something else that caused her to accept the presence of two people who had witnessed a moment of extreme humiliation for her? She reacted normally enough when spoken to, and when the others moved, she moved too, in a perfectly conven-tional fashion; but her answers to remarks were formalised phrases, such as one uses when replying to a conversation to which one is not listening. Really? Yes, I suppose so; and the like. But when she was not speaking she stared before her, in her eyes an expression I can only describe with the melodramatic word 'anguished', while the rest of her face conveyed absence. Not absence of mind in the usual sense, but something near alienation; so much so that I thought she had actually forgotten the occasion on which she met Julie before. Once or twice she looked about her as if wondering what she was doing there, and at me, like one trying to place a chance acquaintance.

Kerenyi offered her a cigarette which she took, and I followed his look towards the hand held out; as he snapped a lighter at the cigarette he continued covertly to examine Agnes' hand, and when I moved an ashtray forward on the table I saw why. Across the back of her right hand, a newly healed scar of smooth tissue crossed just above the knuckles. Agnes herself was now engaged in a discussion with Julie about the pretty beaded handbag of eastern workmanship she carried and which Julie pretended to envy—in reality Julie cared little for modish femininities, in spite of her elegance. I never remember her talking about clothes or personal appointments, while her own adornments always seemed simply part of her. I glanced at Georg and he was looking at me with his shrewd, secretive look. The scar must still have been palpable to Agnes, for she rubbed it absently, as if it itched. She did not touch her wine and when the waiter refilled our glasses she suddenly asked if she might perhaps have a Martini—a 'real American Martini'.

This very strong stimulant was produced for her, she pronounced it excellent and it did seem to revive her. She straightened up in her chair and looked about her, not now at the room, but at Julie and Kerenyi and seemed to focus her attention for the first time.

'Sometimes one really needs a drink,' she said, instead of replying to Julie's remarks about the handbag. 'A good strong slug.'

'These long flights must be exhausting,' agreed Georg and Julie, who twice in the last few years had flown the Atlantic, said something about the strange loss of identity attending journeys that already then seemed too sudden in their changes.

'That's so true,' said Agnes, in a heightened voice, 'I feel as if I were not here really, at all.' She turned with an effect of abruptness to Kerenyi, clearly remembering something.

'I read a review of your book in an American paper,' she said. 'We get them more easily than the English papers, in Bangkok, I don't know why. Is it coming out in London? I rather wanted to try to read it—though I suppose I won't understand half of it. But I—' She stopped, frowning slightly, to collect her thoughts.

'It is coming out this very week in London,' said Georg, 'and if you'll give me your address, I'll ask the publisher to send you a copy. As for understanding it, of course you will. It isn't at all difficult.'

'Your idea of what is difficult is probably rather more intellectual than mine,' and Agnes smiled, looking for a second quite like herself. 'But I wanted . . . this review emphasised the part about personal responsibility, and I'd like to read that. But I'll buy a copy, it will be easier.'

'Please,' he protested. 'Of course I shall send you the book,' and he put his hand inside his jacket to produce a pen.

'But, I can't give you an address,' she said. 'I don't know where I shall be.'

'Are you not going to your mother's then?' I blurted out, and then, aware immediately both of the tactlessness of this remark and of the strangeness of Agnes not knowing where she was going, was stupidly silent.

'Not straight away,' she said. Then she lifted her right hand to show the scar. 'I want to see a cosmetic surgeon about this, first.' She stole quick looks at us, one after the other and went on rapidly. 'Too stupid. I was trying to close the window in one of those sudden storms, and it smashed all over my hand. Terrible mess, and I was alone, and fainted. You should have seen the blood . . .'

It was perfectly obvious she was lying; quite gratuitously for none of us would have thought of asking questions. She was only too clearly in a situation in which people take care never to question anything. And this inevitable isolation, even if she were by now used to it or conscious of it, must have added to her burdens. She glanced from one face to another again, testing out the effectiveness of her story just as the waiter entered the doorway and said quietly that we were served.

She started visibly. 'Oh! I expected him to say something dramatic.' She laughed nervously.

'It is dramatic. Vichyssoise, cold poached salmon and roast lamb.'

'You are becoming a real gourmet, Robert,' said Julie, rising. 'Lali will be complaining about the household bills.'

'I must have some vice,' I explained, pretending to laugh.

'Otherwise I shall get the name of the perfect husband, and nobody can afford that reputation.'

These pleasantries, of a kind we should never have thought of exchanging if Agnes were not there, produced a strong and unpleasing atmosphere of social hypocrisy, and I felt ashamed suddenly of forcing Agnes to pretend instead of trying to help her to tell the truth, whatever it might be.

She reacted by chattering, as we sat down before the soup which was already served.

'Perhaps I could, after all, pick up a copy of the book,' she said to Kerenyi. 'If you really mean it. I could go to the publisher's office? I've never been in a publishing house. I really do want to read it. It would be nice to know what it is one's supposed to . . .'

'I don't know that it could help with any but political matters,' he replied, very gently and seriously. 'It's all about politics, you know.'

Julie shot him a look at this note of intimacy and we both saw that Georg had no intention of playing our social charade.

'Ah, but it's politics I need to know about,' replied Agnes, trying with a flighty air to reject his seriousness. Almost instantly the defence collapsed.

'I just don't understand what it's all about,' she cried softly; but the words were a muffled scream for help. 'In the east—it's all so terrible. The war in Malaya. Korea. The French in Indo-China. People suffer so much. You can't imagine the misery they live in . . .' She stopped speaking, with a deep sigh that was almost a sob, and was unable to continue.

'We all think too much about politics,' said Georgy quietly. 'That is one of the things this book is about that you want to read, as you so kindly say. The world revolution of the last fifty years can hardly be understood—if at all—in our crude terms of right and left, capitalism or Communism. Our whole scale of concepts is quite . . . *verfehlt* . . . Robert, what is that in English?'

'Misplaced, or mistaken.'

'Mistaken, then. It is the technical world revolution that produces changes in power structures, not politics as we know them. The whole process has been personalised by contending propaganda systems that really have little meaning. We feel—if I have understood you, you feel—an involvement, as if the sufferings of other people were your responsibility, even your fault perhaps. But it is no question of colonialism in Malaya, for instance. The fighting and the struggling there would be going on if there were no British troops and would probably be even more frightful for the native peoples, because the organisation of the western world, such as it is in the east, would be lacking, and food and water, roads and communications would be even worse off. The brutality and cruelty would be worse, too, there is no doubt. If you could see the vast struggles as the changeover from a primitive social structure to one founded on techniques, you would be better able to bear the misery you see. For what is inevitable is easier to bear than what we feel is done by the conscious will of men; according to our modern myths, even of one or two men. The struggle everywhere is for the control of techniques and all the illusory superstructure of ideologies only obscures the inevitability of the process. Railways, the aeroplane, radio, chemical fertilisers, they are what is causing the revolutions, and did cause the ones we lived through in Europe.'

The talk gave Agnes time to regain a fragile self-command and he smiled across at Julie now and said, 'I talk too much, and my English is not good enough to talk simply, I am afraid.'

'Your English is almost perfect,' said Agnes. She was only playing with the excellent food, while the rest of us ate heartily. Holding her salad fork loosely, so that it jerked a little in an unsteady hand, she gazed before her, reviewing something, or trying to encompass something. 'But people do believe in ideologies,' she said slowly. 'Believe, so that they will do anything, risk anything, for them.'

'But their beliefs are quite irrational,' I argued, 'adopted unconsciously to make things seem simple.'

'Yes,' she said, giving me a startled look, 'that's quite true.'

'This world revolution, you see,' Georg kept his voice level and even to keep the conversation outwardly impersonal, 'means that we live most of our lives in such a constantly moving state of uncertainty that people with inner weaknesses—and that means nearly everybody—cannot stand the uncertainty. They must find themselves something to hang on to and often they find a false religion, one of the political unfaiths, that they don't really believe. For instinctively the mind rejects a faith that does not reveal and reflect what is real whether seen or unseen. People force themselves to believe in what seems to offer a neat explanation, and the more such people feel that what they believe is unreal or insufficient, the more violently they cling to it for fear of losing even that small comfort. They don't know this themselves, very often, for younger people never knew the world when it contained some absolute certainties. I just remember myself, a world in which those certainties existed, and there was a kind of innocence in those days, in people's minds, that was broken by the first of the great wars. Certainly that world and those certainties must have been falling to pieces before 1914, for otherwise the rulers then would have possessed the confidence to stop the slaughter before it was too late to mend, as they had done a thousand times before.

'Only at times when great and deep changes are taking place in whole societies do wars and revolutions get so out of hand as they have in our times—the last time was the wars of religion, the Thirty Years' War. That is, the first thirty years' war, for the second one ended with 1945. Even the French Revolution and the wars that followed it never broke up the actual base of society—those in power could still talk to each other and form alliances to restrict the damage. But in this century the results of technical inventions, hygienic advances, agricultural discoveries of the previous generations have changed the whole nature of human societies. Of course, you are right when you say that men do believe in the ideologies. They believe in them with the passionate faith of sheer terror of the dark. But the belief is not real, and the unreality accounts for the violence with which men contend against each other's beliefs. A true believer shrugs his shoulders at other men's mistakes; he doesn't want to kill the heretics, only to persuade them.'

'That may all be true in a theoretical way. And I'm sure—I feel—that what you say about the ideologies not being really inwardly believed is true.'

Agnes stopped and there was silence; she could not bring herself to say the word 'loyalty'. It was so clear that Agnes was speaking of a concrete personal question that none of us could answer her, but neither could we carry on with a conversation that concerned something she was not telling us. In the meantime, convention carried us through the meal and we moved from the table to the next room.

Julie poured coffee and I fetched cognac. Some kind of conversation went on, I forget what, for none of us was concentrating, but awaiting a continuation only put off by the fortuitous removal from the table, where we should have continued sitting except that the servants had to be considered. Handing Agnes her coffee, Julie looked into her face with an unsmiling kindness and it occurred to me that lately she lacked the indifference that underlay her every expression when I first knew her; it was completely gone. Agnes too looked straight into Julie's face, and I felt a fleeting impression of shock from their silent look. I felt too, irrationally, that Julie sensed what was happening, although she could not possibly do so for she knew nothing about the Stephensons except that one evening with its dreadful scene.

'Why do you look at me like that?' Agnes said in a frightened voice. 'As if you could see what I was thinking?' She put down her cup with a small clatter. 'You do know, don't you? I believe you have second sight . . . or has Robert told you . . . ?'

'Robert has told me nothing. And I know nothing. But I can see that you are in some great trouble. And indeed, everything you say would tell us that even if I did not know it from my own experience.'

How glad I was that Lali was not there. She would have been frightened and distressed by the distraught tension Agnes injected into the room. She fumbled in the little bead bag for a handkerchief and wiped her hands furtively. Her forehead was damp with perspiration, although it was only pleasantly warm.

'My husband wants to have the children with us,' said Agnes, hastily; words were tumbling out that were quite different from what she intended. 'It's unhealthy for them there, but he misses them so much. I'm supposed to be taking them with me next week, when I go . . .'

'Next week? But a week won't be long enough to get that attended to,' said Julie, glancing down at the scar on Agnes' hand.

'That?' Agnes looked wildly at her own hand. 'What? Oh, yes, I forgot. But can't they do it in a few days . . . ? I . . .' She half rose and then sank back again into her chair as if she felt her knees had failed her. 'How do you know?' she wailed. 'I'm sure it won't take . . .'

'But my dear, don't distress yourself so. You've been told wrongly, if the doctor in Bangkok said it would only take a day or so. A skin graft of that extent will need several weeks, even if it takes at once. I know, because I had one done last year . . . Here, you see, on my head?' Julie pushed up her dark hair and showed the tiny white line that remained of a once disfiguring scar, leaning towards Agnes so that she could see. 'That's how I know the English expression for it, because it was done by that very famous surgeon in England. His name is Archie MacIndoe.'

Agnes stared at Julie's forehead with an expression of terror and disgust so disproportionate to the now almost invisible mark that I thought for a moment she was unhinged.

'How did you get it?' she whispered. 'Did it hurt when they did it?'

'The operation? No, of course not. Don't be afraid of that.'

'No, I mean . . . the scar . . . the scar itself?' Agnes shuddered violently.

Julie did not answer. Her whole body went quite rigid, and her face paled, became gaunt with a terrible look of recalled agony. Kerenyi moved quickly, and she put out a hand which he took in both of his, holding it tightly.

Her look was reflected by Agnes, and from her horror both at Julie's aspect and at what she herself had said, I knew that she had heard some story about that scar; one of those stories that are never told in the immediate circle of the person concerned, but only on the periphery of acquaintance. In the panic distress of her own situation she had said something she knew to be dreadful, the unforgivable betrayal of an evil, gutter rumour.

'It was a war injury,' I said, as calmly as I was able, and heard my own voice echoing as if the silence in the room were vast, endless, the silence of an icy wilderness. Then rage gripped me and I went on savagely, 'And how did you get your scar, Agnes? Because nobody is going to believe that tale about the window breaking!'

'Robert!' whispered Julie imploringly. 'That is unworthy of you.'

I ignored her. 'He did it, didn't he?' I persisted, all my hatred of David Stephenson shaking me; if I could not harm him, any victim would do to revenge that look on Julie's face, and that moment months before when his vile destroyer's imagination touched Lali.

Agnes cried out. Then, trembling and stammering, the tears starting to her eyes.

'He didn't mean to. It's this other man, Johnny Banks, he eggs him on, to drink and drink, and then he doesn't know what he's doing. It was the Canadian's fault, he shouldn't have said those things. He called David a fairy and a traitor, and David was drunk, drunk, he didn't know what he was doing. He just grabbed at the knife—one of those fancy dagger things some fool gave us—and I

360

got in the way . . . I was afraid he'd kill this Canadian. For some reason he can't bear Canadians. It's the same with Americans, but he's afraid of them, usually. Oh God, what am I saying . . . ? Nobody even realised the knife was sharp. I thought it was just a decoration, but I panicked and . . .'

She ceased her wail for a second and drew a great, shuddering sigh, and I heard Georgy say something urgently and Julie's voice answering and then Agnes, her voice rising by several notes, again.

'It's been awful since Johnny Banks came out. He terrifies me. I think he's mad, and he makes David almost mad. Sometimes, since Johnny came, he seems to hate me. And I'm so afraid of taking the children anywhere where he might . . . might get at them, influence them, the way he does David. It was Banks who put the idea into David's head that enemies were watching him, that he's followed wherever he goes. He was so much better until that devil came. He was working hard and everybody liked him . . .' Her voice dropped to a harsh whisper. 'And it's true, you see, they are watching him . . .'

Julie rose and went over to look from the tall, open windows into the dusky garden, now cool with the evening dew; she often did that when she was in this room. And this should have been a happy evening. The Stephensons brought their spiritual wreckage with them, and for the second time, Julie and Georg were dragged into it.

Julie now came back towards us and seated herself beside Agnes.

'Now let us talk about this as quietly as we can,' she said. 'We must try to understand. No, don't cry, we must try to be sensible . . .'

'Oh, forgive me, forgive me,' moaned Agnes.

'Now, now, nothing has happened, nothing has been said. It was just a chance memory, that's all. What is important is to think of your children and what you are to do . . .'

At this moment the outer doorbell rang. I remembered with a mixture of relief and almost comical dismay that Barber was coming in for a drink.

X

And a moment later Barber entered with an air of haste and excitement, speaking almost before he was in the door.

'Hi, everybody. Listen, Robert, there's the most fantastic story on the AP tape. I just came from their office . . .' He went up to Julie to kiss her hand, having adopted, as far as Julie and my wife were concerned, the Viennese custom, and was speaking half over his shoulder in the shaded lights of the large room. Then he saw there was a stranger there and hesitated, glanced sideways, and back at Julie; stopped dead in the act of bending over her hand and came upright again with a sharp movement to turn away towards Agnes. His blunt, open face expressed such ludicrous astonishment and disbelief that our tension slackened like a released catapult, and a burst of astounded and releasing laughter filled the room.

'But, listen—what—Mrs Stephenson—!'

'My dear chap,' I said, with an attempt to reduce a wild hilarity to decent proportion, 'why so surprised? You must have heard of aeroplanes, a travelled man like you?'

'Aeroplanes?' he said and as he stared round at our faces, still distorted in a laughter that was more shock than amusement, he seemed almost to stagger physically with his tremendous astonishment. 'Aeroplanes? Yes, but not in this direction!'

'What are you talking about?' cried Georgy. 'Really, I think we're all a bit *verrückt* this evening.'

'But, is your husband with you?' demanded Barber of Agnes with a manner that changed in an instant to something approaching menace.

'No,' she whispered and we were suddenly all silent, back in the imminence of tragedy that we had, it now appeared, broken into in so unseemly a fashion. Agnes was staring at Barber as he at her, with wide, breathless anticipation.

'Has he gone?' she then said, in a stony, quiet tone.

362

'Gone?' asked Julie, and her clear voice rang with splendour in the pause.

'The story is he left Bangkok in a Russian military aeroplane this morning, ten o'clock their time. His farewell message is just on the AP tape now.' Barber spoke, his loud voice now quiet, with professional bite and conciseness.

'Oh, no!' I cried, seized again with the desire to laugh like a man gone mad. 'Farewell message! It can't be true!'

'It is true, though. It went out on Globe-Reuter and AP copied it—with a commentary, by this time, of course.'

'Globe-Reuter?' I said, the technical details of a trade not my own being beyond me.

'Reuters is British,' Barber explained with a sort of impatient patience. 'They got this message in the form of a handout on British Embassy paper and took it for genuine. The local man would probably hardly understand it, don't you see?'

'Holy God,' said Georgy, in a voice hushed with awe, 'what an incredible nerve.'

Like a blow, the meaning of what we were talking of hit me. Agnes was slumped in her chair, eyes closed, slack with reaction. This was the news she waited for all evening, sweating with anxiety. David Stephenson was gone; by now he was in some central Siberian staging point. She was on her way home to collect her children, to join him; that was the question behind her spoken questioning. Should she co-operate in arrangements most certainly already made down to the last detail? Or should she leave him to his fate, alone, watched for the rest of his life in a land and with people whose very language he could not understand, his only company disguised jailers and the handful of shifty British and Americans who lived outside the foreign community in Moscow. What a prospect—my most savage curses could not have looked for a more dreadful punishment.

The silence lasted so long it seemed it could not again be broken, but at last it was Agnes herself who spoke, her voice dragging and slurred as if she were drugged.

'People will call him a traitor. Nobody will see that he is doing what he believes in. That he's a hero in a way. He knows the Americans are moving towards a new war. It is against war that he worked. And even I let him down. I never could quite persuade myself and he was so alone; he longed for help and support and I gave him nothing.'

'But the Americans are not moving towards another war,' said Barber, gently. 'He is wrong. He deludes himself about the Russians—as I'm afraid he will now find out . . .'

'Ah,' she said, repeating her lesson, 'you don't know everything. In his job he knew much more than you can see on the surface. He knows.'

'We always think we know when we do these things,' said Kerenyi.

'But you can't compare what you did with . . .' Barber's voice was loud with outrage.

'Oh, yes. I was a traitor; my own people said so, and many still think so. And you see, the result of my meddling was to make things worse and not better for my own people.'

'I really don't think these theoretical questions matter much just now,' I protested. 'Surely what matters now is Agnes and the two children . . . ?'

I saw, as soon as the words were out, that Georg meant just that. He was always much quicker-witted than I was. He knew at once that Agnes must be persuaded; and here and now, before it was too late.

'You do see, don't you, why I thought you might be able to tell me about personal responsibility?' Agnes asked him with an infinitely sad trust.

Kerenyi got up with brusque energy and strode down the room and back, to stand scowling in front of the chair in which Agnes half lay.

'Yes, I do see, but I can't help you. I can only talk to you about the State, systems, balances of interests. Stuff that means nothing when the moment comes.' His voice tore with cynical anger. 'I can't help you. Julie can help you, Robert perhaps. I can't.'

'I don't understand . . .'

'You have a decision to make, a decision that will settle your fate and your children's fate for the rest of your lives. You think you've made that decision already. But you must think about it again. Not as you've heard of it, but *as it is*. There is just one thing I can help you with and that is this.'

He sat down again and leaned forward, elbows on his knees and his head stretched forward almost threateningly towards her.

'All the talk you've heard lately, all the arguments, are false. The reason Stephenson went to that Russian 'plane and flew off in it has nothing to do with beliefs, ideals, ideas. You said it yourself, but you won't face it. He was being watched. The police were after him. For a crime. He was passing information to the Russians and the police knew it. That is the real situation, isn't it? Isn't it?'

'Oh, Georgy, you're being abominably cruel,' protested Julie even while she knew quite well what he meant with this. He waved her down and then fished in his jacket pocket for his cigarettes.

'Don't be deceived, Agnes. Look at facts as they are. This man lied to you, to his children, to his friends, to his employers. He lied to you constantly, for years on end, day and night, his whole life was a lie. His lies have put a stain on your children for life. People will point to them and say those are the children of the traitor Stephenson. That is what matters. That and that alone. You didn't let him down. His persuading you of that is a lie like everything else he ever said to you, did with you. You've known this for some time. You knew it when you were last here. It was visible in your face, in your hands, in your voice. That is why I said I can't help you, because I know about theories, ideas. But it's only the primitive loyalty to the people who care for you that matters. That I know little of. I had to learn that from the poor, the helpless, the defeated. Yes, the stupid, who could hardly spell the words I was so clever with, hardly speak the language I now speak to you. This man . . .'

'Stop,' she cried frantically. 'Stop!' You're talking of him as if he were dead . . . !'

He drove on, over her cry, over the tears pouring down her distorted face, over the imploring hands that tried to push him away.

'This man brought children into the world to make himself respectable, to deceive the world into believing he was a normal, decent fellow . . .'

'No! No! He loves them, he does . . .'

'He loves nobody. If he had loved them, he would have found some way out of this horrible entanglement. You know that. Ask yourself. You'd have gone to work as a typist, you'd have scrubbed floors, rather than damage your children, or your husband. Isn't it true? Can you deny it?'

He rose so violently that his chair rocked, and strode hastily away. I heard him fling open the terrace door in the next room, and stride out onto the sharply ringing stone, down the steps into the garden, where he stamped to and fro, cursing aloud in the anger men use for grief.

I remembered the story of the child lost during the war and knew what caused Kerenyi's outburst; and as my eyes crossed Barber's I saw that he was recalling this story, too. Julie I did not dare look at.

After a few minutes, Julie rose and followed Georg out to the garden.

'You can't really mean to take the children and join him,' I said at last. 'Just think what it would mean—what your life would be like . . .'

Agnes did not answer. Though the tears no longer poured down her face, she was in a state of collapse, hardly conscious, slumped in the chair.

I could think of no more arguments, everything seemed remote, blank and meaningless. It was Barber who got up and came to lean over my chair.

'We could take the decision out of her hands,' he suggested softly. 'If we call up somebody in authority . . .'

I stared up at him, not understanding at once.

'She's in no state to make decisions. If we prevent her now from going on with whatever their plans are, she can still change her mind again later—when she's had time to think!'

'We can't take such a responsibility,' I said slowly. 'She's his wife, after all.'

'But the very fact that she came here at all, to you, proves she wants help,' he insisted doggedly.

Before I could collect my wits to answer, to try to formulate some rational course of action, Kerenyi came in from the next room, followed by Julie. There were signs of tears on her face, and she held a handkerchief tightly in one hand. He came straight up to Agnes, and leaned down over her slack form, still shuddering with deep sobs at intervals.

'Forgive me,' he said—his voice sounding cold. 'Forgive me, if you can. The past came up and hit me, and I forgot what I was saying.'

Agnes raised her head, gazing stupidly up at his frowning face, and shook her head a little, the habit of courtesy making her try to speak, even to smile in answer to his apology.

'Barber suggests we ought to . . . to do something. Get in touch with the authorities . . .'

We all stood still, in a group about the chair in which Agnes was seated. We looked at each other, searching for a lead, some sign of certainty in one or other of our faces.

'To give her time to think,' explained Barber, his voice sounding louder than he meant it to.

'If only it were over,' moaned Agnes, 'if only I could be dead, unconscious . . .' She put her head in her hands, gripping at her forehead so that the almost fresh scar went white across her knuckles.

Julie looked sharply down at her, and her face went taut, unfemininely fierce and sharp.

'Barber is right,' she said suddenly, making up our minds for us. 'We must do something. But what? Now, let's consider sensibly. What's the most important thing, the first thing to do?'

'Call . . .'

'I think,' said Barber slowly, 'the very first thing is to get off an urgent telegram to wherever the children are. So nobody can get at them until Agnes gets there.'

'Of course, you're right,' I said, galvanised into sense. 'You draft it. I'll go up and find the address of Agnes' mother. She must have it in her bag, on some letter or something.'

Within half an hour, as if making dispositions about some perfectly ordinary emergency, we sent this telegram—twice to make sure it arrived; we agreed not to cancel Agnes' flight for the next day to London so as not to warn anyone who might be watching at the airport. I argued with the security police and we waited until a broad-set, middle-aged man arrived and took up his position by the house door, with a stolidity that suggested he did this sort of thing every night of his life. We telephoned to the Embassy and hauled an outraged Ambassador from his drawing room in the last stage of a dinner party; finally I informed my own chief.

Only for Agnes herself could we do little. She carried, as I suspected, a variety of sleeping pills in her hand luggage, but shook her head wearily when we offered them to her.

'Lately, if I do take them, I don't sleep,' she said. 'I'm half awake all night only dreaming terrible dreams.'

'I remember that state only too well,' Julie said. 'And I don't believe sleeping pills will do you the least good. What I suggest, Robert, is that we all take a glass of wine.' She moved briskly towards the bell but remembered that both the waiter and Frau Spandela were gone for the night, having finished their work. It did seem the least impossible thing to do, and I went down to the cellar and brought up some fresh champagne.

'We've taken a great responsibility on ourselves,' said Barber quietly. 'The lives of four human beings. I feel as if we were involved in some terrible secret compact. Something that will join us all together for the rest of our lives, like knowing about a murder.'

'In a way,' said Julie slowly, 'it is like knowing about a crime. But remember, the crime is not ours. The crime was already committed and not here by us. We have only put off a decision, a consequence of that crime. Agnes can still make up her own mind. We've only interfered so that she has time to think clearly.'

'I'm afraid you're right, Barber,' said Georgy. 'And I swore I would never again interfere in other people's lives.'

'You both still think in theories,' she said wearily. 'You think of the crime I speak of as political—against some State or nation, I don't mean that at all. The crime was against human beings. You said it yourself—' she turned to challenge Georgy. 'What you said to Agnes was the truth. He lied, he deceived his own family. He married her, as I remember Robert telling us years ago, to get money. Now we know he wanted that money to commit his crimes. He brought children into the world as a cover for his crimes—can you think of a worse thing to do than that? When you talked to Agnes you were making arguments. But it was true, what you said. *That* is his crime and to the devil with nations and State secrets.'

'Julie is right,' I muttered. 'We couldn't stand aside and just let the children and Agnes slide into—into an abyss, where people like Banks can control them.'

'No—we couldn't. But I feel the weight of it,' said Barber.

'So do I,' I agreed. 'But that is because we did it personally, actively. We have no comeback—we can't say we were obeying higher orders. If it goes wrong—if one day Agnes blames us—it's our own personal responsibility. Guilt . . . responsibility . . . in the end they are the same things. Just the positive and the negative words for the same thing.'

'That's just the point. It's our personal intervention that makes it seem so serious. Georgy writing books—me writing newspapers —we interfere indirectly all the time and often wrongly. But to do something so immediate, so personal . . .' He shook his head at

Julie. 'You may be used to the feeling, but it will take me a little time.'

'I don't think so,' she said. 'You are so conscious of it—your responsibility. You know, really, what you do and that what you do is right. And remember—don't forget—we have done nothing final. We've done all that one ever can do with insoluble problems— we've put it off a little. That is bound to be a gain. Don't you see that?'

'And you only need feel responsibility now, at the moment,' I agreed. 'I agree absolutely, it's a serious matter. But what about me? I always knew Stephenson was a wrong 'un. I've known for years. I knew when he married Agnes. But I didn't want to judge him—I didn't dare. Probably I could have done nothing, anyway—I'm not neurotic about it. But just because I was so afraid of doing something that could never be undone, I persuaded myself that I must be wrong. And, really, what did I have to go on, then? If I said something, who would believe me? Nobody—I hardly even believed myself. That's the advantage conspiratorial natures always have —that people who are basically normal can't believe that they are what they are. But I blame myself now . . . God, how I blame myself!'

We were all silent, and then from the chair where Agnes half sat, half lay, came the dragging sign of a voice.

'You couldn't have done anything, Robert. I wouldn't have listened to you or anybody.'

'There was one moment—I could have grabbed the letter that night. Yes, and supposing it contained private papers—not the report that went, as certainly as we stand here, to Banks by military post—but birth certificates so that a close friend could have the banns called for the coming wedding . . . something of that sort? What sort of a criminal idiot should I have been then? You don't do that sort of thing to fellow-officers. You don't demand to look at other people's letters, anywhere, at any time. Before you do things like that, you have to *know*.'

'We've done what we could,' said Julie at last. 'Not very much, but all we could. One must be a little modest about life . . .'

It was the most natural thing in the world that Julie should take her glass and walk over to the long windows that stood open to the night; and that Kerenyi should join her there.

Among all the sensations of that long evening, I felt most

strongly an angry regret that it should have been spoiled for them, when they paid me, of all their many friends, the great honour of spending this particular evening with me. So when Julie began to speak quietly, I was only glad at first that they talked together in the tones of love and harmony.

Gradually, I realised that she was reciting for him. Many times I had watched and listened to her in the theatre; I knew that not only subjectively to me, but to thousands, she was one of the great talents of her world. Now for the first time I heard her incomparable voice in a perfection that for years past must have been lost to it, and was only now recovered. The control of an instrument, the perfect artistry were filled to my ears for the first time, with a quality of spirit which gave the voice more than its lovely sound, and the words more than even Shakespeare's meanings.

She spoke in her own language two of the Sonnets that I recognised but only afterwards identified, as the hundred and twelfth and the fifty-fifth. It is true, they are in German a masterpiece of translation, but the words alone were not the content of what was a declaration for Kerenyi, I knew, but became as well a comfort that could reach even Agnes who understood not a single word.

In the silence as the voice ceased, a whispering echo seemed to hang in the air, and then, as though inevitably, a nightingale from the garden unwound her cadences in a ribbon of glorious delicacy in answer. It was a moment that could never be repeated and never forgotten.

But it was not, in fact, Agnes who watched the sleepless night through; I could hear her heavy breathing of exhaustion, of a collapse from unbearable tension, as I went out into the upper hall now and again, to be sure all was well. It was I who stood at my window leaning out to breathe in the heavy dew as the moon went down and the nightingale ceased for a little while to sing; and still leaned there as the pearly dawn came up into what was never darkness, only a misty twilight. Ghosts walked and visions rose in the June night; ghosts I did not know, would never know, and did not need to know. Events long since dust, and events that could never occur and that I did not even wish for, that were absorbed into living without ever being real.

As if in a dream I imagined that Julie turned to Georg when they were alone, and gripped his shoulders in her hands fiercely, bringing back pain into old wounds where the nerves would never heal, and wanting to cause the pain. And presently, as dawn was rising and I leaned out for the hundredth time to smell the garden, I remembered where that impression came from. The scene of their reunion in the house in the country came back to me; I felt again my juvenile embarrassment at the loaded passions in the half-dark kitchen by the glowing fire, heard again the soup ladle rattle on the stone floor, smelled almost physically the paraffin lamp at the moment I first heard that wonderful voice.

Like a grip in my stomach I felt a fierce longing to be there in that house, to be with Lali and the unborn child, with my real responsibilities and rid of all the involvements of intrigue. Stephenson and the tangled duties of the outside world. I had not yet seen the finished, rebuilt stables to which Tom Wallingham was to bring the first of the horses for the new project which was now, as Barber would have said, all set up.

In the second that I thought of the horses and Tom, longed for the smell of new moist hay just cut, summer flowers, the young trees not yet masking the baldness of the landscape round the house caused by the old timber being stolen; in that moment I saw what the future was going to be.

I should not renew my short-term commission when it ran out, and still less join the regular Army—we had considered that. I should retire to the country and build up the stud into a profitable international business, Lali taking care of the horses and myself the accounts.

A kind of inward laughter began to rise in me. Did Julie know, when she encouraged first friendship, then desire and later marriage, with Lali, that part of my purpose was to be attached to herself—had she used me? Had she always intended me as the protector of her adopted family, using my adoration of herself and my longing for the house, for a home, to establish there a solid foundation against the world outside? She cared nothing for money and never needed to, but she was shrewd where property was concerned; I was perhaps always marked down as the future administrator of her and Nando's property. Was I to avenge her mother's death and other deaths by building it up for a future that only a year or so ago seemed no longer to exist? I saw, with immeasurable satisfaction, how dynasties are founded and carried on.

Note about the author

Author of the best-selling Book-of-the-Month Club Selection NIGHT FALLS ON THE CITY, Sarah Gainham was born in London and lived for many years in Germany and Austria. A regular writer about foreign affairs for *The Spectator,* she has also broadcast for the BBC and West German and Austrian television and contributed to numerous British and American publications, including the *Atlantic Monthly, The New Republic* and the London *Sunday Times.* Her other novels include TIME RIGHT DEADLY, COLD DARK NIGHT, APPOINTMENT IN VIENNA, THE STONE ROSES and THE SILENT HOSTAGE. She now lives in Trieste and Vienna.